PAWFULLY WEDDED

DIANE KELLY

Copyright © 2024 by Diane Kelly

Cover design by Danielle Christopher

All rights reserved.

No part of this book may be reproduced in any form or by any electronic or mechanical means, including information storage and retrieval systems, without written permission from the author, except for the use of brief quotations in a book review.

PRAISE FOR DIANE KELLY'S PAW ENFORCEMENT SERIES

"Funny and acerbic, the perfect read for lovers of Janet Evanovich." — *Librarian and Reviewer*

"Humor, romance, and surprising LOL moments. What more can you ask for?" — *Romance and Beyond*

"Fabulously fun and funny!" — *Book Babe*

"An engaging read that I could not put down. I look forward to the next adventure of Megan and Brigit!" — *SOS Aloha* on *Paw Enforcement*

"Brimming with intelligence, a devious plot and plenty of imagination." — *Romance Junkies* on *Laying Down the Paw*

"A completely satisfying and delightful read. By being neither too 'cute' with its police dog lead, nor too dark with its serious topic, the author delivers a mystery that is a masterful blend of police detective and cozy fiction." — *Kings River Life* on *Enforcing the Paw*

"Four paws up! This is a fabulous series that is sure to win the hearts of mystery fans and dog lovers alike!" — *Books and Trouble*

OTHER BOOKS BY DIANE KELLY

THE HOUSE FLIPPER SERIES

Dead As a Door Knocker

Dead in the Doorway

Murder With a View

Batten Down the Belfry

Primer and Punishment

Four-Alarm Homicide

Dead Post Society

THE MOUNTAIN LODGE MYSTERIES SERIES

Getaway With Murder

A Trip with Trouble

Snow Place for Murder

THE SOUTHERN HOMEBREW SERIES

The Moonshine Shack Murder

The Proof is in the Poison

Fiddling With Fate

THE BUSTED SERIES

Busted

Another Big Bust

Busting Out

THE PAW ENFORCEMENT SERIES

Paw Enforcement

Paw and Order

Upholding the Paw (an e-original novella)

Laying Down the Paw

Against the Paw

Above the Paw

Enforcing the Paw

The Long Paw of the Law

Paw of the Jungle

Bending the Paw

Pawfully Wedded

THE TARA HOLLOWAY (DEATH & TAXES) SERIES

Death, Taxes, and a French Manicure

Death, Taxes, and a Skinny No-Whip Latte

Death, Taxes, and Extra-Hold Hairspray

Death, Taxes, and a Sequined Clutch (an e-original novella)

Death, Taxes, and Peach Sangria

Death, Taxes, and Hot-Pink Leg Warmers

Death, Taxes, and Green Tea Ice Cream

Death, Taxes, and Mistletoe Mayhem (an e-original novella)

Death, Taxes, and Silver Spurs

Death, Taxes, and Cheap Sunglasses

Death, Taxes, and a Chocolate Cannoli

Death, Taxes, and a Satin Garter

Death, Taxes, and Sweet Potato Fries

Death, Taxes, and Pecan Pie (an e-original novella)

Death, Taxes, and a Shotgun Wedding

<u>OTHER BOOKS AND STORIES:</u>

Almost an Angel

Don't Toy With Me

Five Gold-Smuggling Rings

Love, Luck, and Little Green Men

Love Unleashed

One Magical Night

A Sappy Love Story

The Trouble with Digging Too Deep

Wrong Address, Right Guy

ACKNOWLEDGMENTS

Lots of people helped make this book happen, and I appreciate all of you!

Thanks to Laura Kinzie for suggesting the idea of a sassy parrot. Thanks to Carole Pickett and Cecilia Conneely for your helpful input on the draft and excellent proofreading services. Thanks to Brendan Conneely for information about communications involving multiple law enforcement agencies. Thanks to Katie Bosma for providing me with information about high school marching bands. Thanks to Peggy Derryberry Gould and her brother for the description of the tuba sound. Thanks to author Melissa Bourbon for the camaraderie that makes being in this crazy business more fun.

And, as always, thanks to you readers who chose this book. Because of you, I get to do the thing I love, creating characters and stories to entertain you and connect us. I hope you enjoy every word.

1

GARBAGE

The Flamethrower

Friday morning, while the coffee dripped into the pot, the Flamethrower opened the cabinet under the kitchen sink and pulled out the bag of garbage. Until recently, the garbage had been filled with carrot tops, apple cores, and wilted lettuce, evidencing a woman's futile attempts to impose a healthy diet on her household. These days, though, the bags mostly contained fast-food wrappers or frozen pizza roll boxes. The blue recycling bin had undergone a similar transformation. The bin had once housed empty bottles of cheap grocery-store chardonnay and crushed Budweiser cans, but now it held empty bottles of expensive imported beer. He worked hard. He deserved the good stuff. And he was done pinching pennies to save for a future that had become uncertain.

The recycling bin was only half full this morning, so he left it under the sink. He exited the kitchen into the garage, not bothering to put on a T-shirt to cover his bare chest. The cotton shorts he'd slept in covered his naughty bits. That was good enough for running the garbage to the curb. Besides, even though it was only a quarter past seven, it was already hotter than balls outside. Living in Texas had some benefits, but the weather damn sure wasn't one of them.

After dropping the trash bag into the large rolling garbage can, he used his elbow to jab the button on the wall to raise the garage door. He walked toward the door as it rolled up, ducking under it to step out onto the driveway. *Fughhhh ...*

Valerie, the bony, bubbly blonde who lived across the street, stood at her curb in skin-tight purple yoga pants and a matching tank top. As she positioned her garbage can, the rumble of the door caught her attention. She glanced up and spotted him in his driveway. "Howdy, neighbor!" she called. To his dismay, she sashayed across the street toward him, her voice dripping with false southern sweetness. "Hot enough for you?"

Early August in North Texas was too hot for Satan himself. The concrete was frying his feet, and he had to step off into the grass before responding. "Sure is."

Valerie pursed her pink lips and tilted her head. "I haven't seen your wife or son around lately. Everything okay?"

Nosy bitch. Even as she attempted to pry personal information out of him, her eyes flicked to his six-pack abs and firm pecs. The prying pissed him off, but he didn't mind the ogling. He busted his ass at the gym five days a week, and he was proud to still look this good at forty-five. The woman's own husband had a saggy gut that made him look six months pregnant. *Maybe she'll think of me the next time she screws him.*

"We're all doing great," he lied. His wife and son were none of this busybody's business. Besides, his wife would surely come to her senses soon and come back home so they could be a family again. He turned the subject to one he knew would get the woman off the subject of his marriage, even if it meant he'd be stuck listening to her yammer on for the next few minutes. "How are your girls? They ready for school to start up again?"

Sure enough, the woman straightened her head and beamed. "They sure are! Ainsley made the drill team. They've been practicing nonstop for the last two weeks to get ready for the first football game. She's taken dance classes since she was five years old and puts the other girls to shame. Alexis signed up for all advanced placement classes—"

As Valerie rambled on, he smiled and nodded, feigning interest but tuning the woman out, the same way his son did when Ainsley and Alexis flirted with him. The girls made the game too easy, as simple to catch as a pop fly. He was proud his son preferred a chase, refusing to fall for any pretty face.

Finally, the woman stopped bragging long enough to take a breath. "Great to catch up!" he said before she could start up again. He left the garbage can at the curb and backed away at warp speed. "See ya!"

2
BRIDE TO BE

Fort Worth Police Officer Megan Luz

On a Saturday afternoon in early August, my former roommate and best human friend Frankie opened her front door. She gave me a smile as bright as her spiked blue hair and called over her shoulder to the ladies gathered in her living room. "The bride has arrived!"

She stepped back, welcoming me into her home along with Brigit, the oversized shepherd mix who was my work partner, packmate, and best furry friend. Surrounding me were dozens of gifts in pretty bags and wrapped boxes, as well as the women who'd bought the gifts for me. "Hi, everyone!"

A round of greetings and hugs were exchanged before Frankie led me to the recliner, which she'd festooned with what appeared to be a hundred yards of pristine white tulle. Zoe, Frankie's calico cat, had claimed the seat and refused to relinquish it voluntarily. Frankie removed the stubborn cat and held out a hand, inviting me to take a seat. "Your throne, milady."

Zoe cast me a disgusted glance over her shoulder and swished her tail before sauntering off. I sat down and smoothed the skirt of my ruffled white sundress. Meanwhile, Frankie picked up a silver-plated tray and flitted about, passing spinach-stuffed phyllo dough appetizers. "Take as many as you'd like. I made plenty."

Brigit lay at my feet, her head up, keeping a keen eye on the tray of appetizers in case one should fall to the floor. The shepherd mix was large for her breed and as fluffy as a dog could be. She was as cunning as they came, too, smarter than most humans. We shared such an unbreakable bond now that it was hard for me to remember why I'd initially been so resistant to being partnered with the dog. *What's a little fur on your clothing compared to unconditional love?*

Following Frankie with a stack of napkins was my younger sister Gabby. Like me, Gabby got her dark hair from our Mexican-American father and her freckles from our Irish-American mother. Our Catholic upbringing was courtesy of both cultures.

Behind the kitchen counter, Summer raised two glasses of bubbling orange liquid. "Who wants a mimosa?" Summer was one of my fellow female officers from the Fort Worth Police Department. With her sunny demeanor and bouncy blond curls, she lived up to her name. When several hands shot up, Summer filled each one with a drink.

I'd attracted unwanted attention as a child with my stutter and, as a result, didn't generally like being the center of attention. But today, among good friends and family, I was thoroughly enjoying myself. The round diamond glittered from the ring on my left hand as I picked up the first gift bag, which was small, and striped silver and white. The card inside noted that the gift was from Detective Audrey Jackson, who perched on a barstool across the room. The dark-skinned, clever-minded detective had become an invaluable mentor, pulling me into her cases and showing me the ropes. I hoped to follow in her footsteps and make detective one day.

I fished out the tissue paper and reached inside the bag, pulling out a small box containing a wireless video doorbell. *Leave it to someone in law enforcement to give a home security item as a gift.* "What a great idea!"

The detective took the mimosa Summer offered her and readied it for a sip. "With all the burglars and porch pirates hitting houses around town, you can never be too careful."

"So true," Summer chirped as she handed a champagne flute to my mother. When Gabby reached for one, Summer held the glass up, out of reach. "Got some ID, kiddo?"

My auburn-haired mother wagged a reproving finger at Gabby, who had several more years before she'd turn twenty-one. I hoped she wouldn't rush them. Adulting could be great, but it was a lot of responsibility. As much as I loved being a police officer, keeping my community safe and helping solve crimes, the magnitude of my duties and the violence I witnessed sometimes got to me, weighing on my mind and soul. But I wasn't about to spoil this fun event by thinking about work.

I took the mimosa Summer handed me and held it up in toast. "To all of you. The best family and friends a bride could ever have!" I was beyond lucky to have such an extraordinary group of ladies in my life. Each was smart, supportive, and strong in her own way. Frankie had well-defined muscles from years of skating roller derby and working as a firefighter, while my mother had the fortitude to birth and raise five children.

We clinked glasses and I took a sip of the sweet drink, the bubbles tickling my throat as it went down. Setting my champagne flute on the coffee table, I moved on to the next gift. Frankie had bought me a cute ceramic chip and dip tray shaped like a sombrero. No sooner had I lifted the tray out of the box to show the others than Zoe slinked up and climbed into the box. "This tray is so festive! It'll be perfect for serving tortilla chips and guacamole on our next game night."

Mom motioned with her hand. "Open mine next. It's the one in the little pink bag."

Rather than force Zoe out of the box, I set the tray aside to be repacked later. I picked up the bag my mother had pointed out, removed the tissue, and peeked inside. All I could see was a tiny ball of red fabric. I pulled it out to discover it was a sexy see-through lace teddy. Zoe reached up from the box to swipe at the lace, and the group giggled as my cheeks flamed as red as the lingerie. "Mom!" I cried. "This is a bridal shower, not a bachelorette party!"

My fiancé's mother, Lisa, grinned from her seat on an ottoman. "Your mom isn't the only one to blame. I helped her pick out that nightie. We're hoping for a grandchild or two."

"Seth and I haven't even made it down the aisle yet." I stuffed the teddy back into the bag. "It's much too soon to be thinking about kids."

"Don't think too long," Lisa said wistfully. "I've got lost time to make up for."

Lisa had given birth to Seth when she was only Gabby's age, an unwed teenager unprepared to become a mother. Seth's father had never been in the picture. Lisa had never told Seth who his father was, presumably because he'd wanted nothing to do with the son he'd fathered. After giving birth to Seth, Lisa had dropped out of high school. When she found being a teen mom too much to handle, she left Seth in the care of her parents and took off. While Lisa's mother —Seth's grandmother—had been kind and loving, she had died before her time. Seth spent much of his childhood living with a surly grandfather who'd suffered from grief and undiagnosed PTSD from the Vietnam War. Fortunately, the family had recently reunited and begun to heal from their wounds. Lisa had returned to Fort Worth, and Seth and his grandfather had begun to let go of their pain and resentment. They'd lost a lot of years but, with any luck, we'd all have many happy ones ahead of us. I had no doubt Lisa would be a wonderful grandmother someday. For the first time, it dawned on me that my children would have only one grandfather. I felt a little tug at my heartstrings. Forcing the thought from mind, I turned my attention back to the presents.

Summer's gift was a beautiful crystal frame for a wedding photo, while two other friends had gone together to buy an espresso machine. With the odd hours Seth and I worked caffeine was a must. I held up the box for everyone to see. "This machine will get *a lot* of use."

Another friend gave me two sets of hiking poles. I removed them from the package to give them a go. They were adjustable, lightweight but sturdy. I gave her a smile. "These will come in handy on the honeymoon."

Seth and I planned to vacation in Utah after our wedding in late September. The timing would be ideal, after the summer crowds had gone but before the extreme winter weather set in. I couldn't wait to see the rock formations in Arches National Park, the sandcastle-like hoodoos in Bryce Canyon, or the beautiful red cliffs and waterfalls in Zion. Besides the natural beauty, the remote areas sounded peaceful and relaxing, a great place to get away from it all and enjoy a romantic sojourn with a new spouse. Of course, Brigit would tag along with us. She worked as hard as I did and deserved some rest and relaxation. Seth's dog Blast, too. Blast was trained to sniff out accelerants and explosives for the fire department's bomb squad. The skilled dog had earned a vacation as well. Besides, Seth and I would miss our furry, four-footed partners if we didn't take them with us. We'd both grown accustomed to having our dogs at our sides 24/7. To spend a week away from our canines was simply unthinkable.

When I finished opening my gifts and had exchanged dozens of hugs with the guests, Frankie circled again, this time with a platter of finger sandwiches. Although Brigit didn't raise her head from the carpet, I noticed her nose twitch. No doubt she smelled the food coming closer and hoped to get her teeth on one of the sandwiches.

I tipped my champagne flute to down the remains of the mimosa and settled back in the chair, reveling in the moment. I hadn't felt so happy, relaxed, and lighthearted in a long time. I had my wedding and honeymoon to look forward to, and no crime investigation weighing on my mind.

I should have known that carefree feeling wouldn't last.

3
OOPSIE

K-9 Sergeant Brigit

Frankie approached with a tray piled high with sandwiches. With three-hundred million olfactory receptors in her nose compared to a human's mere six million, Brigit could discern exactly what was on the plate. Whole-grain bread. Avocado. Tomatoes. Lettuce. The mock tuna salad made from mashed garbanzo beans, chopped celery, lemon juice, garlic salt, and eggless mayonnaise, one of Megan's—*and Brigit's*—favorites.

Until recently, Frankie and her calico cat Zoe had shared the home where Brigit lived with Megan. Seth and Blast had replaced Frankie when she'd moved out and taken her cat with her. Brigit didn't miss the cat a bit. The useless beast had been arrogant and annoying, acting like she owned the place. Zoe sometimes stole Brigit's spot in the sun, sprawling on the rug and soaking up the rays. She'd often sleep on Megan's bed, too, not seeming to realize she was not part of their pack. She even drank out of Brigit's water bowl! The only good thing she ever did was occasionally knock something off the kitchen counter that Brigit could snack on.

Speaking of snacks . . .

Megan reached her hand toward Frankie's tray. Megan might share a bite with Brigit, but the dog couldn't be entirely sure of her partner's intentions and she wasn't about to take a chance on missing out on those yummy-smelling sandwiches. Frankie was sweet, and Brigit knew she wouldn't want to accidentally step on her paws. The dog wagged her tail, strategically brushing it against Frankie's ankle to make her think she'd stepped closer to Brigit than she really had. As expected, Frankie jerked backed, tipped the tray in her hands, and sent three finger sandwiches plummeting over the edge.

As Frankie gasped in dismay, Brigit snatched the first sandwich out of the air before it could even hit the ground. The second sandwich spent only a millisecond on the carpet before she grabbed it up. The last one lay on the ground slightly longer than five seconds, but dogs have no five-second rule. As soon as Brigit finished the second sandwich, she gobbled up the third one, too. *Yum! Best party ever!*

4
THE SAME OLD GRIND

The Flamethrower

The traffic signal on West Rosedale Street cycled from red to green. *Krrrkkk!*

The Flamethrower's fury ignited as the fifteen-year-old moron he'd fathered ground the gears on his beloved baby, a brand-spanking-new Camaro. The sports car was painted an eye-catching shade that Chevrolet dubbed Riptide Blue, with a black center stripe down the hood. He'd treated himself to the bad-ass ride three months ago for his birthday—over his wife's vociferous objections. *What a relentless nag.* She might not think he deserved these fine wheels, but the Flamethrower thought otherwise. She'd never appreciated him like she should have. That's why he'd barely batted an eye when she'd packed up and left, taking their son and his pubescent funk with her. Of course, she'd first asked the Flamethrower to leave their house. She'd argued that it would be less traumatic for their kid and their mutt if they could remain in the house with her, but the Flamethrower wasn't about to give her the pleasure of seeing him run off with his tail between his legs. If she wanted to go, fine. But hell if he'd leave the house *he* had paid for and make things easy on her. Not after what she'd done. *Whore.*

"The clutch!" he hollered, pointing down at the pedal on the floorboard. "Push harder on the clutch!"

"Sorry, Dad!" One of the tiny rubber bands attached to the boy's braces snapped and ejected from his mouth, landing on the dashboard. The boy bit his lip as he mashed his foot harder on the clutch, but somehow still managed to grind the gears again. *Krrrkk!*

For fuck's sake!

Taking a deep breath, he tried to calm himself. As irritated as he was, he supposed he couldn't fault the kid too much. He'd taken out a mailbox himself when he'd been learning to drive all those years ago. Maybe he should cut the boy some slack. It was hard, though. Every time he looked at his son, he saw *her* face looking back. But while his ginger-haired son might resemble his mother, he had his father's athletic skills. The Flamethrower had led his high school baseball team to a state championship, played well enough to have his pick of girls, and earn a full-ride scholarship to a college in Oklahoma. It was a small, division III school, but he'd been a star pitcher there, as well. He'd even played for three years in the minor leagues before throwing out his shoulder and, in return, getting thrown out of the sport himself. It was just as well. The odds of him being moved up to the majors were slim. Besides, he made good money in his day job and was still involved in baseball as a part-time umpire during the high school baseball season each spring.

Krrrkk! The kid ground the gears for a third time before the driver of the car behind them ran out of patience. *HONK!*

The Flamethrower's patience ran out, too. He made a punching motion with his arm. "Strike three! You're out!"

His son muttered a curse that his mother would've grounded him for, but the Flamethrower couldn't have cared less. Hell, he was glad his son had the balls to utter the word. *I'll make a man out of him yet.* The two opened their respective doors to switch seats. As he rounded the back bumper, the Flamethrower raised a hand in apology to the driver stuck behind them. He slid into the driver's seat and buckled himself in.

His son fastened his seatbelt and sat back in the passenger seat with a huff. "Mom's right. You care more about this car than you care about us."

"That's not true," the Flamethrower said, though at the moment the scale was tipped only slightly in their favor and less so every day that passed without his wife returning. He loved his son. He did. But spending time with a demanding, moody teenager was a chore.

The other car circled around them just in time to race through the yellow light before it turned red again.

As they idled, waiting for the signal to cycle to back green, his son slid him some side-eye. "Doak doesn't get mad when he's teaching me to drive."

Mentioning his mother's lover was a low blow, and the kid knew it. He leaned toward his door as if to put distance between himself and his father. Not that the Flamethrower had ever raised a hand against his son, even when the kid had deserved it.

His grip tightened on the wheel. "That's not a fair comparison. Doak's got an automatic transmission." The Flamethrower added "and a limp dick" under his breath.

His son huffed again, but this time it was a soft snort of humor. A grin tugged at the boy's lips. "That's not what I hear."

The Flamethrower stiffened, his foot inadvertently pushing the gas pedal and causing the engine to roar. His son had the nerve to chuckle. *Little shit.* "You and your mom talk about Doak's dick, do ya?"

His son blushed again, realizing his phrasing had been unfortunate. "I just meant he's a nice guy. That's all."

"Nice guys don't sleep with other men's wives." With that, the Flamethrower shoved the shifter into first gear and took off at warp speed, leaving tread marks on the asphalt. *Screeeeech!*

5
KNOCK ON WOOD

Megan

Brigit and I were scheduled to work the swing shift for the two weeks after my bridal shower. It was my least favorite shift, for a multitude of reasons. Odd and dangerous things happened after nightfall. People tended to be better behaved in the light of day but were more likely to be drunk, high, or belligerent in the later hours. Suspects were more likely to run, too, thinking they could escape into the dark of the night. There wasn't enough time to get much personal business done in the morning before reporting for duty, and I had to keep my eye on the clock lest I be late for work. The swing schedule also threw off my biorhythms. I often found it hard to stay awake, though I was less likely to have that problem tonight. Seth had set up the fancy coffeemaker I'd received at my bridal shower, and I'd prepared two double-shot espressos before heading out on the job. I poured them over ice, added oat milk, and drank one immediately. The other rode along with me in the cruiser's cupholder.

On Friday evening, Brigit lay on her carpeted platform behind me in our specially equipped K-9 cruiser. Besides the fact that the back seat had been turned into a kennel, the car was equipped with safety features to protect my furry partner. If the interior temperature became too warm, the windows would automatically roll down, a fan would turn on, and an alarm would sound. Brigit had a cushy dog bed and an assortment of chew toys in her cage, too. I couldn't let my sweet girl get bored during our shifts, could I? Boredom wasn't a problem at the moment, though. My furry partner was happily dozing on her side, her paws flapping and her nose twitching as she emitted soft *woofs*. She was probably dreaming of chasing squirrels. She'd never managed to catch one in real life. Maybe she had better luck in her dreams.

It was nearing eight o'clock, but the sun still blazed in the sky and the temperature remained sweltering. Some residents preferred to stay inside where they could bask in air conditioning rather than go outside and be immediately coated in sweat. But many others were out and about, and the roads were busy. The Shoppes at Chisholm Trail mall was busy, too, crowds bustling, people taking advantage of back-to-school sales to load up on clothing, backpacks, and items needed to outfit college dorm rooms. Young mothers pushed babies in strollers, while those with older children did their best to corral their errant offspring. Groups of teens wandered about, some made up of girls only, others consisting of just boys, some a mix of the two. I cruised slowly around the outer perimeter of the mall's parking lot, then made another pass, this one following the sidewalk that bordered the building's four wings. Couldn't hurt for people to see a police presence. It would reassure honest folks that they were safe shopping here, and discourage any would-be shoplifters or juvenile delinquents from making trouble.

Seeing nothing of concern, I exited the lot and cruised through the nearby Colonial Hills Country Club neighborhood. There was little to see other than grass and bushes desperately clinging to life, thirsting for the next scheduled watering day. When much of the grass in our yard had given up the fight, Seth and I replaced it with Asiatic jasmine, a thick groundcover that used little water and required no mowing, another win for both the environment and us. I'd also planted drought-tolerant Lantana bushes that produced soft pink flowers, a pretty complement to the mauve paint that covered our rented bungalow in the South Hemphill Heights neighborhood. Of course, the area's golf course greens remained true to their name. The city code allowed a golf course to be watered before ten in the morning and after six in the evening any day of the week. A few of the city's selfish residents had turned their front yards into putting greens in a deviously crafty attempt to circumvent the water restrictions, their rule-bending a middle finger to Mother Earth and local government. I'd argued with more than one of these folks, who insisted they'd complied with the letter of the law, if not the spirit. The city council was in the process of revising the municipal ordinance to clarify that only *commercial* golf courses were exempt from the water-rationing rules.

Brigit and I cruised down University Drive, which passed through the center of Texas Christian University, or TCU for short. Only a handful of summer school students strode about now but, in a couple of weeks, the campus would teem with students returning to school or starting their freshman year. *Go Horned Frogs!* Anxious parents would help move their children into the dormitories, lingering too long as their kids were eager to get settled and meet the other students living on their halls. It wouldn't be long, either, until the bright lights of the stadium would light up the sky on Saturday nights as the Horned Frogs went head-to-head against the Southern Methodist University Mustangs, the Texas Tech Red Raiders, or another college team.

After rolling past the campus, I took a left onto Berry Street, drove for a few blocks, and took another left onto Forest Park Boulevard. As we approached the park, Brigit woke, rolled onto her belly, and lifted her head, her nostrils working overtime as they sought to identify our location. She loved the park. We often stopped there so she could take a potty break and stretch her legs. Occasionally, I'd take her for a longer walk through the city zoo. Not long ago, a clever thief had managed to steal several animals from the zoo, including a rare, endangered rhino. I'd assisted Detective Hector Bustamante in solving the case. It hadn't been easy. I felt proud of the contributions I'd made, proud that the detective had trusted my judgment and appreciated my assistance. Maybe one day, when I became a detective, I'd mentor a young cop who aspired to become a detective, too.

Realizing where we were, Brigit stood in her enclosure and issued a demanding *woof*, letting me know in no uncertain terms that I was to give her a break here now.

"Anything you say, boss." I turned into the park and pulled to a stop in a parking place near an open area. After rounding up her Frisbee from the passenger seat floorboard, I opened the back door to let her out. She slid down to the warm asphalt, her toenails click-click-clicking on the pavement as we made our way to the field. *Sheesh.* I'd taken only a few steps in the late-summer heat and already my armpits and back felt damp.

My partner popped a quick squat to relieve herself. Once she'd emptied her bladder, I held up the Frisbee and waved it around, teasing Brigit. She reared up and pranced around on her hind legs like one of J-Lo's backup dancers. The dog weighed nearly as much as a human, too. But I loved every ounce of my partner, even the seemingly endless tufts of fur she left all around our cruiser and home. Having to sweep up fur bunnies was a small price to pay for having the best partner in the world, one who could chase down suspects I had no hope of catching and snuggle up to keep me warm in bed at night.

I waved the Frisbee one last time. "You ready, girl? Huh? Ready?"

She issued a shrill *arf*, ordering me to stop fooling around with the disc and just throw the darn thing!

I pulled my arm back across my body and sent the disc sailing out over the field. Brigit took off like a rocket, her legs eating up the ground and sending up dirt and dried grass behind her. She leapt high into the air and caught the Frisbee in her teeth before it had even begun to descend. She wasn't just a smart dog, she was an agile one, too, the best and brightest in her training class. While I'd scored high on the written police exam, my physical and gun skills were average at best. Good thing Brigit didn't know she'd been assigned a partner who wasn't her equal. I made up for my shortcomings by spoiling her with toys and treats and belly rubs.

Once her paws returned to the earth, momentum carried Brigit forward another dozen feet before she circled around and ran back to me. We played tug-of-war with the Frisbee for a few seconds before she released it to let me throw it again. I whipped the disc across the field once more and, again, she took off at warp speed, yanking the toy from the air.

A squirrel dared to emerge from the woods to our right, tiptoeing out of the shadows to stand at the base of a tree. He had one eye on Brigit, the other on an acorn that lay a few feet from the safety of the thicket. As Brigit turned and headed back in my direction, seemingly distracted by our play, the little creature crouched and crept forward on all fours, hoping to grab the treasure. I bent over to take the Frisbee from Brigit only to discover she'd been faking. She dropped the disc to the dry grass, pivoted, and bolted toward the squirrel, her legs moving so fast they were nothing more than a blur.

I could have sworn I heard the squirrel squeal in terror, though it could have been my imagination—or maybe the squeal had come from me. The squirrel turned to run into the woods but it was too late. Brigit was on the poor creature.

"Brigit!" I cried. "No!" I knew the dog had natural hunting instincts, and I supposed I couldn't blame her for them. The prey drive was as natural to her as scratching her ears and greeting other dogs with a sniff of their rear. There were even times I was glad for Brigit's innate aggressiveness. But this wasn't one of them. It would break my heart to see her hurt a defenseless little animal when she didn't need to. She had plenty of canned and dry food at home, not to mention the pocketful of liver treats in my pants. "Don't hurt that squirrel!"

I needn't have worried. Brigit scooped the little guy up atop her snout and tossed him a few feet, but humiliating the itty-bitty beast was enough for her. Once he landed, the squirrel skittered up a live oak as fast as his little legs would take him. Brigit barked up at him and wagged her tail, the doggy equivalent of *nyaa-nyaa!* Emboldened on his high perch, the squirrel chastised her for toying with him. He swished his bushy tail and hollered *chit-chit-chit!* Brigit offered him a *rrruff* in return to let him know who was boss, turned, and trotted back to me, her mouth hanging slightly open in what could only be called a canine smirk.

"Bad girl!" I wagged a finger at her. "Pick on someone your own size, Brigit."

Panting, she cocked her head and batted her big brown eyes, acting all innocent.

I pointed to where she'd dropped her toy. "Get your Frisbee. It's time to go."

She dutifully retrieved her plastic disc and trotted beside me as I returned to the cruiser. There, I filled her bowl with cold water, which she slurped up in thirsty gulps. *Slup-slup-slup.* When she finished, I poured the slobbery dregs onto the asphalt.

A young mother came up a pathway nearby. A toddler reclined in the stroller she pushed, and a boy of about four walked beside her. When the toddler noticed Brigit, he sat up straight and pointed at Brigit. "Doggy!"

The older boy stopped walking and looked our way, his eyes bright with curiosity. "Can your dog do tricks?"

Could she ever! I turned to Brigit and raised my brows. She looked up at me and a silent message passed between us. *It's showtime.*

"Down," I ordered. Immediately, the dog dropped to her belly, looking up at me intently. "Sit." She rose to a seated position. "Speak." She responded by raising her chin and issuing a loud bark.

Woof-woof! When I said, "High five," she raised her paw and tapped it against my open palm.

The boy giggled. *He ain't seen nothing yet.*

I directed Brigit to "Assume the position." She rose up on her hind legs and put her paws against the side of the cruiser, like a suspect preparing for a body search. I frisked her, patting down her sides as if looking for a hidden weapon or drugs. She was clean, of course. "Dance." She backed away from the cruiser, performing a canine version of the Texas two-step on her back legs. I formed finger guns, aimed them at her, and pretended to shoot one then the other in rapid succession. "Bang-bang!" Brigit gave an Oscar-worthy performance, collapsing to the ground, closing her eyes, and letting her tongue loll out. I brought her back to life with, "Roll over." She complied, rolling over three times toward the little boy. When she rose to her feet, I said, "Take a bow." She stretched one leg forward and bent her head over it. The little boy smiled and clapped his hands. His baby brother watched him and followed suit in his stroller, mashing his pudgy palms together.

Brigit's performance complete, I fed her three liver treats for her dutiful compliance, then reached into the breast pocket of my uniform where I kept an assortment of lollipops for children I came across on my beat. After getting the okay from his mother, I held out an orange sucker to the boy. "Be good, okay?"

"I will!" He took the sucker and gave me a big smile in return.

I handed another orange sucker to the toddler, who responded by drooling and shoving the plastic-covered candy into his mouth. His mother intervened, removing the wrapper.

After loading Brigit into the rear of our cruiser, I climbed into the driver's seat and drove to the exit to continue our patrol.

The fire station where Seth and Frankie were based sat within my beat. The extreme heat had dried out the grass along the roadsides, and the firefighters had been dealing with an inordinate number of fires started by motorists who recklessly tossed lit cigarettes out car windows. *Seriously, people! The entire state is a tinderbox in the summer.*

Get a clue! Luckily, the firefighters had managed to douse the conflagrations before any had burned out of control and caused extensive damage or injured anyone. The team at the fire station was dedicated and well-trained, and functioned like a well-oiled machine.

As Brigit and I approached the station, I saw that the bay doors were closed. The firefighters must be enjoying a quiet night inside, out of the heat. Though I'd given Brigit a break at the park, I figured I deserved one, as well. I slowed and turned into the parking lot. Frankie's red Nissan Juke was parked next to Seth's seventies-era blue Nova, complete with flames painted down the sides. If only the "Fast and Furious" franchise had launched thirty years earlier, the muscle car could have been featured in the movies.

I eased into the spot next to Seth's car, parked, and let Brigit out of the cruiser. We headed into the station together. Seth, Frankie, and a few of the other firefighters were gathered in the lounge area, watching a movie on a big-screen television. All wore the standard set of station gear, including navy blue fire-resistant pants, a T-shirt bearing the department's emblem, and steel-toed boots.

Seth had served with the army in Afghanistan as an explosive ordnance disposal expert, meaning he'd been trained to defuse bombs and neutralize IEDs. It was a rare and unusual skill that translated to the civilian world, making him perfectly qualified to serve on the bomb squad in addition to his firefighter duties. Seth's broad shoulders and strong arms had been built by workouts at the fire station and thousands of laps swimming the butterfly stroke in the pool at the YMCA. He sported short blond hair, a sexy chin dimple, and a signature pinkish scar the size and shape of a small lemon along his well-defined jawline. Blast, the yellow Labrador retriever dozing on the sofa next to him, had the same blond hair and square jaw, though he had no scar and was trained to locate explosives, not defuse them.

Brigit eyed her sleeping beau and issued a soft *woof*, the K-9 equivalent of "Honey, I'm home!"

Blast opened his eyes and lifted his head as Seth rose to greet me.

On seeing Brigit, Blast hopped down and came over to greet her, too. Tails wagging, the two sniffed each other's snouts and nether regions. Meanwhile, Seth gave me a much preferable hug, pulling me up tight against his shoulder. After a second or two, he released me and took a step back, a sparkle in his green eyes. "This is a nice surprise."

"It's been a slow shift."

Frankie cringed and cursed. "You know better than to say that, Megan! Better knock wood so you don't jinx yourself."

She had a point. A first responder's shift could change on a dime, turning from monotonous to utter mayhem in an instant. I reached down and rapped on the coffee table to keep the bad juju at bay. *Knock-knock.*

Captain MacDougal strode into the room, a piece of paper in his hand. The captain was around fifty, strands of pale silver sneaking into the sandy hair he wore in a trendy fade, short on the sides and longer on top. The guy stood an inch or two over six feet, with a muscular physique built from regularly pumping iron at the station house. "Hey, Megan. Brigit."

I returned the greeting. "Hey, Captain."

Brigit's tail thump-thump-thumped against the sofa as he reached down and stroked her neck. When he straightened up, he ran his gaze across those gathered about. "I'm planning a cookout at my place on Labor Day. All you chumps are invited. Bring your swimsuits so you can enjoy my new pool."

"You got a swimming pool?" said one of the other guys. "Lucky bastard."

Seth concurred in his assessment. "I'd give my left arm to have a swimming pool in my backyard."

The captain snorted. "It'd be hard to swim with one arm."

Seth shrugged. "Don't need any arms to float around in an inner tube. That's what I'd be doing."

"So, Captain." Frankie cocked her head. "Are we going to finally meet this girlfriend you keep talking about? We're starting to think you made her up."

"Yeah." Another firefighter piled on. "She sounds too good to be true. Pretty. Sweet. A good cook."

Seth cut his boss a skeptical glance before piling on. "Captain Mac told me she rubs his feet when he gets home from a shift."

"Ew!" Frankie cried. "No way she's real."

"She's real. You'll see." The captain used a thumbtack to post a sign-up sheet on the bulletin board. "She's also very organized. She wants to know what everyone's bringing to the party."

The male firefighters rounded up a ballpoint pen, walked over, and filled in the top few lines on the sheet. Once they were done, Frankie and I stepped over to take a look. All five of the men had written *beer*.

Frankie scoffed and turned to me. "Looks like it's up to us women to make sure people have something to eat." She shifted her focus to her fellow firefighters. "It's the twenty-first century, you Neanderthals. Men cook now."

One of the men protested. "We cook here at the station. That's enough."

She scowled. "You cook here at the station because it's a job requirement. You can cook at home, too, you know." She tapped the pen against her chin as she considered her options, then wrote *baked beans* on the sign-up sheet.

Seth stepped up next to me. "What are we bringing?"

I cut him a look. "*I* am bringing a fruit salad."

"But we're getting married," Seth insisted. "We're a unit now."

"That doesn't mean you can ride my coattails." I held out the pen.

He harrumphed as he took it from me. He jotted his name on the list, then wrote *beer* in the spot for his contribution to the party.

I snatched the pen from his hand. "Gimme that." I scratched out "beer" and wrote "homemade potato salad."

His brow furrowed. "I have no idea how to make potato salad."

"I've got a good recipe. I'll teach you how to make it."

"Can't wait," he said with the enthusiasm of a patient awaiting a root canal.

Seth and Blast walked Brigit and me out to the parking lot, where we could have a moment in private. My fiancé leaned back against his Nova, looking as hot as the flames painted along the side. I'd fallen in love with him because he was caring and compassionate, fun and sometimes funny. The fact that he made my girly parts tingle was a bonus.

He stretched an arm along the top of the car. "Mom's having trouble finding a dress for our wedding. Think you could help her out?"

"I'd be happy to." Even though Lisa had been a lousy mother during Seth's formative years, she was doing her best to make up for things now. She'd always been kind to me, and appreciative of my efforts to help her family recover from their rough past. "I'll get in touch with her."

"Thanks," Seth said. "It'll mean a lot to her."

I ordered Brigit to get back into the cruiser. The dog issued a long-suffering sigh but obeyed. Blast whined as I shut the door, sorry to see Brigit go. I reached down and patted his head. "Don't worry, boy. You'll see her at home later."

As if he understood, he sat back on his haunches, appeased.

My furry partner and I exited the parking lot and continued to cruise our beat. As we drove through the Fairmount neighborhood, I spotted Dub—real name Wade—walking his dog Velvet, a pit bull mix. Dub was a teenage boy who'd had an even more troubled childhood than Seth. Dub's father had been an abusive type who'd plied and controlled Wade's mother with drugs. Wade ended up in foster care but had been fortunate to find a home with a doting couple who did everything they could to ensure he was happy, thriving, and had everything he might need to succeed. *If only all children could have such supportive role models.* I pulled to the curb and unrolled my window. "Hey, Dub! Velvet!"

Dub turned my way, his lips spreading in a wide smile when he spotted me. He brought Velvet closer and leaned down to look in the window. "Hi, Officer Luz! Hi, Brigit!"

Brigit stood at her window, which I'd also rolled down, and issued a woof through the bars of her enclosure, her tail wagging all the while.

"Ready to go back to school?" I asked Dub.

"After sleeping 'til noon and playing basketball at the Y every day? Hell, nah! Why would I ever want to go back to school?" His grin said he was full of crap. He'd discovered a knack for theater and I'd bet he couldn't wait to audition for the Paschal High School drama department's first performance.

I handed him a lollipop and a liver treat for Velvet. "Stay out of trouble," I said, more out of habit than out of any real concern he'd get into any. He was a good kid.

"I'll do my best." He stepped back and raised his hand in goodbye.

I returned the gesture and drove off, my spirits lifted. Law enforcement officers saw a lot of depressing things on the job, but occasionally we saw people rise above their circumstances, their lives taking a turn for the better. Those positive outcomes, rare as they might be, were what kept us going.

The next time I stopped to give Brigit a potty break, I called Lisa from my cell phone. "Seth says you need help finding a dress to wear to the wedding."

"I do," Lisa said. "Nothing I've found yet has felt quite right, and I keep second-guessing myself."

"I'd be happy to help you pick something out. You busy tomorrow? We could hit the stores when they open at ten, maybe have lunch somewhere." With Seth on duty at the fire station until the morning, he'd sleep a good part of the day tomorrow. Might as well leave him to doze in peace.

"Perfect," Lisa said. "It'll be fun to have some girl time."

I was looking forward to spending time with my future mother-in-law, too. We arranged for me to pick her up at a quarter to ten.

When I drove into the Ryan Place neighborhood, the sky was beginning to dim for the evening, pinkish-orange hues lighting the horizon behind the stately old homes. I was heading south on Fifth Avenue when a beater car came barreling toward me from the other direction. A lighted sign atop the silver Toyota Celica identified it as a pizza delivery car. My dash-mounted radar clocked it going nearly fifty miles per hour. The driver must've spotted my cruiser because he slammed on the brakes. The car rocked forward as the brake lights lit up on the back, and my radar readout plummeted to twenty-two mph. No doubt a lot of cheese and toppings had slid forward inside the pizza boxes.

I flipped on my flashing lights and unrolled my window, putting out a hand to stop the approaching car. The twenty-ish man at the wheel pulled to a stop at the curb and I eased up next to him, the two of us facing each other. As he unrolled his window, the enticing smells of tomato sauce and garlic wafted from his car and my mouth salivated. So did Brigit's. She stood in her kennel behind me, smacking her lips.

The young man raised his hands in surrender. "Sorry! You got me dead to rights. But I've got a shit ton of pizzas to deliver and my boss comes down on me if I take too long."

"I can understand the pressure you're under," I said, "but speeding will only save you a few minutes, at most. If you promise to slow down, I'll let you go with a warning."

"I promise." He put his palms together and glanced upward, thanking the powers that be that a forgiving cop had caught him.

Though I wasn't going to give him a ticket, I nonetheless gave him a pointed look. "If I catch you speeding again, all bets are off. Hear me?"

"Loud and clear."

"All right." Unlike the little boy we'd encountered at the park earlier, this young man was hardly a kid. Still, it couldn't hurt to offer him a gesture of goodwill. I extended a purple lollipop out the window.

"Thanks!" He took the sucker from me. "How'd you know that grape's my favorite?"

"Lucky guess." I made a move-forward motion with my hand. "On your way, pizza guy."

As he pulled away from the curb, I glanced up at the sign atop his car, taking note of the pizza place advertised there. I'd make a stop by the joint, tell the boss to ease up on his drivers. It was the right thing to do. *Oh, who am I kidding?* I just wanted an order of garlic knots for Brigit and me to share.

6

LICKETY-SPLIT

Brigit

Garlic knots! Yum! Brigit snapped each bite out of the air as Megan tossed them to her in the parking lot of the pizza shop. The K-9 had excellent eye-mouth coordination, especially when it came to something so delicious.

When the knots were gone, Megan let Brigit lick the oily remnants from her fingers. Her human partner then wiped her hands with a disinfectant wipe. Brigit's nostrils twitched. She didn't like the antiseptic smell of the towelette. She was glad when Megan disposed of the wipe in the trash can outside the pizza place.

When Megan opened the door to her enclosure, swung her arm, and ordered the dog back into the cruiser, Brigit hopped right in, eager to please her partner. Megan was in a generous mood. Maybe she'd give Brigit another liver treat later if she was a good girl.

7
BURNED

The Flamethrower

DING-DONG!

The Flamethrower glanced into the living room, where his son and three other boys from the baseball team lounged about playing video games on their laptops, each with a headset on, hooting and hollering into the mouthpieces.

Either the idiots hadn't heard the doorbell ring or they'd ignored it. He hadn't looked forward to having a bunch of noisy teenage boys at the house overnight, but it was his son's sixteenth birthday and he had to do something to earn the kid's affection. He wasn't about to come in second place to that bastard his wife was screwing.

He pulled some bills from his wallet and opened the door. The pizza delivery guy stood there, four extra-large pizza boxes in his arms, the white stick of a lollipop sticking out of the corner of his mouth. The Flamethrower had paid for the pizzas online with his credit card when he'd ordered them, but he exchanged the boxes now for a cash tip. Feeding teenage boys with their rocket-speed metabolisms didn't come cheap.

"Thanks!" the delivery guy said with a smile, revealing a tongue turned purple by the grape-flavored sucker. He tucked the tip into the pocket of his jeans and turned to head back to his car.

The Flamethrower was about to close the door when a clean-cut man in khakis and a golf shirt strode up the walkway, a manila envelope in hand. "Steven Quinn?"

"Yeah." *Who's this guy? One of the boys' dads?*

"Have a good evening." The man laid the envelope atop the pizza boxes and turned away.

The Flamethrower looked down at the envelope. "What's this?"

He got no answer. The man strode to a black SUV parked at the curb across the street. The curtain fluttered at the window of the house behind the SUV. Valerie must have been spying on him. *Twat.*

He used his foot to close the front door and carried the pizza boxes into the kitchen. Smelling the food, the boys tossed their headsets aside and were on him like vultures on roadkill, grabbing the boxes out of his hands without so much as a "thanks." The envelope fell to the floor, but none of them made an effort to pick it up. *Teenage boys are dickheads.* "You're welcome!" he snapped.

His son hunched his shoulders in a sheepish grimace. "Thanks, Dad!"

Taking the hint, the other boys murmured words of appreciation —all except Asher Burke, that is. Instead, Asher said, "Isn't feeding their children, like, the bare minimum a father is legally required to do?"

Entitled little shit.

The boys carried the pizzas into the living room and grabbed slices to eat directly out of the boxes, not bothering with plates or napkins. Meanwhile, the Flamethrower picked up the envelope, slid his finger under the flap to open it, and pulled out the contents. He took a moment to scan the document. His wife had filed a petition for divorce, citing "insupportability."

As the world collapsed under him, he involuntarily took a step backward and leaned against the wall, surprised to feel the tightness in his chest and throat. *She's done it. She's actually done it.* She'd taken the first official step toward ending their eighteen-year marriage.

Once he got past the initial shock, his emotions turned to fury and confusion. He consulted the document again. *Insupportability?* Was she accusing him of failing to support her or their son? He'd done no such thing! He'd prided himself on making sure they were taken care of, even after she'd left. He hadn't drained their joint bank accounts or deactivated their credit cards. He'd continued to pay the Visa bill despite the fact that she'd incurred frequent charges at restaurants, enjoying her ladies' nights with friends. She probably spent the entire time badmouthing him, too, but he figured the other women probably complained about their husbands, too. He read on to discover that, for legal purposes, the term "insupportability" meant "discord or conflict of personalities that destroys the legitimate ends of the marital relationship and prevents any reasonable expectation of reconciliation."

Conflict of personalities, my ass! Hot, molten rage welled up in him. He should've filed for divorce first, on the basis of adultery. He'd missed the opportunity to publicly shame her for stepping out on him. *I'll make damn sure to mention her cheating in my response.* It would serve her right for her infidelity to be put in the official court record. Maybe he'd tell Valerie what a skank his wife had turned out to be. Valerie knew everybody in the neighborhood and at the high school. She'd get the gossip mill going.

As tempted as he was to rip the paper to shreds, he knew that doing so would be a mistake. Instead, he crammed the paperwork back into the envelope, stomped to his bedroom, and shoved it into a drawer in his nightstand. He returned to the kitchen and snatched his keys from the hook by the door to the garage. "I'm going out for a bit. You boys behave while I'm gone."

Asher looked up from his pizza, his headset encircling his neck like a high-tech dog collar. "Be cool and buy us some beer first."

Brazen prick. The kid had no manners, no respect for rules or authority. Rumor had it he'd intentionally broken a window on a neighbor's house with a line drive after the neighbor had complained about him playing loud, explicit music in the backyard. When his parents offered not only to replace the window but also to pay the neighbor a thousand dollars for the inconvenience, the matter had been settled. The Flamethrower's wife had feared Asher was a bad influence and had forbidden their son from hanging out with the boy. Unfortunately, Asher was popular and persuasive, the life of the party. Their son had begged the Flamethrower to allow Asher to come to the sleepover, promising he wouldn't tell his mother that they'd explicitly disobeyed her. *As if her domestic decrees mean anything these days.* The bitch didn't live here anymore. She couldn't tell him what to do in his own home. He'd thought he might earn points with his son by playing the cool dad. Still, he had to admit that his wife might have been right to discourage Hayden's association with Asher.

"You struck out, kid." The Flamethrower gave Asher a pointed look as he instinctively raised his right fist and made a motion like he was knocking on a door, the signal for a strike in baseball. "I'm cool. I'm just not go-to-jail-for-buying-alcohol-for-kids cool." Piqued, he said, "Are you boys just gonna play video games all night? Why don't you get off your asses and do something?"

Hayden glanced up at him. "Like what?"

He shrugged. "Have a water gun battle." There were several large pump-action water guns in the garage, amassed over the years. Filled with chilled water, they'd been a fun way to beat the intense Texas summer heat, and much cheaper than installing the swimming pool his son had been begging for.

Asher scoffed, but didn't even bother to look up. "Water guns? Dude. We're not twelve years old."

Asher had a point. Hell, he was nearly full grown. He stood

almost six feet, just a hair shorter than the Flamethrower. Still, the Flamethrower knew he'd better go now or he'd be tempted to shove a greasy slice of pizza down the boy's throat. He stepped into the garage and closed the door behind him. The instant it closed, he heard Asher ask, "Is there any liquor in the house?"

Good thing he'd had the forethought to hide his beer and whiskey in the camping cooler in the garage. He'd covered the ice chest with a tarp, too, for extra measure.

He climbed into his Camaro and drove to his favorite sports bar, Hail Mary's Pub, to see if any of the guys might be around. They'd texted him a few days back about meeting up tonight to watch the game, but he'd declined, citing the slumber party and the fact that he didn't want to leave a bunch of idiot boys at his house unsupervised. Of course, he'd changed his mind once he'd been served with the divorce petition. Now, he could use a distraction. He got lucky. Three of his buddies sat at a square table near the back. He slid into the empty fourth seat, greeting them with a "Hey."

One of the guys said, "Thought you weren't coming tonight 'cause of your kid's birthday?"

"Changed my mind," he replied. "No teenager wants his parents hanging around. I decided to be cool, give them some space."

He hoped they'd believe his explanation. He also hoped he wouldn't go home later to find the house trashed. Before the guys could question him further, a twentyish server in a low-cut tank top and tight denim shorts that barely covered her ass appeared at the table, a round tray perched on her hip. The tattoo running up the inside of her arm read *Live, Laugh, Love*. Not exactly original. While he could appreciate the girl's tight figure, he wasn't about to ogle her like some creep. Hell, he was old enough to be her father. That thought was nearly enough to ruin his appetite, but he ordered a beer and a burger anyway.

She brought the beer right over, setting the bottle on the table in front of him. "It'll be just a few minutes on the burger."

He gave her a nod, raised the bottle to his lips, and took a long pull. The Texas Rangers baseball game played on a big-screen television to his left. An MMA fight was being broadcast on another oversized screen to his right, the two men pulverizing each other. A soccer game played on a third, smaller TV mounted in a corner, but being as he and his buddies were sitting in a sports bar in Texas, none of them gave a shit which teams were playing or who was winning. Soccer was for schoolkids and foreigners and pussies.

Between his beer, his bros, and his ballgames, he could almost forget that he had nobody sharing his home anymore. Not his wife. Not his son. Not even the damn dog. He used to complain about the dog's disgusting habits, but there'd been a few nights recently when he'd have been happy to have the beast lying at his feet, shamelessly licking his empty ball sack. But those days were over for good. He might as well face it. His wife claimed he was a narcissist, that he had only himself to blame for her moving out and taking the kid with her, but she was wrong. There was someone else to blame—the beefy bastard who'd turned him into a cuck.

Speaking of beefy bastards, here comes one now...

The guy slid his black backpack onto the floor under their table, pulled a chair over from an adjacent table, and dropped into the seat. He held out a closed hand to exchange a fist bump with one of the Flamethrower's bros, a Latino guy named Marco who'd played a few seasons for the Fort Worth Cats before the minor-league team folded a decade ago. "Hey, cuz."

The two couldn't have looked less like cousins unless they'd been different species. While Marco stood around five feet seven and had dark hair and brown skin, his cousin stood a half foot taller, with pale skin and hair the same reddish-gold color as the amber lager in the Flamethrower's bottle. No doubt one of the guy's parents was a gringo. The cousin was younger, too, appearing to be only in his late twenties or early thirties, a decade younger than anyone else at the table.

Marco introduced his cousin as Nash, and the guys went around the table, raising a hand or beer in greeting and offering their names in return.

After introducing himself, the Flamethrower cocked his head. "We've spent half our lives in this bar. Why haven't we met you before?"

"I just moved here a week ago," Nash said. "From Oregon."

That explained the guy's pale pallor. Unlike Texas, where the sun beat down relentlessly most of the year, the Pacific Northwest didn't get much sun.

Nash continued. "I'm crashing on Marco's couch until I can find a place of my own. I hope something turns up quick. Marco's wife can't cook worth a shit."

Rather than defend his bride, Marco chuckled and held up a greasy chicken wing. "Why do you think I'm eating here, primo?"

The Flamethrower's wife had been a decent enough cook, though she tended to prepare low-fat meals with lots of vegetables. Any time he'd complained, she'd told him that, if he didn't like the food she prepared, he was more than welcome to take over the kitchen duties.

The Rangers' batter struck out on the big screen TV. Around the table, the guys broke into curses and threw up their hands, as if his failure was a personal affront. The server returned with the Flamethrower's burger. She placed it on the table before shifting her gaze and running it appreciatively over Nash's broad shoulders and firm pecs. Despite the girl's tender age and lame tattoo, a twinge of envy puckered the Flamethrower's gut. Before Nash had showed up, he'd been the fittest guy at the table, the only one whose physique had yet to start giving way to middle-aged dad bod. *No beer gut or man boobs here.*

"What can I get you?" the server asked Nash with a coy smile and a cock of her head.

Nash ordered a draft beer, a burger, and a side of fries. He returned her assessment, overtly admiring her perky ass as she headed off to put in his order with the kitchen. He turned back to the guys and wagged his brows. The Flamethrower fought the urge to roll his eyes. *There's more to life than chasing tail.* Then again, maybe some tail was exactly what the Flamethrower needed to improve his mood. But he hadn't been with a woman other than his wife in twenty years. He wasn't even sure what single people were doing these days. *Is manscaping still a thing?*

As the game played, Nash chatted up the other guys at the table. He had an affable demeanor and a knack for remembering everyone's name and keeping the conversation going without monopolizing it.

When a commercial came on the television, Marco lifted his chin to indicate the Flamethrower. "You and Nash got something in common. You both sell pills."

As a pharmaceutical sales rep, the Flamethrower was used to people making occasional jokes about his career choice, comparing him to a drug kingpin. It didn't bother him. Unlike those who dealt in street drugs, he helped people rather than hurt them, educating their doctors so that they could prescribe the medicines best suited for their patients. The products he sold were developed over years by scientists, and subject to rigorous clinical trials before being approved for sale by federal regulators to treat medical conditions and diseases. He turned to Nash. "What company do you work for?"

Nash beamed. "I work for myself." He reached under the table, unzipped his backpack, and pulled out a small black plastic bottle. He plunked it down in the center of the table.

The Flamethrower picked up the bottle and took a look. *Oh, for fuck's sake.* The logo wasn't from a legitimate pharmaceutical company. Instead, it bore the logo of some shady supplement company. Nash didn't sell real medicine. He hawked snake oil. *Had Marco invited the guys out tonight for a sales pitch?* The Flamethrower returned the bottle to the tabletop.

Nash said nothing but glanced around the table, obviously

waiting for someone to ask about the product. He didn't have to wait long.

A dutiful assistant in the dog-and-pony show, Marco pointed to the bottle. "What's that?"

Nash put his palms together and flexed his arms. "It's that supplement I was telling you about."

The others exchanged glances over their beers, suddenly interested in rereading the menu even though they'd already ordered.

When still nobody asked about the product, Nash went on, undeterred. "These pills build bulk faster than any protein powder and without all the calories."

One of the guys laughed. "Will it keep my dick hard, too?"

Nash raised a jacked shoulder. "It just might." He continued his sales pitch, showing them photos of himself on his phone as proof of the supplements' effectiveness. "My biceps went from fourteen inches to seventeen inches," he said. "You know how hard it is to build calves? Mine were sixteen inches only four months ago, but look at this bad boy now." He lifted his foot and plunked it down on the table, much closer to the Flamethrower's burger than he considered sanitary. As the Flamethrower moved his plate away, Nash pulled up the leg of his track pants to show off his well-developed calf muscle. The Flamethrower couldn't help but be impressed, though he did his best not to show it. He took a long, slow drink of his beer.

When there were still no takers at the end of his sales pitch, Nash said, "I get it. You guys are skeptical. I don't blame you. I was, too, at first." He returned the bottle to his backpack and exchanged it for four small sample packets, each containing a week's supply of colorful tablets. He doled out the packets on the table, like a blackjack dealer dealing out playing cards. "Try a free week on me. You'll have more energy, better workouts, and, yeah, maybe even a harder dick. When you decide you want more, give me a call or shoot me an email." He proceeded to pass out business cards printed with his contact information and social media handles.

The Flamethrower ignored the guy's outstretched hand. Undeterred, Nash tossed the card onto the table. The Flamethrower let it lie where it landed, not bothering to move it away from the circle of condensation left on the tabletop by his dewy beer bottle. He felt his lip quirk in aversion. He'd come here to relax and enjoy himself, not fight off a pushy salesman.

After the server brought Nash his beer, the Flamethrower pointed to the pill packet on the table. "You make a living selling that stuff?"

Nash frowned but answered the question. "My supplement business doesn't pay all the bills yet, but it's growing. I'm looking for a day job here, just until my business gets off the ground."

"What did you do back in Oregon?"

"I was a private firefighter."

The Flamethrower sat up straighter. *Now I'm interested.*

One of his buddies dunked a fry in ketchup, shoved it into his mouth, and talked around it while he chewed. "What's that mean, 'private firefighter'?"

Nash shifted in his seat. "I worked for a company that provided firefighting services for insurance companies. Whenever there was a wildfire, we'd get called out to protect the properties the company insured. Mostly, we taped up vents to keep embers from blowing into them, applied fire retardants to roofs, cut down trees to create fire breaks, things like that. Sometimes we'd stick around too long and end up having to fight the fires ourselves. Other times we were hired directly by property owners, rich folks who didn't want to see their mansions go up in flames."

His buddy picked up another fry. "Didn't people give Kanye West shit for hiring guys like you?"

Nash snorted. "Among other things they gave him shit for. But yeah, some people don't think it's fair that the rich can pay for extra protection for their homes. Never bothered me, though. Life ain't fair. Besides, having more firefighters on duty is a good thing for everybody, keeps the fires from spreading."

"Well, then." The guy brandished the fry like a greasy scepter. "Thank you for your service."

While the others chuckled, the Flamethrower quietly slid Nash's damp card off the tabletop and tucked it into the back pocket of his jeans. He glanced around the group, grateful to see that nobody seemed to have noticed. "Anyone want to split a platter of nachos?"

8

SWATTING

Megan

Frankie was right. I'd jinxed things by mentioning the slow shift. *Should've knocked harder on that wood.*

The sun was slipping below the horizon, daylight turning to dusk, when the radio on my dash sparked to life with an urgent dispatch. It was the type of call a police officer hopes never to hear. "Three men with assault weapons reported at Chisholm Trail Mall! Shots fired!" All officers in the area were ordered to respond.

An active shooter. A law enforcement officer's worst nightmare. And three of them, no less, armed with weapons of war.

Adrenaline rocketed through my veins, every circuit in every system notched up to high. "Hang on, girl!" I cried.

Brigit knew what to do. She hunkered down on her belly, legs splayed for stability. I switched on my flashing lights and siren, made a quick check for cars, and hooked a squealing U-turn. *Screeeeech!*

Pressing the gas pedal to the floor, I swallowed the lump of terror in my throat and forced myself to take a deep, calming breath. *Please, God! Don't let anyone get hurt or die!*

Woo-woo-woo! In less than a minute, I roared into the mall parking lot. But even though my response had been fast, an automatic weapon could fire a barrage of bullets during that short timeframe. There was no telling how many people might have already lost their lives.

To my surprise, everyone in the lot seemed to be going about their business as usual. No one was rushing or looked panicked. I knew not to take appearances at face value, however. People often discounted the sound of gunfire, writing it off as fireworks or machinery. Besides, the mall was big. People at one end could have no idea what was going on at the other.

I zipped into the reserved spot for law enforcement too fast, and my front tire slammed against the curb stop, rocking me forward in my seat. I cut the engine and grabbed the mic for my public address system. In active shooter situations, potential victims had three options. The best option was to get the hell out of Dodge and bullet range. The second was to hide and hope the shooters didn't find them. The third option was one I hoped nobody here would have to face—to fight back against the attackers.

The lights in the parking lot flickered on as I pushed the talk button and shouted into my microphone. "Active shooters reported! Leave the area immediately!" I opened my door and stood by my cruiser, motioning frantically with an arm toward the exit of the parking lot as I repeated the message. "This is Fort Worth Police! Leave the area! Active shooters reported!"

People might have been dawdling a moment ago, but they weren't dawdling now. Everyone within earshot ran for their vehicles, some dropping their shopping bags and picking up their children. A toddler fell and his mother dragged him along for several feet, skinning the poor child's knees before she realized he'd fallen. She reached down, yanked the shrieking child up into her arms, and bolted into the parking lot. A car nearly ran them down, veering at the last minute to slam into the back fender of a parked pickup truck. The truck's alarm activated as the driver of the car backed up and took off again, leaving the damaged pickup behind.

Moving as fast as I could, I grabbed my riot gear from my trunk. Every second counted, but I'd be no good to anyone if I was injured and unable to return fire. I donned my helmet and chest protector. The latter had hard shell pieces that curved over my shoulders, like modern-day high-tech knight armor. Being designed for men, it also had a triangular-shaped padded flap in front in case someone tried to kick the officer wearing it in the nards. Not so much a problem for me. Now outfitted, I released Brigit from her enclosure and swiftly slid her ballistic dog vest over her back. I fastened it tight and ordered my K-9 partner to follow me. "C'mon, girl!"

Out of the corner of my eye, I saw the Fort Worth Police Department's armored SWAT vehicle careen into the parking lot. Though the SWAT team would be better equipped and protected than me, I couldn't wait for them to deploy. Lives could be lost in the interim. Every second counted.

I rushed forward with my bullhorn in my left hand, my gun in my right, and Brigit by my side. The mall was shaped like a large X, the four wings extending from a glass-enclosed center atrium that contained a food court and administrative offices. I ran down the nearest wing, yelling into my bullhorn. "Leave the area! Active shooters reported!"

I hurried along, my ears peeled for gunfire, but heard nothing other than the screams of frightened shoppers, the pound of their footsteps as they ran past me for the parking lot, and the panicked pulse of my heart. Either the shooters had stopped to reload, or they were moving intently about, seeking specific targets. The thought made my guts squirm. Brigit hustled along rigid and ready beside me as I scanned the shops and walkways ahead, looking for blood, bodies, or bullet casings, any sign that might tell me which way the shooters had gone. But I saw nothing. *Where are they?* I continued to holler into the bullhorn, directing people to leave the scene. "Active shooters reported! Leave the area immediately!"

People stampeded past me. Tires squealed. Horns honked. Sirens wailed. But still, no sound of gunshots. *What's happening? Had the shooters fled?*

Footsteps thudded behind me as several members of the SWAT team rushed forward, overtaking me and my partner. One of them was my former partner Derek "The Big Dick" Mackey, a rusty-haired jackass with testicles the size of bowling balls—metaphorically speaking. He lived for this type of situation, loved to exercise his bravado. He held his gun at the ready as he ran past me.

Ahead, the door to the sporting goods store opened and a man exited. He was dressed in black and had something long and black in his hands, the end resting on his shoulder. *Holy shit! Is that a rifle?* Derek stopped, crouched behind a large potted plant a few steps ahead of me, and took aim. As momentum carried me forward, I realized the man was dressed in black bicycle shorts and a spandex racing shirt. The black tubular item resting on his shoulder was not a rifle, but a tire pump. *Derek's going to shoot an innocent person!*

"Nooo!" I dropped my bullhorn, shoved my gun into its holster, and launched myself at Derek, going airborne just like Brigit did when taking down a suspect. As I landed on his back, he sprawled forward over the heavy pot, his arm swinging downward just as he pulled the trigger. *BANG!* The muzzle flashed and the bullet disappeared into the pot, sending up a spray of green leaves and soil, and shattering the ceramic exterior. I hit the pavement shoulder first, rolling as I'd been trained to disperse the power of the impact. Good thing I wore extra protection or I'd have been seriously bruised.

The man Derek had targeted simultaneously dropped the bike pump and his jaw. A wet stain spread across the crotch of his bike shorts. A tinny ringing noise replaced the pulsing heartbeat in my ears. Shoppers screamed as they raced past us. Brigit stood a few feet away, trembling with nervous energy, waiting for me to issue an order. I called her back to my side.

Derek pushed himself up from the remains of the pot. His SWAT uniform bore a smattering of dirt and his face had an expression of *Oh, Shit!* Having discharged his weapon, he'd have to file a report and justify his actions to a review board. No doubt I'd be called in to give my story. He might have shot the man with the bike pump if not for my intervention. We officers had to make split-second decisions that could mean life or death. He'd made the wrong decision. But what if it had actually been a gun in the man's hands? The guy could've taken out innocent civilians.

Though Derek had made my life hell while we'd been partnered together—farting in our squad car, making me clean the cruiser, constantly taunting me with sexist jokes—at the moment I felt awful for him. A cop's worst nightmare is accidentally hurting an innocent person. I stood, reached over, and put a hand on his shoulder, giving it a supportive squeeze. Though he said nothing, he cleared his throat, speaking volumes with the sound. The normally tough, unaffected guy was overcome with emotion.

I stood close enough to Derek to hear the voice of the SWAT captain come through his earpiece. "Where'd that gunshot come from?"

Derek cleared his throat another time before pressing the button on the earpiece to activate his microphone. "This is Officer Mackey. That was my weapon, sir. Accidental discharge."

"Any injuries?" the captain asked.

"No, sir."

"Good. Anyone see evidence of a shooter?"

A chorus of voices responded over the airwaves, all in the negative.

The captain cursed. "Looks like a false report."

False report?! I slumped as the tension in my body eased, my shoulders coming down from my ears. Thank goodness there were no gunmen! But how had this situation come to be? Had someone truly thought they'd seen three men with guns enter the mall, and inadvertently made an incorrect report? Or had someone purposely tried to mislead law enforcement? No doubt the department would thoroughly investigate. I looked forward to hearing the results.

Through the glass walls of the atrium, I could see the SWAT officers who'd come up the other mall walkways gathering for a huddle in the food court. Meeting eyes with Derek, I lifted my chin to indicate the man who'd peed himself. Not that I blamed the guy one bit. I'd wet myself the first time I'd been attacked by a trained K-9, despite being protected by a thick bite suit. "That man could use a clean pair of shorts," I said. "I'll talk to him. Go join your team."

Derek managed to eke out, "Yeah. Okay. Whatever." It was as close to a thank you as I'd ever get from him.

As Derek hustled to the atrium, I walked over to the man in the soiled bike shorts. Brigit trotted along beside me. "You all right, sir?"

"All right?" he squeaked. He gave me an incredulous, wide-eyed look and barked a laugh. "I guess I'm as all right as a man who thought he was going to get his head blown off and pissed himself could be." His adrenaline fading, the man swayed on his feet.

"Take a seat over here." I took his arm to steady him and walked him over to sit on a bench—a bench that would later need to be disinfected.

Brigit nudged his bare knee with her nose. He looked down as if noticing her for the first time, then reached down to pet her. The motion seemed to calm him. K-9s were good for much more than sniffing out drugs and chasing down suspects. They served as emotional support dogs on occasion, too, both for their handlers and for victims or witnesses.

"Sorry about the situation," I said. "We received a report of three active shooters here at the mall. Law enforcement arrived expecting to find armed men. From back there—" I jerked my head to indicate the shattered pot—"your bike pump resembled a rifle."

The man swallowed hard. "Thank goodness you tackled that other officer before he could get a shot off."

As the man sat and stroked Brigit, I took down his name and contact information in case it would later be needed by internal affairs. Meanwhile, the SWAT team members moved methodically up and down the walkways, opening the doors to the stores, peeking in, and calling out to make sure everything was okay. One of the SWAT officers stepped up next to us. After pulling open the door to the sporting goods store a few inches, he peered inside. "Just verifying that everything's okay in there!" he called, probably to a cashier or other staff member nearby. "We received what seems to be a false report of active shooters."

A faint male voice called back to the officer. "We haven't seen anyone with a gun, but we heard a loud bang from outside a few minutes ago. Sounded like a gunshot."

"We've identified the source," the officer said. "There's no threat." With that, he moved on to the next store.

I turned my attention back to the man on the bench. "What size bike shorts do you wear?"

"Large," he said.

"I'll run into the store and get you a new pair so you won't have to drive home in wet shorts. I'll see if they sell underwear, too."

"No need," the guy said. "Bike shorts are designed for going commando."

I hadn't been aware of that fact, but it made sense given how tightly the shorts clung to the body. Victoria might keep secrets, but bike shorts sure didn't.

I signaled Brigit to follow me as I went into the store and bought the man a new pair of bicycle shorts. I opted for a pair on the more expensive end of the range, hoping the gesture would buy goodwill. We might need it.

When I returned to the bench, the man took the shorts from me, offering a quick "Thanks, officer," before heading to the men's restroom to change.

Just after the man left, Derek emerged from the atrium with one of the other SWAT officers. The two headed my way.

I intercepted Derek as he walked past. "You owe me sixty-five bucks."

Derek waited until his cohort had continued on before turning to me and issuing a snort. "Buying the guy new shorts wasn't *my* idea."

"Paying me back is the least you could do." *You asshat.* "If not for me, you could be facing a manslaughter charge."

He looked away. "Maybe I wasn't even going to shoot. Maybe you shoving my arm down is what made the gun go off."

Seriously? I debated arguing with him, but there was nothing to be gained. He seemed to be trying to convince himself he hadn't almost made a terrible mistake. Denial was probably some sort of psychological defense mechanism. Besides, the video footage would show exactly what happened here. At least I hoped it would. Depending on the angle, the footage might be difficult to interpret. Besides, it had begun to get dark outside and everything had happened in a split second.

I debated whether to go back out on the beat but, frankly, I wanted to see how things would play out here. I'd never been involved in anything remotely similar to this situation, and I was curious how the department would handle it. With Brigit tagging along, I made my way up and down the sidewalk, collecting bags that shoppers had dropped. I'd take them to the mall management in the hopes that whoever had paid for the merchandise would return to claim their items.

It wasn't long before Detective Hector Bustamente arrived on the scene. Bustamente was a clever, corpulent man who didn't get easily ruffled. His calm nature was an asset in his line of work. He'd handled thousands of cases during his tenure, and had one of the highest closing rates in the Fort Worth PD. He stopped in front of me and Brigit and gave us a nod. "Hello, Officer Luz. Heard y'all had some excitement here tonight."

I chuckled mirthlessly. "That's one way to put it." Now that things had settled down, the adrenaline that had spiked through my veins earlier was wearing off. I felt cold and shivery. My teeth tried to chatter, but I clamped my jaw down tight to prevent that from happening. Through gritted teeth, I asked, "Why would someone call in a fake active shooter report?"

Though I'd meant the question to be rhetorical, he gave me an answer. "Because it gives them a kick to get everyone in a dither and force a response from law enforcement. Makes them feel like a big shot."

In other words, a power trip. Now that he'd explained the *why*, I wanted to know the *who*. "What did dispatch tell you about the caller?"

"That she sounded frantic."

He raised his cell phone, tapped a few buttons, and replayed the phone call for me. *"Send help!"* a high-pitched voice cried. *"There are three shooters at Chisholm Trail Mall!"* A sound could be heard in the background, a *pop-pop-pop* that could have been gunfire or fireworks or even someone repeatedly hitting a nail with a hammer. *Who knows?* Before the dispatcher could ask for more information, the caller cried, *"They're coming my way! I have to run!"* The line went dead.

I pondered things for a moment. Though the voice was high-pitched like a woman's, it was natural for a person's voice to rise an octave or two when they were under stress. The voice might have belonged to a man. Of course, if the caller was pulling a fast one and knew there were no actual shooters at the mall, the high pitch could have been an intentional affectation to disguise their normal voice. "Are you sure the caller was a woman?"

Bustamante shrugged. "Dispatch tried to reconnect but nobody answered the phone. I've tried the number three times since, but no one has picked up. We've got the tech team working on pinging its location."

"Do you know who the number belongs to?"

"No. The phone's on a prepaid plan."

"A burner, then." Cheap burner phones were commonly used by criminals or others who were up to no good, like cheating spouses.

"Maybe," Bustamante said, "or the phone could belong to

someone who simply can't afford a regular plan. Not everyone has a grand to drop on the latest iPhone. I suppose we'll find out soon enough."

He glanced around, taking note of the security cameras along the wing. "I'm going to see about getting the camera footage. If this was a prank, it's possible the cameras caught something. People usually want to see the results of their hoax, so it's likely the culprit was here, enjoying the chaos they'd created."

Sheesh. If the person wanted to see some excitement, they could've just bought a movie ticket. The theaters could use the business.

Bustamente gestured toward the parking lot at the end of the building. "As much as I enjoy chatting with you, Officer Luz, they could use your help out there."

"Yes, sir." I raised the bags I'd collected. "Okay if I drop these with the mall management first?"

"I'll take them for you. I'm on my way to speak to the manager now."

I handed the bags over. "Good luck with the investigation." I signaled Brigit to follow by my side and we made our way back to the parking lot. Cars clogged the exits, having crashed into each other in the drivers' mad attempts to escape what they thought would become a scene of mass carnage. A dozen cop cars remained on site, as well as two ambulances. Medics tended to people who'd been hurt in the mayhem—*mayhem I'd inadvertently helped to create.* The thought made the half-digested garlic knots in my stomach twist themselves up again.

After securing Brigit in our cruiser with the windows down, I donned my white gloves and grabbed my traffic wand. It was nearly ten o'clock by then, and fully dark. An officer stood at what was normally an entrance only, but which was being used as an exit now to help alleviate the backup. I waved my light and motioned with my hand, directing cars out of the lot. As I directed traffic, I eyed the drivers and glanced around, wondering if the person who'd called in the report might be in the vicinity or in one of the vehicles, watching as things wound down. I could only hope that, if the incident was indeed a prank and not a mistake, the caller wouldn't make another false report. Someone could have easily lost their life in the chaos this evening. We might not be as lucky next time. *Please, God. Don't let there be a next time!*

As I waved my flashlight, my ears detected sirens activating in the distance. The deep blare of a horn told me a firetruck was leaving the station. Looked like it was going to be a busy night for Seth and Frankie, too. *So much for knocking wood.*

9
K-9 CONFUSION

Brigit

Brigit lay in her kennel in the back of the cruiser, panting and gazing out through the metal bars as Megan directed traffic. The dog had been trained to remain calm and still, even when the loud *bang* of bullets sounded around her. Megan took her to the shooting range often so she'd get used to the noise. But while Brigit might be used to it, she didn't like it. The loud noise hurt her ears, made her want to bolt or bite. When that cop fired his gun earlier tonight, it took every bit of her restraint not to sink her teeth into his leg. She knew Megan didn't like the guy. Megan stiffened up every time he was around, and she spoke her words differently, too, faster and shorter and louder. If Megan didn't like the guy, it went without saying that Brigit didn't like him, either. Their pack stuck together.

Besides the noise, the mall had been awash in scents, too. Perfume samples that women and teen girls tried on at the cosmetics counters in the department stores. The smells of all kinds of food wafting out of the food court in the center atrium. And especially human adrenaline. The people running out of the mall had been terrified. Megan had been, too. But she hadn't let it stop her from going in the opposite direction of everyone else.

When Brigit had smelled Megan's adrenaline, she felt sure that she'd soon be deployed to chase someone. She'd looked forward to running after a fleeing suspect and tackling them to the ground. It was fun, like a game to see how quickly she could catch the person. But Megan had never issued the order. Megan had tackled that other officer herself. Brigit had long since accepted that humans could be strange and unpredictable. She only wished she understood what, exactly, had been going on.

10

OVERSHADOWED

The Flamethrower

He arrived home to find the boys huddled around the television, watching the local news. *Since when do kids watch network TV anymore?* His son usually preferred to stream shows on Hulu or Netflix or one of the million other streaming services they'd signed up for.

He feigned ignorance as he walked into the living room. "Breaking news?" *A fire, maybe?*

His son continued to stare at the screen. "Something about shooters at Chisholm Trail mall."

That wasn't what he'd expected to hear, yet it wasn't much of a surprise, either. Seemed every time you turned around there was another mass shooting. "Was anyone killed? Did they catch the guys?"

Asher cut a look his way. He appeared amused, but it was hard to tell. The punk wore a perpetual smirk. "Wasn't anyone to catch."

"What do you mean?"

Asher stuck his hand into a plastic bowl on the coffee table and grabbed a handful of pretzels. "They're saying it was a bogus report."

"You mean there was no shooter? Nobody got hurt or killed?"

"Nope." Asher made a popping sound with his lips on the P.

"Well, at least that part is good news." The Flamethrower gestured to the screen. "Anything else?"

His son looked back over his shoulder. "Like what?"

The Flamethrower shrugged.

Asher scoffed. "Dude. What news would be more important than active shooters at the mall?"

He hated to admit it, but the little shit had a point.

Asher cocked his head. "Any chance you've changed your mind about buying us beer?"

The Flamethrower snorted. "Not on your life, buddy."

11
SHOPPING TRIPS AND GUILT TRIPS

Megan

Once the crowd had been cleared out, Brigit and I stuck around the mall Friday night to ensure calm while the management and maintenance dealt with the aftermath of the evacuation. They secured the stores that had been abandoned by the staff. They gathered remaining articles shoppers had dropped, including merchandise that had been run over in the parking lot. They cleaned up drinks and food items left behind. They also made sure the grills, fryers, and ovens were turned off in the food court.

When our shift was finally over, Brigit and I drove home through the nearly empty streets of Fort Worth. The streets seemed even darker than usual, but perhaps my perception was affected by my mood. *What kind of cretin would call in a false report of three active shooters?*

Besides untold numbers of skinned knees and bruises amassed

by the fleeing crowd, a teenage girl had broken her wrist when she'd tripped over a curb and reflexively put out a hand to halt her fall. A man suffered a heart attack and collapsed in the parking lot on the other side of the mall. According to my fellow officers, several shoppers had run past the man or hurdled his body before two heroic TCU students stopped, grabbed his legs, and dragged him to safety between two parked cars. They'd stayed with the panicked man until medics could get to him. *Situations like this reveal a person's true character.*

After giving Brigit a crunchy dog biscuit, I poured myself a glass of red wine, stripped off my sweat-soaked uniform, and filled the bathtub with warm water and lavender bubble bath. I lit a candle, turned off the lights, and soaked, eyes closed, forcing myself to take deep calming breaths like we did in the yoga classes I took on occasion. *Breathe in, two, three, four. Breathe out, two, three, four.* After several rounds of deep breathing, I tossed back a large gulp of wine. I repeated the process until the wine was gone, then simply soaked until the water went cold. Brigit came to check on me two or three times, but made the mistake of sampling the flowery water only on her first visit.

Once I'd brushed my teeth and donned my nightgown, I joined Brigit in the bed. Though she couldn't know precisely what had happened tonight, the perceptive pup sensed my distress. I didn't want to imagine how much worse things could have been, how much more traumatized everyone would be had there actually been three shooters—or even just one, for that matter. Brigit licked my cheek, whimpered softly, and licked my cheek again, trying to comfort me in her sweet doggy way. I ruffled her ear. "Thanks, girl."

I slept fitfully, tossing, turning, and twisting, wishing I had Seth to snuggle up to. But anyone who paired up with a firefighter soon learned they were lucky to share their bed with their beloved four nights a week. At least the time apart gave us a chance to miss each other, kept things romantic.

I woke Saturday morning to the smell of fresh coffee brewing and the *thud* of Brigit's paws hitting the floor as she slid off the bed. *Seth and Blast are home.* I sat up, angling my head one way and then the other to crack my tight neck. After a body-wakening stretch, I slid out of bed, too, and padded to the kitchen. Seth was there, dressed in a pair of shorts and a T-shirt. He must've slipped into the bedroom to change while I was still asleep.

He eyed my wild hair before fishing a mug out of the cabinet, filling it with coffee, and handing it to me. "You look like you could use this."

"I'll try not to take that as an insult." I took the mug from him and added a dash of flavored oat milk creamer from the fridge. Turning back to him, I said, "You hear what happened at the mall?"

"That someone reported a gang of gunmen? Yeah. The medics filled us in. They were concerned about whether it was safe to go in and help people. Thank God it wasn't true."

Thank God, indeed. "Detective Bustamente played the nine-one-one call for me. There was a noise in the background that sounded like gunfire, but it could have been something else. He's not sure if the caller was mixed up on what was happening and mistakenly made a false report, or if the whole thing was a hoax from the start. The call was made from a prepaid phone. Last I spoke with him, the tech team was trying to ping the device."

"I hope they figure things out," Seth said.

"Me, too." I took a sip of my coffee. "I heard the firetrucks head out last night, too."

Seth filled me in on the details. "There was a dumpster fire behind a fitness center on Stanley Avenue. It was intentionally set."

"How do you know?"

"We found flammable materials."

"Gasoline? Lighter fluid?"

He shook his head. "Fritos."

"Fritos?" I repeated, holding my coffee mug halfway to my lips. "The corn chips?"

"Yep. Believe it or not, they can be used to start a fire. Corn chips are incredibly greasy."

I'd heard of Frito pie, but never a Frito pyre. Still, I supposed it made sense. Cooking oils caused many kitchen fires, and the chips were fried in oil. If the chip was heated by a flame, the absorbed oil could ignite. I knew from personal experience that the chips contained excessive amounts of oil. They always left a greasy coating on my fingers when I ate them.

Seth went on. "There weren't any security cameras on the back of the building, but we're guessing it was kids experimenting, maybe after seeing a video online. Probably somebody on TikTok posted a recording of themselves doing it."

Social media stunts got a lot of attention and encouraged risky behavior. Reports came in regularly to the police department about someone doing something dangerous while someone else filmed it. The Tide Pod challenge was probably the most notorious, but there were also stunts where people jumped from moving boats. There was even one stunt called the skull breaker challenge where three kids would jump into the air, and the two on the sides would kick the legs out from under the one in the center, making them fall backward and smack their heads on the ground. Needless to say, that stunt had led to several serious concussions.

"The fire probably wouldn't have gotten far," Seth said, "but the fitness center had just thrown out a bunch of old towels and some cleaning rags covered in the oil they use to lubricate the machines. The dumpster was a tinder box and went up like the fourth of July. Thank goodness the flames were contained and didn't spread to the houses behind the strip center."

The fire was another unfortunate and scary situation, but I told myself to look on the bright side. Nobody had lost their life, home, or business in either incident last night. Things could have been a whole lot worse.

Given that Seth had made the coffee, I supposed I should reciprocate by fixing us something to eat. Though it was morning and I'd be eating breakfast, I realized the meal would be more like a dinner to Seth given his twenty-four-hours-on/twenty-four-hours-off schedule. "Want some avocado toast? There's also leftover pesto fettuccine if that sounds better to you."

"Toast is fine."

Seth took the dogs out back for some playtime while I rounded up the whole-grain bread and gave our supply of avocados a squeeze to see which ones were ripe. I slid two slices of bread into the toaster and turned to retrieve the Tajín seasoning, a perfect blend of lime, chile peppers, and sea salt. When I did, my eyes spotted a small package sitting atop a brochure on the counter. I picked up the package to examine it. One side was clear, allowing me to see the five bright orange tablets inside. If not for the fact that there was no S or M imprinted on them, I might have thought they were Skittles or M&M candies. The other side of the package was black and printed with a neon green logo that read PHYSICAL FORCE SUPPLEMENTS in all caps. These particular tablets were identified as Mass Formula tablets. Below the product name appeared a mathematical formula: MASS = VOLUME X DENSITY. The company's website was also listed.

I picked up the brochure. It touted the benefits of the company's line of supplements. Larger muscles. Increased strength. Enhanced vitality. The image of the grinning, ripped guy surrounded by three gorgeous women said what the words didn't: *These pills will get you laid.* Sheesh.

The salesperson had scrawled his name—Nash Goshen—on the designated line on the back of the brochure. He'd also jotted his phone number, which began with area code 541. I wasn't familiar with that area code. Either he wasn't a local, or he'd purchased the phone somewhere else and decided to retain the number rather than going through the hassle of updating it.

As the bread toasted, I poured two glasses of orange juice and set them on the table, along with two napkins. I topped the toasted bread slices with a thick slathering of mashed avocado, sprinkled the zesty spice over the top, and set the plates on the table. If I didn't make something for the dogs to eat they'd demand some of our food, so I prepared each of them a bowl with half a can of wet food, a cup of dry kibble, and three baby carrots. Dogs, though often thought of as carnivores, were actually omnivores. Brigit loved to crunch on carrots and slices of apple. So did Blast. The low-calorie snack would fill their tummies while helping them stay in shape so they could do their important jobs.

I walked to the back door and opened it to call Seth and the dogs inside. "Food's ready!"

The dogs came running at full speed, tails wagging. Seth jogged up behind them. I set the bowls on the floor, and Seth and I took seats at the table. I pointed over to the little package on the counter. "Where'd you get those supplements?"

Seth picked up a slice of avocado toast. "Some guy came by the station selling them. He had a bunch of different types, some for bulking up and others for energy. He said he'd worked as a firefighter in Oregon so he knows how critical it is to stay in shape for the job."

While some people swore by supplements and I took a daily multivitamin myself, I tended to believe that the best ways to stay in shape and feel your best were to eat a healthy diet and exercise regularly. I was skeptical of the infomercials that claimed supplements could do everything from keeping a person looking young to enhancing their sexual performance. Besides, I'd tried ginkgo biloba once in college because it purportedly helped with focus and memory. All it had succeeded in doing was giving me a headache. "You planning to try them?"

"No," Seth said. "My usual routine seems to be working fine. Why mess with it?" Seth swam dozens of laps at the YMCA pool on his days off to stay in shape and, like me, he ate a relatively healthy diet to avoid putting on the pounds or ending up with a cholesterol problem. Not that we didn't cheat now and then. "Besides," he added, "those tablets cost a small fortune. A month's supply of the energy booster pills alone is eighty-nine bucks."

I did the math. At around three dollars a pill, the supplements were indeed expensive.

Seth went on. "The guy said we could join his distribution team as downline sales reps. He claimed the pills were a goldmine." He snorted a laugh. "He might have been more convincing if he hadn't asked whether the fire department was hiring."

I certainly couldn't blame this Nash guy for trying to make a buck, but I knew the city was short of firefighters and actively seeking new applicants. Firefighter salaries weren't exactly high to begin with, and tight city budgets meant small pay raises, if any. The job was demanding, both physically and psychologically. It wasn't easy to carry heavy hoses and equipment, along with the weighty emotional burden from witnessing traumatic events. Some firefighters had quit due to burnout over short-staffed stations and the demands of the job.

After we finished eating, Seth gathered up our plates and took them to the sink. As he prepared to wash them, I stood from the table. "I'd better get ready. I'm picking your mother up to go dress shopping."

"I hope she'll have better luck finding a dress with you along."

"Me, too. A second opinion is always helpful."

I cleaned up, dressed, and headed out in my personal vehicle, a tiny blue Smart Car. As I passed the police station, I spotted Derek's black pickup truck in the lot. A tacky pair of rubber truck nuts hung from the rear, as usual. *No wonder he's single.* I turned into the lot and pulled up behind his truck. After retrieving the receipt for the bicycle shorts from my wallet, I circled the total with a pen, climbed out of my car, and slid it under the windshield wiper on the driver's side where Derek couldn't miss it. On my way back to my car, I pulled my foot back and gave his truck nuts a solid kick.

My task there completed, I drove to pick up Lisa at Seth's grandfather's house. The place was an older single-story model, made of wood siding and chipped orange brick. But while it had appeared neglected and dismal the first time I'd seen it, the home was much cheerier now. Seth had repainted the siding a nice shade of cornflower blue. Lisa had hung baskets of pink petunias from the eaves, affixed a wreath of faux sunflowers on the front door, and placed a gnome in sunglasses and a Speedo on the front porch, the silly decoration a nod to her son's love of swimming. Fortunately, Seth wore a more traditional bathing suit when he swam, forgoing the tight, tiny trunks that left nothing to the imagination, much like the bike shorts the man at the mall had been wearing the night before. The misshapen oak tree had been trimmed, and Seth and his grandfather Ollie had planted grass sod so that the yard was no longer mere dirt and weeds.

Lisa spotted me through the front window, waved, and stepped out onto the porch, a tote bag slung over her shoulder. Lisa had dishwater blond hair and the family's trademark chin dimple. Though she'd been painfully thin when she'd first returned to town a while back, she'd gained some weight and was a healthy lean now.

After turning to lock the deadbolt behind her, she cut across the lawn, climbed into my car, and placed her tote bag on the floorboard. A pair of shiny beige pumps were nestled in the bag. The neutral color would match any dress she might try on, and allow her to visualize the complete look.

After she fastened her seatbelt, she turned to face me. "I heard what happened at the mall last night. Were you involved?"

"Brigit and I responded when the call came in. It was chaos. Detective Bustamente is investigating. He's trying to determine if the caller genuinely thought there were gunmen entering the mall or if the call was a swatting incident."

Swatting, as the action came to be called, involved someone making a false report of a serious violent situation that would trigger a large and immediate police response. The most famous incident occurred in 2017 and involved a twenty-five-year-old man named Tyler Barris, who lived in Los Angeles. After a dispute involving an online video game, Barris called in a false report to the Wichita, Kansas police department, claiming to have already shot his father and to be holding his mother and brother hostage in their home. Barris believed that Shane Gaskill, one of the men involved in the video game dispute, still lived at the address he gave to the dispatcher. In reality, Gaskill had moved from that address and lived elsewhere. Law enforcement was dispatched to the address. The current resident, a twenty-eight-year-old man named Andrew Finch, had no idea why law enforcement was surrounding his home. When he came outside, multiple officers issued different commands, causing him understandable confusion. Finch was fatally shot by an officer who believed he was reaching for a weapon, though Finch was actually unarmed. *So tragic and heartbreaking.*

Upon investigation, it was discovered that Barris had called in multiple false reports to police departments across the country. He was tried for involuntary manslaughter and sentenced to twenty years in prison. The district attorney determined that the police officer who shot Finch had followed department policy and declined to bring charges against him, but Finch's family subsequently filed a civil suit for excessive force. Had I not tackled Derek, the Big Dick could be facing a similar fate. *He owes me.*

Lisa shook her head. "People can be so awful."

She didn't know the half of it, but I wasn't about to educate her about the horrific things I'd encountered on the job. Ignorance is bliss, after all.

We drove to the closest bridal store. A clerk wandered over shortly after we entered. Her eyes went to my left hand, noting my engagement ring. "Looking for a wedding dress?"

"No, I've already got my dress." I'd commissioned a custom gown from a widow named Beverly who was a professional seamstress. I'd met the lovely woman while working an attempted burglary case. I'd later introduced her to Ollie, and the two had been dating ever since. I held out my hand to indicate Lisa. "We're hoping to find something for the mother of the groom."

The woman turned to Lisa. "Got anything specific in mind?"

"Not really," Lisa said. "I rarely wear dresses, so I'm not sure what style would look good on me."

"I'll round up some different options for you to try, then."

The woman gathered up several dresses and hung them in a dressing room. Lisa tried all of them on, but most of the stock was traditional and frumpy, in subdued hues and unflattering styles seemingly intended to keep the wearer from having any chance of overshadowing the bride. None were right. We thanked the clerk and returned to my car to try the next store.

We had slightly better luck there. A plum-colored sheath dress flattered Lisa's figure and the price was reasonable. The garment was a little plain, though, and we weren't yet sold. The saleswoman didn't want us to leave without a dress in hand, and came at us with the aggressive tactics of a car salesman. "Some sparkly jewelry would do the trick. Or a colorful shawl or scarf. If you don't buy the dress now, I can't guarantee it'll be here when you come back."

"I'll keep it in mind," Lisa said. "We've only just started looking." With that, we slipped out of the woman's grasp and aimed for the door.

Our next stop was the Chisholm Trail Mall. If I hadn't responded to the active shooter call myself the night before, I wouldn't know anything unusual had happened here. The shattered pot had been removed and the dirt had been cleaned up. People strolled calmly about, chatting, sipping drinks, window shopping. It was nice to see that things had returned to normal so quickly. I wondered whether Detective Bustamente had made any progress yet, traced the prepaid phone to a location, or received any information from the service provider. Though I knew he'd contact me with an update, I also knew it would not be instantaneous. His first priority was figuring out what, exactly, had taken place. For all I knew, he'd already pinged the phone and made an arrest. *If only we could be so lucky.*

A blonde coed was on us the instant we crossed the store's threshold. *She must work on commission.* "Hey, y'all," she said, her voice dripping with southern sweetness. "Looking for something to wear to a special occasion?"

The place was a formalwear shop. Everyone who walked in the door was looking for attire for a special occasion. But I didn't insult the girl by pointing this out. She was only doing her job.

Lisa gestured my way. "This beautiful young lady will be marrying my son in two months. I'm having trouble finding the perfect dress for their wedding."

The sales clerk turned to me. "So happy for you! Tell me about the big day. Will it be an indoor or outdoor wedding? Super dressy, black tie only? Or more casual and relaxed? Will there be dancing?"

My hopes were lifted. She was asking all the right questions to ensure Lisa found just the right dress.

"It will be an indoor wedding," I said, "but not overly formal. We're planning on lots of dancing. Mostly, we want it to be a fun celebration, a party."

Her head bobbed as she listened. When I finished, she said, "Gotcha." She motioned for Lisa and me to follow her. She led us to a rack on a side wall. While some of the dresses bore shiny rhinestones or sequins and looked more appropriate for a New Year's Eve soirée, several of the options were the perfect blend of fancy and fun. She pulled a number of them from the rack, holding them up in front of Lisa and issuing various noises depending on her conclusions. An *nnn* meant no. A head tilt and *hmm* meant maybe. And the "ooh!" she issued when she held up a fitted teal number with three-quarter length sleeves and ruffles along the crossover neckline and skirt said this might be the one.

The sales clerk led us to a large dressing room. While the two of us waited outside, Lisa slipped into the teal dress. From over the top of the door, we heard her gasp in delight. She opened the door to show us, and her lips spread in a big smile. The dress appeared to have been specially made just for her. Everything from the color, to the fit, to the style was flattering.

My hands reflexively covered my mouth, stifling my cry of glee. "Lisa! It's gorgeous!"

She turned side to side, beaming. "It is, isn't it?"

"It's not *the dress* that's gorgeous," the clerk said. "*You* are what's gorgeous."

I gave the girl a nod. "You really know your stuff."

"Thanks. I'm majoring in fashion merchandising, so that means a lot." She gestured with her hand, directing Lisa to raise her arms. She proceeded to check the fit, moving her hands down the side seam, tugging gently to see where it might be roomy. Her movements were similar to the pat-downs police officers gave suspects. "We could take in a half inch around the hips if you'd like, but I'm not sure it's necessary."

I didn't think so, either. "Gotta leave some room for a big piece of wedding cake."

Lisa concurred. "I don't want it to restrict me on the dance floor." She improvised the dance move commonly known as the cabbage patch, and we all shared a laugh.

I snapped several photos of her with my phone before she slid out of the dress and carried it to the checkout counter to pay for it. Luckily, the price was the perfect size too, and remarkably affordable. Lisa had dropped out of high school and worked as a hotel housekeeper for years. She didn't have a lot of money to spend on a dress. But when Seth had offered to buy her wedding outfit, she'd refused him. *"I've taken enough from you,"* she'd said with a sob. *"Your whole childhood."* Of course, getting pregnant with Seth had cut Lisa's childhood short, too.

The clerk put the dress in a fancy vinyl hanging bag to protect it and handed it over. "Enjoy the wedding."

"I will!"

After Lisa thanked the clerk again and promised to write a five-star review online, we returned to my car and I drove her home. When we reached her house, I stepped out of the car to give her a goodbye hug.

As she released me and stepped back, tears brimmed in her eyes. "I feel so lucky, Megan. I couldn't ask for a better wife for my son, or a better daughter-in-law for myself."

Tears pricked at my eyes, as well. "I couldn't imagine a better mother-in-law, either. Aren't you supposed to be critical and interfering?"

She laughed, but then her expression darkened. "Does Seth ever—" She stopped herself, as if unsure she wanted to continue.

Though I didn't want to pressure her, it wasn't good for her to keep things bottled up. I could tell whatever she wanted to talk about was weighing on her. She might feel better if she got things off her chest. "Does Seth ever ... what?" I held up a palm, inviting her to finish.

She bit her lip, then blurted, "Does he ever talk about his father?"

What would there be to say? Seth's father had never been in his life, and Lisa had never told Seth who his father was. Seth had confided that he'd been curious as a child but, as he grew up, he came to the conclusion that, if his mother didn't want him to know who his father was, the guy must be a real loser. After all, what kind of guy knocks up his teenage girlfriend and then totally drops out of the picture?

"Seth doesn't talk about his father." Even so, I wasn't about to lie to Lisa. "It will always be an issue for him, though. He'll always wonder why his father didn't help you out, or care enough to meet his son even once. But it's not something he dwells on."

Seth had suffered abandonment and attachment issues, not only due to his father's lack of involvement but also when his young mother left him in the care of her parents and took off for long periods of time. When Seth had first realized he had serious feelings for me, he'd backed away, an instinctive reaction to protect himself from vulnerability and potential hurt. He'd broken my heart. Fortunately, he realized rather quickly that he'd made a mistake and come back with his tail between his legs, begging me to give him another chance. In light of his background, I was willing to cut him some slack and move past it. Things had been great since, nothing more than the usual minor relationship snags.

Lisa looked off into the distance as if trying to look back in time and see what she might have done to prevent her son from suffering. But it was too late for that. The best she could do was be a good mother to him now, even if he no longer needed much from her.

I gave her a second warm hug, for good measure, and stepped back. "For what it's worth, he's forgiven you."

At that, her lips quivered for a second or two before she burst into a sob. I'd hoped my words would console her, but they seemed to have the opposite effect. I pulled her into another embrace, and she cried on my shoulder for a long moment before getting herself under control, lifting her head, and backing away again. "I'm so sorry, Megan. I just … I just wished I hadn't messed everything up so badly. I'm so glad he's found happiness with you, and the chance to have a real family of his own."

"I'm glad about that, too." I reached out and squeezed her hand. "See you again soon." With that, I returned to my car, feeling misty. *Poor Lisa.* She'd had a difficult life and carried such a heavy burden of guilt. I wished there was some way to lift it.

12

PACK 'N PLAY

Brigit

Their whole pack was together tonight, all four of them—Megan, Brigit, Seth, and Blast. Brigit loved it when her pack was complete. Megan and Seth were curled up on the couch watching a movie on the television, while Brigit and Blast wrangled on the rug.

"Who wants popcorn?" Megan called.

Immediately, Brigit and Blast stopped playing and sat at attention. *We do!*

Megan went to the kitchen to prepare the popcorn under the watchful eye of the two dogs. When it was ready, she poured it into a large bowl and returned to the couch, where she and Seth tossed popcorn into the air for the dogs to catch. Brigit knew the ones Megan tossed were intended for her and that the ones Seth tossed were intended for Blast, but she had no qualms snatching Blast's popcorn out of the air when he moved too slowly.

"Brigit!" Megan scolded. "Let Blast have his fair share."

Knowing Megan couldn't resist when she played cute and contrite, Brigit flopped over and rolled onto her back, exposing her underside. Sure enough, Megan shook her head but reached down and scratched the dog's belly. *I've got Megan wrapped around my paw.*

Blast, on the other hand, glanced over at her, his ears back and his tail still. He didn't appreciate Brigit stealing his treats. She wriggled over on her back, lifted her head, and gave his mouth a quick swipe with her tongue. He still sat rigid. She rolled back over onto her belly. When Megan tossed her the next bit of popcorn, Brigit intentionally let it fall to the floor, then nudged it in Blast's direction. He looked from her to the popcorn, then lowered his head to eat it. Once he'd gobbled it down, he wagged his tail again, letting Brigit know she was forgiven.

13
LEGAL ROBBERY

The Flamethrower

First thing Monday morning, he got on the phone to see about getting an attorney to represent him in the divorce. He figured hiring a female attorney might earn him some brownie points with the judge, but he wanted a ballbuster. He searched online, reading over the reviews, and found one who "fights hard," was a "shrewd negotiator", and "doesn't take sh*t from anybody." *That's my girl.*

After a few minutes on the phone with the law firm's receptionist, the Flamethrower grasped his hair in a death grip. He didn't expect that hiring legal representation would be a pleasant process, but he didn't expect to feel like the attorney was trying to screw him over just like Gretchen was. "Five grand? Are you kidding me?"

The receptionist was nonplussed, evidently used to complaints about the firm's fees. "That's a typical retainer for a divorce. These matters can be time-consuming, especially if the parties are uncooperative."

He didn't want to cooperate. Hell, he didn't want this divorce at all! But he was up against a deadline for responding to his wife's divorce petition, and he could get screwed if he failed to respond on time and protect his interests. "Fine," he spat. "How soon can you get me in to see the lawyer?"

He'd been pacing the house during the phone call to burn off his anxious energy. He found himself in his son's room, though pig sty might be a more appropriate term. The space reeked of teenage funk. *When was the last time the kid had washed his damn sheets?* Dirty, rumpled clothes were strewn all about—on the back of his desk chair, his dresser, the bed, and wadded up on the floor. Gretchen had always done Hayden's laundry and washed his bedding, but the boy was old enough to take care of these things himself. The Flamethrower wasn't about to coddle the kid. Hell, some of the mess wasn't even his Hayden's. Asher had left his water bottle on the floor. It was a large navy blue one with a built-in straw, a Yeti brand bottle, one of the most expensive. If Asher wasn't going to respect his property, the Flamethrower felt no obligation to, either. He took his frustrations out on the bottle, kicking it under the bed.

The receptionist came back on the line, offering a thirty-minute appointment two days later. The Flamethrower could either take the appointment or waste precious time calling other law offices, hopelessly seeking a lower retainer and better hourly rate. He exhaled sharply, not bothering to turn the microphone away even though he knew the noise might hurt the woman's ears. "Put me on her calendar."

14
INTERNAL AFFAIRS

Megan

The mail carrier had delivered our wedding invitations on Monday afternoon, and Seth and I sat down at the kitchen table Tuesday morning to assemble them. My penmanship was far better than his, so we decided I should be the one to address the envelopes. I carefully made out the first envelope and handed it to Seth. He added a postage stamp to the front, then turned the envelope over to insert the invitation and reply card. Curious what the humans were doing, Brigit strode up to the table, her mouth hanging slightly open. Seth had raised the envelope to his lips to seal it, but he glanced down at the dog and apparently got a better idea. He lowered the envelope and ran the adhesive strip over Brigit's tongue to moisten it. After pressing the flap into place, he rewarded her with a dog biscuit. He performed the same routine with the next envelope. Brigit didn't seem to mind.

I gave my fiancé the evil eye. "There better not be crumbs on that seal." I got up and wet the kitchen sponge at the sink, squeezing the excess water from it. I handed the damp sponge to Seth. "Try this instead."

Brigit huffed in disappointment. No more trading her tongue for treats. Having been unceremoniously fired from her envelope-licking job, she wandered to the living room.

I sat back down, and Seth and I continued to work. My hand grew cramped as I wrote out address after address, but eventually we finished with the invitations and slid them into a bag so I could drop them off at the post office before my shift. I changed into my police uniform and gave Seth a kiss goodbye. I gave Blast a goodbye kiss, too, though I applied it to his forehead rather than his lips. I knew where that mouth had been.

"C'mon, girl!" I called to Brigit, signaling with my hand. "Time to go to work!"

She slid down from the couch and performed a full-body stretch, then trotted with me to the door. Seconds later, we were in our cruiser, aimed for the post office. Rather than force others to wait behind me as I shoved them into the outdoor mailbox, I decided to go inside. Brigit came into the lobby with me and watched the patrons pass by as I deposited the invitations into the outgoing mail bin. There were invitations for Detectives Jackson and Bustamente, of course, as well as the other officers and administrative staff who worked in my sector. I'd felt obligated to invite Derek, too, though I prayed he'd decline. The last thing I wanted to see on the happiest day of my life was his stupid face.

As I turned to exit, the branch manager spotted me. He was a seasoned employee, just a stone's throw from retirement. "Officer Luz!" He waved me and my furry partner up to the counter. "Do you and Brigit have time to inspect some suspicious packages?"

Local law enforcement agencies often assisted the post office in determining whether packages might contain illegal drugs or explosive materials. Senders often wrongfully believed that parcels sent via the United States Postal Service were exempt from search and seizure. They weren't. Stained or leaking boxes were a red flag to postal service employees, as were boxes packaged or wrapped in a way that seemed intended to thwart inspection, such as boxes that were entirely encased in clear strapping tape. A box that emitted a ticking sound was also a dead giveaway.

"Happy to help." This wasn't our first rodeo. Brigit and I had inspected packages at this branch several times before. "How have you been, Mr. Baldwin?"

"Fair to middling," he replied. "My back hurts constantly from all those years lugging a heavy mail sack, but I'm still alive so I suppose that's something."

Baldwin unlocked a door to allow Brigit and me into the rear sorting area. There, he removed three packages from a locked cabinet and set them atop a table. The first was a large flat-rate priority mail box with tiny brown granules leaking from a corner.

I placed the box on the floor and gave Brigit the order to sniff. She lowered her head, gave the box a once-over, and sat, issuing a passive alert. "Yep, there's drugs in the box." I bent down, tapped my finger on the brown granules that had leaked from the box onto the floor, and lifted my finger to my nose. Sure enough, even a mere human like me could recognize this particular scent. "Coffee grounds." Though commonly used in an attempt to thwart drug detection by trained K-9s, coffee grounds were overhyped as a deterrent and rarely prevented a competent canine from scenting illegal substances.

"Thanks." Baldwin picked up the box and returned it to the cabinet.

The second box was stained from a clear liquid having spilled inside. The box gave off a light floral scent. Brigit thoroughly sniffed the box when I set it down in front of her, but did not issue an alert. I picked it up and handed it back to the clerk. "This one's clean." Brigit's nose was never wrong.

The third box was a repurposed Amazon delivery box, approximately twelve inches by twelve inches square. Thick, bright orange duct tape had been applied along every seam to thoroughly seal the contents, and the word FRAGILE had been written on each side in red marker along with a drawing of a smiley face that might have been intended to be disarming. I placed the box in front of Brigit and issued the order for her to check it out. She sniffed intently along the tape at the left edge, followed it across the top, then sniffed along the right edge. When she finished, she again plunked her hindquarters down on the floor, issuing a passive alert. "Something's in that box that shouldn't be."

Baldwin gave Brigit a pat on the head. "Thanks, Brigit. We can always count on you."

I scoffed in jest. "What am I? Chopped liver?"

"By comparison?" Baldwin teased. "Yes." He looked down at Brigit again. "I don't have dog treats, but I've got half a turkey sandwich left over from my lunch. Could I give it to her?"

Brigit might not have understood exactly what Baldwin said, but she recognized the word *turkey* and hoped it had something to do with her. She looked from Baldwin to me, her tail wagging in a canine plea. How could I deny her the special treat? Especially when she'd just taken illegal drugs off the streets? "Sure," I said.

Baldwin hustled to his office and returned with the half sandwich in a clear bag smeared with mayonnaise on the inside. The sandwich was cut on a diagonal. *Fancy.* He pulled it out of the bag and held it out to my partner. She took one sniff, snatched the sandwich out of his hand, and wolfed it down in three gulps, not bothering to chew. She licked the mayo from her lips and belched. *Brrrrp!*

I looked down at her and wagged my finger. "You need to work on your table manners, girl." After bidding goodbye to Baldwin, my furry partner and I headed to the exit.

Before we reached the door, a woman stepped into the lobby. She had a cardboard box in her hands and a colorful parrot perched on her shoulder. The bird looked down at Brigit, spread her wings, and said, "Woof-woof" in an amazingly dog-like way. If I hadn't seen with my own eyes that it was a bird barking, I would have sworn it was a dog.

Brigit stopped in her tracks and cocked her head, staring up at the bird with a *what-the-heck?* expression on her face.

The woman and I shared a laugh. "I have a terrier mix," she said. "My bird loves to imitate him. I'm not sure exactly what the barks are saying but, apparently, it's quite insulting. The terrier gets all riled up."

Brigit, too, seemed insulted. She gave the bird a low growl and a single *arf* in response. The bird laughed as we walked out the door. "Ha-ha-ha!"

We spent the afternoon cruising our beat. I issued a few traffic citations, all of which were warranted and none of which were appreciated. One of the recipients had been doing fifty-eight miles per hour in a thirty zone, nearly double the speed limit. Despite this fact, he had the nerve to mutter "bitch," under his breath as I'd walked away from his window. I could understand being upset by the ticket and the fine he'd have to pay, but he only had himself to blame. I wasn't going to let some jerk ruin my day, but I wasn't above giving tit for tat, either. I turned back to eye him and raised my brows in question. I kept my tone cordial, not because I was being recorded by my body cam, but because it drove jerks crazy when an officer didn't get ruffled by their rudeness. I cupped a hand around my ear. "Excuse me? I didn't quite hear you. Could you repeat that?"

He glared at me. "I didn't say anything. Even if I did, it's my right as an American to say whatever I want to. It's right there in the Constitution after 'We the people.'"

Such a patriot. "Actually, sir, free speech was not mentioned in the original Constitution. It's in the Bill of Rights. The First Amendment." *Someone didn't pay attention in their high school history and government classes.* I lowered my hand from my ear to straighten the body cam on my chest. "If you'd like to exercise this right, I'd be happy to come closer to ensure your words are recorded clearly."

His eyes flicked to the small lens then back to my face, and a purple blush rushed up his neck as he realized he'd been caught on camera acting like an ass. His mouth spread in a fake grin but anger still lit up his eyes. "No need, officer. Thank you for your service."

"You're more than welcome, sir." *You big turd.* "Drive safely." I turned around, rolling my eyes as I returned to my cruiser.

My butt had just settled in the driver's seat of the patrol car when my cell phone came alive with an incoming call. I checked the screen. *Internal Affairs.* Though I'd been expecting their call, a sense of dread nonetheless spread tendrils through me. Last Friday at the shopping mall had been a nightmare. I didn't want to relive it, but I'd have to. I tapped the button to accept the call. "Officer Megan Luz."

The investigator identified himself. "Can you swing by to speak with us? We've got some questions about what happened at the mall last week."

"Sure." I was between calls and could head to headquarters immediately. "I'll be there in a few minutes."

I drove to the Fort Worth Police Department's headquarters on West Felix Street and brought Brigit inside with me. We rode the elevator up to the Internal Affairs division, checked in with the administrative assistant at the desk, and were directed to a conference room. Three fifty-ish men sat on one side of the table inside. Both their hair and their business suits were gray, though in varying shades. They stood, introduced themselves, and shook my hand before the lead investigator invited me to take a seat across from them. Brigit settled on the floor at my feet, lying on her belly.

The man pushed his legal pad forward a few inches, set his pen atop the pad, and leaned back in his seat, his casual behavior seemingly intended to put me at ease. "Tell us what happened at the mall, start to finish."

"Sure." As my mind went back to that terrifying night, my throat clogged with emotion. I swallowed to clear it. "I wasn't far from the mall when the call came out for officers to respond to a report of three shooters. B-Brigit and I r-rushed over." *Ugh. There goes my stutter.* I took a calming breath and slowed my speech. "When I drove into the mall parking lot, I noticed everyone was acting normal, like nothing unusual was going on."

As I spoke to the men, another internal affair began in Brigit's belly below me. It started with a gurgle, followed by an elongated growl. There was a muted *pfft*, and the odor of canine flatulence filled the air. In retrospect, letting her wolf down that mayonnaise-soaked sandwich at the post office had been a mistake. "Sorry about my dog."

One of the men picked up the legal pad and fanned the air. "Were you surprised?"

"Somewhat," I replied, "but it's a large mall. I thought maybe the shooters were on another side of the mall and that the shoppers on my wing weren't aware yet. I pulled out my bullhorn and directed everyone to clear the area. Then I put on my riot gear as fast as I could and got Brigit out of her enclosure. We were heading into the mall when I saw the SWAT truck enter the parking lot." I told them how Derek came running past me down the wing. "A man came out of the sporting goods store up ahead. He was dressed all in black and had a long black tube in his hand, with the other end resting on his shoulder. My immediate impression was that he was carrying a rifle, but then I realized he was wearing biking gear and that the tube was a tire pump. Officer Mackey had stopped behind a potted plant and was raising his gun. It looked to me that he had been mistaken about what the man was carrying, too. I thought he was about to fire, so I dove at him to force his arm down. The gun discharged into the pot. The SWAT captain must have heard it because he came over the radio asking about the gunshot. Officer Mackey told the captain that his gun discharged accidentally. I told Mackey that I would talk to the man with the bike pump while he regrouped with the SWAT team in the mall's atrium."

One of the other men eyed me intently. "I understand the man soiled himself and that you bought him a new pair of bike shorts."

It was more a statement than a question, but I knew he was awaiting confirmation. "That's correct."

"Did the shopper demand that his clothing be replaced?"

"No, sir," I said.

"Was the purchase intended as an admission of guilt?"

"Guilt?" I wasn't sure if they were referring to guilt on my part or Derek's but, either way, that thought hadn't crossed my mind at the time. Yes, the shopper wet himself in reaction to seeing a SWAT officer aim a gun at him, but the person most to blame was the caller who'd set the entire course of events into motion. I was no fan of Derek, but he had reacted on instinct and training. He could have made a horrific mistake Friday night, but it would have been just that. A mistake. *Thank God it hadn't happened.*

The third man men chimed in. "Perhaps 'responsibility' is a better word than guilt."

I realized the man had lost bladder control as a result of Derek's actions, but did causation necessarily constitute responsibility? It was a complex question. "I didn't think about guilt or responsibility at that moment. I bought the shorts as an act of goodwill. I figured the man might be embarrassed or uncomfortable. I was trying to make things better in the only way I could."

The lead investigator sat up now. "Did you come into contact with Officer Mackey's gun when you dove at him?"

"I don't think so," I said, "but everything happened very fast. I only meant to prevent him from taking a shot."

His head bobbed slowly. "Might Officer Mackey have already been lowering his arm when you rushed him?"

I knew they were only trying to get a complete picture of what went down, but the direction this question had taken made my guts squirm. Were they implying *I* had done something wrong? "I didn't notice him lowering his arm. I wouldn't have thrown myself at him if I had."

The man angled his head ever so slightly, his features and voice softening. "Is it possible you overreacted? That Officer Mackey was only positioning himself to be ready in the event he needed to fire his weapon, but that he had not yet finished his assessment of the situation and had not begun to pull the trigger?"

Had Derek told them this story? Could it be true? Had I jumped the gun, so to speak? Not being able to read Derek's mind, I couldn't speak for him. I could only tell them the truth as I saw it. "It appeared to me that he was about to take a shot. My response was reflexive." I could no more have just stood there and observed than I could have performed a triple backflip.

As if sharing her opinion on the subject, Brigit released gas much louder this time. *Pfffft.* The fumes were even more noxious than they'd been before.

While the lead investigator again fanned the air with the legal pad, one of the others opened a laptop computer that had been sitting on the table next to him. He brought up a video clip and turned the screen to face me. He clicked on the arrow to play the clip, and the scene I'd just described unfolded from the viewpoint of a security camera on a light post along the wing. Here I came, rushing up the walkway toward the camera, hollering through my bullhorn, my gun in my other hand. Brigit sprinted beside me, looking up at me, waiting for orders. Derek rushed up from behind and passed by me, virtually screeching to a stop as the man appeared in the doorway of the sporting goods store. I had nearly caught up when Derek raised his arm. My bullhorn dropped from my hand. Brigit tripped over it, falling forward, her chin skidding along the concrete. Until I saw this recording, I hadn't even realized she'd fallen. *Poor baby! That must've hurt.* I glanced down at her. Her head rested on her paws and her eyes were closed as she catnapped.

I returned my attention to the screen. Still in motion, I shoved my gun into the holster on my hip and launched myself at Derek. A split second after impact, his gun flashed as his arm swung downward. The pot exploded into pieces. I rolled down the walk like a drunken, unskilled gymnast. Brigit rose to her feet and rushed after me. Derek stumbled forward a step or two into the mess of pottery and potting soil, but managed to right himself. His mouth fell open as he turned his head. His gaze went first to the man in the doorway, then over to me as I rose to my feet.

The investigators stared at me for a moment or two, observing and assessing. I didn't argue with them, and I didn't attempt to defend my interpretation of the events. They had a difficult decision to make, and I didn't envy them the responsibility for trying to read what had been in Derek's mind and mine. Whatever they determined, I knew we'd all been lucky. At the end of the day, while the events had taken an emotional toll on everyone involved, there'd been no loss of life. I wasn't sure if there were any lessons to be learned from that night. Because my actions had been instinctive rather than conscious, I wasn't sure I could do anything different should I find myself in a similar situation again. I also wasn't sure I should. I still believed I'd done the right thing. I told them so. "I did what I thought needed to be done."

After a long moment of silence, the lead investigator finally dismissed me. "That's all we need for now, Officer Luz. Thanks for speaking with us."

I gave them a nod, nudged my partner with my toe to wake her, and waited while she leveraged herself to her feet. She issued a final fart at the door as we exited the room.

Behind us, one of the men gasped. "What the hell is she feeding that dog?"

As we rode the elevator down to the main floor, Brigit again let one rip. I apologized to the two crime scene techs who were stuck in the elevator with us. Once we reached the first floor, I hurried her outside and onto the lawn, where she promptly popped a squat. Naturally, it was at precisely that moment that Police Chief Garelik walked up. He glanced in our direction, his nose quirking in disgust. The chief and Derek were hunting buddies and, while the chief couldn't deny that Brigit and I had been instrumental in solving a number of high-profile cases, it was no secret I wasn't his favorite underling. Nevertheless, I raised a hand and called, "Good afternoon, Chief!"

He offered a mere grunt in reply, not a warm greeting by any means, but at least an acknowledgment. He stopped and said, "Were you here to meet with internal affairs?"

"Yes, sir."

Technically, internal affairs reported to the chief of police, but they were intended to operate as an objective, impartial body. Chief Garelik would think twice before going against their recommendation if they suggested Derek Mackey be permanently relieved of his duties. The chief's lips moved, as if he wanted to ask me another question, but was holding back. He must have decided that questioning me was not advisable. He gave me a nod and went on his way.

I cleaned up Brigit's mess, tossed the poop bag into an outdoor trash can, and opened the back door to secure her in our cruiser. She hopped into her kennel, then turned around to face me. Before I could close the door, she whipped out her tongue and gave me a kiss on the cheek. I ran a hand over her head. "Thanks, girl. I needed that."

15
DON'T SWEAT IT

Brigit

Brigit was glad her kiss made Megan happy. She'd smelled the scents Megan had put off while they were in the room with those men. Megan smelled of sweat, the kind that humans produce when they are scared or worried. It smelled different than the sweat they produced when exercising. Brigit wasn't sure why those men had made Megan fearful, but she was glad it was over.

16

ASSETS AND ASSHOLES

The Flamethrower

Wednesday afternoon, he sat in the attorney's office, waiting and listening to the wall clock tick-tick-tick up his bill as she looked over the list of assets he'd been instructed to bring. She was a broad, bullish White woman with a square face, her spiky red hair sticking up from her head like bloody knives. She wore a slate blue pantsuit with a white button-down. No jewelry. No makeup. No nonsense. He speculated she might enjoy the company of women.

She looked up when she finished perusing the list. "Which assets are you hoping to keep for yourself?"

He realized he hadn't given the matter much thought, even as he'd been putting the summary together. Truth be told, none of the property meant much to him other than his Camaro, and he'd even soured a little on the car. He'd felt like the king of the world when he'd driven it off the car lot but, now, it seemed to represent everything selfish and bad in him. If he thought Gretchen would let their son drive it, he'd give the car to Hayden. But Gretchen wouldn't be comfortable with their kid in a vehicle designed for style and speed rather than safety. He wasn't sure he wanted the house, either. He'd initially refused to leave the house in the hopes that Gretchen would decide to stay. He'd remained there after she left in the hope she'd come back home. But he didn't want to live there long term without her. He'd rather get a new place, one unencumbered with memories and a cabinet full of fancy china they rarely used.

"Just my car, I guess," he told the attorney. "If Gretchen wants the house, she can have it. We can split everything else fifty-fifty."

"If she takes the house, I assume you'll want her to buy out your share of the equity?"

He shrugged. "It's just money. I earn a good living, so it's not like I need it. Gretchen quit work years ago to stay home with our son, and she's only worked occasional part-time jobs since. She doesn't have much earning potential. I don't want her to struggle." That wasn't exactly true. He just didn't want Hayden to see his mother struggle. He knew his son would blame him for it.

"You're being remarkably magnanimous." The attorney cocked her head. "You feeling guilty? Did you cheat on your wife or something like that? Best you tell me now so I can be prepared. I don't like being blindsided at mediation or in court."

He shook his head. "I didn't cheat." *She did.* But for some reason, he didn't tell the lawyer that. Though he'd been furious when he'd been served with the divorce petition, he'd given things more thought the past couple of days. He didn't want to shame Gretchen for seeking the companionship and attention he'd stopped giving her. Besides, he knew Gretchen, how much she valued family and relationships. He believed her when she said that nothing had happened with Doak until after she'd told the Flamethrower she wanted to separate and had moved into the guest room. If there was even the faintest hope of getting her back, he needed to show her that he'd changed, that he wasn't only out for himself, that he could put her needs before his own.

It struck him how ironic things were now, that he was so desperate to maintain his marriage to Gretchen when he had considered himself out of her league when he'd first asked her out back in college. They'd had a biology class together, and he'd repeatedly caught her casting furtive glances at him. He could tell she had a major crush. She was pretty, sure, but he could have bagged an even prettier girl. A curvier one, too. Gretchen had been on the scrawny side before getting pregnant with Hayden and putting on a few pounds. But he'd got off on the adoration, if he was being honest, and he knew dating down came with an upside. A girl who felt lucky to have him would be more accommodating. She had been, at first, putting up with his boys' night bar crawls, never complaining that he rarely took her out and that their dates mainly consisted of cheap movie nights at his apartment. She even wrote a few papers for him so he'd have more time to work out with his pals from the baseball team. But as the years went by, Gretchen seemed to realize she might not have been so lucky, after all. Steven no longer felt out of her league. He realized he'd been the one to marry up. *I didn't deserve her.*

The attorney cocked her head in the other direction and arched a thick brow. "You sure you won't change your mind about the assets? I don't want to draft a settlement offer only to have to immediately revise it."

He didn't like being talked to like a child. "I won't change my mind. Trust me. The last thing I want to do is run up my legal fees. I'm already paying you an arm and a leg."

The bitch had the nerve to chuckle. "Well then," she looked up at the clock, "let's conclude this meeting before the next six-minute billing increment."

The Flamethrower stood. "Consider me gone."

17
PHONE PHONY

Megan

Wednesday morning, Brigit and I were patrolling our beat when my cell phone buzzed with an incoming call. The screen told me it was Detective Bustamente on the line. I whipped into the parking lot of a gas station, veered to the side where my cruiser wouldn't block customers, and braked to a quick stop that sent Brigit scrambling for purchase in her enclosure behind me. "Sorry, girl!" I called before tapping the icon to accept the call.

Bustamente greeted me with a curt. "Mornin', Officer Luz. Got some news to share with you."

"Have you arrested someone?"

He chortled. "I appreciate your faith in me, but no. Not yet, anyway. But I got a search warrant and contacted the cell service provider."

The cell phone company could give us critical account data, such as when the phone service was turned on, what numbers were called from the phone, and the source of incoming calls. The provider could give us texting history, as well. I knew better than to get my hopes up too high, though. Clever criminals knew to change phones often to avoid leaving a detailed trail. On the flip side, most criminals weren't all that clever, and rarely as smart as they considered themselves to be.

"Have you heard back from the provider yet?" I asked.

"Just a few minutes ago. The phone was a Tracfone."

Tracfones were cheap, common burner phones used by all sorts of criminals for all sorts of nefarious purposes. During my time on the force, I'd come across dozens of the phones in the pockets, cars, or homes of lawbreakers. Of course, many people used Tracfones for legitimate purposes, too, preferring the company's budget-friendly options over high-priced name-brand models.

I'd learned from earlier investigations that prepaid cell service had been provided to Tracfones via the Verizon network since Verizon acquired Tracfone in late 2021. I'd also learned that all mobile devices were identified by an Electronic Serial Number, ESN for short, as well as a Mobile Equipment Identifier, sometimes referred to as an MEID, or an International Mobile Equipment Identity or IMEI. The MEID or IMEI could be found in the phone's settings. The unique identifying number could also be found on the physical device under the battery, below the battery, or on the back of the phone, depending on the particular device. The number was used by cell phone companies and law enforcement to stop service to lost or stolen phones. The number could also be used to determine where a phone had been purchased, which might help identify who'd bought it.

Bustamente continued to fill me in. "The phone was activated Friday morning, just hours before the call came in to dispatch. The only activity on the phone was an incoming spam call from one of those car warranty outfits and the outgoing call to nine-one-one. No texts. No pics. No app downloads. No subsequent incoming or outgoing calls."

In other words, no data that might provide a clue as to the caller's identity.

Bustamente went on to say that the phone had been sold at a Dollar General store. "The company couldn't immediately pinpoint which store. Their manufacturing facility shipped boxes of phone inventory, including the one we're looking for, to a regional distribution center in Longview, so I had to contact the distribution center for the information. The distribution center told me the phone was shipped from their warehouse to the store located on East Berry Street four months ago. I thought you might want to come to the store with me. I've already cleared it with Captain Leone."

"Of course!" I was grateful the detective was willing to let me shadow him, and that my captain was willing to spare me. I was also grateful that it was a slow morning for lawbreakers. I might not have had this opportunity otherwise.

"Pick me up at the station," Bustamente said. "Pronto."

Brigit and I made a beeline to the station, where my partner took a quick potty break on the grass. We picked up the detective and got on our way again. At the stoplight just before the store, a sunburned white man in tattered tennis shoes, jeans, and a faded T-shirt sat on an upended five-gallon paint bucket, a crudely written cardboard sign in his hand. The sign read COMEDIAN ON A MEDIAN. CLEAN JOKES $1. DIRTY JOKES $2.

I had to give the guy credit. He'd come up with a good schtick. As we waited at the light, I unrolled my window and held out a single. The man stood, took the bill, and said, "Knock-knock."

"Who's there?" I asked.

"Dishes," he replied.

"Dishes who?"

"Dishes the police!" He pointed a finger gun at me. "Put your hands up!"

Bustamente and I laughed. "Good one," I told the guy.

"I got more if you want to hear 'em."

The traffic light cycled from red to green. "I'd love to, but we gotta go."

He waved goodbye as I punched the gas. We made the turn and took an immediate right into the parking lot. I let Brigit out of her enclosure, attached her leash, and we strode inside. I followed Bustamente as he stepped up to the register, where a thin, middle-aged woman with dark brown hair pulled up in a topknot was bagging cleaning products for a customer. As soon as she'd finished the transaction, Bustamente asked to speak to the manager.

The cashier cupped her hands around her mouth and called, "Hey, boss! There's cops up here that want to talk to you!"

The manager poked his dark, balding head out from around an aisle, where he'd been stocking the shelves. "I'll be right with you." He took a few more seconds to empty the box he'd been working on, flattened it, and carried it with him up to the counter. He looked at us expectantly. "What can I do for you?"

"I need information about sales of a particular model phone made at this store." Bustamente walked over to the locked phone display and pointed through the glass. "That Tracfone right there."

After a brief discussion, the manager circled around the checkout counter and ran the cash register records for the four months ending last Friday. He consulted the information on the screen. "We've sold seventy-one of those phones in the last four months." He printed out the sales transactions on register tape and handed the long strip of paper to Bustamente. Unfortunately, the records didn't identify the phones by their unique number, only the bar code for the model.

The detective consulted the strip of paper, slowly moving it through his fingers as he looked it over. "Looks like some of the phones were purchased with debit or credit cards. We don't need to be concerned with those."

I knew why he'd dismissed those sales. If someone had bought the phone for a nefarious purpose, they wouldn't have used a payment method that could be linked to them. They would have paid in cold, hard, untraceable cash.

After finishing with the tape, Bustamente looked back up at the manager. "We'll need to see your security camera footage. Let's start with the most recent cash sales and work backward."

The manager glanced over at the stack of boxes he'd been unpacking and frowned. "Tell you what. I got a big load delivered this morning, and I've got to get things out on the shelves ASAP. How 'bout I show you how to run the feed, and you can use my office as long as you need? Would that be okay?"

"That would be fine," Bustamente said. Law enforcement generally preferred to review evidence privately, when possible.

The man took us back to a small, windowless office in the stockroom, logged into his computer, and showed us how to run the feeds for the various cameras before leaving us to our work. I sat on an uncomfortable metal folding chair while Bustamente sat in the padded rolling desk chair. Brigit flopped down on the cool tile at our feet, softly panting.

The detective started with the first sale prior to the phone being activated Friday morning and selected the camera aimed at the checkout stand. Per the register tape, the transaction had taken place at 4:48 last Thursday afternoon. As we watched, the jokester from outside strolled into the store, grabbed a blue Gatorade from a refrigerated display, and walked over to the phone case. He turned and called back to the cashier, which happened to be the same one working today. She came out from behind the check stand, unlocked the glass case, and pulled a small box from a stack at the bottom of the case. She carried it up to the register herself, where she rang it up along with the Gatorade. She placed both items in one of the store's signature bright yellow plastic bags, took the cash the man offered her, and made change. As she pushed her till closed, he picked up his bag from the counter and strode outside. The exterior camera showed only the parking lot and part of the street. We watched until he walked out of view.

"Go get him," Bustamante ordered. "Bring him back here. I'll keep going in the meantime."

I rousted Brigit and we walked out of the store, side by side. I crossed with the light to the median where the panhandler sat. A man in a pickup truck waited at the light, his window down. I heard only the tail end of the joke but, judging from the punchline, he'd paid the $2 for a dirty joke.

"Excuse me," I said to the comedian-on-a-median. "We need you to come into the Dollar General store for a moment."

He went stiff, no longer chuckling along with his customer, his eyes wary. "Why's that?"

"We think you might have witnessed a crime."

He shrugged. "Not that I know of."

I hoped he wasn't going to give me a hard time. It was hotter than Hades out here and I didn't want to wrangle with him. I debated threatening him with my K-9 partner, but instead decided I'd catch more flies with honey. I motioned with my hand. "Come with me. I'll buy you a cold drink."

His face brightened and his features relaxed. "Now you're talkin'!"

I held out a hand, inviting him to lead the way so I could keep an eye on him from behind. Brigit and I followed him into the store, where he selected a blue Gatorade from the refrigerated case, just like he'd done last Thursday. He also grabbed a full-size bag of tortilla chips from a nearby snack display. "Mind if I get these, too?"

"No problem."

I paid for his items and we headed to the stockroom. On the way, we passed the pet section. Brigit sniffed at a stuffed pink dog toy shaped like a donut with colored sprinkles. After giving it the once over, she took the toy in her teeth and pulled it off the peg. It gave off a loud squeak—satisfying to her, annoying to us humans. She carried it with her as we went to the office. *This visit is adding up.*

I closed the door behind me and invited the comedian to take a seat on the folding chair.

Detective Bustamente introduced himself and offered his hand. "May I have your name, sir?"

"Matt Treacy," the man said, giving the detective some sort of a casual low-five soft slap rather than a handshake.

"Got any ID on you?" Bustamente asked.

"Yep." The man reached into his back pocket, removed his wallet, and pulled out a driver's license, holding it out to the detective.

Bustamente took a look at the license, then handed it back to the man. "Thanks." He pulled up the camera feed on the screen and angled his head to indicate the monitor. "Tell me what's going on here."

Treacy watched as the camera showed him enter the store, grab the Gatorade, then summon the cashier to the phone case. "That must've been from last week. Some guy walked up to me on the street and said he'd pay me twenty bucks if I'd buy the phone for him."

"Some guy?" Bustamente repeated. "You didn't know him?"

Treacy shook his head. "No. Never saw him before. Not that I remembered, anyway."

"Did he give you his name?"

Treacy shook his head again. "No. He just said he needed a new phone but that he didn't want to go into the store because his girlfriend worked there. He said she'd bought him a phone there using her employee discount, but that he'd lost it and needed to replace it before she found out and got mad at him."

"What did the guy look like?"

He shrugged. "Just like a regular guy."

Regular wasn't helpful at all.

"How old was he?" Bustamente asked.

"I don't know," Treacy said. "Mid twenties, maybe? It was hard to tell because he had sunglasses on." He circled a finger in front of his eyes. "The kind with mirrors for lenses. He wore a hat, too, one of those winter beanies that kids used to wear year-round a few years back." The trend hadn't lasted long in Texas, where wearing a knit cap in the heat of summer was a surefire way to pass out from heatstroke. "He was vaping, too, so his hand covered the bottom part of his face." Treacy mimed using a vape pen, showing us how his fingers covered his mouth and chin.

"What else was he wearing?" Bustamente asked.

"Regular clothes."

Bustamente's glower told the man he needed to step things up.

"Jeans," Treacy clarified. "At least I think it was jeans. I didn't pay his clothes much mind. Plain white T-shirt. That, I remember. Not grungy, but not brand new, either. Didn't pay any attention to his shoes, but if they were anything other than everyday running shoes, I might have noticed."

"What about his race?" the detective asked. "White? Black? Asian? Latino?"

"White," Treacy said.

"Dark or light hair?"

Treacy's eyes narrowed, as if he were trying to picture the guy. "Wish I could tell ya. I guess he must've had short hair if I don't remember. It must've been covered by his cap. I suppose he could even be bald."

"What color was the cap?"

"Black."

"Any logo on it?"

"Nope. Just solid black."

"Did he have any distinguishing characteristics?"

"Not really," Treacy said. "He stood about my height. I'm five-eleven. Kinda thin, but not so much he looked like a tweaker or anything like that."

"What about his voice?" Bustamente asked. "Did he have an accent? Use any unusual words?"

"Not that I remember."

"Was it high-pitched or low?"

I knew why the detective was asking. The person who'd called in the report of the three shooters at the mall had sounded female but, of course, if the caller thought there was a threat, the high pitch could be the result of terror tightening his vocal cords.

"His voice was just regular," Treacy said. "Not especially high or low that I recall." His expression changed, and he huffed. "His nose got a little out of joint when he saw that I'd bought a drink along with the phone. I offered to tell him two dirty jokes to cover the cost of the drink, but he just took his change, handed me the twenty he owed me, and went on his merry way."

"His merry way," the detective repeated. "Where did he go? Did he get into a car?"

"No," Treacy said. "He just walked off down the street. That's the last I saw of him."

Bustamente stood and motioned for Treacy to follow him. "Show me."

Brigit and I followed the two to the front of the store, where I assured the cashier I'd be right back to pay for my partner's new toy.

Out front, Treacy pointed to the left. "He walked behind that building. I don't know where he went from there."

Just past the other building, the parking lot gave way to a broad railroad easement that demarcated the edge of the Morningside neighborhood and continued on for miles until it curved around to the rail yard on West Vickery Boulevard. Someone could sneak about the easement unnoticed and out of range of security cameras. The man could have exited anywhere along the long stretch and walked to his residence, or caught a bus or Uber to somewhere else entirely. It would be virtually impossible to determine.

Bustamente asked a few more detailed questions. "Was he clean-shaven, or did he have a beard or mustache? Stubble?"

"Clean-shaven, I think," the man said.

"Did he move in any identifiable way? Like with a limp or pigeon-toed, anything like that?"

"No."

"You got a phone of your own?"

"Right here." The man reached into the back pocket of his jeans and pulled out a phone.

Bustamante took the phone from him and removed the basic blue protective case. The Tracfone logo—three concentric circles—was printed on the back of the phone. The model appeared to be the same one he'd allegedly purchased for the unidentified person last Thursday, though the condition of the screen, scratched and dull, said he'd likely owned this phone much longer. Bustamante held the phone out, screen up. "Mind unlocking it?"

Treacy did as he'd been instructed, reaching over to type in his passcode. Bustamante reviewed the settings and the call log, before sending himself a text from the phone. He returned the device to Treacy, then pulled a business card from his breast pocket and handed it over, as well. "If you see this guy again, call me immediately. But don't let him know you're doing it, okay? Don't say anything to him."

"Okaaay," Treacy replied, elongating the word in curiosity. "This guy must've done something bad if you're putting this much effort into finding him. What did he do? Kill somebody? Steal a car? Sell drugs?"

"Sorry. I can't share that information at this time." Bustamante wiped away the sweat that had gathered on his brow in the short time we'd been outside. He cocked his head. "Mind if we frisk you? Make sure you don't have another phone on you? You understand, I have to be thorough."

Treacy raised his arms out to his sides, exposing pits damp with sweat and releasing a barrage of body odor. "Be my guest."

Bustamante patted the man down, going so far as to run his hands over Treacy's calves to ensure he hadn't secreted a phone in a sock. When the detective was done, he reached into his back pocket, pulled out his wallet, and removed a single. "How about another joke before we go?"

Treacy eyed the bill, grinning with mischief. "What's a word that starts with F and ends with U, C, K?"

The detective frowned. "I paid for a clean joke, not a dirty one."

"Firetruck!" Treacy cried, raising his hands skyward as if he'd just shared the funniest quip ever.

Bustamente and I thanked the man for his help and headed back to the store. There, Bustamente went to the register. While she rang up Brigit's donut toy, he asked the cashier if she'd bought a phone in the store for her boyfriend.

"I don't have a boyfriend," she said. "Not since last year anyway."

As I tapped my credit card against the screen to pay, Bustamente broadened his inquiry. "Have you ever bought a phone here, for someone you were dating or anyone else?"

"No." She pulled a phone from her pocket and held it up. "Just this one, and I bought it for myself." She slid it back into her pocket and handed me the receipt for the toy.

The detective glanced around as if looking for other employees. "Who worked with you last Thursday afternoon?"

She looked up in thought. "I believe it was Ernest, Stuart, and him." She gestured toward the manager again.

"You were the only female on duty?"

She reached under the countertop for a stapled document. She placed it atop the counter facing us. "This is a printout of the schedule if you want to take a look."

Sure enough, the document indicated that she'd been the only female on duty for the shift ending at 5:30 last Thursday.

Bustamente thanked the woman, then walked across the front of the store until he spotted the manager stocking paper towels down an aisle. I followed him as he turned down the aisle and approached the manager.

"I hate to bother you again," he said, "but I need contact information for all your female employees."

"All right." We returned to the manager's office, where he jotted down phone numbers and addresses for the female employees not currently on duty, and handed the list over to the detective. Bustamente thanked the man and we returned to the cruiser, where we cranked the air conditioning up to full blast.

"What do you think?" I asked. "Now that we know the caller had someone else buy the phone, does that make it more likely the call was a hoax?"

"Probably," Bustamente said. "The story the guy gave Treacy was flimsy. If he lost the phone his girlfriend had given him, he could have bought a replacement at a different Dollar General store."

To ensure we'd considered all angles, I said, "Maybe he doesn't have a car, and it would take too long to get to another store by bus."

Bustamente volleyed with, "He had twenty bucks to pay Treacy. He could've taken an Uber to the next closest Dollar General store for less than that."

"Point taken."

We spent the next couple of hours stopping at businesses that backed up to the greenbelt along the train tracks, asking to see their security camera footage, hoping to discern where the man who'd bought the phone had gone after transacting his business with Matt Treacy. Unfortunately, it seemed to be a lost cause. He didn't appear in any of the footage, and there were too many places in between where he could have sneaked out into a residential area.

Detective Bustamente was silent on the drive back to the station but, while his lips weren't working, the deep lines between his brows told me his mind was laboring over the evidence we'd gathered today and where to go from here.

I pulled to the curb near the entrance. "Thanks for letting me shadow you today."

"It was nice to have company." He turned, gave Brigit a "bye, girl," and slid out of my patrol car, heading into the station with his shoulders slumped. No doubt he'd hoped for a quick and easy resolution to the case. Behind me, Brigit squeaked her new toy again. Maybe that's what Bustamente needed. A squeaky donut to take out his frustrations on.

18
NEW TOY

Brigit

Squeak! Squeak-squeak! Squeak!

The noise was like music to Brigit's ears, giving her the illusion that she'd caught and terrified some elusive prey. The fact that the stuffed toy resembled a pink donut with sprinkles was of no consequence. She felt like a powerful apex predator, a wild wolf after a successful hunt. *Squeak-squeak!* She lifted her head to the heavens and howled in victory.

19
SPOUSAL SUPPORT

The Flamethrower

It wasn't enough that he continued to give his estranged wife unfettered access to *his* earnings, she'd asked him to babysit their son again for eight straight days. She hadn't said why she needed him to supervise their son over what was supposed to be *her* weekend, and he didn't ask. He both did and didn't want to know. Most likely she was going to visit her folks. Maybe her mother would talk some sense into her, convince her to give her marriage another go. But Gretchen might be going away somewhere with her new fuckboi, and he didn't want to think too much about that. Still, if he had any hope of winning her back, he needed to be accommodating and cooperative, nothing like the self-centered asshole she'd accused him of being. So, when she'd texted him to ask if Hayden and the dog could stay with him, he'd typed back Sure. Would love more time with our kid.

It was Friday, trash day again. But he was up earlier this time, hoping to avoid another encounter with the nosy neighbor.

He collected the bag from the kitchen and carried it out to the large plastic bin in the garage. He raised the lid to find the greasy, sauce-stained pizza boxes from his son's birthday party the weekend before crammed haphazardly inside. As he rearranged the boxes to make room for the bag, several small broken pieces of black plastic slid out of a box. Obviously, the boys had broken something and hidden it in the box. *But what was it?* His first thought was that it was the television remote, but he hadn't noticed it missing. He hadn't noticed anything else missing, either.

After setting the bag of trash atop the boxes and closing the bin, he jabbed the button to open the garage door. He was halfway down the driveway with the bin when the garage door across the street began to ascend. He spat a curse as Valerie emerged, rolling her garbage bin out to the curb, too. It was almost as if she'd been watching for him, waiting for a chance to corner him and dig for information …

At first, he was tempted to turn around and go back inside to avoid her nosy chitchat, but a moment later he realized the situation offered him an opportunity. He continued rolling his bin forward, his lips spreading in a fake, friendly smile as he made his way down to the curb. "Hey, Val!" He'd never called her by the nickname before, but he'd heard his wife use it.

Valerie parked her bin, put one hand on her hip, and raised the other in a wave. "Howdy, stranger!" As expected, she sauntered across the street to join him at his curb. "How ya been?"

"Doing great." *What a lie.* Without his wife at home, he'd been lonely, frustrated, and suffering a severe case of blue balls. Not to mention the fact that he couldn't find anything in the kitchen, had accumulated a pile of dirty laundry a mile high, and watched so much porn he'd lost interest in it. *Is it too much to ask for a semblance of plot, or dialogue that went beyond "ooh," "aah," and "harder!"?*

Valerie cocked her head. "You sure you're okay? A little birdie told me that Gretchen and Hayden moved out."

He wasn't sure who the little birdie was, but if he found out, he'd wring that birdie's neck. "Gretchen and I are taking a little break, that's all. I'm sure we'll sort things out." *What marriage didn't suffer a few rough patches?* As if to prove that things were still relatively normal, he added, "Hayden had a sleepover for his birthday here last weekend."

"I heard," she said. "Asher Burke told Ainsley about it."

No doubt Asher was the little bird who'd spilled the beans about the separation, too. *Shithead.*

Valerie cupped a hand around her mouth and leaned in as if to share a secret. "I think Asher has caught some feelings for Ainsley."

She wagged her brows and grinned, as if her daughter being admired by the entitled punk was happy news. She might not feel the same if she'd heard the raunchy things Asher said he'd like to do to the big-breasted female characters in the video game the boys had been playing. And why was she using Gen Z lingo? It didn't make her sound younger. It made her sound ridiculous and pathetic.

"Speaking of Ainsley," the Flamethrower said in a subtle attempt to change the subject, "is she excited for the drill team performance tonight?"

"Is she ever!" Valerie clasped her hands at her chest. "They've practiced so much she's got blisters on blisters on blisters. But she can't wait to get out on the field in front of a crowd. It'll be extra fun that it's a big game."

The rivalry between Arlington Heights High School and Paschal High School, the school their kids attended, had been going on for decades. Last spring, the Paschal baseball team had lost to Arlington Heights by just one run scored in the last few seconds of play. His son and the rest of the team had vowed to beat them this school year. Starting the football season with this particular match up would ensure a big turnout at Farrington Field tonight. "You'll be at the game, right?"

"Of course!" Valerie said. "I wouldn't miss seeing my daughter dance for the world."

From the corner of his eye, he saw Gretchen's green minivan turn onto their street, just as he'd hoped. She'd been driving the ugly thing since she'd gotten pregnant with Hayden. At the time, they thought they'd eventually fill another seat or two with children, but Hayden had been such a colicky baby that the Flamethrower decided one child was enough and had refused to compromise on the subject. The Flamethrower still got a migraine when he thought of those three torturous months when their son screamed bloody murder all day and night. Though he'd never touched his neighbor before, the Flamethrower reached out and put a hand on Valerie's shoulder. "Enjoy the game."

Valerie's eyes flicked to his hand. She looked puzzled for a second or two before a smug smile played about her lips. He fought the urge to roll his eyes. *Don't flatter yourself.*

As the minivan drew up to the curb, he realized how outdated it looked. *I should've bought Gretchen a new car rather than getting myself the Camaro.* Gretchen's gaze went to his hand as he removed it from Valerie's shoulder, and her eyes narrowed. *She's jealous. Good.*

Hayden hopped out of the passenger seat, then opened the back to let Mickey, named after old-school baseball star Mickey Mantle, out of the backseat. The wire-haired gray mutt trotted into the center of the yard and promptly squatted to drop a deuce. Hayden reached into the van to retrieve his backpack, slung it over his shoulder, and shut the door. He didn't waste a beat before pulling his cell phone from his back pocket. His eyes locked on the screen, he started up the drive to the open garage without even greeting his father. The Flamethrower knew it was typical teen behavior, but he felt a twinge in his heart nonetheless. The dog scuttled after Hayden, following him into the garage.

After saying, "See you later" to Valerie, the Flamethrower walked up to Gretchen's window and gave her his best smile, the one she'd said caught her eye from across the room when they'd been in college.

She unrolled her window just two or three inches, enough to be able hear him while keeping a barrier between them.

"Hi, Gretch." He tried his best to sound casual. "How have you been?"

"Fine."

Her curt answer wasn't going to deter him. He ran his gaze over her face. One of her many complaints during their marriage was that he never noticed the effort she put into looking good for him. "Did you get your hair done?"

She rolled her eyes. "No."

Liar. He'd seen the recent debit for her hairdresser when he'd checked their joint bank account the evening before. Undeterred, he said, "Well, you look fantastic." She might have been lying, but he wasn't. She looked prettier than ever, her lips pink and plump, her ginger hair shimmering a coppery gold in the morning sunshine. *How had he stopped noticing?* His head must have been up his ass.

When he heard the garage door close across the street and knew Valerie could no longer hear their conversation, he stepped closer to the window, raising one arm up to rest it on the luggage rack. It was as close as he could get to putting an arm around her. "I miss you, babe. Hayden, too. Come home. Let's be a family again." He waited a beat or two before adding "please" for good measure.

She turned her face away and stared straight out the windshield, saying nothing for a moment.

Maybe she just needs a little more encouragement. "I'm sorry for not treating you as well as you deserve, Gretchen. I was just going through something, I guess. But things will be better now. I promise you. Let's chalk it up to a mid-life crisis and focus on the future."

"Mid-life crisis?" She turned and gave him an incredulous look. "You've acted this way our entire marriage. I was just too blind to see it at first."

"Come on," he encouraged. "No marriage or person is perfect.

You've made mistakes, too. I'm willing to forgive and forget." Okay, *now* he was lying, too. He'd never be able to forgive her for leaving him for another man, and he'd never forget it, either. But he'd do his best to pretend if it meant he could have his family back. "I won't ever make you feel guilty or—"

She raised a palm in a stop motion. "It's too late," she said softly. "I've moved on and you should, too." She cast a glance at the house across the street before facing him. "I'm sure there are plenty of women who'd be happy to keep you company."

But they aren't you! He thought the words, but he couldn't quite bring himself to say them aloud, no matter how much his heart squeezed in his chest. It would be too damn humiliating. He wasn't going to grovel any more. "You're right," he said, fighting hard to keep the venom out of his voice. "No sense hanging on to something that's broken beyond repair." With that, he stepped back from the van and raised a hand in goodbye. "Have a fun week." *Whore.*

She looked down for a moment and swiped at her eyes. *Holy shit. Is she crying?* Maybe there was hope yet. Or maybe she wasn't feeling regret and sorrow, but was merely emotional about what might have been if things had worked out. He wasn't sure how to take her tears. Before he could say anything else, she'd rolled up the window and put her foot to the gas pedal, slowly easing away from him once again.

She'd gone only a few feet when he changed his mind. He would put aside his pride and grovel. He would tell her how much he wanted her back, how much he loved her, how he'd never stopped loving her, how he'd been a damn fool to put himself before her and their son. "Gretchen!" he called, raising a hand in the hope it would catch her attention. "Gretchen, wait!"

But either she didn't see him or she ignored him. The minivan continued on to the corner, where it turned and disappeared from sight. He was the one with tears in his eyes now.

He walked back into the garage, punching the button with his fist to lower the door. *Damn that hurt!* Cradling his bruised knuckles, he walked into the kitchen to find his son at the toaster, waiting for a strawberry Pop-Tart to finish toasting. *Speaking of things that are broken beyond repair ...* "I saw some shards of plastic in the trash. You think I'm an idiot and wouldn't notice? What did you break and try to hide from me?" He knew it wasn't fair for him to take out his hurt feelings on his son, but he couldn't help himself.

Hayden's eyes flashed in alarm and his mouth hung open for a second or two, revealing thousands of dollars of orthodontics in progress. "It was just a video game controller. Asher accidentally stepped on it at my sleepover last weekend."

Asher! Figures. "I'm not replacing it," the Flamethrower snapped. "If you want a new one, you'll have to use your allowance to pay for it." His son's shrug only added to the frustration he was feeling. "Better yet, get a job. You're sixteen now, too old for an allowance." When the Flamethrower had been his son's age, he'd worked at the local mini golf. His kid could get off his ass and start earning his own way, too.

Hayden's expression brightened with hope. "If I get a job, I'll need a way to get there." He hesitated a few seconds as if waiting for his father to fill in the blank. When that didn't happen, he said, "Maybe you could buy me a car? It wouldn't have to be new. We could get a cheap used one. I'm not picky."

Not picky?! Hayden was starting to sound as entitled as Asher. Fresh fury boiled in him, but then he realized he could work this angle to his advantage. "I'd be able to buy you a car if I wasn't looking at thousands of dollars in legal fees for this divorce your mom wants."

When he saw the disappointment on his son's face, he felt a pucker of guilt in his gut. None of this was the kid's fault and, as upset as the Flamethrower was, he knew his son was suffering in his own way, too. Before he could think things through, he heard himself say, "Tell you what. You can borrow my Camaro to drive to the game tonight. How's that sound?"

"Really?! You're the best!" Just as his son's face broke into a big smile, the pastry popped up from the toaster, the edges charred. The burning smell reminded the Flamethrower of the odor of his gears grinding. He hoped he wouldn't regret allowing his son to take his car.

The brakes of the approaching school bus squealed outside. Hayden shoved the Pop-Tart into his mouth and held it between his teeth as he grabbed his backpack. He called something out as he ran out the front door to catch the bus, but his words were muffled by the pastry. Context said it was probably "goodbye".

As soon as the door swung shut behind Hayden, the Flamethrower felt more alone than he'd ever felt in his life, despite the dog sitting at his feet staring up at him. He picked up his cell phone, scrolled through his contacts until he saw the name he was looking for, and tapped the screen to place a call. "You free tonight?"

20
DOWN, SET, HIKE

Megan

On Wednesday afternoon, a report came in of an active shooter at an industrial facility just north of the city. Because the location was in another precinct, I didn't learn about it until later. Patrol officers and SWAT responded to find, like before, that there was no actual shooter. The call was quickly traced to a disgruntled employee who'd been fired the previous month for his poor attitude and substandard performance. He'd assumed turning off the burner phone he'd purchased would be enough to make it untraceable. He'd been wrong. He was found drinking a beer in his underwear at his apartment. He was taken into custody kicking and screaming, while his neighbors snapped photos of him in his saggy underpants and handcuffs.

On Thursday, I pulled up to a four-way intersection with stop signs on each corner. Before I could put my foot on the gas pedal to proceed, Officer Mackey approached in his cruiser on the perpendicular street to my left. The fact that Derek was back on the beat told me that Internal Affairs had cleared him to return to regular duty. I certainly hadn't missed him.

Though I had the right of way, the Big Dick laid on his horn, punched the gas, and sailed into the intersection without stopping. As he passed in front of me, he turned my way, stuck out his tongue, and held up a hand with his index and pinky finger sticking up. He probably intended the sign to represent devil horns but, since he hadn't tucked in his thumb, he'd actually said *I love you* in American Sign Language. *Dipshit.* I flashed my bright beams at him.

Later that day, another copycat phoned in a threat, though this caller's modus operandi, or way of doing things, was slightly different. Rather than calling nine-one-one, this caller phoned the county tax office, warning that a man armed with semiautomatics and suppressors was on his way. The building went into lockdown, and patrol officers and SWAT again responded. In this case, the phone had been tossed into a dumpster after the call was made. While there were no fingerprints on the phone, the tax office employee recognized the caller's voice and readily identified him as a resident who'd appealed his property valuation last spring but lost. He'd raised a ruckus after the appeals board rendered its decision, promising they hadn't heard the last from him. He was arrested when his car was spotted two blocks away by an alert officer. The man was sitting inside, binoculars to his eyes, enjoying a front-row seat to the mayhem he'd caused. This call, too, was outside of my beat, in the northeast part of the city. While I was glad not to have to face something so terrifying and traumatic again, I didn't want my fellow officers to face it, either, and especially not the civilians who'd feared for their lives.

While these two copycat cases were quickly resolved, neither seemed to have a connection to the call reporting shooters at Chisholm Trail Mall. That call remained a mystery. *Who had made that bogus report and why?* I hoped Detective Bustamente would soon find out. I also prayed we'd seen the end of the swatting calls. In such a high-intensity situation, when everyone's nerves were on edge, it would be all too easy for something to go wrong.

At half past five, I turned into the parking lot of the Shoppes at Chisholm Trail Mall. As I circumnavigated the perimeter, I noticed Detective Bustamente's unmarked cruiser parked in one of the spots reserved for law enforcement vehicles. I turned into the open spot next to it and cut the engine. Brigit stood in her enclosure, her tail wagging. I climbed out and let her out of the back so we could stretch our legs. Of course, being the aspiring investigator that I was, I'd keep an eye out for Bustamente, see if I could find out what he was up to here. *Has he gotten a new lead I haven't heard about yet?*

I glanced around for the detective as Brigit and I strolled up the wing, but saw no sign of him. As we entered the food court, a variety of aromas greeted us. The warm smell of pretzels baking. The savory scent of fried rice. The spicy scent of onions and peppers frying on a grill. Drool dripped from Brigit's mouth and she smacked her lips, hoping for a treat. I reached down and ruffled her ears. "You got it, girl."

We made our way over to the kabob stand, where we found Serhan Singh, a Turkish man I'd first met when I was a rookie and a bomb had exploded here in the food court. Though it wasn't all that long ago, it felt like eons. So much had happened since. A tornado had flipped my cruiser over with Brigit and me inside. We'd pursued a peeping tom and a drug dealer. We'd surveilled a cult compound and searched for animals stolen from the city zoo. To say my career had been eventful was an understatement.

When Singh spotted us, his mouth curled up in a broad smile and he raised his arms in welcome. "Hello, friends! Would Brigit like her usual?"

Before I could respond, my partner answered for herself. *Woof!* Translation: *Yes, please!* Brigit's usual was a paper basket full of beef tips, sans the onions, peppers, and the kabob stick, which she'd undoubtedly try to eat as well. Couldn't risk her getting splinters in her gums.

"Coming right up," Singh said. "Anything for you, Officer Luz?"

I stuck with vegetarian fare. It was hard enough to stay in shape as a police officer given that I spent most of the day sitting in a car. I wasn't about to add greasy burgers or fried chicken to the mix. "I'd love a veggie kabob."

He gave me a nod and strode back to the food preparation area to make our order. As we waited, I glanced around the food court area. Though it was the dinner hour and relatively busy, few of the customers were teenagers. No doubt most of the teens who lived nearby would be at the big football game tonight, the first match of the season, when rivals Arlington Heights High School and Paschal High School would go head to head. I had graduated from Arlington Heights, and my sister Gabby attended school there now, so it was an easy guess who I'd be rooting for. *Go Yellow Jackets!* Brigit and I would be at the game later. Though Farrington Field didn't technically lie within our usual beat, as a K-9 team Brigit and I could be summoned to put our special skills to work anywhere in the city. We'd been asked to work the entrance tonight, the hope being that a K-9 presence would deter drug activity at the stadium.

Singh returned in less than a minute with our food in paperboard trays. After I paid for our meal, Brigit and I walked over to a table. She sat on the floor beside me. Between mouthfuls of my own dinner, I picked up bits of beef one by one, blowing on them until they were cool enough that they wouldn't burn her mouth. I placed them in my cupped hand where she could take them, careful to keep my fingers out of the way of my eager dog. She enjoyed every bite.

We'd just stood to throw away our trash when I spotted Detective Bustamente emerge from the hallway that led to the mall's management offices on the other side of the atrium. I stood and tossed our trash in a nearby can before rounding up my partner. With Brigit trotting beside me, I hurried over, raising a hand and my voice to halt him. "Detective! Wait!"

Bustamente stopped and turned in our direction. "Hey, Megan. Brigit." As we stepped up, he bent over and treated Brigit to a nice scratch under the chin. "Who's a good girl?"

Brigit opened her mouth and released a beef-scented belch. She might be a good girl, but she had bad manners.

"Has there been a development?" I asked.

"Unfortunately, no." Bustamente stopped scratching my partner and straightened. "We still haven't been able to locate the cell phone used to call in the active shooter report. It looks like the device has been permanently disabled. If the phone were legit, the owner should have turned it on again since making the call." He gestured around in a general manner. "I've talked to the mall management and the store managers to see if a disgruntled employee might have pulled the prank in retaliation for being disciplined or terminated. I was given a few names and followed up with the employees, but none of them seemed upset enough to have taken such a drastic measure. One was fired for allegedly stealing products from the cosmetic counter where she worked. She admitted that she'd bent the windshield wipers on her supervisor's car afterward, but that's as far as things went. Besides, she sounded nothing like the caller." He raised his palms and shrugged. "I've hit a wall."

"I'm sorry to hear that." After all, the phone call hadn't been a harmless prank, like the *is-your-refrigerator-running* variety of prank calls that pre-dated caller ID. Multiple people had been injured trying to flee the mall, and would likely suffer ongoing psychological trauma. Property had been damaged. Derek had nearly shot an innocent man—at least it had looked that way to me.

Bustamente might have hit a wall as far as investigating went, but that didn't mean he was out of ideas. "I'm going to talk to the chief about offering a reward for information. Whoever made the call might have bragged about it to friends, or maybe someone out there can identify the caller's voice, even though it's likely they tried to disguise it. We'll get the recording out to the news sources and post it on social media, ask the public to call in with tips."

"Good luck."

"Thanks," he said on a sigh. "We're going to need it."

He walked away, his slumped shoulders telling me just how much the case was weighing on him. *I wish there was something I could do to help.*

Brigit and I returned to our cruiser. As I settled in my seat, I glanced at the clock. *Time for us to head over to the stadium.* I started the engine, backed out of the spot, and aimed for Farrington Field.

21

BACKSEAT DRIVER

Brigit

As the cruiser rolled along, Brigit lay quietly on her belly in her rear enclosure, keeping tabs on their progress and location not so much by looking out at the scenery but by lifting her nose in the air and scenting the ever-changing and unique combination of smells. The odors of hippo and kangaroo poo told her they were passing the zoo. Next came the aroma of onions, peppers, and refried beans from a Mexican restaurant. The acrid odor of gasoline told the K-9 that they were passing a gas station. This unique progression of scents told her they were heading north on the major road that would soon take them past the botanic garden. Sure enough, the next thing Brigit smelled was the sweet scent of roses.

Megan didn't come this way often. It wasn't part of their usual beat. Curious, Brigit pushed herself up to a sitting position. Where was Megan taking them?

22
SHOPPING LIST

The Flamethrower

As the Uber carried him across town, he scrolled through the messages he'd received on the various dating apps. All the women who'd contacted him were either looking for a sugar daddy, too pretty in their profile pics to be real, or had too much baggage. *Twice divorced with four kids under the age of ten? No thanks.*

He had the driver drop him at a bowling alley five miles from his house. Once the car had gone, he walked a quarter mile down the street to a grocery store, slipped inside, and proceeded as surreptitiously as possible to the feminine hygiene section. There were dozens of places he could have purchased tampons between his house and this store, but he didn't dare shop closer to home where he might be recognized by a neighbor. The Flamethrower had allowed Hayden to use his Camaro for the evening, so he'd had to take an Uber down here and would have to take another back home. *The expense and inconvenience better be worth it.*

He stood there, staring at the products, feeling the same embarrassment he used to experience when his wife sent him to buy her monthly supplies. Fortunately, the blush on his cheeks was obscured by his disposable paper mask. Not many people in Texas wore masks these days. Hell, not many had worn them during the peak of the Covid pandemic, certain the virus was a hoax or that God would keep them healthy, even though the Big Man had made no such promise and had allowed some of his most devoted followers to suffer in horrific ways in Bible stories. But at least a mask didn't draw attention the way it would have prior to 2020.

Besides the embarrassment, he felt the same sense of confusion as he stood there, too. Nash had told him to buy tampons with cardboard applicators, but most of them seemed to be made of plastic. There was one brand that came with no applicator at all. Would those work for their purposes? He wasn't sure. Gretchen had always gotten agitated when she sent him to the store and he'd come back with the wrong thing, accusing him of failing to listen to her. In reality, he had no interest in standing in front of the dish soap, shampoo, or feminine hygiene products, trying to match the products to the items written on her list. He'd grab the first thing that seemed to fit the bill and drop it into the cart. After all, if it wasn't the right thing, maybe she should do the shopping herself.

A woman in the store's trademark red knit shirt approached, pushing a cart loaded with adult diapers, which were displayed next to the tampons and pads. He tried to ignore her, but she seemed to sense he was having trouble. "Can I help you find something?"

Lest he be identified later, he didn't turn her way. He was hesitant to speak, too, but he didn't want to be standing here all night. He waved a hand to indicate the tampon display and spoke in a deeper voice. "I'm looking for the cardboard kind."

She stopped her cart and, not missing a beat, pointed to several blue boxes on a lower shelf. "Down there."

"Thanks."

As she rolled on a few feet further, he leaned in to read the boxes more closely. Though all had cardboard applicators, they came in varying sizes. Regular. Super. Super plus. *Shit.* Nash hadn't told him which size to get.

To make sure their bases were covered, he grabbed a box of each and dropped them into his basket alongside the lighter fluid he'd picked up three aisles over. He strode up to the checkout lanes, where he snatched a plastic butane lighter from a peg and added it to his collection. He continued on to the self-checkout, feeling totally conspicuous and as self-conscious as an adolescent. He hurriedly scanned the items. *Beep. Beep. Beep.* After placing them in a plastic bag, he returned his basket to the stack by the entrance and exited the store, wondering if he hadn't only lost his wife, but also his damn mind.

23
GATEKEEPERS

Megan

Brigit and I headed down University Drive, making our way north under the Interstate 30 overpass. Shortly after passing the beautiful botanic gardens, we reached Farrington Field. The original construction of the iconic art-deco-style stadium took place nearly a century ago, in 1937. With its proximity to the city's arts district, the old stadium sat on extremely valuable land. There'd been talk in recent years about the school district selling the property to raise much-needed funds. Residents got up in arms about the idea of selling the nostalgic stadium, but they'd also voted against a bond proposal that would have funded new stadiums, citing the improvement of academic performance being a greater concern than having modern sports facilities. *Who would've ever guessed that Texans would value education over football?*

A couple of school buses were parked in the lot, having transported the players here from Arlington Heights and Paschal High School. A few other cars were in the lot as well, most likely belonging to members of the booster clubs who volunteered to run the concession stand and had to arrive early to get the hot dogs loaded into the electric roller, the cheese heated for the nachos, and the displays of chips and candy set out. I pulled my cruiser up near the main gates, where it would be the most visible. With all the crazy things happening in the world today, seeing a law enforcement presence at events gave people assurance they were safe.

Brigit and I exited the cruiser into the sultry Texas evening. A Fort Worth police officer who worked as an SRO, or School Resource Officer, at Paschal High School stood by the ticket booth. Because tickets were sold online these days, the booth was obsolete and empty. However, three women in purple shirts stood in a row at the adjacent entrance, ready to make sure everyone entering had a pre-purchased ticket and complied with the stadium's bag policy. If a bag could hide a gun, it couldn't be brought inside. No large purses, backpacks, or fanny packs were permitted, though they did allow small cross-body style purses and clear plastic or see-through mesh bags. Though I was glad there was a policy in place, I knew it couldn't guarantee the spectators' safety. Someone intent on causing mass casualties might find some subterfuge for sneaking a large arsenal and ammunition into the stadium. The smallest semi-automatic pistols were only around five inches long, and could easily be hidden in large pockets or boots, or tucked into a waistband under a loose shirt.

The resource officer raised a hand in greeting as we approached. "This would be a good spot for the two of you."

I agreed. Everyone who entered on this side of the stadium would have to pass by us. Our presence could deter crime. As Brigit and I took over the post, the officer begged off to patrol inside.

Despite the fact that she'd been fed at home earlier and eaten the bonus kabob—Brigit drooled on smelling the popcorn, nacho cheese, and hot dog aromas coming from the concession stand inside the gates. I'd get her a hot dog once the game began.

Traffic into the stadium's large lot picked up, parents and students arriving for the game, some wearing the blue and gold colors of the Arlington Heights Yellow Jackets, others wearing the purple and white colors of the Paschal Panthers. Despite the oppressive heat that had yet to relent, the crowd buzzed with excitement.

A sporty blue Camaro with a black stripe down the hood rolled slowly past. Despite the high outdoor temperature, the windows were rolled down. No doubt the four boys in the car wanted to make sure they were seen in the sweet ride. A dark-haired boy in the passenger seat glanced our way, spotted Brigit, and raised his head to the sky to howl. "Arooooo!" The other boys laughed. Heck, I laughed, too, as Brigit responded by lifting her head and issuing a howl of her own. *Arooooo!*

A few minutes later, I spotted a boy named T.J. approaching with a small group of friends. T.J. had unceremoniously dumped my sister Gabby after meeting another girl at a debate tournament last school year, and Gabby had been absolutely devastated—for approximately three seconds. Upon learning she was unattached, a boy named Aiden who'd had a crush on Gabby for years finally mustered up the courage to ask her out. The two had been dating ever since. T.J. glanced my way, looking a little sheepish. I raised a hand in greeting and gave him a smile, letting bygones be bygones. He raised his hand in return, appearing relieved.

Over the next half hour, Brigit and I greeted students and adults as they approached the gate. A couple of times, after seeing a uniformed police officer and K-9 at the gate, students stopped, turned around, and scurried back to the parking lot. While Brigit and I weren't in a position to chase down these potential lawbreakers, we'd at least deterred them from attempting any shenanigans here tonight.

Gabby and Aiden arrived ten minutes before kickoff, meaning they'd have to climb all the way up to the nosebleed section at the top of the stadium to find empty seats. "Hey, sis." Gabby crouched down and dug her fingers into the fur around Brigit's neck, giving my partner a good scratch. Brigit's eyes closed and her tongue lolled in ecstasy.

Aiden's brother was a second-string offensive lineman, so I figured Aiden might have the inside scoop. "What does your brother think of our chances tonight?"

Aiden tilted a hand one way and then the other in a gesture of uncertainty. "He thinks it'll be a tight game, but we could get lucky and pull it off. It would be great to start the season with a win, especially against Paschal."

Knowing money could be tight for teens, I whipped a twenty-dollar bill out of my pocket and handed it to my sister. "Popcorn and drinks are on me."

Gabby smiled. "Thanks, Megan!"

Aiden repeated the sentiment, and they turned to walk to the concession stand, where a group of women in purple and white Paschal shirts worked to keep the hot, hungry crowd fed and hydrated.

A few minutes later, the incoming crowd dwindled and the announcer's voice came over the loudspeaker, inviting each team to run onto the field while their respective band played their fight song. Once the players, coaches, and cheerleaders were in place on the field, the crowd quieted and stood for the national anthem. As the song concluded, the stands erupted in applause and kickoff commenced. I waited another five minutes for stragglers to enter, then stepped inside the gate and led Brigit to the snack bar. She promptly put her front paws on the counter, her tail wagging behind her.

The women working the counter exclaimed in excitement and came over to see her.

"Can we pet her?" one asked.

"Sure." I was lucky my partner wasn't just skilled, she was also friendly. I never had to worry about her snapping at anyone who didn't deserve it.

The women fawned over Brigit, rubbing their hands down her neck, scratching her under the chin and behind the ears. A health inspector would surely find some sort of violation in their behavior, but they were not professionally trained food handlers, and I wasn't tasked with enforcing the city' health and sanitation code. Anyone who ate food served by volunteers at a football game did so at their own risk. It was an implied social contract.

When they'd gotten their fill of petting my partner, I said, "One hot dog, please."

"Coming right up." One of the mothers used tongs to select a hot dog from the glass-enclosed roller, and plunked it into a cheap bun. She slid the whole thing into a small white paper bag and exchanged it for the two singles. She pointed to a condiment stand behind me. "Ketchup, mustard, and relish are over there. Napkins, too."

"Thanks." I wouldn't need any condiments, but a napkin would come in handy. I walked over and snatched one from a dispenser, then pulled the hot dog from the bag and tore it into bite-sized chunks. Brigit gobbled them down as fast as I could toss them to her. Meanwhile, a *pop-pop-pop* came from the concession stand behind us, a signal that fresh popcorn was on its way.

From our location under the bleachers, we couldn't see exactly what was happening in the game. The noise told us there was a lot of excitement going on, though. Between each school's band launching into their fight song every few minutes, we heard the roar of the crowd, mass groans when things didn't go the way some fans had hoped, whistles blowing, and airhorns sounding. We could also hear the faint yells of the cheerleaders. "Move that ball!" "Fight, fight, fight!" We could hear the announcer, too. From what he said, it sounded like the teams were well matched, each side's defense preventing the other's offense from making much headway.

The atmosphere took me back to my high school days, when I'd been a twirler with the Arlington Heights High School marching band. I pulled my police baton from my belt, flicked my wrist to extend it, and twirled it between my fingers, the familiar *swish-swish-swish* as it rotated taking me back to the time when I twirled on the field.

"Wow!" called one of the mothers from the concession stand. "Did you learn that in the police academy?"

"No. I twirled in high school." To show off my skills, I bent down, prepared, and sent the baton sailing up a dozen feet over my head before catching it on its descent. *Brigit isn't the only one who can snatch things out of the air.* I proceeded to do a four-finger twirl in an arc from my right to left, along with a knee bend and dip to add flair.

The ladies at the concession stand broke into applause and I took a bow. Seeing me bend over, Brigit followed suit, stretching one leg out in front of her to perform her canine version of a curtsy.

Since our work at the gate was done for now, I led Brigit up a ramp so that we could watch the game and also be seen by the crowd. The Paschal High drill team sat nearby, the girls chatting and smiling, full of energy, ready to dance at halftime. I walked Brigit up to the railing and we circumnavigated the stadium at a reasonably fast clip so we wouldn't block anyone's view for more than a second or two.

Six minutes into the game, Arlington Heights scored a touchdown. The Yellow Jackets fans erupted in noise and applause. An official in a black and white striped shirt and white ballcap raised his arms straight up over his head to signal the score, resembling a human goalpost. Arms still raised, he turned his body so that his signal would be visible to those in the announcer's box and spectators watching from other angles. I'd never paid much attention to the officials' signals before but, seeing them do their work here tonight, I couldn't help but think how their motions were similar to a police officer directing traffic.

The celebration died down a few seconds later as the game continued. The boys played aggressively, and the refs signaled a series of penalties and fouls. After a ref bent one arm up in front of himself and grabbed his wrist with the other hand, the announcer called a personal holding foul. Another ref later put his palms to the back of his head, elbows out. Though it looked as if he were preparing to dance the Macarena, he was signaling the loss of a down.

Eight minutes in, Paschal scored a field goal. As the sun descended, the bright overhead lights came on, bugs flitting about under them. An occasional bat soared in to snatch a snack from the air.

My alma mater got lucky again halfway through the second quarter, scoring another touchdown. The extra point was good, and the score was 14-3 in our favor. The clock continued to count down toward the end of the first half. The announcer's voice came over the loudspeaker. "Arlington Heights is at the three-yard line." A hush settled over the audience as I watched from a ramp. A few seconds later, the Yellow Jackets carried the ball into the end zone. The west side of the stadium erupted in cheers, and the announcer's voice cried, "Touchdown!"

I fought the urge to throw a victorious fist in the air. I wanted to be true to my school and all that, but I figured a law enforcement officer ought to give the appearance of impartiality. A few seconds later, as the ball sailed through the uprights, the announcer's voice sounded again. "The kick is good!" AHHS had scored the extra point once more, putting the score at 21-3. Fresh cheers came from the Yellow Jackets side of the stands.

"Megan!" Gabby called.

I looked up to see my sister waving from her place in the stands, only a few rows from the top, where she sat with Aiden and an assortment of friends. I waved back. She gestured to the scoreboard, then pumped her palms up over her heads in a raise-the-roof motion. I gave her what I hoped was a discreet thumbs-up sign.

It was half past eight and the last rays of sun lit the horizon when the clock counted down to indicate that two minutes remained in the second quarter. Many spectators would come down from the bleachers during halftime to use the restrooms or to get a drink or snack. I figured it was best to get Brigit out of the way so her paws wouldn't get stepped on. I led her down the ramp back down to the concession and restroom area. Just in time, too. A shuffling sound came from above as the marching bands and drill teams descended the bleachers and headed down to ground level to get in place for their halftime performances. A flow of people came down the ramp behind them, bringing loud chatter with them.

I backed up under the bleachers, where Brigit and I would be out of the way but could keep a close eye on things. Though it seemed to be a typical game, an eerie feeling invaded my gut. There were a lot of people here tonight, probably the largest public gathering in the city. The recent armed shooter report at the mall still had me rattled. I couldn't help but think of the 2017 shooting in Las Vegas, where nearly sixty people were shot to death and hundreds wounded when a man fired down on the open-air arena from a casino hotel room across the street. The people in the crowd had been sitting ducks.

There'd been a multitude of fatal mass shootings more recently and closer to home, too, in various towns and cities in Texas, including the 2017 shooting at a church in Sutherland Springs, the 2018 shooting at Santa Fe High School near Houston, the 2019 shooting at a Walmart in El Paso, and the 2022 elementary school shooting in Uvalde. In 1991, a man had opened fire at a Luby's cafeteria in Killeen, just a couple hours' drive south of Fort Worth. In 1999, when I was just a young girl, a man had gone into the Wedgwood Baptist Church here in Fort Worth during a Wednesday night event, shooting and killing seven people. More recently, a man in disguise pulled a shotgun from under his coat and killed two members of a congregation in the Fort Worth suburb of White Settlement. That gunman was shot and killed by a member of the church's security team, who was a former law enforcement officer. The fact that the church felt the need for a security team said so much.

These days, nowhere was safe.

24
LOUD CROWD

Brigit was not a fan of crowds. The more people milling around, the more likely one of them might step on her paws. She didn't like all the noise the people made, either. The racket made it harder for her to hear Megan's commands. But the dog had a job to do, and she wouldn't let her partner down. She stuck close by Megan's side, keeping her eyes peeled and her ears pricked, watching, listening, and awaiting direction. With any luck, maybe she'd get another hot dog later, or at least a couple of the liver treats Megan always carried in her pocket.

25
FIRE DRILL

The Flamethrower

He had the Uber drop him off in the parking lot of a hotel, a Hyatt frequented by parents of children attending Texas Christian University. The hotel sat just a few streets west of his house. He walked into the lobby and stopped to peruse the display of sightseeing brochures, giving the Uber driver time to pull away.

Once the coast was clear, he exited the hotel and made his way home, carrying the grocery bags with him. At the house, he rounded up a dark blue hooded windbreaker, the heat-resistant grilling gloves he'd purchased at Ace Hardware on his lunch break, and the clear eye protectors his wife had bought him a few years back after hearing about a man who'd been blinded by an errant rock while weed eating. He'd refused to wear the goggles, told Gretchen she was being ridiculous and paranoid. But while he used to find Gretchen's constant worrying excessive and annoying, looking back he realized it was a sign she that cared. No one gave a damn about him now. *I should've just worn the stupid goggles.*

After taking the items he'd purchased out of their packaging, he shoved them into an old backpack his son no longer used. He donned the jacket, slung the backpack over his shoulder, and left the house on foot, aiming for Paschal High School. Though he still wore the face mask, he kept his head down as he walked, trying to make sure he couldn't later be identified by any of the people driving past. He hoped the jacket wouldn't draw attention. Only a nut job or criminal would wear a jacket in August in North Texas. The nylon windbreaker didn't breathe, and already his T-shirt was drenched in sweat underneath it. With nervous energy warming him even more, he'd be lucky if he didn't pass out before they finished their task.

As he drew closer, he pulled up the hood on the jacket and donned the eyewear, more to disguise himself than for protection. He circled around to the back of the school, giving the building a wide berth and staying in the shadows, sliding his hands into the heat-resistant gloves as he moved.

As planned, Nash waited for him in the dark funk behind the dumpsters. Nash was dressed in dark running shoes, black track pants, and a short-sleeved black T-shirt. A balaclava covered his face and hair, making him resemble one of those Mexican wrestlers, a luchador. He held a large plastic toolbox in one hand which, like the Flamethrower's, was covered by a grilling glove. Nash motioned downward with his free hand and whispered, "Wait here until I whistle."

Nash slipped out from behind the dumpster. The Flamethrower bent down and peeked around the corner of the bin, glad the mask muted the disgusting odors emanating from it. Floodlights attached to the back of the building provided dim illumination. A series of security cameras ran across the rear of the structure, too. Nash stopped about thirty feet away from the first security camera he reached, which was positioned on a corner about twelve feet high. He set his toolbox down on the concrete, unlatched it, and removed something. *A can of spray paint?* A moment later, a brilliant beam came from the object, telling the Flamethrower that it was not a can, but rather some type of high-powered flashlight or shop light. Nash placed the light on the ground and angled the beam directly at the lens of the security camera. Though Nash hadn't explained himself, it was clear from context that the bright lights were intended to provide cover by essentially blinding the lenses. *Clever.* Spray paint would have made a mess, and left residue on their clothing. Lights were a much better method for disabling the cameras. The Flamethrower wondered where Nash had learned this trick, whether he used it before. Then he realized it might be best if he didn't think too much about it.

Nash picked up his toolbox and hustled, hunched over, to the next security camera, which was located over a rear door. He repeated the process, then scurried to the third and final camera at the other end of the building. When he was done, he turned and motioned to the Flamethrower.

The Flamethrower darted out from behind the dumpster, keeping his head turned away from the building as he hurried along in case any of the security cameras might somehow still be able to record his movements. Nash stood in a dark spot halfway between two lights mounted on the building. He held a cordless drill with a long, large bit attached. Unlike a regular drill bit, this one had an arrow-shaped tip.

The Flamethrower gestured to the tool. "What's that for?"

"Watch and learn." Nash turned toward the building and placed the drill bit against the mortar between two bricks. The drill whirred to life, the bit disappearing into the mortar and cutting a quarter-sized semicircle in the bottom of the brick above. After a few seconds, the drill jolted forward, having made it through the brick and mortar, and into the building's frame. "The trick," said Nash, "is to make sure you use a masonry drill bit. A regular bit won't cut it." He held out his hand, like a doctor asking for a surgical instrument. "Tampon." As the Flamethrower unzipped the backpack and riffled through it, Nash explained the process. "Public buildings like this are made with fire-resistant materials. It's nearly impossible to burn one down from the outside. Bricks aren't flammable, and steel has to get really hot to melt. You've got to get through the outer layer to the internal flammable materials to make the fire spread."

"Got it." He handed Nash a super-plus size tampon. *The bigger the better, right?*

Nash took one look at it and grunted. He removed the paper covering and tried to insert the tampon into the hole he'd drilled, but it jammed after going in only two or three inches. Nash pulled it out, blew hard into the hole to clear out the dust, and tried again. "Dude! It's too big. Tell me you got some smaller ones!"

Nash sounded like Gretchen when the Flamethrower arrived home with the wrong product. Fortunately, he'd foreseen this response. "I got every size they had."

Nash snorted. "Good. You'll be prepared when you get your period."

The Flamethrower used to wonder why women got so upset when men blamed their bad moods on their period, but if it was anything like he felt right now he could understand their rage. He rummaged in the backpack again and found the box of regular size. He tore it open and pulled one out.

Nash grabbed it from him, tore off the paper wrapper, and dropped the wrapper to the ground. He carefully inserted the tampon as far into the hole as far as it would go, leaving an inch of string hanging out. He held out his hand again and wiggled his fingers in a gimme motion. "Lighter fluid."

The Flamethrower pulled the can of lighter fluid from the backpack and handed it to Nash. Nash shot a steady stream of the flammable liquid into the hole, soaking the tampon and string, before handing it back. Before their eyes, the cotton expanded to fill the space. *It's like we're planting improvised dynamite.*

Nash handed the lighter fluid back to the Flamethrower and picked up his toolbox. "We need to move faster. Now that you see how this works, I'll drill the holes and you take care of filling them and dousing the cotton. Got it?"

"Got it." Excitement replaced the Flamethrower's aggravation. He felt like MacGyver or a soldier on a top-secret special forces mission, taking out an enemy stronghold. He hoped it would work. He wanted nothing other than to humiliate the man who'd stolen his wife and turned him into a cuck. *What better way to humiliate him than to expose his incompetence?*

26

SHOWSTOPPER

Megan

The Paschal marching band had just taken the field to perform their halftime routine when it happened. Again.

Dispatch came over the radio with the type of call a police officer hopes never to hear, let alone twice in such a short timespan. "Attention officers at Farrington Field! A caller has stated they intend to open fire during the halftime show. The call was pinged to a phone inside the stadium. Initiate evacuation procedures immediately. SWAT and mobile command are en route. Keep all communications open for updates."

Though the dispatcher had remained calm, my heart rate had ratcheted up so high it was a wonder my veins didn't explode. *The caller is here! In the stadium! These people's lives are in my hands!*

Farrington Field had a seating capacity of 18,500. While it wasn't full tonight, at least eighty percent of the bleachers had been occupied. That meant thousands of lives were at stake. If the shooter had an automatic weapon, law enforcement could be outgunned.

My bullhorn was back in my cruiser, so I cupped my hands around my mouth, yelling as loud as I could over the sound of the marching band. "Emergency! Clear the stadium! Proceed calmly to the exits!"

While a few people in the immediate vicinity glanced my way, nobody responded, unable to hear over the roar of the crowd welcoming the band to the field. I tried yelling again to no avail. I grabbed my whistle and blew it as hard as I could, nearly suffering a self-induced aneurism. But, after hearing the officials blow their whistles repeatedly through the first half of the game, the crowd was immune to the sound.

Desperate, I looked down at my furry partner, who was quivering with barely restrained energy beside me. Brigit could sense my tension. "Speak!" I ordered.

Brigit lifted her snout. *Woof! Woof-woof! Woof!*

Thank goodness my partner was a K-9. On hearing a dog barking, people stopped talking and looked in our direction. I raised my hands in the air, motioning for people to move toward the exit gate. "Clear the stadium!" I hollered, fighting to keep my voice steady. "Proceed quickly and calmly to the exits! Now! There's been a threat!"

People stood still for an instant before my words sunk in, then they turned en masse and ran for the exit. The exit was normally secured by a double-paneled chain-link gate. Only one panel was open now. As the crowd surged, people were squashed against the chain link on the closed side of the gate. Several screamed in terror that they'd be crushed to death. *Oh, no!* Fortunately, before I could move, someone had the sense to raise the drop rod on their way out and the other side of the gate swung open, too, allowing the crowd to flow more freely. Luckily, nobody fell as the gate opened or they might have been trampled.

The marching band launched into their first song as the women in the concession stand ran for the door to get out of the booth. When they jammed in the doorway, two of them crawled over the counter instead. One of them caught her foot on the candy and chip display, sending bags of Flaming Hot Cheetos and Skittles to the ground where they were promptly crushed by the feet of the surging crowd.

Everyone was pulling out their phones, frantically trying to contact family or friends elsewhere in the stadium. *Oh, my God! Gabby's here!* I sent up a quick prayer for her safety while frantically sending her a text in all caps. LEAVE NOW! SHOOTER THREAT!

While those who'd come down to the area under the stands to use the restrooms or buy refreshments knew to evacuate, those who'd remained in the stands to watch the halftime show had no clue they were in danger. *I have to get them out of here!*

Keeping Brigit by my side, I rushed as fast as I could up a ramp, hollering to everyone I passed to leave the stadium. "Evacuate! There's been a threat!"

I reached the inside of the stadium and looked up to see Gabby, Aiden, and their friends rushing down the steps while calling out to those seated nearby and motioning for them to follow. I hoped their movements wouldn't draw the attention of the shooter. I'd never forgive myself if my warning had made her a target.

On the field, the Paschal band marched in precise formation, forming various figures as they moved about in their colorful uniforms and high-feathered hats. I turned to the crowd and waved my hands over my head, yelling at the top of my lungs, trying to draw their attention away from the field. But while they might have watched the officials' signals during the game, they overlooked mine now. Only the people seated in the first few rows noticed me. They stared at me slack-jawed, unable to hear me over the loud music.

I grabbed the arm of a man on the first row and pulled him from his seat, pointing to the exit. After exchanging confused glances, a few more took heed, gathering their things and heading toward the ramp. But the vast majority still sat, watching the band, not knowing this could be the final moment of their lives. I waved my hands toward the exit ramp and mouthed, "Go! Shooter!"

A woman on the third row looked at me, her eyes narrowed in question. She mimed shooting pistols. I nodded vigorously. *Yes! Guns!* She stood, turned, and hollered to those behind her, but the band music drowned out her voice just as it drowned out mine.

I have to get these people out of here! But what could I do? I looked up to the announcer's booth at the top of the stadium, rows and rows above me. As high up as it was, it might as well have been the summit of Mount Everest. It would take forever for me to climb all those steps. Too bad I couldn't send Brigit to deliver the message. My partner had endless energy. She'd have no problem bounding up the steps.

Frantically, I glanced around, trying to figure out a better way to get the word out. On the sidelines stood a referee wearing an electronic headset over a black ballcap. *Maybe he can communicate with the booth!*

I swung a leg over the railing that separated the bleachers from the sideline, climbed over, and dropped to the ground. Brigit squeezed through the bars and hopped down after me. I ran to the ref and cupped my hands around my mouth to shout into his ear as a sousaphone *wahh-wahh-wahhed* its way past us on the field. "There's been a shooter threat! We have to clear the stadium! Tell the announcer!"

The man stared at me for a split second, his eyes wide in shock, before moving the mouthpiece directly in front of his mouth and pushing a button on a controller attached to his belt. He relayed my message to the announcer's booth and, seconds later, the order came over the loudspeakers. "Attention, ladies and gentlemen. Fort Worth Police have ordered that everyone clear the stadium immediately. Please move quickly and carefully to your nearest exit."

Unfortunately, though it was clear something was being announced over the loudspeaker, it was impossible for the spectators to make any sense of the broadcast over the sound of the music coming from the field. People exchanged glances, some unsure, some irritated that the announcer had interfered with the band's performance. The only way the crowd would hear the announcement was if the music stopped. *I have to stop the band!*

Brigit and I took off running onto the football field. An entourage of woodwinds came at us. I waved my hands over my head in a stop motion but they continued on, having been instructed never to get out of formation and to march through any obstacles they encountered. Heck, I recalled band members colliding with a judge who'd inadvertently stood in their way at a marching band contest when I'd been in high school. But while their pace didn't change, their expressions did, all of them looking confused and concerned to discover a cop and a K-9 in their midst. I dodged left and right as if I were playing football myself, trying to avoid a collision with a trumpet, trombone, or French horn as the brass section came my way. Brigit did a great job of staying with me, just as she was trained to do.

Glancing around, I saw the drum major up on a podium, her hands moving in front of her as she directed the band. I sprinted to her podium and up the steps. Brigit jumped around at the bottom of the platform. The girl turned her face to me, but kept her arms moving. "You've got to stop the band!" I cried. "There's been a report of a shooter!"

Like the referee, the girl spent an instant in shock while the information processed. Then she raised her whistle to her lips, blew it with all her might, and forced her hands forward in a *stop* motion. While the crowd under the stadium had ignored the sound of my whistle, the band members were trained to respond to the sound. They turned en mass to look at the podium, each of them coming to a stop at a slightly different time. There was one final *oom-pah blrrt* from the tuba player, like the call of a depressed elephant. The *rat-a-tat-tat* of the drum line continued until only one percussionist, who couldn't see over his bass drum, let out a final three *boom-boom-booms* before realizing he was the only one on the field still playing. With me and my partner wreaking havoc on their practiced routine, the band's perfect formation now appeared nothing more than a messy mob on the field. But at least the stadium was quiet now.

"Go!" I told the girl, motioning her down with both arms. Up on the platform, she'd be much too easy for a shooter to pick off.

As she clambered down the steps, the announcer seized the silence to repeat the instructions, his voice audible this time. "Folks, law enforcement has ordered that the stadium be cleared immediately. Proceed to your nearest exit and leave the premises in a calm and orderly fashion. I repeat, proceed calmly to the nearest exit and leave the premises immediately."

There'd been so many mass shootings in the country, many at packed stadiums and other crowded events, that the spectators could easily surmise the reason for the evacuation. If they hadn't clued in yet, the swarm of approaching sirens would spur them. They wasted little time getting in motion, parting like the Red Sea in the center of the rows as people filed toward the aisles on either side. When the steps got log-jammed, many resorted to walking down the bleachers rather than exiting at the ends of the rows. Like I'd done only minutes before, spectators climbed over the railing surrounding the field and dropped to the turf in the hopes of getting out of the stadium faster. They merged with the Paschal band members who were on their way to the exit at the south end of the field.

There was nothing Brigit and I could do then except stand back out of the way and try not to look panicked. The task was much easier for my partner than for me, though the way she stared at me said she knew something was up, and that whatever was up was something big. She remained sitting as ordered, but trembled all over. I trembled along with her, though I trembled in fear, not excitement. We could be called into action at any second, and we needed to be ready. I kept a sharp eye on the crowd, constantly scanning our surroundings. An active shooter would want to take out anyone who might stop them. That meant me and other members of law enforcement. Standing here without our riot gear, Brigit and I would make easy targets.

A group of girls in blue and yellow drill team uniforms came down the ramp, faces contorted in horror. A few were crying outright. Tonight would have been their first public performance of the season. No doubt they'd been looking forward to it for weeks, and now it was ruined. They were followed by the Arlington Heights marching band, the bright stadium lights glinting off the metal of the instruments. The tuba player was essentially wearing his instrument and was jostled about by others squeezing past him. The instrument slammed against the metal railing with a clang. No doubt it was dented now.

Once the stadium was halfway cleared, I went with the flow to keep an eye on things under the stadium. The crowd was denser there and moving slower. If a shooter wanted to do some real damage at close range right now, here under the stands would be the place to do it. *Gulp.*

Sounds came from the parking lot outside—tires squealing, horns honking, people shouting. No doubt it was mayhem out there. I hoped the officers outside could get it under control. People tended to disobey orders when they were panicked.

I kept my ears peeled for the sound of gunfire and my eyes peeled for anyone holding a gun. I saw a marching band member with a piccolo, and another with a clarinet, but nobody with a lethal weapon. Over my radio, the precinct captain announced his arrival on site and the establishment of a mobile command unit in the small employee parking lot at the northwest corner of the property. Officers chimed in, confirming that they had detoured oncoming traffic at nearby intersections to allow a faster flow of vehicles out of the stadium parking lot. They also confirmed that it was pretty much every man for himself out there, with SUVs and pickup trucks exiting the lot by driving over curbs and grass.

We were near the condiment table when another surge of people passed, jostling us. Brigit yelped as a man inadvertently stomped on her paw. I backed her up against the stand, stepped in front of her, and spread my legs to protect her. She stuck her head out between my thighs to keep an eye on things, too. I probably appeared to be riding her like a stick pony, but at least her paws were safely out of the way of the stampeding feet.

I scanned the area for anything suspicious but, with a constant flow of people rushing by, it was hard to see much of anything. *I need to get higher.* I was debating whether to climb atop the condiment table when a horrifying sound met my ears. *Pop-pop-pop!*

Screams came from the crowd. People pushed and shoved. Several fell to the ground. *Dear God, please don't let them be trampled to death!*

My head snapped in the direction of the sound, my heart leapt into my throat, and my heart pounded so hard in my ears that it muffled the sounds of the crowd. I yanked my gun from my belt, ready to confront a shooter. But the sound wasn't gunfire at all. The sound came from the concession stand popcorn machine, innocently overflowing with a fresh warm batch, though no one remained to serve it. *Pop-pop-pop!*

"It's just the popcorn machine!" I yelled, hoping to reassure those who could hear me that they weren't under a barrage of bullets.

Pop-pop-pop!

I blew my whistle and put up my hands to slow the crowd while people helped those who had fallen get back on their feet. One of the girls who fell was bleeding from her brow. The stream of blood mixed with her terrified tears to form a pink trail down her face. I snatched a handful of napkins from the dispenser at the condiment table and handed them to her as she lurched on, sobbing.

Surrounded by the crowd, I could see precious little. I yanked my baton from my belt and flicked my wrist to extend it. I held the baton out lengthwise over Brigit to protect her as we made our way across the flow of people to the concession stand. Brigit's paws would be safe in there, and I could get up on the counter to better survey the surroundings.

Pop-pop-pop!

As soon as we'd entered the stand, I ran over to the popcorn machine and yanked the electrical cord out of the wall to stop it from terrorizing the crowd. Though no longer receiving power, the kettle remained hot enough to explode a few more kernels. *Pop-pop-pop!* I yanked open the glass door, grabbed the handle inside, and turned it to upend the kettle, filling the space below with freshly popped corn. At any other time, I'd be tempted to grab a handful, but this was no time for a snack.

After ordering Brigit to stay put, I climbed up onto the counter and stood, hanging on to edge of the roof for leverage. I ran my gaze over the crowd, but all I saw was a sea of heads. Dark heads. Light heads. Bald heads. Heads wearing ball caps. Heads wearing cowboy hats. Heads with ponytails, buns, braids. I saw no glint of gunmetal, no barrel, no one taking aim.

My eyes spotted Derek and another SWAT officer in their riot gear attempting to enter the stadium. With the congestion at the gate, they'd never be able to work their way in against the crowd. But from my vantage point I could see that they'd be able to get inside if they climbed through the ticket booth window and came out the back door of the booth. I squeezed the talk button on my radio. "Mackey! Enter through the ticket booth!"

Derek motioned to the other SWAT officer, and the two edged sideways to the ticket booth. One after the other, they dropped their shields through the window and grabbed the frame, pulling themselves up and into the booth. They picked up their shields and left the ticket booth through the back door, first Derek then the other, swimming against the current as they headed for the ramp to enter the stadium.

I stood and waited for further direction from the mobile command, continuously scanning the crowd. The seconds ticked away much too slowly. I was aware of each and every one.

How will this end?

27
OUCHIES

Brigit

Humans were idiots. That stupid man had stomped right down on Brigit's paw as if she wasn't even there. Why didn't he look where he was going? He was lucky she didn't nip his butt as he rushed away. Would've served him right. If not for the fact that she knew Megan would be angry, Brigit would've done it.

She was glad they were away from the people now. She was even more glad that they were in the place where Megan had got her a hot dog earlier. Maybe Megan would give her another one. The hot dogs were right there on the counter, rolling back and forth inside that glass box, just waiting to be eaten. But Megan was on the counter now, too distracted for Brigit to get her attention. She'd have to wait. *Sigh.*

28

INFER-NO

The Flamethrower

He and Nash made their way down the building. They'd planted seven tampons when the Flamethrower felt his phone vibrate in his pocket. He was tempted to ignore it, but Nash had just started drilling a new hole. The Flamethrower had already prepared the others with cotton and lighter fluid, and it would only take a second or two to check his phone. He was damn glad he did. A message from his son was displayed on the screen. Game canceled. Gonna hang at Waffle House.

His anal sphincter pucker. *What the hell?* He had no idea why the game had been called off, but he knew it meant the school buses would soon return to the campus with the football players, cheerleaders, and drill team, and the school would be swarming with students and parents.

Nash finished drilling the hole as the Flamethrower looked up from his screen. "The game was canceled. We've got to get out of here before everyone comes back."

Nash exhaled sharply and rolled his eyes. "Let's at least make an exit."

Nash gestured to the hole, and the Flamethrower quickly jammed a tampon inside, dousing it with a generous squirt from the can of lighter fluid.

Nash held out his hand. "Lighter?"

The Flamethrower handed the butane lighter to Nash. Nash held the lighter to the tampon string, wet with the flammable liquid, and flicked the spark wheel. The end of the string burst into flame. The blaze raced up the string and into the wall. The next thing the Flamethrower knew, flames were shooting out of the hole Nash had drilled.

They hurriedly retraced their steps. Nash stopped at each spot to light the strings. They'd reached the last one, leaving a trail of tampon tiki torches behind them, when the Flamethrower heard a rattle and rumble coming from the street in front of the school. He peeked around the corner of the building. A school bus approached, its brakes squeaking as it slowed to turn into the drive.

The Flamethrower turned to Nash. In his panic, his brain went on autopilot. He raised a fist over his head, grabbing the wrist with his other hand, the baseball umpire's signal for spectator interference. "A bus is coming!"

"Shit!" Nash flicked the lighter three times in an attempt to light the last string, but the device refused to ignite.

The school's fire alarm activated, blaring an earsplitting warning. Nash gave up and shoved the lighter into his pocket. The two broke out in a run.

29
THINGS HEAT UP

Megan

The seconds ticked slowly past until, eventually, the surge of spectators slowed to a dribble. The last to exit the stadium were mostly people with mobility issues and their family members or friends. Several of the stragglers were in wheelchairs. Three used canes. One had a rollator. Thankfully, all of them made it safely to the exits.

I climbed down from the counter and let out a long breath before drawing in another to calm myself. Not a single shot had been fired. There'd been no bloodshed. I could only hope there were no serious injuries as people fled. I closed my eyes and thanked the heavens, adding an extra prayer for all of those who had not been so lucky, who'd lost their lives or a loved one in a mass shooting incident.

Now that the threat seemed to be over, my body gave way. My legs went weak under me, and I sank to my knees on the concrete floor beside Brigit. She turned her head my way and, seeming to sense my emotions, gave me a supportive lick, wetting me from my jawline to my hairline with saliva that smelled of hot dog. I put an arm around her and pulled her close. "Thanks, girl. I needed that."

Though it was possible the shooter had changed their mind and decided not to go ahead with their plan to open fire at halftime, the report could have been another hoax, an empty threat meant to cause panic and pandemonium. If so, mission accomplished, asshole. I wondered if tonight's threat came from yet another copycat caller, or whether the caller might be the same person who'd dialed 9-1-1 last Friday to report the alleged shooters at the shopping mall. The details were different, of course. The first caller only reported having seen shooters, while the caller tonight claimed to be a shooter himself. And while the phone used to call in the earlier report seemed to have vanished into thin air, the phone used tonight had been traced to the stadium. I wondered if the department still had a location on the phone and was tracking the caller right now.

Brigit's ears pricked and I stood, cupping hands around both of my ears to listen. Barely audible in the distance was the wail of a fire engine siren, most likely from Seth and Frankie's station. Sure enough, dispatch came over the radio asking for units to respond to a fire at Paschal High School. *First a report of a shooter here at the Paschal/Arlington Heights football game, and now Paschal High is on fire? Are the two incidents related?*

I had no time at the moment to ponder the matter. Detective Bustamente walked through the open gate dressed in a ballistic vest and helmet. Two SWAT officers flanked him, their guns at the ready. Bustamente held his cell phone to his ear. He glanced in my direction, doing a double take. He raised a finger to his lips in a shush signal.

He turned and headed in my direction, a look of intense concentration on his face as he listened to the person on the other end of the call. As he approached, he met my gaze and used his meaty index finger to draw a triangle in the air and then point to his cell phone, telling me that he was communicating with a tech specialist who was triangulating the phone used to call in the threat.

He and the officers slipped silently into the concession stand. In the now-quiet night, I could hear the voice come over the phone line. "You're right on it, Detective." In other words, the phone was in the immediate vicinity. *Does that mean the shooter is in the concession stand, too? Is he hiding somewhere in here?*

My heart sputtered in panic and my skin broke out in a cold sweat. The detective, the SWAT officers, and I glanced around, looking for places someone could hide. A large cabinet stood along the side wall, big enough to hold a human being. Both doors were closed. Bustamente motioned for me to crouch down for safety. I did as he'd directed, holding my gun at the ready in case a shooter burst forth from the cabinet. Bustamente eased over and crouched down next to me.

He made a motion, and the SWAT officers carefully approached the cabinet, taking up positions on either side. One of them mouthed a silent countdown of three, two, one, and they each yanked open a door. But no shooter burst forth. The only thing the cabinet held was a stock of paper goods—napkins, cups, popcorn bags, and the like.

A refrigerator stood next to the cabinet. The two SWAT officers repeated the process, though it seemed less likely the caller would be hiding in the fridge, where he could suffocate. The fridge was opened to reveal only a few cans of soda cooling inside and the fetid odor of curdled baby formula emanating from a half-filled plastic baby bottle. Judging from the gray-green color of the contents and the swollen condition of the container, the bottle had been sitting in the fridge for months.

Bustamente glanced about some more before breaking the silence by addressing the tech on the phone. "We don't see anyone or the phone. Can you call it? Maybe we'll hear it ring or vibrate."

The four of us stood in hushed silence for a moment. Even Brigit seemed to realize that she should be quiet. She stopped panting and closed her mouth.

Three seconds later, a techno ringtone burst out so loud next to me that I jumped. I turned to see a repurposed cardboard pickle box sitting on a shelf under the service counter. Someone had scribbled LOST AND FOUND on it with a ballpoint pen.

The ringtone continued to assault our ears as Bustamente came over, pulled the box out from the shelf, and set it on the counter. The two of us peered down into it. Inside the box sat a small stuffed zebra, probably purchased at the zoo down the street. A pair of cheap plastic sunglasses. Two dental retainers. *Ew.* One silver hoop earring. And, finally, a flip-style cell phone, the screen lit up with the words FTW POLICE.

Bustamente ended his call with, "We found it. Thanks." He slid his cell into his pants pocket.

I grabbed the hot dog tongs and quickly washed them with dish soap and hot water at the sink. After drying them with a paper towel, I handed them to Bustamente and he used them to lift the cell phone from the box. It was a basic flip phone with the Tracfone logo—three concentric circles—printed on the hard plastic case. While it was the same brand as the phone used to report the alleged shooters at the mall, it was a different model. *Does that mean the person who called dispatch earlier tonight isn't the same person who called in the threat at the mall? Is this another copycat? Or had tonight's shooting been thwarted somehow?*

The detective looked down at the phone, as if willing it to talk to him. "Who do you belong to?"

"There was a group of moms working the concession stand tonight," I said. "Band boosters, I think. Or maybe athletic boosters. I'm not sure which, but they were dressed in Paschal gear. The football coach or band director could put you in touch with them. Maybe they'll know something."

"Good idea." Bustamente used his radio to get in touch with the commanding officer and the head of the SWAT team. "We found the phone abandoned. You can call off your team. Let's gather at the concession stand."

Minutes later, the SWAT team and other officers were gathered in front of the concession stand, waiting to be debriefed. I remained inside the booth, perched atop a folding stepstool I'd found by the brooms and mop.

Derek pointed to the hot dog machine. "Yo, Luz. Gimme a hot dog."

I arched a brow and talked to him as if he were a child. In many ways, he was. "What do you say when you're asking for a favor, Derek?"

"Jeez!" He muttered a curse. "Will you *please* get me a hot dog?"

While the hot dogs and buns had been bought by the booster group, it was clear the food would go to waste if not eaten tonight. It might even attract rodents or bugs. I'd already fed some of the food to my partner. Might as well feed the SWAT team, too.

While I'd turned off the popcorn machine earlier to put an end to the popping sound, I hadn't turned off the hot dog warmer or the crock pot containing the melted cheese for the nachos. I found myself taking orders and preparing food for the SWAT team, all of whom on site tonight were men. I supposed it might seem sexist for the only female officer here to be serving them—maybe it even was—but these officers had rushed into a potentially dangerous situation when everyone else was rushing out. I could prepare them a snack without getting my panties in a wad.

After serving the last of the hot dogs, nachos, and popcorn to the assembled crew, I did my best to clean what I could. I scraped the burnt, congealed cheese from the crock pot and washed the pot in the sink, along with the ladle and tongs. I wiped down the popcorn and hot dog machines with a degreasing agent I found under the sink.

Meanwhile, the commanding officer consulted with Bustamente, then stepped over to give us officers a rundown. "The phone used to call in the threat was located. It's unclear at this time whether the threat was a hoax or whether the shooter aborted his plans but, either way, you all are to be commended for your performance here tonight."

After thanking the officers, he dismissed them. As they headed back to the SWAT vehicle parked just outside the gates, Bustamente came over to the concession counter to address me. "Meet me at Paschal High. The firefighters at the school found evidence of arson. I want to see if there's any evidence that connects the fire to what happened here tonight."

"Yes, sir." I, too, thought it was suspicious that there were two events on the same night involving the same high school, and I was curious to learn more.

I rolled down the metal window gate on the concession stand, rounded up my partner, and led her out of the structure, closing the door behind us. We headed out to our cruiser and drove south, arriving at the high school a few minutes later.

It was nearing ten o'clock and fully dark now. While I saw no flames as I approached the school, flashing lights lit up the area behind the school. I walked around the building to find two fire trucks parked in the rear drive. Several firefighters milled about, rolling up hoses. One of them was Frankie. She raised a hand in greeting as Brigit and I pulled to a stop next to Detective Bustamente's car in the student parking area nearby. I raised a hand back to her, then we turned our attention to our official duties.

To keep Brigit safe from debris and hot embers, I left her secured in the back of my cruiser with the windows down to allow for air circulation. I met the detective in front of our vehicles, and we walked over to where a tall, thin man with a thick mustache and stylish eyeglasses stood speaking with Seth. Blast sat at Seth's feet, his tail wagging as he saw me approach. *Sweet boy.* The dog wore four little rubber booties to protect his feet as he performed his tasks.

Bustamente introduced me. "Officer Luz, this is arson investigator Lewis Hamrick."

I shook the man's hand before he held out a hand to indicate

Seth. "This is Seth Rutledge and his dog Blast. They're part of the department's arson team."

Seth winked at me before turning to Hamrick. "Officer Luz and I met a while back, when the bomb exploded in the food court at Chisholm Trail Mall. In two months, she'll be my wife."

I put the back of one hand to my forehead, feigning a swoon. "Sparks flew when I met him."

Hamrick's brows rose as he looked from one of us to the other. "That's certainly a unique way to meet. Congratulations."

I thanked him with a smile.

Now that introductions had been exchanged, Bustamente informed the fire investigator why I was tagging along with him. "Officer Luz is an aspiring detective. Having her take a look around will be good for her and us both. She's got a sharp eye and mind, and might be of help. Then again, she just might steal my job." He cut me a sly look before turning back to the men. "Mind showing us what you found?"

With Blast at his side, Seth led us over to the building. He stopped before the wall and pointed to the left and right. "A series of holes were drilled along this wall, then flammable materials were inserted and ignited."

Hamrick used a high-beam flashlight like a laser pointer to illuminate various spots along the rear that were marked with black soot stains starting at about four feet high and trailing upward along the brick. Below each stain was a quarter-sized hole in the brick and mortar. We followed along until Seth, Blast, and Hamrick stopped before a hole in the wall near the end. No soot marred the wall above this hole. Rather, a short white string hung out of it. While Hamrick kept the flashlight fixed on the wall, Seth hung back to allow Bustamente and me to take a closer look at what he and Blast had discovered.

I peeked into the hole, which reeked of lighter fluid. Inside, I saw a tube of wet cardboard filled with compressed cotton, a string hanging from it like a fuse. "Is that what I think it is?"

From behind me, Hamrick said, "It is. When doused with a flammable liquid, those products make excellent fire starters." He shined a flashlight down at the ground below, which was covered in grayish dust. "That's from the mortar. Whoever made the hole must have used a cordless drill. If they'd chiseled the holes, they wouldn't be so perfectly round and uniform."

I thought aloud. "Maybe some kid borrowed his dad's drill." *And his mother's feminine supplies.* "A school seems like a place an angry teen would target." After all, schools were a favored target for disgruntled teenagers with guns.

"Could be," Hamrick said, "but I doubt we're dealing with total amateurs here."

Seth was naturally handy, and had also learned a lot from his grandfather, who'd been a tank mechanic with the U.S. Army in Vietnam. He added his two cents. "They knew to use a masonry drill bit. A regular bit wouldn't have made such clean holes."

Hamrick nodded in agreement. "Whoever did this seems to have some training and knowledge of fire science, or maybe they read up on arson and formulated this scheme, practiced the techniques beforehand to ensure everything went smoothly. They could have found some information on the internet and run with it. But it seems pretty clear this was planned, not just a crime of opportunity or something done on a whim."

I mulled things over for a moment. "The holes make it clear this fire was set intentionally. Don't arsonists usually try to hide the fact that a fire was set on purpose?"

"It depends," Hamrick said. "When people set fire to their own property for the insurance money, yeah, they try to make it look like an accident. I'm working such a case, in fact. The homeowner filed an insurance claim that included a large amount for damaged art, including an oil painting. It was destroyed by a fire that purportedly started when a cinder escaped the fireplace and ignited a cleaning rag lying atop a stack of logs on the hearth. He'd used the rag to polish the mantle with a flammable furniture polish. His insurance company thinks he orchestrated things. I do, too. It was suspicious that he left flammable materials so close to an open flame. Plus, the guy is an avid art collector and would have known better than to hang a valuable oil painting over a fireplace. The heat can dry out the paint and make it crack, and the particles in the smoke can stain the art."

Seth frowned. "I remember that fire. The guy raked us over the coals for not getting there fast enough even though we reached his house only three minutes after he called. He complained that we caused water damage to his artwork and knocked over some priceless figurines."

A first responder's job could certainly be thankless at times.

Hamrick shook his head before returning to my question about arson. "When someone isn't trying to collect on insurance, when they're trying to scare people or make a point, they don't attempt to make the fire look like an accident. They want it to be clear that the fire was set intentionally."

I mused aloud. "If the shooter was thwarted at the stadium, could he have decided to come here and set this fire instead?"

"Like a plan B?" Bustamente considered it, but he didn't seem to fully buy into my theory. "It's possible, I suppose. But most criminals stay in their lane. They commit the same types of crime over and over rather than branching out."

"A gang, then?" I suggested, looking from the detective to Hamrick. "Some of them could have started the fire here, while another called in the shooter report from the stadium." Maybe the crimes had been an initiation ritual, or high-stakes pranks.

Bustamente shrugged. "Might be a coordinated attack. Might not."

Rather than further entertain my theories, Hamrick pointed up at a security camera mounted on the wall. "I'm hoping the camera footage will tell us something. I'm just glad it wasn't a school day and that the building was empty. Nobody was on site except a janitor buffing the floors."

Bustamente's brows lifted. "You talked to him?"

"I did," Hamrick said. "He didn't see anyone, but he smelled the smoke. He grabbed a fire extinguisher and got most of the fires put out before the alarm even activated. When it did, he left the building and called nine-one-one, but the department was already on its way."

Blast could sniff for accelerants, but he wasn't trained to track a suspect who'd fled. I pointed back to my cruiser, where Brigit stood at the open window, watching us. "Should I see if Brigit can pick up a trail? She had the best nose in her training class."

"Sure," Hamrick said. "Let's give her a whirl."

Seth hiked a thumb at the fire truck. "I'll get her Blast's spare booties."

I went to my cruiser and let Brigit out of the back. Seth came over and we put the booties on Brigit's feet. She didn't much like them, but she tolerated them. They were a heavy-duty variety, much thicker than the ones I put on her feet when we spent extended periods of time on hot asphalt. I led her over to the back wall of the school and issued the order for her to track. She sniffed around, found a trail, and began to follow it. Seth, Blast, Hamrick, and Bustamente followed along with me. We'd gone forty yards or so when she stopped at a curb. She made several false starts in various directions.

Seth frowned. "That's where the school bus parked to let the football players out."

No wonder she was confused. There were too many trails to follow. What's more, the water from the fire hoses had flowed down the asphalt, carrying the scents with it.

She sniffed around some more, then doubled back, stopping at a storm drain and sitting down, issuing a passive alert.

"She's having trouble," I explained. "The boys from the bus must have disrupted the trail, and the water must have carried the scent down the storm drain." I peered down at the opening, noticing the inside of the storm sewer was dimly lit. *That's odd.* Was it merely a reflection from the lights on the school, or something else? "Is it just my imagination, or does it seem like there's light coming from inside the sewer?"

Seth dropped to his knees and peered into the drain. "There's something glowing in there." He removed the heavy metal manhole cover, and we peered down into the drain. A heavy-duty LED flashlight glowed from atop the concrete at the bottom, the beam pointed away down the drainage pipe.

Hamrick said, "That flashlight must have been washed down into the sewer with the water."

"It's not one of ours," Seth said.

Hamrick looked down at the flashlight, then over at Brigit. "Good eye, young lady."

Good *nose* was probably the more correct response, but Brigit knew when she was being flattered. She beamed nearly as bright as the flashlight, her eyes gleaming and her tail wagging.

Hamrick pulled a pair of latex gloves from his pocket, slid his hands into them, and carefully lowered himself into the sewer to retrieve the flashlight. He slid the device into a clear plastic evidence bag, placed the bag on the ground next to the manhole, and pulled himself back up to ground level. He whipped a black marker from his pocket and documented the date, time, and place he'd found this potential piece of evidence. He wrote both my name and Brigit's on the bag, as well.

He turned to me. "Thanks, Officer Luz. This could be an important clue."

Though I knew my role as a K-9 handler was important, I knew the bulk of the credit belonged to my furry partner. I reached into my pocket and retrieved three liver treats to reward her for her find. Despite having eaten half her weight in extra food today, she happily gobbled them down.

The detective and I wrapped things up here, and headed back to our vehicles, parting ways in the lot. Though I continued to cruise my beat at an average of thirty miles per hour, my mind was doing a hundred or more. *Who is behind tonight's incidents, and how can we find out?*

30
SUNRISE STROLL

Brigit

Bright and early Saturday morning, Brigit's ears picked up the sounds of Megan slipping out of bed, moving slowly and carefully so as not to disturb Seth, who lay softly snoring beside her. Brigit lay on the foot of the bed next to Blast. She opened one eye to see what her partner was up to. *Is Megan just taking a potty break, or is she going to the kitchen?*

When Megan motioned for Brigit to follow her, the dog slid down from the bed. She turned back and nuzzled Blast's chin. *Come on, lover boy. Rise and shine.*

The dogs padded after Megan, who closed the bedroom door behind them. After Megan let them out to relieve themselves and fed them their breakfast, she washed up in the bathroom and dressed in shorts and a T-shirt. When Brigit spotted Megan pulling her sneakers out from under the couch where she'd left them, she began to dance around. She knew what those shoes meant. *We're going for a walk! Woo hoo!*

After Megan tied her shoes, she leashed both Brigit and Blast and led them out to Seth's car. The three of them wouldn't fit in Megan's tiny Smart Car.

Minutes later, she'd parked and was leading the dogs along the Trinity River Trail. Brigit loved walking here. Sometimes Megan would even let her off leash to cool down in the river. Brigit loved swimming around and chasing the ducks, though she never seemed to be able to catch one. Darn it!

Brigit enjoyed the walk, and she could tell it was good for Megan, too. Megan had been very tense last night. Brigit could smell her adrenaline, the pheromones that said she felt fearful. She didn't know what had caused it, but she was glad Megan seemed more herself today. She was also glad her bruised paw felt much better this morning.

Brigit pulled to the side to pop a squat on the grass. After depositing her droppings, she waited while Megan bagged them. Blast lifted his leg and peed where Brigit had just pooped, adding his scent to the mix. They continued on until Megan had four full doggie doo-doo bags in her hands and the sun had risen high enough that it was no longer enjoyable to be outdoors. But just before they reached the parking lot, Megan let the dogs off leash for a minute or two so they could swim in the river. The water was cool and refreshing, and Brigit lapped it up as she swam around. When Megan called them back, Brigit and Blast dutifully returned to her side and allowed her to reattach her leashes. They climbed into the backseat of the car, and Megan rolled their windows down far enough that they could hang their heads out, but not so far that they could fall out of the vehicle. What a great way to start a day!

31
CRIME DOESN'T PAY AND IT WILL COST YOU, TOO

The Flamethrower

At five o'clock on Saturday afternoon, he drove to Hail Mary's and parked at the far end of the lot. He glanced around. Though he didn't see Nash's Jeep in the lot, he spotted the man himself, heading his way with a large black box. Printed on the side in neon green print was FORCE = MASS X ACCELERATION. The Flamethrower had no real interest in the supplements, but Nash had made it clear that his help came with conditions, one of which was that the Flamethrower purchase a six-month supply of the tablets Nash was having a hard time unloading. The guy might be skilled at setting fires, but he sucked at sales. The Flamethrower could teach him a thing or two.

The Flamethrower climbed out of his car, took the box from Nash, and stashed it in his trunk.

Nash fished his phone from his pocket and inserted a small credit card reader into the port. He held out the phone, and the

Flamethrower tapped his credit card against the device. A beep told him the charge had been processed. As the Flamethrower returned his credit card to his wallet, Nash texted a receipt to his phone. "Nice doing business with you."

It was nice for Nash, sure. But at nearly $1,200 for the supplements, it wasn't so nice for the Flamethrower. He could've used that money on seat protectors for his car or deposited it in Hayden's college account. The fire they'd started at the high school had burned for only a short time, causing minimal damage. The Flamethrower supposed he couldn't blame Nash for that. The guy couldn't have known people would be returning to the school early any more than the Flamethrower could have predicted it. He only hoped the fire, though small, would cause concern where it counted.

32
FAMILY REUNION

Megan

At half past five on Saturday, Seth and I picked up his mother, his grandfather Ollie, and Ollie's girlfriend Beverly, the professional seamstress who'd designed my wedding dress. I'd met the small, snowy-haired woman on an earlier case, and later introduced her to Seth's grandfather. Both of them were widowed and had been ready for new companionship. They'd been an item ever since.

Seth and I had invited the others to dinner to celebrate Ollie's birthday. Once they were all loaded into the car, we headed north to Joe T. Garcia's, an iconic Fort Worth Mexican restaurant that had been in business for nearly nine decades. The establishment had served a slew of celebrities over the years, including Bruce Springsteen, Bette Midler, Reba McEntire, and Harrison Ford, to name a few. Seth and I had enjoyed many date nights at the restaurant.

The day was partly cloudy and the outdoor temperature hovered in the high 80's, surprisingly cool for summertime in North Texas, where we'd suffered three consecutive weeks with highs of over one-hundred degrees in a recent year. The delicious aroma of spices and simmering beans greeted us as we entered. Living in Texas acclimates a person to higher temperatures, and we asked to be seated on the restaurant's extensive patio, knowing the shade trees and frozen margaritas would help keep the heat at bay. The server led us to a table next to a colorful tile fountain in the shadows of a long-limbed tree. Ollie rolled his oxygen tank under the table where it would be out of the way.

While one server passed out menus, another placed two baskets of tortilla chips and individual bowls of fresh salsa on the table, returning a moment later with large glasses of ice water. Once she'd set them down, she pulled a pencil from behind her ear and a pad of paper from her apron. "Margaritas?"

"All around," Seth replied. "Frozen, with salt."

"As the good Lord intended," Beverly added with a nod.

While we waited on our frozen drinks, I scooped up salsa with a tortilla chip, and turned to Beverly for an update on her business. "Have things slowed down for you now that the summer wedding season is coming to an end?"

"Not at all!" She took a sip of her water, "I'm doing fittings for a dance studio that's putting on the Nutcracker in early December. I've got sixty-three costumes to alter between now and then." Her smile said that, despite being well past retirement age, she was happy to have the work. She wasn't the type of woman who'd be content sitting around all day watching soap operas.

Ollie had recently joined a darts league at the VFW. He was relatively new to the sport. I asked him how things were going. "Having any luck?"

"Luck?" He snorted around the oxygen tubes in his nose. "Haven't won a game yet. But I'm getting better bit by bit. The other guys are showing me the ropes."

Despite his losses at darts, Ollie was having fun socializing with the other veterans. He'd spent decades in self-imposed isolation, grieving his dead wife and suffering from PTSD, before finally coming around and venturing out, reconnecting with army buddies he'd served with in Vietnam and making new friends, as well. He was a very different man from the surly curmudgeon he'd been when I'd first met him.

A family of four came out of the back door of the restaurant, and a hostess led them in our direction. The two boys appeared to be in their mid teens, and had light brown hair and broad shoulders like their handsome father, who wore cowboy boots and a short-sleeved madras shirt tucked neatly into his jeans. Their mom was petite, a tad plump with the curves that often come with motherhood and middle age, but she wore the extra pounds well and looked stylish in a pale pink prairie dress and tan cowgirl boots. Her highlighted blond hair was swept up in a lively twist held together with a plastic banana clip.

Lisa had just raised her water glass to her lips when the family approached our table. The boys passed by first, then their mother. She glanced up as the man followed them, then did a double take and froze. The man stopped in his tracks, staring down at Lisa. Her water glass slipped from her grasp and fell to the table, toppling over and sending a tsunami of cold water and ice across the tabletop.

The man's brows rose and his mouth gaped. "Lisa?"

While Beverly and I used our napkins to sop up the spill, Lisa stared up at the man, her expression equal parts surprised, terrified, and pained. She said nothing, seemingly shocked speechless. *Who is this guy?*

"It *is* you!" The man's eyes brightened and a broad smile spread across his face. "Wow, how long has it been?" He shook his head slowly in disbelief. "Thirty-something years, right? What have you been up to?"

Lisa shrank back against her seat, her shoulders curving inward as if she were trying to disappear inside herself. Her lips parted slightly, but no words emerged.

When his mother still said nothing after a few seconds, Seth rose from his chair. Though his expression was confused, he politely extended a hand to the man. "I'm Seth, Lisa's son."

As I watched them, I noted that the two were the same height. Their noses were similar in shape, too.

The man took Seth's hand. "Tommy Wainwright." Though he addressed Seth, his eyes were on Lisa. "Your mom and I dated in high school. Maybe she mentioned me?"

Tommy's face looked so hopeful it was a shame Seth had to bring him down. Still, Seth did his best to soften the blow. "I don't recall her mentioning your name, but you know how sons are. We don't pay much attention to anything our mothers say."

Tommy chuckled as he released Seth's hand. "You got that right." He stared down at Lisa, though she had yet to make eye contact with him. "You look great, Lisa. Hardly changed at all."

Lisa barked an involuntary laugh, and flung a dismissive hand, venturing a quick glance up at him. "Oh, Tommy. That's bullshit and you know it."

Beverly chimed in. "At least it's nice bullshit." She punctuated her sentence by biting into a chip. *Crunch.*

Seth had yet to sit back down. His eyes narrowed as he scrutinized Tommy, taking in the broad shoulders that were so like his own. He cast a questioning glance at his mother before addressing Tommy again. He pointed from Tommy to his mother. "What happened with the two of you?"

"Your mom's the one that got away." Tommy shoved his hands into his pants pockets, and rocked back on his heels. "I was a senior and Lisa was a sophomore when we dated. She ended things when I headed off to Duke. I didn't want to go to school so far from home, but they offered me a swimming scholarship. Full ride." He shrugged. "Couldn't say no to that, could I?"

Oh, my God! The resemblance. The timing of Tommy and Lisa's relationship ... *Could it be?*

Seth, too, had put two and two together—or perhaps one and

one. He looked from Tommy to his mother, and cocked his head. "Mom, is this the guy?"

Tommy's actions mirrored Seth's. He looked from Lisa to Seth. "*What* guy?"

Seth's gaze met Tommy's. "My father."

Tommy jerked his head back as if someone had thrown a punch at him. A sob burst from Lisa, and she covered her face with her hands, her shoulders shaking. Tommy looked at her, and his eyes went wide. Though he appeared flummoxed, he didn't deny the possibility that he could have fathered Seth. Though Lisa and Tommy had said nothing, their reactions spoke volumes. Tommy Wainwright was Seth's father, the man he'd never known, never before met.

I reached out to put a comforting hand on Lisa's shoulder.

When Tommy spoke, his voice had gone up three octaves. "I'm ... *what now?*" His gaze darted between Lisa and Seth.

Lisa removed her hands from her face, looked up at Tommy, and choked back a sob. Unable to speak, she merely nodded.

The two locked eyes for a long moment before Tommy turned to Seth, looking him up and down as if making a visual confirmation. "You're my son?"

None of us had noticed Tommy's wife heading back our way, and she stepped up just in time to hear Tommy's words. I had no idea what her voice sounded like normally, but it squeaked like Minnie Mouse now. "Your son?!" She looked from her husband to Seth to Lisa, then back to her husband again, her mouth hanging open and her eyes wide now, too.

Ollie rose from his seat, jabbing a finger at Tommy, the surly old man back with a vengeance. "You no-good son-of-a-bitch! You knock up my daughter then skip town? I ought to clobber you!"

As a police officer, I regularly found myself in the middle of awkward and emotional situations. It was natural for me to step in to mediate. I stood and made a downward motion with my palms. "Let's all take a deep breath. This is a big surprise, but I'm sure we can talk things out." First, it was only fair to let Tommy's wife know who she was talking to here. I extended my hand. "I'm Megan Luz." I held out a hand to indicate Seth. "Seth is my fiancé." I gestured to Ollie and Beverly. "Ollie is Seth's grandfather and Beverly is his date." I turned to Lisa now. "Lisa is—"

"*Lisa?!*" The woman put her hand to her chest and stared at Lisa, slack-jawed. "You're Lisa? *The* Lisa?"

Uh-oh. Tommy had told his wife about Lisa. The only question now was what, exactly, had he told her?

When Lisa said nothing, but just looked up at her with her lips trembling, the woman turned to her husband in question.

Tommy exhaled a shaky breath. "Yeah. She's *the* Lisa."

The woman looked a bit faint, taking an inadvertent step back. Seth noticed and offered her his chair. She plopped down into it, shaking her head in disbelief. Once she'd collected herself, she looked around the table and said, "I'm Pamela. Tommy's wife." She turned back to Lisa, her expression surprised but without malice. "Is it true? Is Seth Tommy's son?"

Lisa stared at Pamela for a long moment, her pursed lips moving from one side to the other, no words making it past them. Finally, she just nodded.

Pamela slumped back in the chair, gobsmacked.

Seth jumped in, turning on Tommy. "How could you not know my mom was pregnant?" he demanded, though he kept his voice steady. "How could you just dump her and move on?"

Tommy cleared his throat. His voice was hoarse, and barely above a whisper when he said, "I didn't dump her. I had no idea." Tommy opened his mouth to say more but hesitated, as if wanting to defend himself, to explain his actions—or inactions—but as if he were reluctant to throw Lisa under the bus. He paused for a beat or two, trying to figure out what to say. His voice was soft when he spoke again, his tone matter-of-fact rather than accusatory. "I'd wanted to keep things going back then, but your mother wasn't interested in a long-distance relationship. She ended things cold turkey, wouldn't return my calls or letters. She ghosted me, though that term didn't really exist back then. Broke my eighteen-year-old heart." He looked to Lisa, putting a hand over his heart and forcing a smile though there was pain reflected in his eyes, a wound that time hadn't fully healed. He shifted his focus back to Seth, his gaze full of guilt and regret and apology. "I had no idea," he repeated, "or I would've stepped up, done the right thing."

"I know you would have!" Lisa choked out, her hands fisting atop the table. "That was the problem!"

Tommy's brow furrowed. "The problem?" he repeated. "What do you mean?"

Lisa gulped down her motion. "I'm so sorry, Tommy," she rasped. "I should've told you when I found out I was pregnant. But I was so scared! And I knew you wouldn't go off to college if I told you. You were so excited about swimming for Duke. I didn't want you to feel stuck, with me or in Fort Worth. You had a bright future ahead of you, and I didn't want to mess things up for you." She turned to Seth and gulped down a fresh sob, her eyes dark with sorrow and regret. "Instead, I messed them up for everyone!" She put her face in her hands.

"You were a child, Lisa." I gave her trembling shoulder a squeeze. When she removed her hands from her face to look at me, I said, "Besides, it's never too late to make amends."

Her expression brightened ever so slightly.

"Speaking of amends," Tommy eyed Seth, chuckling softly, "I suppose I owe you thousands in allowance."

"Don't forget the child support you owe Lisa!" Ollie snapped.

Both Lisa and Seth cut Ollie a look that told him to keep his mouth shut. The financial ramifications of the situation were the least of their concerns at the moment.

Pamela inhaled a deep breath, then released it through her mouth before turning to Lisa. "I was on the diving team at Duke. That's how Tommy and I met. He pined for you our entire freshman year. I had a big crush on him, but he wasn't interested, in me or any other girl. His heart was back here in Texas with you. I'd just about given up on him when he finally came around." From the seat Seth had relinquished to her, she reached out and took one of his hands in hers, taking Lisa's hand with the other. "This is a big surprise. I'm not going to pretend otherwise. But we're family now. Let's get to know each other."

Lisa nodded and gave Pamela a grateful smile through fresh tears. The rest of us relaxed in relief. This could have gone so much worse. Pamela could have been jealous and angry and protective, but she wasn't. She must have considered her marriage to be solid, her husband's long-ago, teenaged indiscretion no threat to her family. It was amazingly magnanimous of her.

I stopped the server as he walked past. "Any chance we can pull another table over and add four chairs?"

Fortunately, a group had just vacated the adjacent table. The server pulled it over, a busboy quickly cleaned it off, and we rearranged our seats. Tommy raised a hand in the air to signal his two boys to come over from their table and join us. Being typical teens, their focus was on the screens of the phones in their hands and Tommy's gesture went unnoticed.

Pamela whipped her phone from her purse. "I'll text 'em and tell 'em to get their butts over here." Her manicured thumbs moved furiously over her phone.

A few seconds later, the boys stepped up to the table, their faces befuddled.

"Guess what?" Pamela said. Not bothering to wait for them to hazard a guess, she hiked a thumb at Seth. "He's your half-brother. Your dad knocked up his high school girlfriend and didn't know it."

"Dude!" The older boy barked a nervous laugh and eyed his dad. "For real?"

Tommy raised his shoulders. "For real."

The younger one cringed. "Ew! Is this why you kept talking about condoms when you gave us 'the talk'?"

"Well, yes," Tommy said, his expression sheepish. "I didn't want there be any accid—" As if realizing he might inadvertently insult Seth with his wording, he stopped himself and instead said, "I didn't want you getting into a situation you weren't prepared to handle."

Seth's expression was mildly amused. He seemed to take pleasure in Tommy's discomfort. Was it nice? No. But after he'd spent years having to field questions from school personnel and nosy neighbors about his unknown, absentee father, he probably felt like Tommy deserved to suffer the same sense of shame and embarrassment. Fortunately, Seth wasn't going to make his half-brothers, who were innocent of wrongdoing, feel any such shame. "Hey, bros." He made a fist and held it out so they could bump knuckles with him. "I'm Seth."

The older boy reached out and bumped fists with Seth. "I'm Dallas."

The younger boy followed his brother's lead. "My name is Austin."

We all took our seats. After placing our orders, Tommy proceeded to ask both Lisa and Seth a series of questions that would enable him to piece together the years he'd missed. Of course, with so many years having gone by, they hit only the highlights.

Tommy seemed both impressed and proud of Seth's service as an ordnance disposal specialist in the army, and his work as a firefighter and on the city's bomb squad. He was delighted to learn that Seth, too, enjoyed swimming. "What's your best stroke?"

"The butterfly," Seth said.

Tommy threw up his hands, happy to know he'd passed something positive down to his son, even if unwittingly. "That's my stroke, too!"

"Mine, too," Austin chimed in.

"Cool," Seth said. "Did your dad give you some pointers?"

"He told me to keep my chin down and wait to breathe until late in the stroke."

"Good advice," Seth said. "All I heard from my grandfather was 'Don't slip and fall! We can't afford to take you to the doctor!'"

Tommy, Pamela, their sons, and Beverly shared a laugh, thinking it was a joke when, in actuality, Seth was telling the truth. Dealing with his own demons, Ollie hadn't been the most supportive grandparent, especially after losing the wife who'd humanized him.

The server brought our food, and we all dug in.

As I sipped of my margarita, Pamela's gaze went to my engagement ring. "When's the wedding?"

"Late September," I said. It was hard to believe the big day was only a few weeks off. "We're going to Utah for the honeymoon."

"Utah is gorgeous," Pamela said, clasping her hands in delight. "We've taken the boys skiing in Park City a couple of times."

Skiing was an expensive activity. It was only natural for Seth to wonder about his father's occupation. He turned to Tommy. "What do you do for a living?"

"I'm a manager at the G.E. Aviation manufacturing facility in Asheville, North Carolina," Tommy said. "We build parts for airplane engines, specifically ceramic matrix composite components."

The words were gibberish to me, but Seth knew exactly what his father was talking about and dumbed it down for me. "That's relatively new technology. Things made of CMCs can handle extremely high temperatures. There are applications in fire protection. Heat shields. Fire barriers. That kind of thing."

We continued to make small talk until we'd finished our dinner and had to relinquish the table to waiting guests. As we stood outside the restaurant to say our goodbyes, Tommy turned to Lisa and Seth. "Any chance you two could meet me for breakfast in the morning, just the three of us?"

Pamela and I exchanged a glance, both of us feeling a little left out while at the same time understanding why it was important the three of them have some time to speak privately, to come to terms with their situation.

Lisa nodded. Seth said, "Works for me. I'm off duty until Monday."

They arranged to meet at the Ol' South Pancake House on

University Drive at nine the next morning. Hugs and handshakes were exchanged all around, though Ollie offered his handshakes begrudgingly.

Once we were seated again in Seth's car, Seth snorted a laugh. "Well, that was an interesting dinner." He glanced back over the bench seat at his mother. "You okay, Mom?"

The fact that he could be concerned for her emotional welfare when she was obviously feeling like she'd deprived him of a father's love and support all his life was too much for her to bear. She burst into fresh tears. "I've made such a mess of things!"

"It's okay, Mom." Seth met her gaze in the rearview mirror. "Please don't cry."

I glanced back at Lisa. She'd dammed up her emotions for years, and now that dam had burst. There was no fixing it. The only thing to do was let the emotions flow until they ran dry. "She needs to cry," I told Seth. "This was ... a lot."

Lisa nodded vigorously through her tears, giving me a small, grateful smile.

As I turned back to face forward, I found myself tearing up, as well. Apparently, I needed to cry, too.

33
DOGGIE BAG

Brigit

Brigit didn't much like being left home. Without Megan, being home was boring. At least Blast was here, and the two could be bored together.

The dogs tussled on the rug. When a young man skateboarded past on the street, they ran to the window and barked up a storm, letting him know this was their turf. They spent a quarter hour exercising their teeth and gums on their nubby chew toys. They curled up side by side on the sofa and took a nap. Then, they repeated the entire process, though this time the focus of their barking was a girl on a bicycle rather than a boy on a skateboard.

Both dogs pricked their ears and raised their heads from the rug as a recognizable engine approached and turned into the driveway. A few seconds later, they heard the car doors slam and murmurs of conversation. Brigit's nose picked up the scent of the fajita meat before Seth and Megan even opened the door. She met the humans as they stepped inside. Blast stepped up beside her, both of them wagging their tails in anticipation of a nice treat. Megan and Seth didn't let the dogs down. In less than a minute, the two dogs were face down in their bowls, wolfing down bits of seasoned beef.

When Brigit finished, she lifted her head, issued a satisfied belch, and issued a bark in thanks. "Arf!"

Megan ruffled her ears. "My pleasure, partner."

34
SMOKESCREEN

The Flamethrower

Sitting in front of his laptop Sunday morning, he searched for reports about the fire at the high school. He thought by now that word would have spread, even if the flames hadn't. The fire he and Nash had set at the school had been quickly snuffed out by a janitor who'd been on site to clean the locker room and band hall after the football team and marching band packed up and went home. The brave man hadn't waited for the fire department to arrive. Rather, he'd grabbed an extinguisher and put out the flames himself, minimizing the damage. *Effing wannabe hero.*

The Flamethrower muttered a curse. The only reference to the fire was a mere postscript to a long, detailed article about the evacuation of the stadium. Once again, some asshole had called the police with a bogus shooter threat and stolen his thunder. But he'd be damned if he'd let that happen again. He was going to be like Thor, the god of thunder. To do that, he had to get his thunder back.

35
THINGS COOL OFF

Megan

While Seth went to breakfast with Lisa and Tommy, I took the dogs for a walk. We'd made it only to the corner before they were panting so hard I feared they'd succumb to heatstroke. "Let's go home," I said. The fact that they obeyed me without hesitation said a lot. Those two lived for walks.

Leaving the dogs at home in the air conditioning, I drove to the nearest Walmart, intending to buy a plastic kiddie pool for the dogs to cool off and play in. But when I spotted the last of their easy-installation above-ground pools, I realized a full-size pool would be fun not only for the dogs, but also for us humans. With summer nearly over, the pool had been reduced to half price. *I'd be a fool to pass up this deal.*

The box was quite large and, according to the specifications thereon, weighed 195 pounds. While I wasn't foolish enough to pass up the low price, I was foolish enough to think I could wrangle the box into my cart. Despite my best efforts, I managed only to walk the box off the low shelf and onto the tile floor. I was going to need some help, not only here in the store, but getting the pool home, as well. There was no possible way it would fit in my tiny car.

I whipped out my phone and dialed Frankie. "Any chance you and Zach can meet me at Walmart?"

When I told her why I needed her help, she said, "We'll be there in fifteen minutes. Don't let anyone else get that pool!"

While I waited, I looked up the instructions online on how to care for the pool, and snagged some chemicals from a nearby shelf. I grabbed a couple of pool noodles as well, plus four inflatable loungers, a beach ball, and two small splash balls, which were made to absorb water and fun for playing catch in a pool on a hot day. Frankie and Zach arrived in no time, both wearing their bathing suits. Zach, who was tall and dark-haired, had paired his swim trunks with a T-shirt, while Frankie had covered her bikini with a colorful knit coverup. Zach picked up the large box as if it weighed nothing and set it in my cart.

"Impressive," I said. "You been working out?"

"I have." He flexed his biceps and turned side to side, giving us girls a gun show. "Thanks for noticing."

An elderly gray-haired woman pushed her cart by us and issued a wolf whistle.

Zach dipped his head in appreciation. "Thank you, ma'am."

Frankie returned her attention to me. "Zach's been working out more, but he also took some free supplements a guy gave me at the firehouse."

"The Physical Force brand?" I asked. "In the black and neon green package?"

"That's them," Frankie said. "I say they're snake oil, but Zach swears by them."

He flexed again. "These guns don't lie."

Despite his impressive biceps, I sided with Frankie. I thought the supplements were mere snake oil, too. They weren't regulated by the Food and Drug Administration, and standard dosages hadn't been established. Still, I supposed they were far better than taking steroids. Besides, Zach was an adult. Surely, he'd weighed the pros and cons before taking them. Maybe they had a placebo effect that made those who took them feel stronger and more energetic. "Seth brought a sample home, but he doesn't plan to use them. He said they cost a small fortune." I turned to Zach. "You're welcome to them."

"I'll take you up on that."

The pool securely in the cart, we headed to the refrigerated section where we grabbed six-packs of beer and hard lemonade, then rolled to the front of the store. I paid for the items at the self-checkout, showing my receipt to the greeter on our way out the door. We continued into the parking lot, where Zach slid the pool and other items into the back of his pickup.

Frankie opted to ride to my house with me rather than Zach. Along the way, I gave her an update.

Her mouth hung open. "Seth's dad just showed up out of the blue? That had to be a shock."

"It was," I said. "Seth and his mother are having breakfast with him right now."

She cocked her head. "How did Tommy's wife take it? I can't imagine she was happy to learn she had a stepson she'd never heard of before."

"Pamela surprised me," I said. "She seemed to take it in stride—as much as anyone could, anyway. Same with their boys." *Thank goodness.* If any of them had been openly upset or angry, it would have only made things that much harder. Still, I wasn't naïve enough to think that Tommy and Pamela wouldn't have to work through this big news, come to terms with things over time. Seth's stepbrothers, too. Changing the subject, I asked if Frankie had heard whether the fire investigator had any leads on the arson at the high school.

"Not as far as I know," she said, "but it can take a while for information to trickle down."

I hadn't heard anything from Detective Bustamente about the investigation into the shooter call at the stadium, either. But I knew no news didn't necessarily mean no progress.

When we arrived at the house, I opened the gate and Zach, Frankie, and I carried the heavy box into the backyard. After ensuring the gate was latched, I let Blast and Brigit out through the backdoor. Curious, they ventured over to sniff the box and the parts as we pulled them out. When they realized none of the materials were edible, they lost interest and walked over to their favorite spot under a tree to relax. Both used their front paws to dig up the dirt until they reached a moister, cooler level. Though the digging would ensure they tracked dirt into the house later, it was hotter than Hades out here and I wasn't about to stop the poor beasts from trying to cool down.

The pool was eighteen feet in diameter and fifty-two inches high, with a volume of 4,400 gallons, a fairly large size for a do-it-yourself above-ground pool. It took over an hour for Zach, Frankie, and me to get the pool properly set up, and another half hour to fill it to ankle level.

"This is taking forever." Frankie picked up the green garden hose and shook her head. "Too bad we can't use a fire hose. I'd have this baby filled in ten seconds flat."

Not only was the water taking a long time to fill, it wasn't cold. The extreme Texas heat had warmed the underground pipes.

While the water continued to run, I went inside, emptied the ice cube trays, and refilled them. Frankie pushed aside everything in the freezer to make more room, and I filled bowls, baking dishes, and plastic cups with water, placing them all in the freezer to produce more ice. She and Zach started a bucket brigade, filling my stock pot and pitcher with water at the kitchen sink and taking turns carrying them out to fill the pool faster.

I ventured back outside, where I eyed the ladder that had come with the pool. While humans could easily climb it, the apparatus was too steep to be useful to the dogs. *Hmm.* Though our house was a rental, Seth had completed a variety of repairs our landlord had dragged his feet on, such as fence repair. I went to the garage to see what leftover materials I might find inside. Neatly stacked at the back of the space were several cinder blocks, as well as a dozen two by fours. While Frankie continued to fill the pot and pitcher in the kitchen, Zach helped me move the materials to the backyard. Together, we built makeshift steps for the dogs to use to access the pool. The top step served as a narrow platform or deck, which would also be convenient for us humans.

By the time Seth arrived home from breakfast and opened the back door at half past noon, the water in the pool was still only knee deep. Even so, Frankie, Zach, and I were standing in it, cold drinks in our hands. The dogs were in the pool, too, leaping around and splashing, having the time of their lives.

Seth stepped outside, his expression brightening. "I leave you home alone for a few hours, and you put in a pool?"

"I couldn't help myself," I said. "It was too hot to walk the dogs this morning. I went to the store to buy a kiddie pool for them, but then I saw this one. They were practically giving it away."

"Hey, I'm not complaining." He walked over to the pool. Blast barked up at him from inside, as if begging him to get in, too. Seth reached over the side, having to bend way over to touch the water. "Too bad we can't hook a hose up to the hydrant down the street. We'd have this pool filled in no time."

Frankie put her hands on her hips. "I said the exact same thing!"

I lifted my foot and kicked some water at Seth. "Put on your suit and join us."

He used the back of his hand to wipe sweat from his brow. "You won't have to ask me twice."

He disappeared into the house, returning a moment later in his swim trunks, a cold bottle of beer in his hand. He checked out the makeshift steps, making sure the design was safe and secure. "Not bad," he declared.

Although I was dying to know how the breakfast with his parents went, I didn't want to pressure him to talk about it, especially in front of Frankie and Zach. Seth had a history of shutting down emotionally, a self-protective reaction that had become a habit during his tumultuous childhood, but he was working on being more open. I knew he'd give me the details when he was good and ready.

As the water continued to slowly rise in the pool, we grabbed the inflatable rafts to blow them up.

Frankie turned the inflation process into a competition. "Last one to fill their air mattress is a rotten egg!"

It was a childish dare, but that didn't stop the rest of us from taking it. We all blew as quick and fast as we could to inflate our respective air mattresses. My head went light with each exhale.

A minute later, Frankie lay her mattress atop the shallow water, flopped down on it, and declared herself the winner. "I smoked y'all!"

Zach snorted. "That's only because you're full of hot air."

Seth, Zach, and I finished blowing up our floats and joined Frankie atop the water's surface. Though the water was only three feet deep, it was enough to keep us afloat. We relaxed and engaged in casual conversation as the water continued to rise. When it became too deep for the dogs to stand, Seth and I helped them up to the platform, where they could rest and dry off.

Later that afternoon, Seth fired up the grill. While he prepared spicy black bean burgers and roasted corn, Frankie and I threw together a fruit salad for dessert. Rather than endure the blistering heat while we ate, we enjoyed our meal in air-conditioned comfort in the kitchen, the happily exhausted dogs napping at our feet on the cool floor.

As we finished up, I remembered the supplements I'd offered to Zach earlier. I retrieved the package from the cabinet where we kept the vitamins, and handed them to Zach.

Seth cocked his head and eyed Zach. "How are those working for you?"

"You tell me." Zach again raised his arms, flexing his biceps to show off his muscles. He raised a brow in question.

Seth intertwined his fingers, rested his chin on them, and batted his eyelashes. "You look absolutely dreamy."

"Back off, Bucko." Frankie glared at Seth in jest. "He's taken."

The four of us shared a laugh.

I remembered that the Physical Force distributor had expressed an interest in working as a firefighter. "Do you know whether Nash Goshen applied to the fire department?"

"The guy who was selling the supplements?" Seth replied. "Yeah, he put in an application and took the preliminary written test. He got a sixty-seven. You have to score at least seventy to be considered, but most people who get hired score much higher. The captain told us he encouraged the guy to try again, but the test is only offered twice a year. Most people who don't pass the first time give up and move on to something else."

At that point, Frankie and Zach begged off.

"It's been fun," Zach said, as he took his plate and silverware to the sink, "but we better hit the road. Let's do this again soon."

"Yes!" Frankie said. "Let's."

Seth and I walked them out to the driveway, where I thanked them again for making the pool possible.

Once they'd gone, we cleaned up both the kitchen and ourselves, and snuggled up on the couch with the dogs. Seth had been quieter than usual since his breakfast with his mother and father that morning, but he seemed ready to talk about it now.

He scrubbed a hand down his face. "Tommy—*my father*—is extremely upset that my mother kept something so important from him." Seth said Tommy's emotions had run the gamut. He was happy to learn the truth, but he resented Lisa for robbing him of a chance to know and raise his son, and for robbing his parents, who still lived in town, of the chance to know their grandson.

"Understandable," I said, though it made my heart twinge to feel like I was betraying Lisa. After all, she'd been only a girl at the time. It was hard to fault her for making a bad decision.

Seth released a long, loud breath. "Tommy said he thought they could have made it work."

While I was a sucker for first-love stories, I thought Tommy's claim was a bit idealistic. "The odds would have been against them, unfortunately. Teen marriages rarely last."

Seth cut me a look. "I think he really loved her. Seems like she really loved him, too."

"I don't doubt it. It must have been hard for her to let him go."

"She said again that she thought she was doing what was best for him. Tommy came from a large Catholic family, nine kids. His parents struggled to make ends meet. He'd had to get a job at sixteen to help pay the family's bills. His parents couldn't afford to send him to college. The scholarship offer was a godsend. He knew it would change his life forever, that he could get a good job and help his family out after he graduated so they wouldn't have to keep living hand to mouth. My mom knew it, too. She didn't want to hold him back, derail his dreams."

"What about *her* dreams?"

Seth shrugged. "She wasn't academically oriented and didn't plan to go to college. Her aspiration back then was to get a job at a department store at the mall, maybe work her way up to manager."

Getting pregnant at fifteen had gotten in the way of Lisa's plans, too. She was pregnant before she was even old enough to work at a store. *Poor Lisa.*

Seth wrapped things up. "Tommy seemed relieved to know that he'd meant as much to my mom back then as she had meant to him, and that she hadn't dumped him because she'd stopped caring about him. He seemed to be trying to understand her predicament and decisions, trying to forgive her." He inhaled a shaky breath. "He asked how things had been for me growing up. I sugarcoated things, mostly for my mom's sake, but for his, too. I could tell he felt guilty, responsible. I told him I was glad to learn that my father hadn't knowingly left my mother in a bind. We've decided to try to put the past behind us, and focus on moving forward."

Forgetting the past would surely be easier said than done. Seth would need time to process things. His father would, too. Lisa would also have to come to terms with the consequences of her decision.

I rested my head on his shoulder. "I hate that you and your mother had it so rough, but I'm glad you're here with me now."

A grin tugged at his lips as he looked down at me. "How about you show me how glad you are?"

Grinning now, too, I stood, took his hand, and led him to the bedroom.

36
PARTY POOPER

Brigit

Brigit had hoped that Megan and Seth would allow her and Blast to play in the water again Monday morning. It had been fun to splash around and cool off. But when Brigit saw Megan putting on her work uniform, she knew it wouldn't be happening. She normally enjoyed work, but it wasn't nearly as fun as romping around in the water. She flopped down on her belly, rested her chin on the floor, and issued a resigned doggie sigh.

Megan reached down and ruffled her ears. "Off to work we go. But if you're a good girl today, you can get in the pool this evening."

Brigit lifted her head. She didn't entirely understand what Megan meant, but she recognized the word *pool*. Megan, Frankie, Zach, and Seth had used that word many times yesterday, and she knew it referred to the big tank with the water in it. Maybe she'd get to play in the water again today, after all!

37
BLOWING SMOKE

The Flamethrower

Early Monday morning, the Flamethrower was standing at the sink, washing a week's worth of dishes and taking an occasional sip of coffee, while Hayden was eating his usual morning Pop-Tarts at the breakfast bar, tossing the crusts down to the eager mutt at his feet. Hayden's phone lay on the counter. The screen lit up with an incoming text. It was an image of Gretchen and her new lover standing in front of the Eiffel Tower, their arms encircling each other's waists. *The fucking Eiffel Tower. Most romantic place on earth.* Gretchen had begged the Flamethrower to take her there for their tenth anniversary, but he'd refused. He wasn't into museums and cathedrals, and had no interest whatsoever in visiting the Louvre or Notre Dame. *I should've done it anyway.*

Hayden glanced down at the screen, then up at his dad, before slipping the phone into the back pocket of his jeans.

The Flamethrower's blood felt as hot as the steaming water in the sink, and he had to turn his head away so that his son wouldn't see the fury on his face. When he finally got himself under control, he turned back to Hayden, forcing his voice to remain calm. "Your mom's in Paris?"

"Yeah." A look of guilt skittered across Hayden's face. "She didn't tell you?"

"No," the Flamethrower said. *She damn well should have!* "What if there was an of emergency and I needed to get in touch with her?"

Hayden pointed out the obvious. "Her cell phone works over there. You could still call or text her just like when she's here."

And she could ignore those calls and texts, just like she had when she'd first moved out. But the Flamethrower knew there was nothing to be gained by putting his son in the middle of their marriage problems. Hayden had nothing to do with their issues. Other than the colic, their son had generally been a bright spot in their marriage. The Flamethrower had enjoyed teaching Hayden how to play baseball when the boy was young, enjoyed watching his games. He had happy memories of their family camping trips at Eagle Mountain Lake. *What had happened to them?*

He knew the answer. He'd been prone to selfishness to begin with and things had only gotten worse over time. As middle age approached, he'd found himself in the throes of a midlife crisis. He'd felt bored and restless, unfulfilled, resentful of the responsibilities of taking care of his family and their home. He'd been acting like a big damn crybaby instead of a man. That's why his wife was in Paris getting her ooh-la-la from another man. The thought ignited fresh, hot fury. *If that bastard hadn't come along, Gretchen and I could have gotten through this.* His wedding vows might have proved meaningless, but he'd never renege on his most recent vow: *That guy will pay for ruining my marriage.*

The Flamethrower glanced at the clock on the microwave. "The bus will be here soon. Better hurry up."

A few minutes later, to his son's obvious utter horror, the

Flamethrower walked outside with him as the kid went to catch the bus Monday morning. Hayden rushed ahead, as if he were being stalked by a zombie. He joined Ainsley and Alexis at the curb as the big yellow bus rolled to a stop. He climbed on as fast as he could, and didn't glance back.

The Flamethrower knew Valerie always watched from behind the curtains as her girls waited for the bus. Gretchen used to do the same thing, hiding out of sight a few steps back behind the blinds so Hayden wouldn't know. They were both good mothers, if excessively protective.

He raised a hand to wave to Valerie, but quickly turned his hand around and motioned for her to come outside. He headed across the street, meeting her on her porch as she stepped out her front door. After quick niceties were exchanged, he said, "Someone tried to set fire to the school last weekend. Did you hear about it? Gretchen is worried they might try again. Our kids could get hurt." He heaved a shuddering breath for dramatic effect. *"Or worse."*

He might not have been able to get a blaze going Friday night, but he was blowing plenty of smoke now. Gretchen would indeed be worried about the fire—if she knew about it. Not knowing where she was and having had no contact with her since she dropped their boy and dog off Friday morning, the Flamethrower had no idea whether she'd even heard about it. But he knew that Gretchen and Valerie had a little thing going, a sort of surreptitious competition to see who was the better mother. The Flamethrower knew if he mentioned Gretchen's alleged anxiety, Valerie would strive to out-worry his wife to show she was the superior mother. Maybe he could use that to his advantage.

To his surprise, Valerie refused to take the bait. "From what I heard, the fire didn't do much damage. It was probably just kids pulling a prank. Besides, if it happens again, the fire alarms will go off just like they did before and the kids will evacuate. They know what to do. They have drills for it. Besides, the school's sprinkler system would kick in. I'm much more worried about the shooter report at the football game. I can only imagine the death toll we might be facing if they hadn't evacuated the stadium so quickly."

His gut and fists clenched. He was tempted to point out that the students had undergone active shooter drills just as they had fire drills, but he knew the two threats weren't at all the same. Hell, he'd felt a little freaked out when he'd learned about the call to 9-1-1 Friday evening. Thank goodness that, by the time he heard about it, he knew his boy had safely evacuated and was on his way to eat cheap, greasy breakfast food with his friends. Still, with another shooter hoax having happened only days before, he didn't take the shooter threat quite as seriously as he would have otherwise.

The Flamethrower decided to push a little harder. He cocked his head and forced his face into a judgmental frown. "I'm surprised at your reaction, Val. Our children's lives could be at stake. I always considered you a role model for the other moms, but you seem to be taking the fire lightly."

She stiffened, her eyes flashing.

Before she could argue with him, the Flamethrower twisted the knife. "I figured you and the others on the PTA board would put some pressure on the fire department to find out who did this, to make sure the arsonist doesn't set another fire at the school. The fire department wouldn't listen to just one parent like me, but the PTA represents a large group. Y'all have power. They'd pay attention to what you had to say. But if it doesn't matter to you—"

"I didn't say it doesn't matter to me!" she snapped, crossing her arms over her chest. "I'm concerned about anything that might harm my girls or the other kids. I just meant that a shooter is a greater risk than a fire."

"Only if there actually is a shooter, which there wasn't. Either time." He raised one shoulder in a half shrug, then backed up, palms raised. "But you do you, Val. I've got to get to work." A sly grin captured his lips as he turned around and put his back to her. He'd seen the indignant rage flare up in her eyes. No doubt she'd bring the matter of the fire up to the other demanding PTA moms. Those spandex-clad ladies were a force to be reckoned with.

38
THINGS HEAT UP

Megan

Finally, my swing-shift rotation was complete, and I was back to working the day shift. I was standing along the back wall at roll call Monday morning, Brigit sitting at my side, when Detective Bustamente stuck his head in the door of the meeting room. He glanced around, caught my eye, and motioned me forward.

From behind the lectern, Captain Leone looked over at the detective from under his caterpillar-like wiry black brows. "You borrowing my best officers again?"

The room erupted in noise as my fellow officers expressed outrage, each insisting that he or she was the best officer in our precinct. The captain chuckled at the rise he'd gotten out of them. As he resumed updating the shift on the latest updates on burglaries, road repairs, and recent arrests, I eased my way through the crowd of uniforms to the door. As I attempted to squeeze past Derek, he extended a leg to make my going more difficult and hissed in my ear. "Kiss ass."

I rolled my eyes. Derek was jealous that Detective Bustamente had taken me under his wing and included me in several of his investigations, but the detective certainly hadn't done it out of pity. I'd worked hard to prove myself, to learn, to be an asset to the department. Besides, while I might have brainpower on my side, Derek certainly had brawn on his. His physical prowess had landed him that coveted spot on the SWAT team. Why he bothered to be jealous of me I'd never know. Could be he was a misogynist who felt threatened by intelligent women. Could be he was nothing more than an asshole who simply enjoyed giving me a hard time.

Once Brigit and I had joined the detective in the hall, he reached down to stroke her head. "Who's a good girl?"

Brigit wagged her tail.

Bustamente wore rubber-soled loafers, along with khakis and a pink button-down shirt that had been worn soft after many years in his wardrobe. He had a holstered gun on his hip and held a soft-sided faux-leather briefcase in his free hand. After a few more pats, Bustamente returned his attention to me. "I tried the Dollar General store again first thing Saturday morning, but turns out they don't carry the flip-phone model used to make the call on Friday night. I'm still waiting to hear back from the cell phone company to find out where the phone was sold." He told me he'd spent some time online, and discerned that the model was sold at Walmart, Target, and Best Buy stores, as well as Family Dollar stores, 7-11 convenience stores, and the major chain pharmacies.

I sighed. "There's a bunch of those stores in our precinct, probably a hundred or more across the city."

"Exactly. Rather than waste time trying to hit them all, I figured I'd wait for the phone company to narrow things down for me. As far as the M.O., it's the same as last time. The only call made from the phone was the call to nine-one-one from the purported shooter. There was no other activity. This time, the phone was activated only two hours before the call was made."

"That's an even shorter time period than before." I supposed it made sense that the caller would activate the phone only a short time before it was used. It would be a waste of money to pay for service when they intended to make only a single call.

While Bustamente might be waiting to hear back from the cell phone company, he hadn't let any grass grow under his feet. "I tracked down the ladies from the booster club over the weekend. The first two didn't know where the phone came from, but the third told me an algebra teacher had turned it in at the concession stand. How would you like to chauffer me to the school so we can interview Mrs. Pollard?" A sly grin played about his lips. He knew I'd never turn down a chance to be involved in an investigation.

Proving his point, I'd already pulled my key fob from my pocket. "I'd be happy to."

We strode out to the parking lot. On the way to my cruiser, I stated the obvious. "None of the prints on the phone matched anyone in the system, then. Otherwise, you would have made an arrest already."

"That's correct," he confirmed. "There was only one set of prints on the phone, plus a partial palm print. The woman working the concession stand said she never touched the phone. She said she held out the lost and found box, and Mrs. Pollard dropped the phone into it. Whoever the fingerprints belong to hasn't ever been arrested. Most likely they're Pollard's."

"What about the security cameras at Farrington Field?" I asked, knowing he had probably already taken a look at the footage. "Did they tell you anything?"

"No," he said. "The system is minimal there, just one camera over the entrance to the district's athletic department under the west stands, and a few cameras along the exterior to discourage vandalism. The facility is old, and outfitting it with a bunch of high-tech equipment would be costly, without much benefit. Most events there are large, with plenty of potential witnesses who could capture images on their cell phones."

The decision made sense. Large crowds tended to act as a natural deterrent for most crimes. Criminals generally don't like witnesses, after all. But a large crowd would have the opposite effect for someone planning mass violence. The number of people would be a draw when witnesses would be obliterated and the criminal doesn't necessarily expect to survive the event. *Gulp.* Even if there had been footage, it might have been difficult to discern much with a big crowd milling about, anyway. Still, it was nice when video surveillance could pinpoint a perpetrator, and provide police with a quick arrest and prosecutors with a slam-dunk case.

After I loaded Brigit into the back of my cruiser, we took off for the high school. I parked in a visitor's spot in front, and we headed to the doors, Brigit's claws rhythmically click-click-clicking along the pavement like a ticking clock.

Standing watch out front was one of the resource officers permanently assigned to the campus. He'd conspicuously parked his car at the curb, either to deter anyone who might come to the school with nefarious intentions in mind, or to assure students and parents that the campus was safe. Probably both. He lifted his chin in greeting as we approached. "You here about the fire or about the shooter call?"

Before we could answer, a voice came from behind us. "I'm here about the fire. They're here about the phone call."

Detective Bustamente and I turned to see Lewis Hamrick strolling up the walkway.

Bustamente extended his hand in greeting. "Any prints on the flashlight from the sewer?"

"Unfortunately, no," Hamrick said as he took Bustamente's hand and gave it a quick shake. "We found two others, same model. One was by the rear doors. It had rolled into the bushes. It wasn't on, and the lens was cracked. My guess was it got damaged when the firefighters were working. The other was still on. It was on the ground, pointing up at the building. At first glance, I'd mistaken it for a floodlight. No prints on those devices either."

Bustamente issued an empathetic grunt.

"Three flashlights," I mused aloud. "Does that mean three people were involved in setting the fire?"

"Possibly," Hamrick said.

Bustamente's head turned from me back to Hamrick. "Gonna ask the principal about disciplinary cases?"

"Yep. Figured the fire could be an act of revenge."

"Disciplinary information might be relevant to my investigation, too," Bustamente pointed out. "No sense making the principal repeat everything. Mind holding up a few minutes? I got a teacher I need to speak with first."

"I'll come with you," Hamrick said. "After all, we might be chasing the same person."

The three of us headed to the front office, where we checked in with the stern-faced woman behind the desk. Despite the fact that I was in uniform, she asked all three of us to present identification. While we humans produced our driver's licenses, Brigit stood on her hind legs and put her paws on the counter. The name BRIGIT on the metal rabies tag hanging from her collar served as her ID.

Once the woman had input our names into their visitor monitoring system, she gave us Mrs. Pollard's room number. She gestured out the door and to the right. "Take a right down the main hall, then turn down the first hall on the left. Her room is the second one you'll come to."

We thanked her and headed to Mrs. Pollard's room. With me being both female and in uniform, Bustamente and Hamrick thought it best that I be the one to knock on the door. An unknown man peering through the window of the classroom might be disconcerting.

I took a quick peek through the window to see a fortyish Black woman with loose bronze curls leaning over a machine that projected an image of equations full of X's, Y's, and numbers onto a whiteboard at the front of the class. The blackboards and chalk of yesterday were sorely outdated now. I positioned myself so that I was easily visible through the glass rectangle on the door and raised my hand to rap on it.

As Mrs. Pollard turned my way, I smiled and waved in greeting. Her eyes sparked in alarm. She lifted a finger in an I'll-be-right-with-you gesture, then turned back to address her class. She rose from her stool and came to the door, her eyes sparking again when she saw Brigit and the two men flanking me. She opened the door just enough to slip outside, then put her back to the glass so that the students couldn't see out. Her gaze ran over the four faces looking at her. "How can I help you?"

After quick introductions were made, Detective Bustamente got down to brass tacks. "Do you recall finding a cell phone at the stadium last Friday night?"

"Yes, I do," Mrs. Pollard said. "I turned it in at the concession stand. They keep a lost and found box under the counter."

"Where did you find the phone, exactly?"

"Behind the ketchup pump at the condiment stand." Her eyes narrowed. "Why?"

Bustamente gave her a pointed look. "That phone was the one used to call in the threat."

"The threat?" she repeated. Her eyes snapped wide when she realized what he meant. "The *shooting* threat?!"

He nodded. "We need to determine who it belongs to."

Her mouth hung open as her head slowly turned side to side in disbelief. She seemed more than a little jarred to realize she'd had an unwitting brush with a criminal.

Bustamente pressed her for more information. "Did you see someone leave the phone behind?"

"No," she said. "I just spotted it there when I went to get a napkin. I figured someone had put it down when they fixed their hot dog, then forgotten about it and walked away. I called out to a student who'd just left the stand, a sophomore named Asher Burke.

He was in my first-period class last year. He said the phone wasn't his. He even laughed at the suggestion. He said it looked like a toy or a piece of cheap junk, and that it probably belonged to someone's grandparent who'd come to the game. He had his own phone in his pocket. He showed it to me."

Bustamente's head bobbed as he took in the information. "Was anyone with Asher when you spoke to him?"

"No," Pollard said. "As far as I could tell, he was alone. He walked over to the ramp by himself and went up to the bleachers. Another boy had just left the condiment stand, too. One of the football players. I didn't know his name and he was walking away too fast for me to catch him. I hollered after him but he never turned around. I figured if the phone was his, he'd realize it was missing pretty quick and come back for it. Teenagers can't seem to keep their hands off their phones for more than two seconds."

Hamrick had perked up at the mention of the football player. "What did the football player look like?"

"I only saw him from behind." Mrs. Pollard looked up in thought, as if trying to visualize him. "He was White. Shaggy auburn hair. Big." She raised her elbows at her sides to imply biceps so large they made his arms stick out.

"What about a jersey number?" Hamrick asked.

The woman brightened then, realizing she had a salient piece of information to offer. "Seventy-three. I'm sure of it."

Leave it to a math teacher to take note of a number.

"Seventy-three," Hamrick repeated. "An offensive lineman."

Mrs. Pollard suddenly stood straighter and bit her lip. "I hope I didn't mess up any fingerprints that might have been on the phone when I picked it up."

"If you did," Bustamente said, "we know it was unintentional. But would you allow me to take your fingerprints for comparison?"

"Of course," she said.

Laughter came from inside the unsupervised classroom, and she glanced back at the door.

"It'll take a minute or two." Bustamente gestured my way. "Would you like Officer Luz to keep an eye on your class while I get your prints?"

"I'd appreciate that."

I signaled Brigit, who'd been softly and patiently panting at my side. Together, we entered the classroom.

"What the ..." breathed a boy on the front row.

"Oh, my gosh!" squealed a girl wearing the false eyelashes that had recently come back in vogue after decades of being worn primarily by stage performers and drag queens. "Your dog is so cute!"

Brigit could indeed be cute but, when she went after a suspect, she was all fangs and ferocity, as far from cute as she could get. Still, I'd accept the compliment on her behalf. "Thanks."

Murmuring excitedly, the students leaned to the sides, some standing and craning their necks to get a better look at the K-9 who'd interrupted their class.

I put a finger to my lips to shush them. "If y'all stay quiet, I'll have Brigit show you some of her tricks."

They quieted down, though several in the back moved to the front of their rows, kneeling down to get a good look as I took Brigit through her paces. I started with the simple, unimpressive commands.

"Sit."

Brigit sat.

"Shake."

Brigit lifted her paw to shake my hand.

"Heel."

She stood at my side, looking up at me.

"Roll over."

She dropped to the floor and performed three perfect rolls.

When Brigit rose to her feet, I formed a gun with my index finger and thumb. Ironic, given that I was here to investigate a shooting threat. I pointed it at her. "Bang-bang!"

Brigit collapsed to the floor in dramatic style, letting her head loll, tongue hanging out, playing dead. The kids loved it, exclaiming in amazement.

"Assume the position." I pointed to the wall at the front of the room.

Brigit stood and put her front paws up on the wall, glancing back over her furry shoulder. I pretended to frisk her. The kids erupted in muted laughter, putting their hands over their mouths to stifle the noise.

I proceeded to recite the Miranda Rights to my partner. "You have the right to remain silent. Anything you *bark* can be used against you in a court of *paw*."

As she'd been trained to do, Brigit emitted a soft growl.

"If you cannot find an attorney who will work for dog biscuits, one will be appointed for you." Naturally, I couldn't say the word biscuit without offering her one. Fortunately, I had a stash in my gun belt for just such an occasion. I fed them to my partner, who crunched them loudly, crumbs falling to the floor.

That was pretty much the extent of our act, so I told the kids if they'd retake their seats, I'd allow them to pet her and take pics. I walked her slowly up and down the aisles, giving the kids the chance to snap selfies with Brigit. She ate up all the attention, as well as a piece of bologna one of the boys had removed from the sandwich in his lunch bag and offered to her. I hoped he wouldn't regret sharing his food come lunchtime.

Mrs. Pollard reentered the room just as the last student gave Brigit a belly rub. "Thanks for watching my class."

"Our pleasure," I said, speaking on behalf of myself and my partner. I was thankful not to be back in high school, with homework every night. Then again, I supposed detective work was homework, in a sense. I knew Detective Bustamente didn't stop thinking about his cases at the end of his shifts, and I didn't, either. The all-consuming nature of investigative work was one of its downsides. Even so, it didn't stop me from wanting to become a detective. I felt called to it, the way other people were called to the ministry or medicine or the arts.

I stepped into the hallway to see Bustamente sliding the fingerprint card into a clear protective sleeve. I noticed he'd not only taken Mrs. Pollard's fingerprints on the front, but that he'd also taken a palm print on the back.

He tucked the card into the outer zipper pocket of his briefcase. "We'll need to head back to the office and find out where the boys are now so we can talk to them. If the phone doesn't belong to one of them, maybe they saw something that'll help us out."

We returned to the front office, where Bustamente stepped up to the counter. "We need to speak with a student named Asher Burke. Can you tell us where we can find him?"

While the woman behind the desk turned to her computer, I ran a quick search of social media to see if Asher had posted anything Friday night. TikTok was the platform most preferred by teens, so I checked there first.

Sure enough, Asher had a TikTok account. His profile image was a cartoon character I recognized from my childhood. It was the dark-haired Ash Ketchum, a primary human character in the Pokémon universe. My three younger brothers were addicted to the show back in the day, and they'd overruled me every time I begged to watch something else on TV after school. My guess was Asher Burke had chosen the character to represent himself due to the similarity in their names.

Asher had amassed an impressive number of followers, over eight thousand. A quick glance at his content showed that it mostly contained clips of him playing baseball or working out, though he'd uploaded two videos Friday night. Bustamente and Hamrick watched over my shoulder as I played the videos. In the first clip, four teenage boys danced next to a late-model blue Camaro in the parking lot at Farrington Field. The stadium loomed in the background as they performed simple hip-hop dance moves to a song I recognized from one of the "Fast and Furious" movies I'd watched with Seth. The boys' loose technique told me that none had any formal dance training, but they were entertaining nonetheless and looked like they were having fun. Four thousand people had liked the video so far. I remembered seeing a new blue Camaro Friday night. It's hard not to notice a flashy sports car like that, especially when a teen driver is at the wheel. The other clip from Friday showed four boys around a table at Waffle House, challenging each other to a biscuit-eating contest. Asher emerged victorious, swallowing an entire biscuit in under six seconds while his friends choked, gagged, and coughed out dry bits of bread. Asher had tagged the three other boys in the video. Their names were Micah Peters, Hayden Quinn, and Cade Cox.

The clerk had accessed Asher's records and looked up from her monitor. "Asher's in A-P biology right now." A-P was shorthand for Advanced Placement, meaning Asher was likely a good student and college bound. She jotted down the teacher's name and room number on a sticky pad, pulled off the sheet, and handed it to Bustamante.

He gestured to my phone. "Give her the other names, too."

I rattled off the names of the other boys in the videos, and the woman wrote their classroom numbers down on a second sticky note.

When Bustamante inquired about the football player Mrs. Pollard had mentioned, the clerk said, "I don't have a record of who wears which number jersey, but Coach Knapp can tell you. He coaches the varsity team. You'll find him in the field house."

Bustamante thanked her and we left the office, once again striding down the halls. We reached Asher's classroom to find the window dark. Inside the dimly lit room, the students were watching a video on genetics, a twisty strand of DNA twirling like a ballerina. Again, I was given the task of summoning the teacher. I stood at the glass and rapped on the door.

A moment later, a sixtyish man with wiry gray hair and silver-rimmed glasses opened the door a few inches. Unlike Mrs. Pollard, he remained in his classroom. Though he said nothing, he arched his brows in question.

Keeping my voice low, I said, "We need to speak with Asher Burke, please."

The man turned back to the class. "Asher." He jerked his head our way. "You're wanted in the hall."

Though I tried to duck back out of sight, I was too late. As the boy headed toward the door, a taunt followed him. "Uh-oh, it's the po-po! Asher's in trouble!"

Asher chuckled and looked back over his shoulder. "No tea here, bro. I've got nothing to be in trouble for."

Once the boy had stepped into the hallway, Bustamente reached over to pull the door closed.

Asher looked from me, to Hamrick, to the detective. He was a tall boy, already standing almost six feet despite having several more years to grow. He was attractive, too, with dark, shiny hair and chocolate brown eyes, not the slightest hint of acne on his face. He had either good genes or a fantastic dermatologist. He wore sneakers with a stylish pair of lightweight jogging pants and a short-sleeved tee made by one of the pricy, trendy brands. He looked calm but confused. He greeted us with a casual yet tentative, "What's up?"

"We just spoke with Mrs. Pollard," Bustamente told him. "She said you were at the condiment stand at Farrington Field Friday night when she found a cell phone. Was it yours?"

"*That* phone?" He issued a soft snort. "No. It wasn't mine." He unzipped the side pocket of his joggers and pulled out a cell phone housed in a rubbery protective case. He held it up for all of us to see. "*This* is my phone. It's the brand-new iPhone. Apple just dropped it a few weeks back." He shoved the phone back into his pocket. "The one Mrs. Pollard found was a cheap flip phone, like the kind a poor person would buy or old people like 'cause they're easy. I think it's called a Jitterbug or a Cricket. I've seen their commercials on TV."

The phone used to make the 9-1-1 call was not a Jitterbug phone and not on the Cricket Wireless system, but Bustamente didn't correct him and I didn't either. I knew better. In any investigation, information was shared on a need-to-know basis only.

Bustamente scratched behind his ear. "Did you notice anyone leaving it behind?"

Asher shook his head. "No. Sorry."

The detective cocked his head. "Who else was in the area when you were at the condiment stand?"

Asher shrugged. "I didn't pay any attention. I just went down to grab a hot dog and get back to the game. I heard Mrs. Pollard call after one of the football players. He'd been at the stand, too. He didn't turn around, though. He just kept going."

"Do you know who the player was?"

"No," Asher replied. "I might recognize him if I saw him, but I don't know his name. This is a big school. It's hard to know everyone."

He had a point. Paschal's student population was over 2,200, more than five hundred kids in each grade. It would be easy not to know another student's name, especially if they weren't on the same academic track.

"How did you get to and from the game?" Bustamente asked. "Did you drive yourself?"

"No," Asher said. "I won't be sixteen until February. I've only got a learner's permit. I rode to the game with friends. After the announcer told everyone to evacuate, we went to Waffle House to hang out." Asher's gaze locked on Bustamente's, his head cocked. "What's going on? Is there some big deal with the phone?"

Again, Bustamente kept his cards close to his vest. "The person it belongs to might have been a witness to a crime."

"A witness to a crime?" Asher's face tightened in confusion for a moment before suddenly exploding. His brows shot up and his mouth fell. "Oh, my God!" His wide eyes gleamed in the bright lights of the hallway as he launched a barrage of questions at Bustamente. "Did they see someone with a gun? Did they call the police to report it? Is that how the shooting was stopped? They'd be, like, a hero!"

"Sorry." The detective raised his palms. "I can't share any details with you." Asher opened his mouth to ask a follow-up question, but the detective shut him down. "Thanks for the information. You can return to class."

Asher's face darkened. He appeared disappointed that he hadn't gotten more details from Bustamante. Kids that age loved to be in the know. He'd probably hoped to impress his classmates with insider news about the shooter investigation. But he did as he was told and returned to the classroom.

Once he was gone, I held up the sticky note with the other boys' classrooms jotted on it. "Where should we go next?"

Bustamante's eyes narrowed in thought. "Let's keep those boys on the back burner for now." He gestured toward the door of Asher's classroom. "We've already set the rumor mill in motion, and I don't want to get a lot of kids and their parents riled up if there's nothing to be gained."

He had a point. After all, we had no evidence linking Asher to the phone, other than the fact that a teacher had noticed him in the general vicinity after finding the device abandoned. There'd probably been lots of other people milling about, too. Better to stay focused on finding clear, hard evidence.

Bustamante glanced up and down the hall. "Either of you know the best way to the field house?"

"This way." Hamrick motioned for us to follow him.

As we made our way down the hall, I asked the detective what he thought about Asher. "You think he was telling the truth?"

"His behavior was consistent with someone who was telling the truth," Bustamante said. "He seemed calm. Curious."

I concurred. "That was my sense, too."

The detective cut me a sideways glance. "It was also consistent with someone who knew they might be questioned and had prepared for it."

"Meaning either he'd guessed the abandoned phone might have been used to call in the shooter report," I mused aloud, "or he was the one who'd called in the report himself and then ditched the phone?"

Bustamente issued a curt *mm-hm*.

If the boy had been pretending the phone wasn't his when it actually was, he'd done a pretty convincing job. Maybe he should consider auditioning for the next school play.

39
NO SCRAPS TODAY

Brigit

As they passed the cafeteria, Brigit twitched her nose. It wasn't lunchtime yet, but she could smell the food that the workers were in the process of preparing for the students. Dough. Tomato sauce. Cheese. Yep, it was pizza day. She could also smell the hot oil used to fry the French fries and chicken nuggets, as well as the flatulent smell of steamed broccoli. Suddenly, the breakfast she'd eaten at home and that half bologna sandwich seemed so long ago. She slowed her stride, hoping to snag another handout. She wasn't asking for a whole slice of pizza, just a slice or two of pepperoni. To her disappointment, Megan ordered her on.

40
A PRESCRIPTION FOR TROUBLE

The Flamethrower

Finally, a bright spot after an especially shitty few weeks. He'd just spent a half hour regaling a team of doctors with the benefits of the latest drug to treat hypertension. Unlike a daily pill regimen, which could be difficult for some patients to adhere to, this drug required only a single injection every six months. The doctors were excited about the new medication, and their patients would be, too—though they might not be happy about the price tag.

The Flamethrower was under no illusions, and he knew some people looked upon pharmaceutical sales reps with distaste. People complained about the cost of prescription drugs in the United States, which had the highest prices in the world, but they also elected legislators who refused to put in place a universal, single-payer healthcare system, which would give the government more bargaining power and keep costs down. *You can't have it both ways.* At any rate, with this new drug to market, he saw a big bonus in his future. Maybe he'd buy Hayden a Camaro just like his. Hayden was a good kid, if a typically messy teenager, and the Flamethrower needed to do something to win back his son's affection. Then again, the cost to insure a teenage driver was already astronomical. With a sports car, it would cost a small fortune. Maybe he'd buy the boy a used pickup truck instead.

As the Flamethrower drove to his next appointment, he passed a retirement home. A heavyset middle-aged woman helped a frail, gray-haired woman with a walker make her way up the front walkway. The Flamethrower had been to the facility before, pitching a medication that treated atrial fibrillation. A high number of the residents were on some type of treatment for Afib. He'd made a pretty penny that day, too.

And that's when he got a devious idea.

People might not give a shit about other adults, but they cared about children and old people. He'd started the fire at the school because he thought it would rile people up if their children's safety was at risk. Children were just starting out, especially vulnerable. But the elderly were especially vulnerable, too, right? People got upset when older folks were mistreated or suffered unnecessarily. If he and Nash set a fire at a nursing home, there'd be even more pressure on the fire department, more focus on their response. *And if I can delay their response, even better ...*

41
BLINDED BY THE LIGHT—BUT NOT QUITE

Megan

We followed Hamrick as he led us out the back of the school. Another resource officer was stationed out back, his cruiser likewise parked in a conspicuous spot. Bustamente and I raised our hands in greeting, and continued on to the field house. There, we found a female coach leading a group of girls through a weight-training circuit. One of the girls was bench pressing over a hundred and thirty pounds. *Impressive.*

"Excuse me," Bustamente said to the coach. "Can you tell us where we might find Coach Knapp?"

"Practice field." She hiked a thumb over her shoulder. "He's putting the players through some drills."

"Thanks."

We ventured back outside and over to the practice field. While it was a standard-size football field, it was bare bones, with only a small set of bleachers on each side and a much smaller scoreboard than that at Farrington Field. On the turf, two dozen boys ran through a tire course. Lest they catch a toe on a tire and fall flat on their face, they lifted their knees high, mimicking the exaggerated gait of Tennessee Walking Horses. I remembered running the same drills in the police academy. It wasn't easy. My thighs and calves ached for days afterward. I'd tripped once and fallen, bruising my ribs. I'd made sure to lift my legs even higher the next time around.

We walked over to the coach, a White man of about fifty with a shaved head and salt-and-pepper goatee. He wore a short-sleeved purple golf shirt with black athletic shorts. Despite being middle aged, he'd managed to maintain a muscular physique. Two deep vertical frown lines and one horizontal line formed a goal post shape between his brows. Fitting for a football coach.

"Coach Knapp?" Bustamente extended his hand. "I'm Detective Hector Bustamente from the Fort Worth Police Department." He proceeded to introduce me, Brigit, and Hamrick. He turned and pointed to the group of boys running the drills. "Does one of these boys wear jersey number seventy-three?"

The coach's expression soured. "That would be Gunther Fertig." He jerked his head to indicate a White boy who was bent down, tying his cleat, the only player on the team who had yet to cast a curious glance in our direction. The coach grunted. "What did that boy do now?"

Bustamente's brows rose. "Is he a troublemaker?"

"He's disrespectful, doesn't take direction well, argues calls. He likes to throw his weight around with the other boys, too. He always hits harder than necessary. Last week, he got too rough in practice and injured another player, my star quarterback no less. Caused a tear in his rotator cuff. Back in my day, a kid would've gotten himself paddled for acting like that. He's lucky I only benched him for last Friday's game."

"If he was benched," Bustamente asked, "did he still wear his uniform?"

I'd been wondering the same thing, whether someone else could have stolen or borrowed Gunther's jersey.

Coach Knapp quickly disavowed us of that theory. "Yes. I had him suit up in case one of the boys on second string couldn't play for some reason. We didn't end up needing him, of course, what with the game ending early. In hindsight, having him put on his jersey was a mistake."

"Why's that?" the detective asked.

"During the second quarter, he asked if he could go to the restroom. Do you know that boy had the nerve to come back with mustard on his jersey?" The coach shook his head. "The fool had gone to the concession stand without permission. The athletics budget is already tight, and now I'll have to order a new jersey. A mustard stain is impossible to get out."

Bustamente and I exchanged glances. If Gunther had used the mustard dispenser, he could have easily slid the burner phone behind the ketchup container in the process.

Coach Knapp exhaled sharply but, when he spoke again, his voice had softened. "I have half a mind to kick him off the team, but football is all that kid's got. I'd hate to take that from him. I'm hoping he'll turn himself around. He's a solid player with a lot of potential. Makes decent grades. He could probably get a scholarship to a division three school like Hardin-Simmons or McMurry University if he can learn to control himself."

Bustamente's head bobbed as he processed the information. "Do you know if Gunther had his cell phone with him when he went to the concession stand?"

"If he did, he wasn't supposed to," the coach said. "I want the team paying attention to the play on the field, not the latest dance craze on TikTok. They're supposed to leave their phones in the locker room."

Bustamente cut his eyes to the boy then back to Coach Knapp. "May we talk to him for a moment?"

The coach grabbed the whistle hanging around his neck and

blew a quick *tweet* to get the team's attention. When the boys turned his way, he released the whistle and it dropped down to his chest, where it bounced off his rock-hard pecs. "Fertig!" He motioned with his arm. "Get over here!"

Gunther jogged over to where we stood. He might still be a boy, but he dwarfed us all. He stood at least six-foot-three, maybe more, and weighed a good two-twenty, a solid wall of muscle. Though it was still only mid morning, the outdoor temperature was already in the nineties. A sheen of sweat coated the boy's skin, and he smelled like he'd been giving it his all. He didn't turn his head to look at me, Brigit, Bustamente, or Hamrick. He kept his eyes on his coach. "Yeah?"

"*Yeah?*" Coach Knapp skewered the boy with his gaze. "Let's try 'Yes, sir?'"

Gunther's chest inflated then fell as he huffed a frustrated breath. His voice carried a forced calm when he spoke. "Yes, sir?"

The coach held out a hand. "These folks want to talk to you." With that, Knapp stepped away and blew his whistle again, directing the boys to begin a new drill as he jogged over to them.

Bustamente stepped directly in front of Gunther. "Could you remove your helmet, please?"

I could see why Bustamente had made the request. It was difficult to see the boy's eyes and expression with the helmet obscuring his face. Gunther loosened the chin strap and pulled his helmet off to reveal a sweat-dampened mass of reddish-brown hair. Hamrick, Brigit, and I stepped up beside Bustamente and, with the four of us forming a semi-circle in front of him, the boy could no longer avoid looking at us.

Bustamente told the boy who we were, then said, "We've got some questions for you."

"What about?"

"Last Friday's game against Arlington Heights."

Gunther shrugged, his shoulder pads making a clunking sound

as the hard plastic pieces knocked against each other. "I didn't get to play. You should be talking to someone else."

"No," Bustamente said, undeterred. "You're the one we want to talk to. One of the teachers said she saw you at the condiment stand shortly before halftime."

"She was mistaken." Gunther looked down and toed the turf with his cleat. "The team isn't allowed to eat during games."

He's lying. Why? I put my hands on my knees and bent over, looking up at him, making him look me in the eye. "Your coach knows you ate something, Gunther. He said you asked to use the restroom during the second quarter and returned with a mustard stain on your jersey."

Gunther froze, though he didn't avert his gaze from mine. "He told you that?"

Coach Knapp must have let the stain slide. "He did," I said, rising to a full stand once more. "You want to come clean with us now?"

"Okay! Jeez." He huffed another angry breath. "I got two hot dogs at the concession stand. Since when is eating dinner a crime?"

His snide response said he was feeling defensive, which could mean he feared being found out. Of course, it could just mean he didn't appreciate having his practice interrupted or being called on the carpet for a minor infraction.

Having come across numerous instances of neglect during my time as a police officer, I asked, "Didn't you eat dinner at home before coming here to catch the bus to the game?"

He turned his head slightly, looking past us, as if the answer might be there. "I didn't go home after school."

"Why not?" I asked.

He looked directly at me now. "Because my mother runs a daycare out of our house. There's always a bunch of kids running around, screaming and crying and pooping their diapers. I went over to the church across the street." He gestured in the direction of a nearby Methodist church. "They've got good air conditioning, and they don't mind if you're there as long as it looks like you're praying. Sometimes I close my eyes and take a nap sitting up."

It sounded like Gunther got little peace, privacy, or sleep at home. I was beginning to see why the kid had an attitude problem. I was also beginning to see why the coach had cut the kid some slack and allowed him to remain on the team.

Bustamente picked up where I'd left off. "You forgot your cell phone at the condiment stand. It was found behind the ketchup dispenser."

Gunther shook his head. "That's not right. I didn't have my phone on me. Coach doesn't let us have them at the games. Besides, I've got my phone. It's in the locker room." He gestured back toward the building.

"I'm talking about your *burner* phone," Bustamente said.

"Burner phone?" Gunther's expression was equal parts perplexed and annoyed. "I don't have a burner phone. Did somebody say I did? 'Cause I don't." After a beat, he asked, "What's this all about anyway?"

Ignoring the boy's question, Hamrick jumped in now. "Did you ride the bus back to the school with the rest of the team?"

"Yeah," Gunther said. "Who else would I ride with?"

"A parent, maybe?" Hamrick suggested.

Gunther snorted. "Not likely. My mother has only made it to two games since I started playing ball in junior high. She says weekends are *her* time. On Friday nights, she usually goes out with whatever idiot she's dating that week. My father lives in Mississippi. He's never seen me play. Not even once."

Although he was much bigger than me and a person of interest in our current investigation, I had to fight the urge to step forward and give the boy a hug. Seemed like he could use one. Brigit seemed to sense he'd said something sad, too. She issued a soft whimper as she looked up at him and nuzzled his hand. He used his fingers to rub one of her ears.

"Are you having trouble with your teachers?" Bustamente asked.

"Dude." Gunther rolled his eyes. "We've only been in school a week."

"What about last year?"

He looked down and toed the ground again. "I got detention a few times for back talking, but I never got expelled or anything like that."

Hamrick gestured to the field. "You're good at football. Are you good with tools, too?"

"Tools?" Gunther looked confused. "What do you mean?"

"Hammers?" Hamrick suggested. "Screwdrivers? Drills?"

Gunther flapped his shoulder pads again. "Not especially." He looked back to the field, where the team was now working on passing drills. "Look, I don't know what y'all are getting at here, but whatever it is, I had nothing to do with it. Can I get back to practice now?"

"All right," Bustamente said. "I'm sure Coach Knapp wants you back out there, too. He said you need to work on your self control, but that you're a good player with a lot of potential."

Gunther cocked his head, his eyes brightening and the tiniest hint of a grin pulling at the corners of his mouth. "He said that? Really?"

"He did," Bustamente said.

I followed up with some quick words of advice. "Your coach has cut you some slack, Gunther. Maybe you should return the favor?"

Gunther seemed to think about it for a moment, then said, "Yes, ma'am." As he turned and jogged back to join his teammates on the field, he called out to Coach Knapp. "I'm back, sir!"

The coach turned and cast an impressed glance back in our direction, raising his palms as if to ask *what did y'all say to this boy?*

I raised a hand in goodbye.

Hamrick angled his head toward the main building. "Ready to watch the footage now?"

"Lead on," Bustamente said.

As we approached the back of the building, I ran my eyes across the wall. The holes that had been drilled to ignite the fire had since been filled with fresh mortar that didn't quite match the pre-existing mortar. The dark gray circles looked like a line of bullet holes, as if a firing squad had performed executions back here. *There's a happy thought.*

Bustamente, too, ran his gaze over the building. "Looks like there's three sets of cameras back here." He raised a finger to point them out. "There's one over the rear doors, and one at either end of the building."

As we stepped inside, I had another thought and voiced it aloud. "Paschal doesn't offer automotive classes, but Trimble Tech does. Construction technology, too. A student in one of those programs might know how to handle a drill." Trimble Tech was a specialized high school that offered focused career programs of both vocational and pre-college varieties. The courses of study ranged from the popular animation and architecture programs, to cosmetology, culinary arts, and robotics. Students across the Fort Worth Independent School District could apply to attend the school. "Maybe a former Paschal student who transferred to Trimble Tech drilled those holes out back. They might have had a bad experience here, and requested the transfer as a result."

Bustamente must have found my theory potentially viable. "We'll ask the principal about that."

We returned to the front office, where we asked to meet with the principal. The clerk used her desk phone to buzz the principal's office. "There's law enforcement here that would like to speak with you." Though we couldn't hear the response, the principal must have told the clerk to bring us back. The clerk hung up the phone, stood, and said, "Follow me."

We strode down a hall to a door that was cracked open only an inch or two as if to say *it's okay to interrupt me, but it better be important.* The nameplate on the door read PRINCIPAL LIENA ZHAO.

As the clerk turned to retrace our steps back to her post, Hamrick rapped on the door frame. A voice called from within. "Come in, please."

He pushed the door open to reveal a woman who appeared to be in her mid forties. Her dark hair framed her face in a silky bob that came to stylish points on either side of her chin. She was dressed in a forest green pantsuit accessorized with a striped ivory and gold scarf, her look classy and professional.

After introductions were exchanged, she held out a hand, indicating the seats facing her desk. "Please sit." Once our butts settled in the seats, she surveyed the three of us. "What can I do for you?"

Hamrick led the charge. "We need to see the school's security camera footage from Friday night. We'd also like information about any students who have had disciplinary problems, or who transferred to Trimble Tech. It's possible one of them made the call about the shooter at Farrington Field or started the fire here."

She offered a curt nod and turned to her computer. After a few minutes of tinkering with the machine, she had the security footage ready for viewing. She turned her monitor so that we could all get a look. The screen was divided into twelve sections, one for each camera. There were two facing in opposite directions at each corner of the building, one each over the rear and front doors, and one over both the entrance and back door to the field house. Of course, we would focus on the images from the rear of the building, where we knew for certain the arsonist had been.

Zhao started the footage at sunset, fast-forwarding through it until the sky went dark and the floodlights turned on, dimly lighting the school grounds. For a few beats, there was nothing, then for a brief instant, in the feed from the rear left camera, a figure in dark clothing appeared—*a big, beefy figure.* Before I could get a good look at the prowler, a bright flash lit up the screen, blinding me and rendering the camera useless. It might as well have been filming the surface of sun. *What the heck?* In quick succession, the scurrying dark form likewise rendered the other rear cameras useless. All they showed was an intense glow of light.

"What happened?" I asked. If Jesus had suddenly appeared amidst the brilliance, I'd understand what was going on. But given that the messiah had yet to return for His second coming, I was still in the dark here.

Hamrick's nostrils flared in irritation. "He aimed LED flashlights at the lenses. It disables them. Like I said, we're not dealing with an amateur."

Earlier, I'd assumed the three flashlights Hamrick had recovered from the scene Friday night meant that three people had been involved in setting the fire. Now, I wondered if there was a single arsonist, and the number of flashlights simply correlated to the three cameras along the rear of the school. *Hmm.* I understood the evidence pointed to a skilled fire starter. Still, I couldn't fathom a good reason for someone to go to such lengths to start a fire at a high school. A school wasn't private property. There would be no insurance for an individual to cash in on. "What would a professional arsonist have to gain by setting a fire at a school?"

"If we knew," Hamrick said, "we'd have an easier time figuring out who it was."

Principal Zhao forwarded through the feeds. Two of the rear cameras continued to show only the bright light. At first, it was the same for the feed from the camera at the north corner, where firefighters had found the tampon that had *not* been set on fire. But then the light suddenly shifted away from the lens and we could see another figure, a tall and lean one, also dressed in black, with a white medical mask and what appeared to be protective goggles over his eyes. This figure stepped to the corner of the building and raised both arms over his head. Though the image was shadowy and grainy in the dim light, he appeared to put his right hand to his left wrist for a beat or two. Then again, maybe the footage simply froze for an instant while he was waving his arms. He disappeared out of camera range and that was all we saw for two minutes until firefighters showed up and the streams of water from their hoses washed the flashlights aside. Then, we saw the firefighters milling about, including Seth and Frankie.

Hamrick pointed to Zhao's computer screen. "Go back to when the guy shows up at the corner."

She complied, and we watched again as the tall man stepped to the corner and raised his arms over his head, grabbing a wrist.

I squinted. "What's he doing?"

Hamrick speculated. "He could be signaling a third person in front of the school, maybe. Possibly a lookout or getaway driver."

I gestured to the feeds from the cameras on the front of the school. "I don't see anyone out front. Just the school bus approaching."

Hamrick shrugged. "If there was a lookout, he could have been hiding out of camera range across the street." He asked Zhao to run the footage again, and had her stop it when each of the men first reappeared on the screen. He leaned in to take a closer look before turning to the detective and me. "I can't tell much about them but, judging from what little I can see of their faces, they both appear to be light skinned."

Bustamente concurred with a nod and looked to Zhao. "Any chance you recognize either of those people?"

Zhao pursed her lips. "I wish I could say 'yes,' but they're dressed all in black with their faces covered. That doesn't give me much to go on. If they're students, they're likely juniors or seniors, judging from their size. Few lowerclassmen are that tall."

Except Asher Burke. As soon as the idea entered my mind, I realized the theory had holes. He said he'd evacuated the stadium with his friends. In other words, he had a verifiable alibi. *Unless his friends were also involved in setting the fire* ... Of course, the TikTok video showed them at Waffle House that evening, shoving biscuits into their mouths. But while the app showed the date the video had been uploaded, it didn't show the time.

Both Hamrick and Bustamente had brought thumb drives for the purpose of downloading the surveillance camera footage. They handed them over to the principal, and she inserted each of them in turn into her computer, transferred the footage, then handed them back to the men. The task complete, she cocked her head. "You had questions about the disciplinary cases?"

"We do," Hamrick said. "I realize it's early in the school year, but are there any students who've been especially problematic? Any who've made threats to the school or a teacher? Maybe the administration?"

"One with a grudge to settle, you mean." Principal Zhao looked up in thought for a few seconds before returning her focus to the two men. "We haven't had any significant problems yet this school year. Two boys got into a shoving match in the hall, but other students broke it up. As far as I know, their anger was directed toward each other, not at a teacher or the school. We had a boy last spring who broke into other students' lockers and stole electronics. Tablets, phones, Bluetooth earbuds, that type of thing. The school resource officer caught him red-handed. I believe the boy was given probation."

If the boy was accessing the lockers, he must have used a tool, right? "How was he breaking into the lockers?" I asked.

"With a small screwdriver." Zhao mimed as she spoke. "He stuck it between the frame and the locker door, and pried them open. Bent the metal out of shape."

Using a basic flathead screwdriver to pry open a locker was a rudimentary task, no advanced skills or specialized equipment required. Though both the thefts and the fire required a tool to complete, the circumstances were different enough that I doubted the boy was one of the arsonists. Bustamente and Hamrick seemed to feel the same. Though they took his name, neither sparked with sudden interest.

Zhao took a sip of coffee from a mug that read LADY BOSS before continuing. "I've referred a couple of students for psychological evaluations this week. Both were cutting themselves. I've also dealt with an online bullying issue. None of the posts the student made were connected with the school in any way, so it tied my hands legally. But she's been warned that no bullying will be tolerated on campus."

Sadly, childhood was not always the carefree time it was often portrayed to be. Children could be unbelievably cruel to each other.

Zhao shook her head slowly. "I'm glad social media didn't exist when I was a teen. It puts too much pressure on these kids."

Bustamente and Hamrick, both of whom were middle aged, murmured in agreement. I, on the other hand, had been young when MySpace launched, and had witnessed the rise of Facebook, Snapchat, and Instagram. I'd created accounts on the social media platforms, not so much because I liked to share about myself, but because it was interesting to lurk on the sites and see what my peers were up to. I'd quickly realized that almost everyone was putting on an act, pretending their lives were far more interesting than they really were. That's when I'd returned to reading mystery novels and romances. I figured if I was going to be reading fiction, it should at least be professionally written.

Bustamente turned the discussion to a particular student. "Have you had any issues with a student named Asher Burke?"

"Asher Burke?" Zhao's eyes narrowed and she looked up. "The name rings a bell." She turned back to her computer and pulled up Asher's file. After running her eyes over it, she said, "I recognize him from his student ID photo. He's fairly popular, from what I can tell. I make a point of standing in the hallways each morning and at the end of the day, to keep an eye on things. Between classes, too, when I can." She gestured at the screen. "This boy Asher is often walking or talking with other kids in the hall." She maneuvered her mouse, clicked a couple of times, and leaned in to consult the screen. "His academic performance is commendable. Good grades. Advanced placement classes. His record notes that he was on the freshman baseball team last year." She clicked again, pulling up another screen and quickly scanning it. "He got detention once last year for being tardy to class too often, but there's no record of any disciplinary referrals."

"What about Gunther Fertig?" Bustamente asked.

Zhao scoffed and leaned back in her chair. "Gunther is an entirely different story." She didn't have to consult the boy's file to give us an update. "No problems so far this year, but he was sent to my office at least three times last year. One time he kicked a desk over. Another time, he threw a half-eaten burrito at another student in the cafeteria. A third time he tossed his dirty jock strap onto the desk of a girl he claimed called him a 'dumb jock.' Nothing too extreme, but hardly exemplary behavior. He can't seem to control his anger. I gave him in-school suspension each time and referred him to the counselor. She's been working with him. He has a part-time job at a fast-food place. He works until the place closes at least two or three times a week on school nights. It's likely he's not getting enough sleep, and that's exacerbating the problem. I've tried contacting his mother, but she never returns my calls or e-mails."

Once again, I found myself feeling sorry for the kid. He seemed like he could use some TLC. I hoped he hadn't made the call to 9-1-1 Friday night in a desperate cry for attention.

Bustamente's last question involved students who had transferred from Pascal to Trimble Tech. "Were there any who transferred that seemed especially glad to leave this campus?"

"Not that I'm aware of," Zhao said. "If there'd been an obvious and significant problem, someone would have informed me. Besides, only a handful of students have elected to transfer."

Having obtained the footage and information we'd come for, we thanked the woman and stood to go. She escorted us to her door. "Have a good day. I wish you luck getting things sorted out."

We checked out with the clerk, and walked out the front doors. The resource officer stood at the curb speaking with a trio of women, presumably mothers of students. One was a thin blonde in workout gear. One was a redhead in jeans and a T-shirt. The third was a dark-haired Latina wearing capri pants and a lightweight peasant blouse. Their faces were pensive, their body language tense. When the officer spotted us making our way to our vehicles, he called out to stop us. "Detective Bustamente! Captain Hamrick! Hold on a second!" He headed in our direction, and the women fell in line behind him like baby ducks following their mother.

The officer informed Bustamente, Hamrick, and me that the women had been asking him for updates on the fire investigation. "Is there any information you can offer them?"

Before Hamrick or Bustamente could respond, the blonde said, "Our children attend school here. We're concerned for their safety." She put a hand to her chest. "Me, most of all."

The other women cut her irritated looks that said they considered themselves equally concerned, if not more.

Hamrick took the lead. "We're doing all we can to figure out who started the fire. We've reviewed the security camera footage and spoken with the administration."

The woman's brows rose and she tilted her head in question. "You saw the camera footage? Do you have a suspect, then?"

"Not yet," Hamrick admitted.

"What about fingerprints?" demanded the dark-haired woman. "Or footprints? Tire tracks?"

The redhead entered the conversation, too. "Maybe the bad guy dropped something, like a gum wrapper or a glove with his DNA on it."

The three flashlights had been left behind by the arsonists, but Hamrick apparently didn't want to share that information. "I can't share the specific details of the case, but trust that we've made it a top priority."

The women frowned and exchanged sour glances, clearly disappointed and unsatisfied. Real-life investigations never moved as quickly as they did on TV, and clear-cut physical evidence was rarely as readily available. The phenomenon was known in law enforcement circles as the CSI Effect. The show had led the public to have unrealistically high expectations about the availability of forensic evidence like hair, blood, or fingerprints, and made it more difficult for prosecutors to obtain convictions in some cases.

The redhead put her hands on her hips and issued a declaration that seemed more threatening than hopeful. "We expect to hear soon that you've got the culprit in custody."

With that, the ladies stepped away. As soon as they were out of earshot, Hamrick muttered, "Bunch of Karens."

I didn't blame him for being annoyed. I was, too. We were doing everything we could to figure things out, and it was insulting for them to imply that we weren't working hard enough.

Detective Bustamente and I bade goodbye to Hamrick and the resource officer, and returned to my cruiser. I tossed a liver treat into the rear enclosure, and Brigit jumped right in after it.

Once I'd taken my seat, I cast a glance over at the detective. His face was pensive. "What are you thinking?"

"I'd hoped that visiting the school would give me some new leads on the shooting call." He stared at the building as if willing it to talk to him. "We now know there were at least two people involved in starting the fire here, but I'm not sure that helps my case in any way."

Two arsonists, yes, one of whom was beefy like Gunther Hertig. But Gunther had been on the football bus at the time the fire was set. It couldn't have been him. The leaner one had looked to be about the size of Asher Burke. *Had he been lying when he said the phone wasn't his? Would he and his friends have had time to get from Farrington Field to the school and set the fire before heading off to Waffle House and posting the video to TikTok?*

I turned to the laptop mounted to my dashboard, booted it up, and logged into my TikTok account.

The detective watched me with interest. "What are you doing?"

"I'm going to see if I can find out exactly when Asher made that video of him and his friends choking down those biscuits. It'll tell us whether they had time to get back here to set the fire before going to Waffle House." We had nothing linking the kid to the phone used to call in the threat other than a teacher seeing him in the vicinity of the phone around the time the call had been made. It was a weak link, at best. We had even less connecting him to the fire at the school. While Asher was tall and lean like one of the people in the surveillance video, so were a lot of other people. Still, I might as well be thorough and see if we could rule him out as one of the arsonists, right? After all, he could have left the game with his friends and they could have started the fire. None of the boys in the TikTok video had been beefy, though. If Asher was the taller, thin arsonist, who was the other one?

The detective watched over my shoulder as I clicked on the word View on my toolbar. I then clicked on Developer, then View Source. Doing so brought up a page of computer code. I ran my eyes over the technical mumbo jumbo until I came to words I recognized: create time. The code indicated that the video had been created at 9:08 p.m.

Bustamante issued a *hmph*. "Couldn't have been Asher who started the fire, then. The fire alarms went off at eight fifty-three. He wouldn't have had time to drive from here to the closest Waffle House, order, get his food, and shoot the video in just fifteen minutes." Bustamante lifted a shoulder and let it drop in a shrug, nonplussed by this news.

I, too, felt no big disappointment. Nailing Asher for the fire had been a long shot, anyway. At least now we could rule him out for that particular crime.

I started the engine, drove the detective back to the station, and headed out on patrol, hopeful we'd have some new leads to pursue once Bustamante heard back from the cell phone company about the flip phone found at the stadium.

42
ALL WORK AND NO PLAY MAKE BRIGIT A DULL K-9

Brigit

Visiting the school had been fun. There'd been so many interesting smells in the building and on the grounds. The scent of sex hormones had been nearly overwhelming, though. Smelled like most of the students were going through puberty.

Now that the workday was over, she and Megan were cooling off in the new backyard pool. Megan had ordered her a heavy-duty vinyl raft to rest on, as well as a floating dog toy that Brigit could swim after in a wet game of fetch. Brigit's favorite thing to do was to run up the makeshift steps and leap off the platform, landing in the water with a splash that rained down on Megan and sent her raft rocking on waves. Brigit adored Megan, but it could be fun to tease her partner, too. *Heh-heh.*

43
CASING THE PLACE

The Flamethrower

On Tuesday morning, the Flamethrower pulled his Camaro into the parking lot of the Magnolia Villa retirement home and parked in one of the visitor spots up front. He'd debated whether to rent a car, or to park elsewhere and walk to the building to avoid his license plate being picked up on the security cameras, but he figured that if he did anything out of the ordinary now it could raise suspicions later. It was perfectly normal for a pharmaceutical sales rep to visit such places, after all. He'd visited this very facility in the past, several times. His visits were documented in his logs and sales reports. He just hadn't paid much attention to the layout of the place when he'd come here before. Today, he would.

He climbed out of his car and slung the blue bag bearing the logo of the pharma company over his shoulder. Leaving his sunglasses on, he strolled inside, attempting to glance around without turning his head too much. He didn't want it to look like he was gathering intel. *Bingo.* The dining hall sat directly ahead, in the center of the long building. The double doors were open, and he could see people seated at tables inside, enjoying oatmeal, pancakes, or today's special which, according to the chalkboard sign situated by the doors, was a southwestern omelet. The diners' hair appeared to be in grayscale, ranging from dark pewter to snow white, though a few outliers continued to dye their hair brown, red, or blond. Beyond the dining room, swinging doors with round, porthole-style windows led into the kitchen. On either side of the dining room were activity rooms with glass walls. One was set up for an exercise class. The other contained a piano, as well as easels and art supplies.

The layout was perfect. He and Nash could start a fire in the rear of the kitchen. His goal was to give the fire station's captain some hell, but he didn't want anyone to get hurt in the process. He wasn't that kind of guy. Fortunately, there was no risk of collateral damage. A glance at the ceiling confirmed the place had an extensive automatic sprinkler system that would extinguish the flames long before they could spread through the dining room and activity rooms to the residential wings.

He forced a smile to his face and stepped up to the reception desk. Though he recognized the woman who worked the desk, he didn't remember her name. Fortunately, the nametag pinned to her chest gave him the information. He pulled off his sunglasses and tucked them into the breast pocket of his button-down shirt. "Hello, Catherine. Good to see you again." He lifted his bag and placed it on the counter. "I don't have an appointment scheduled with the doctors today but, if you don't mind, I'd like to leave them some literature on a new Afib medication. It produced amazing results in the clinical trials, and could really help their patients." He pulled a small stack of brochures from the bag and handed them over, along with a half dozen inexpensive promotional plastic pill cutters. "I'll give the docs a few days to read over the information, then I'll call to schedule a meeting with them."

"Sounds good." Catherine swept the items off the counter and set them on her desktop, beside her monitor.

The Flamethrower thanked her and headed out to his car, which had already heated up in the morning sun. He cranked up the air conditioning, and placed a call to Nash. "I need your help again. How much more of your snake oil do I have to buy?"

44
REDIAL

Megan

On Wednesday morning, Brigit and I were cruising through a residential area on our beat when my mobile phone chimed with an incoming call. Detective Bustamente's name appeared on the screen. Eager for an update on the swatting/shooter investigations, I pulled over to the curb and tapped the screen to accept the call. The background noise told me he was on the road, using speakerphone to keep his hands free for driving. "Got news, Detective?"

Indeed, he did. "The fingerprints on the cell phone matched Mrs. Pollard's."

Ugh. "The prints are a dead end, then."

"Not necessarily."

Huh? "What do you mean?"

"The fingerprints were Mrs. Pollard's, but the palm print on the lower back of the phone wasn't."

My mind took a beat or two to process the information. This could be a huge clue! Maybe even break the case. But I was getting ahead of myself, wasn't I? After all, the phone had been found abandoned. Someone else could have touched it between the time it was left there and when it was found. Still ... "The palm print could belong to the person who made the call."

"That's what I'm thinking. Of course, I first ruled out that the palm print didn't belong to the woman who took the phone from Mrs. Pollard when she turned it in at the concession stand. I've also verified that the other women working the booth never touched the phone. Unless somebody else held the phone after the caller ditched it behind the ketchup and before Mrs. Pollard found it, the palm print is likely the caller's."

Most people didn't realize that a palm print could be used to identify a person. The caller could have wiped their fingerprints off the phone before leaving it behind and missed cleaning the palm print, or maybe they'd worn latex gloves when they'd handled the phone, and the gloves hadn't been pulled on fully or had curled up at the wrist, exposing the heel of their hand. A variety of scenarios could explain how things had occurred. Regardless, the palm print gave us some hard evidence. Unfortunately, palm prints weren't taken when people are arrested, so it couldn't be processed through a database in search of a match. However, it could later help us ensure we had the right suspect—assuming we gathered enough other evidence to arrest someone. It could also provide forensic evidence that would help the district attorney obtain a conviction. In other words, while the palm print might be helpful down the road, it didn't give us anything to move forward on right now. "Has the cell phone company given you any info yet?"

"They have. The phone was purchased at the Walmart Supercenter on Jacksboro Highway. I'm on my way there. Meet me at the store?"

"Sure! See you in a few."

We ended the call and I mapped a route to the location. The store sat north of Interstate 30, not too far from Farrington Field. I made it there in fifteen minutes. Bustamente waited near the customer service counter at the front of the store. As soon as Brigit and I stepped up next to him, he headed to the counter to speak with a clerk.

He showed the woman his badge and business card. "We need to speak with the manager, please."

She picked up a phone, dialed a number, and listened for a few seconds before saying, "There's a detective and a cop here that want to talk to you." A beat passed before she said, "Okay," and hung up the phone. She pointed to a heavy-duty metal door to her left. "He's coming to let you in."

The face of a middle-aged Latino man appeared in the small square window. He opened the door and led us down a short hallway to his office. Three large TV screens were mounted on the wall, playing feeds from the security cameras so he could keep an eye on the entire store, the parking lot, and the receiving area in the rear, where three men were currently unloading a large semi-trailer adorned with the Walmart logo. "How can I help you?" the manager asked.

"We need information about recent sales of a particular model phone." Bustamente handed the man a sticky note on which he'd written the model information.

The manager's brows rose in curiosity. "Was the phone used in a crime?"

"It was," Bustamente said without elaborating.

The manager looked disappointed not to learn more, but he seemed to realize no further details would be forthcoming. He called back to the electronics department and directed an employee to bring him one of the phones. While we waited, he knelt down on the rug and ran his hand over Brigit's back. "What a beautiful girl you are!" She wagged her tail, and he looked up at me. "I'm a sucker for dogs. Got three of 'em myself. Heinz fifty-seven mutts, all of them." He proceeded to show me pics of his dogs on his phone. One appeared to be mostly husky, another mostly black lab. The third was such an odd-shaped mix of multicolored curly fluff that it was impossible to discern her lineage. She appeared to have a little bit of every breed in her. "Can your dog do any tricks?" he asked.

"She can, and she loves to show off." I ran Brigit through her list of tricks. *Speak. Play dead. Assume the position. Roll over.*

When she rose to her feet after executing three rolls, the man treated her to a round of applause. "Bravo, pooch!"

A knock sounded on the door down the hall, and the manager left the office, returning seconds later with a new phone in a box. He logged into his computer, scanned the phone with a handheld device, then turned to us. "How far back should I go?"

"Two weeks," Bustamente replied.

The man printed out a summary of recent sales. He handed the list across his desk to Bustamente. I leaned in to look over the detective's shoulder. Three dozen of the phones had been sold in the last two weeks. We could ignore any that had taken place since the call came in to dispatch last Friday. Bustamente ran his finger down the list until he found the first sale prior to the bogus shooter report being called in. I checked the time of the transaction. The phone had been purchased just minutes before the caller's cell service had been activated.

Bustamente placed the paper on the desktop and pointed to the sale. "I need to see the security camera footage from the electronics department at the time this sale was made."

"No problem." The manager brought up the footage, just as Principal Zhao had done at the school.

On the screen, we saw a crowd of people milling about the electronics department while three clerks attempted to help them with televisions, computers, phones, and assorted accessories. A line five people deep waited at the register. One was a tall, White young man in a black beanie and mirrored sunglasses. He fit the description given to us by Matt Treacy, the Comedian on the Median, who'd been paid to purchase a phone at the Dollar General store on Berry Street.

We watched as one-by-one, the customers ahead of him completed their transactions and turned to go. Finally, his turn came and he stepped up to the register. Now that nobody else stood in front of him, we could see that he wore jeans and a bright blue T-shirt with yellow lettering that spelled out ARLINGTON HEIGHTS YELLOW JACKETS. He held an enormous fountain drink cup to his face. The cup was so tall that only an inch or two of the plastic straw stuck up from the top. He took a sip from the straw, but didn't lower the cup to speak. With the beanie covering his hair and the cup hiding his nose and mouth, it was obvious the boy was trying to obscure his face. His lean frame said he definitely wasn't Gunther Fertig. *Could he be Asher?* Given the disguise, the distance from the camera, and the quality of the image, it was impossible to say for certain.

He said something to the clerk, and she left the counter with a key to unlock a nearby glass case where the cell phones were stored. She retrieved a box, returned to the register, and rang up the phone, as well as two other small items he'd carried up to the register. The boy took the bag, turned, and walked out of camera range, keeping the cup at his mouth as he headed to the front of the store.

Bustamente and I exchanged a glance. While the kid couldn't be easily identified with his face hidden behind the sunglasses and cup, the Arlington Heights High School T-shirt offered a clue.

The detective pointed to the screen. "Follow him through the store."

The manager switched camera feeds, and we watched as the boy continued down the main aisle and out the front door. I hoped we'd see him get into a vehicle outside, but instead the outdoor feed recorded him circling around to the back of the building. A security camera on the rear showed him walk off across the greenbelt behind the building.

"Can you go back?" Bustamente said. "I want to see how he got to the store."

The manager took the footage back further in time, playing the various exterior camera feeds until we saw the boy approach the store on foot from the greenbelt at the rear. He walked up the side of the building and entered in the front. He headed to the health and beauty section, walked up and down the aisles, then stopped in front of a display. He grabbed a small box off the shelf before making his way to the electronics department. There, he pulled something small off a peg near the locked phone case.

Bustamente turned back to the manager. "Besides the phone, what did he buy?"

The manager pulled up the details of the transaction on his computer. "He bought a fifteen-dollar prepaid phone card and a box of Band-Aids. Tru-Stay Clear Spots, fifty count. Two dollars and fifty-six cents."

"Any chance the clerk who rang him up is working today?"

The manager consulted a printed schedule on his desk. "She is." He picked up his phone, dialed a number, and asked the person who answered to come to his office.

The woman, who appeared to be in her late thirties, arrived a few minutes later. Unfortunately, she had little recollection of the transaction or the customer. "Friday nights are insane." She groaned. "We're always super busy and the customers get annoyed when they have to wait for us to unlock the cases. I barely have time to look up. I vaguely remember a guy with a beanie because it seemed outdated, like nineties grunge, or early hipster. Plus, he had to be nuts to be wearing a winter hat when it was a hundred degrees outside." She shrugged and raised her palms. "That's all I remember about him."

After she'd left the office, Detective Bustamente had the manager download the security camera footage to a thumb drive and thanked the man for the information. We left the office, as well, and went to the health and beauty section to take a look at the bandages the boy had purchased.

I ran my gaze over the display until—*Bingo!*— my eyes spotted the Tru-Stay Clear Spot Band-Aids. "There they are." I reached out and pulled the small box from the shelf.

Bustamente and I looked over the package. The Band-Aids were very small, just 2.2 centimeters—or less than an inch—square. They had a tiny bit of cotton padding in the center and a clear adhesive border to make the bandage less noticeable. As small as they were, they'd be of limited use. They could cover a small nick, or maybe a needle prick after an immunization. "They'd be perfect for covering fingerprints without being noticeable."

"Whoever he is," Bustamente said, "he's a smart cookie."

"You think it could be Asher, after all?" I asked. "He's tall. Smart, too."

"Possibly," Bustamente said, "but there are lots of tall young White men. The body type could be coincidence. Before we approach him again, I'd like to see if we can find some concrete evidence. Let's see where the caller might have gone when he left the store."

I returned the product to the shelf and we walked outside, the heat feeling even more oppressive as it radiated off the concrete and asphalt, broiling us from below. Lest Brigit's paws burn, I hustled her along in the shade next to the building. She immediately began to pant. We circled around to the back of the building and headed out onto the greenbelt, where I looked around and considered the possibilities. The boy could have made a wide U-turn to head over to the Cowtown Bowling Alley, which sat next door to the Walmart. He could have continued on straight ahead through Anderson Campbell Park, though he wouldn't have gotten far before he'd have found himself at the bank of the west fork of the Trinity River. With the Rockwood Park Golf Course to the east, it seemed unlikely he'd have headed in that direction. Golfers didn't appreciate interlopers on the course. Logic said he'd probably headed west, into the residential area.

Bustamente stopped and glanced around for a moment before

turning toward the neighborhood. He must have reached the same conclusion I had.

We came out of the greenbelt onto Ohio Garden Road. On a curve some distance ahead sat a convenience store with a sign out front identifying it as the Quick Sak. We turned and made our way first down Pumpkin Drive, where Bustamente kept an eye on the row of single-wide mobile homes, looking for any with security cameras or smart doorbells, making note of a few. When we'd walked the length of the horseshoe-shaped street, we continued to the other side of Ohio Garden Road, where we stopped and glanced up and down Ichabod Crane Road.

Bustamente hiked a thumb over his shoulder. "Let's head back to Walmart. I'll get my car and make the rounds of this neighborhood, see if I can get any footage from doorbell cameras. I'll try the Quick Sak, too." He handed me the jump drive. "Run over to Arlington Heights High. See if anyone in the office recognizes the kid. If they don't, try Paschal. You know why, right?"

I did, and I was proud of it. "The kid went to great lengths to hide his face, so it seems odd he'd wear a shirt that could help identify him." There was a good chance the shirt was a farce, meant to mislead law enforcement. The boy who bought the phone might not be a student at Arlington Heights High. He might attend the rival school they'd played football against Friday night—Paschal High. He might be a former student. Or he might have no relation to either school, and have simply realized that the football game was the largest public gathering taking place in the city last Friday night, an opportunity to maximize the terror and chaos.

I tucked the thumb drive into my breast pocket and we walked back to our vehicles. After loading Brigit into her kennel, I followed the detective out of the lot, continuing on when he turned into the neighborhood we'd just walked through.

Minutes later, I parked in the visitor lot at Arlington Heights High School. I released Brigit from her kennel, gave her a few seconds to tinkle and sniff around the grounds, then led her inside. At the front desk, I held up the thumb drive. "I need to find out if anyone in the administration recognizes a student on this video. We believe the student might have been involved in a crime."

"A crime?" The gray-haired clerk arched a brow. "And here I thought it was going to be another boring, ordinary day." She leaned toward me and whispered, "Is this about the shooting hoax?"

It didn't take a genius to put two and two together. Still, I knew it was best not to share information with anyone not in law enforcement or a leadership position. "I can't say. Sorry."

She scowled, but summoned the campus police officer, as well as the principal and two vice principals. I was led to an office, where I showed them the video. All four leaned in to get a good look at the screen.

The officer shook his head. "He's doing a darn good job of hiding his face."

The principal squinted at the screen. "This video isn't ringing any bells for me. But the kid's wearing one of our shirts. He must attend school here."

"Not necessarily," I said. "The shirt might have been intended to throw us off."

The principal suggested we allow the front office staff to view the video. "They interact with the kids and parents all day long, and they often overhear gossip. They might know something."

Realizing he had a point, I agreed. He invited the staff to the office to watch the video but, unfortunately, none of them could positively identify the boy, either.

I thanked them and drove over to Paschal High, where I repeated the process to equal disappointment. Nobody could say for certain who the boy was.

My assigned task completed, I texted Detective Bustamente a baseball emoji along with a message: I struck out. Brigit and I set back out on our beat. I issued two speeding tickets, provided water to a homeless woman sweating on a street corner, and cruised through Forest Park, keeping an eye out for suspicious activity. I saw none. Hardly anyone was out and about. It was too hot to be outside without a very good reason for doing so. Even the squirrels appeared sluggish, lazing on the tree limbs.

After my shift wrapped up, I decided to swing by my parent's house. Teenage girls kept a close eye on teenage boys. Maybe my sister Gabby would recognize her purported classmate who'd bought the burner phone at Walmart.

45
CATS VS. DOG

Brigit

While Megan and Gabby sat at the kitchen table and stared at a computer screen, Brigit inched toward the bowl of cat kibble on the floor. Brigit liked coming to Megan's family's house. They were always happy to see her, and the fishy kitty food she always managed to steal was a nice treat.

The dog thought she'd been subtle until Megan turned from the computer and pointed a finger at her. "No, Brigit!"

Brigit looked away, playing innocent. Three identical cats stood in the kitchen doorway, watching and swishing their tails. Brigit wasn't about to let those inferior beasts see her cowed by a mere human. She knew she shouldn't, but sometimes it was better to beg forgiveness than get permission. In defiance of Megan's direct order, Brigit darted over to the bowl and gobbled up the food.

When she finished, she looked up at Megan. Her partner stood over her now with her hands on her hips. "Bad girl!"

Brigit faked contrition, lowering her head and putting her tail between her legs. She slinked toward the living room, forcing the three cats to part ways to let her pass. But as she went by, one of them had the nerve to swipe at her hindquarters with their razor-sharp claws. *Yelp!* She dashed forward a few steps before turning to glare back at them. She wasn't sure which of the three had dared to touch her, but all three sat smugly now, one of them licking its paw with nonchalance as it eyed her. *Nasty, useless creatures!*

46
LIGHT UP THE NIGHT

The Flamethrower

At 2:00 Thursday morning, the Flamethrower sat in the bed of a rented pickup truck, virtually hidden behind a stack of junk Nash had collected at the city dump. When Nash stopped at an intersection, the Flamethrower stood in the bed, grabbed a rusty stepladder, and tossed it into the street. He followed it with a rickety wooden bar stool to ensure both sides of the road would be impassable until the debris was cleared. People often didn't properly secure their things when they were moving them, and stuff was forever falling out of pickup trucks and ending up in the roads. Mattresses. Drawers. Sofa cushions. He figured it was unlikely the debris would be tied to the fire, but he was careful not to leave fingerprints anyway. He banged lightly on the top of the cab to let Nash know he could get moving again, and sat back down. They made their way a block over, where the Flamethrower tossed a cracked concrete birdbath into the street, along with a faded and torn patio umbrella. *That'll slow them down.*

The most direct routes from the fire station to the nursing home now obstructed, they parked down a dark side street and turned their attention to starting the fire. They skulked through the neighborhood and sneaked up behind the nursing home. They were armed with the cordless drill, more tampons, and a full can of lighter fluid, as well as two LED flashlights with swiveling heads. The nursing home had only two security cameras on the back of the building. They were centered over the rear that led into the kitchen and were aimed in opposite directions. Odds were that nobody was currently monitoring the camera feeds, but they'd work fast, just in case.

Nash wore the balaclava he'd worn to the high school, and the Flamethrower wore the medical mask and goggles, along with the hooded windbreaker. Both wore barbecue gloves again, to avoid leaving fingerprints or burning their hands. Although it was unlikely they could be identified, as an extra precaution they held their flashlights in front of their faces, the bright beam shining outward as they approached the cameras. The Flamethrower set the flashlight on the ground and swiveled the head to aim it directly at the lens of the security camera that faced east. Nash did the same a few feet away, blinding the camera that faced west.

They repeated the procedure they'd used at the high school except, rather than drilling holes down the entire length of the building, they limited the range to a twenty-foot expanse to ensure the fire would be contained to the kitchen. There were elderly people living here, after all, and the Flamethrower didn't want to cause them any physical harm. They'd be upset enough being roused from their slumber by the sound of the smoke alarms and fire trucks—assuming they could hear the noise without their hearing aids.

As Nash drilled each of the five holes, the Flamethrower followed behind, shoving a tampon into the space and dousing it with lighter fluid. After Nash drilled the final hole, he left the Flamethrower to finish his tasks, and returned to the first hole to light the string. As the Flamethrower shoved the tampon into the hole, his nose caught a whiff of something foul smelling, like rotten eggs. He paused, sniffed, and glanced around. The garbage dumpster sat only a few yards away. It was probably full of kitchen discards and old food. *The smell must be coming from there.* He returned his attention to his task, shoving a tampon into the hole and wetting it with the lighter fluid.

The other holes were blazing when Nash scurried up and lit the final string. The two turned and ran. They'd made it only a few steps when *KABOOM!* The force of the eruption behind them knocked them flat on their faces. Broken pieces of brick fell to the ground around them.

"Holy shit!" From his prone position on the asphalt, the Flamethrower turned back in horror to see flames shooting twenty feet into the air, fueled by far more than a few squirts of lighter fluid. The mystery of the rotten egg smell was solved. *Nash must have nicked the gas pipe. Some fire pro he'd turned out to be!*

As the building's smoke alarms activated, the Flamethrower pushed himself to his feet and took off as fast as his feet could go.

47
NOSING AROUND

M^{egan}

Gabby hadn't recognized the boy in the security camera footage from Walmart, but I was glad I'd stopped by the house anyway. It had been nice to check in with my sister and parents. With Seth only recently becoming acquainted with his father, stepmother, and half-brothers, it made me realize how much I'd taken my family for granted all these years. I offered to take everyone out for Italian food. Seth met us at the restaurant, and we had a nice meal together.

Seth and I were sleeping off that meal when my cell phone erupted at 3:30 AM on Thursday. I sat bolt upright, grabbed the phone from the nightstand, and checked the screen. It was Detective Bustamente calling. I jabbed the button to accept the call and swung my legs out from under the covers. Though Brigit raised her head from the foot of the bed to look at me, she made no move to get down. I hurried out into the hall and closed the door behind me. "Hello?" I whispered. A late-night call was never good news.

"We need your particular set of skills," Bustamente said, mimicking Liam Neeson's speech from the movie "Taken."

"What for?" I asked.

"Someone started a fire at a nursing home. Residents suffered smoke inhalation. One had a heart attack, though it appears to be a minor one, thank goodness. Another fell and fractured her ribs. The M.O. is the same as the fire that was set at the high school. Feminine products shoved into holes, doused with flammable liquid, and lit on fire. We'd like to see if Brigit can track the culprits." Bustamente gave me the address.

"We'll be there A.S.A.P." I ended the call and tiptoed back into the bedroom.

Seth rolled onto his back and scrubbed a hand over his face. "Duty calls?"

"Yeah," I said softly. I circled the bed and kissed him on the forehead. "Go back to sleep. I'll fill you in later."

He reached out and took my hand. "Be careful."

I gave his hand a squeeze. "I will."

After rounding up my uniform, my shoes, and my partner, I dressed, brushed my teeth, and splashed cold water on my face to make sure I was fully awake to drive. "Let's go, girl."

Brigit followed me out to our cruiser and climbed in.

We pulled up to the nursing home a few minutes later. An ambulance with flashing lights rolled out of the driveway with what I assumed was the last of the injured residents. I turned my attention to the building. *Whoa.* While the damage at the high school had been minimal, the center of this building had been entirely incinerated. The roof was gone, leaving a gaping, soot-rimmed hole in its place. Smoke from smoldering embers rose through the hole. The glass front doors were open, and firefighters moved about inside the lobby, finishing their work. Frankie was among them. Residents in pajamas, nightgowns, robes, and slippers huddled on the grass, some in wheelchairs, while nurses in scrubs tended to them. Many of the residents were on their cell phones, probably calling family to make temporary living arrangements.

I drove into the parking lot, took the first available spot, and released Brigit from her enclosure, attaching her long leash to her harness. We walked over to Detective Bustamente and Investigator Hamrick, who stood a few yards to the side of the building's entrance.

"Thanks for coming," Hamrick said.

"Brigit and I are always happy to help." The statement wasn't entirely true. Brigit and I did indeed want to help, but the *always* part that was a white lie. *Why can't criminals pick more convenient times to commit their crimes?*

Hamrick led us around to the back of the building, where he showed me the holes that had been drilled into the bricks. Sure enough, whoever had started the fire here had used the same tactics as those who'd started the fire at the high school. Only here, they'd been much more successful—assuming wanton destruction could ever be described as success.

I pointed at the last hole on the right, which was jagged and much larger, approximately a foot in diameter. "What happened there?"

"Whoever drilled the hole hit the natural gas line to the kitchen. The gas caused a small explosion and fed the fire. That's why the flames spread so quickly."

I recalled the gas well explosions I'd seen on the news. They were huge, like super-powered flamethrowers being aimed at the sky, and extremely difficult to extinguish. Many of them had been deadly. "It's a wonder the damage wasn't worse."

Hamrick nodded solemnly. "If the nighttime desk attendant hadn't kept a cool head, realized what was happening, and known how to turn off the gas feed, we'd be looking at widespread casualties, maybe even fatalities."

The thought that innocent people could have perished here

made me feel sick to my stomach. "Do you think the arsonists meant to kill people here?"

"Hard to say. I hope not. The place has a sprinkler system. If not for the gas feed, the fire wouldn't have gotten far. The fact that the pipe was only nicked tells me it might have been an accident. They might have intended to cause only a small fire, get some attention."

"But why?"

"Hell if I know," Hamrick said. "But I'm determined to find out."

I was determined, too, and would help him and Detective Bustamente as much as I could. I looked down at Brigit. She looked back up at me, eager to work, her eyes bright and alert. I gave her the order to track the disturbance. She put her nose to the ground and snuffled around for a few seconds before heading off in one direction. I gave her a long lead and trailed along behind her. As before, she stopped at a sewer drain. But unlike last time, she didn't issue an alert. Nothing in the drain interested her this time. She turned and headed off in another direction before circling back to the building and tracking to another storm sewer at the opposite end of the parking lot. *She's having trouble again.* Though I was disappointed, I knew I was asking a lot of her. Even the most skilled nose would be challenged to find a distinctive trail among all the disturbances caused by the arsonists, residents, staff, and firefighters.

After letting her lead the search for several minutes, I tried a different tack. Assuming the arsonists left the scene on foot, I led her to the outer perimeter of the nursing home property to see if she could pick up a trail there. We had more luck now. In just a few seconds, she found a scent and trailed it off the property and down the street. I jogged along behind her as she turned down one residential street, then another. She stopped a few blocks away in an unlit area along a side street. She dropped to her haunches, issuing a passive alert. *This must have been where the arsonists got into their vehicle.* It was a clever place to park. None of the houses faced the side street, so it was unlikely the vehicle would be picked up on doorbell cameras.

I made a note of the two closest intersections, and walked back to the nursing home to inform Bustamente and Hamrick of the location.

"Thanks," Hamrick said. "That'll give me a place to start. I'm not sure when I'll be able to get the security camera footage, but it's likely to be useless, anyway. I found a couple of flashlights, so my guess is they blinded the cameras again."

I wished him luck, bade Bustamente goodbye, and led Brigit to our cruiser. By the time we arrived back at our house, it was 6:00 in the morning and the horizon glowed with the promise of sunrise. With my alarm set to go off in only half an hour, there was no point in returning to bed. Instead, I undressed, showered, and washed the smell of smoke from my hair, then put on a fresh uniform. I fixed myself a bowl of oatmeal and a triple espresso. After losing three hours of sleep to the fire investigation, I'd need all the caffeine I could drink to get through the day.

Seth padded into the kitchen, Blast puttering along behind him. While Seth prepared an espresso for himself, Blast performed a series of stretches, putting one leg out behind him, then the other, then reaching his front paws out in front of him and lowering his head to elongate his back. While the espresso processed, Seth turned and leaned back against the counter. "Catch me up."

I told him about the gas-fueled fire at the nursing home, and Brigit trailing the arsonists to what appeared to be their parking spot. "Several of the residents were injured when they evacuated the building. One had a heart attack."

Seth glowered. "This isn't good. The fires are escalating. Three mothers came to the station this week and put Captain MacDougal on the spot about the fire at Paschal High. They demanded to know what the captain was doing to ensure their children were safe at school. He told them that the school has a good alarm system, and that the station has adequate manpower and equipment, but they weren't satisfied. They wanted to know how he planned to prevent another fire." He threw his hands up. "I don't know what they're expecting. The fire department can't control what some whack job might do. The incident at the nursing home is only going to get the moms more riled up."

I could relate to the fire department's dilemma. The public sometimes had unrealistic expectations of law enforcement, too. We did our best, of course, but we couldn't always predict if and when a lawbreaker would commit a criminal act. There's a reason we were called *responders*, not *prophets*.

Changing the subject, Seth said, "Tommy and Pamela have offered to pay for our rehearsal dinner."

"Really? That's very nice of them." It would be one less expense for us. *Who knew even a modest wedding could be so expensive?* "Does this mean they're coming to the wedding?"

Seth nodded. "My half-brothers, too." He took a sip of his espresso. "It still feels weird to say that. Brothers."

I stepped over and wrapped my arms around him. "I hope it will stop feeling weird soon. Tommy seems like a good guy, and Pamela has been surprisingly cool with everything. It's good you're getting to know your family." I gave him a kiss. "Soon they'll be my family, too."

Seth released a soft sigh. "Mom's still beating herself up over how she handled things. She'll be glad to know Tommy wants to be more involved. He sent me a text yesterday inviting you and me to visit them in Asheville."

"I'd love to go." I'd heard that Asheville, North Carolina was a beautiful, artsy place, and who wouldn't want to spend some time in the mountains? "Maybe they can teach us how to ski."

"I'd be game for that. I'll let him know."

I glanced at the clock on the microwave. "I'd better get going. My shift starts soon." I only hoped I wouldn't get drowsy after losing so much sleep. I left Seth with another kiss on the lips, while Blast had to settle for one on the head.

I heard nothing more from Detective Bustamente on Thursday but, on Friday afternoon, while Brigit and I were cruising past the Texas Christian University, my phone pinged with an incoming text from him. Got video. Help?

I texted him back. OMW. I arrived at the station a few minutes later and headed down the hall to Bustamente's office, my laptop in my arms and my furry partner at my knee.

The detective and I were well beyond formalities now. He pointed to a chair facing his desk and simply said, "Sit." He handed me a thumb drive. "I've collected footage from eight cameras in the neighborhood near the Walmart, including footage from the Quick Sak convenience store. You review the videos on that thumb drive, I'll take a look at the others."

I inserted the thumb drive into my computer. The first camera was a doorbell camera on a mobile home on Pumpkin Drive. Unfortunately, the device had very limited range. While the stoop was visible, the viewing field was blocked by a scraggly crepe myrtle tree to the left, which prevented the camera from recording more than a sliver of the street. Still, I did my best, working slowly through the footage to see if the young man from Walmart appeared. He didn't. All I saw were three squirrels chasing each other and a hummingbird flitting about, looking for nectar.

The next feed was from a camera situated over the entrance to the Quick Sak. I went through the feed, pausing it each time a customer entered or exited. None of them wore a blue Arlington Heights shirt, mirrored aviator sunglasses, or a beanie hat, though several of them were tall, lean young men in jeans and sneakers. I jotted down the license plates of the few who had arrived in a vehicle with visible plates. I searched the license plate records for their names, and ran them through the criminal database. One of them had a record for shoplifting batteries. Another had a record for a hit and run. Their crimes were distinctively different from phoning in a bogus active shooter report. I knew that criminals tended to stay in their lanes and commit the same general types of crimes. But for every rule there's an exception, right? Maybe one of them had decided to branch out, and thought that a shooter hoax would be a good way to take revenge on the police department for their arrest and conviction. I printed out their criminal reports for Bustamente to review.

While the detective looked over their records, I moved on to the third camera. This one was a doorbell camera on a mobile home situated on a curve on Ichabod Crane Road. Unlike the other doorbell camera, this one covered a fairly wide field of vision. Cars slowed as they rounded the corner, allowing me to get a look at their license plate numbers. Per the time stamp, eight minutes after the burner phone had been purchased at the nearby Walmart, a lean boy strode quickly up the road. Though he wore jeans like the guy in the store's security camera footage, he held no cup, carried no Walmart bag, and wore neither a knit beanie nor the blue T-shirt. Rather, he wore a fitted charcoal gray athletic shirt, what trendsetters called athleisure wear. But what caught my eye was his sunglasses. They were mirrored aviators, the same type of sunglasses the guy who'd purchased the phone had been wearing. He passed the house and disappeared out of view.

Eleven seconds later, a flashy blue Camaro with a black center stripe down the hood came from the direction in which the boy had gone. *Didn't I see one just like it at the stadium Friday night?* I was fairly certain I had. A boy inside the car had howled at Brigit. Unfortunately, I couldn't recall what the driver looked like. It hadn't seemed important at the time. *Could it be this boy?*

My heart beat faster as I paused the feed. The tint on the car's windows was too dark for me to tell if the boy was driving the vehicle or whether anyone else was inside, but the street had been relatively inactive and the timing seemed too close to be coincidence. The odds seemed good that he'd gotten into that car. I moved the feed forward three more seconds and paused it again, making note of the license plate.

I brought up the DMV records and ran the license plate. The car was registered at an address within my beat, not far from Paschal High school, and belonged to a Steven Quinn. *Why does that last name ring a bell?* It took a beat or two, but then my mind sparked. "I think I've got something!"

Bustamante looked up. "What did you find?"

I turned my computer so Bustamante could see my screen, and replayed the footage. "This boy is wearing the same type of sunglasses as the guy who bought the phone." I paused the video for a few seconds so the detective could take a good look, then resumed the feed. The boy walked out of camera range. I paused the feed again as the Camaro appeared and rounded the curve, heading to the exit for the neighborhood. I pointed to the car. "He could have gotten into that Camaro. It's registered to a Steven Quinn at an address near Paschal High. Quinn is the last name of one of the boys who was in the Waffle House video Asher Burke posted on TikTok." I brought up another window, logged into the social media site, and played the video for Bustamente. "See? Hayden Quinn is tagged in the video."

Hayden was lean and on the tall side, though not as tall as Asher. The bright sun in the doorbell camera footage made it difficult to discern the exact color of the boy's hair as he walked by, though it did not appear to be blond. In the TikTok video, Hayden appeared to be ginger haired. *Was that Hayden Quinn in the doorbell footage?* He might have been the one who called in the shooter prank, then ditched the phone behind the ketchup dispenser. Hayden might have been near the condiment stand with Asher when Mrs. Pollard found the phone. If she was unfamiliar with Hayden but knew Asher, it would be only natural for her to call out to the student she recognized. *Had Asher and the other boys been in on the prank?* I wasn't sure how things had played out, but my tingling nerves and the fact that Bustamente was rising from his seat told me we'd soon have some answers.

48
NAUGHTY PUPPY

Brigit

Brigit stood on the porch, waiting by Megan's side. She could hear a dog inside. He was jumping up on the inside of the door and scratching it with his claws. He was barking, too. *Arf! Arf-arf!* His overly excitable behavior and the scent he'd left all over the front yard told her he was a young dog, barely out of puppyhood.

The door opened and the dog ran out. Brigit was on duty and knew she should ignore him, but it wasn't easy when he shoved his cold, wet nose into her butt. *At least buy a lady a dog treat first!*

49
ANOTHER DAY, ANOTHER LAWYER

The Flamethrower

The Flamethrower was in the kitchen, gathering plates and silverware for their dinner, when Hayden went to the front door to get their food delivery. The dog was yapping up a storm but, between yaps, he heard Hayden gasp. *What the hell?*

Leaving the plates and forks on the countertop, he stepped into the hallway. The front door was open but, rather than a delivery person from DoorDash on the porch, it was a uniformed female police officer. A paunchy Latino in a cheap sport coat stood on one side of her, and an enormous German shepherd mix stood on the other. His heart jumped into his throat. *SHIT-SHIT-SHIT! Had they found out he and Nash had started the fires? Was he going to be arrested in front of his son? The fire at the nursing home would never have been so big if Nash hadn't fucked up and nicked the gas line. It was all Nash's fault!*

He stepped up behind Hayden and forced a pleasant smile to his lips. His throat was so choked with anxiety he could barely force the words out. "Hello. Can I help you with something?"

"We hope so," the man said. "Are you Steven Quinn?"

"Yes, I am."

The man extended his hand. "Detective Hector Bustamente."

Steven took his hand and gave it a firm shake, hoping his grip would exude confidence.

The detective handed him a business card, then introduced the uniformed officer. "This is Officer Megan Luz and her canine partner Brigit."

Steven gave the young woman a nod in greeting, took the business card she held out, and looked down at the dog. The damn bitch had her snout in the air and was flexing her nostrils, as if she smelled something that interested her. When her eyes met his, he wondered if the interesting thing was *him*. Meanwhile, his son's mutt danced around behind the shepherd, shamelessly giving her fluffy butt a thorough inspection. The K9 sat and looked up at her handler.

He returned his focus to the detective. He did his best to sound clueless, and to refrain from shitting his pants. "What's this about?"

Bustamente said, "The call made to nine-one-one to report a shooting."

On learning the cops hadn't come about the fires, Steven felt a rush of relief. But, before he could respond, Hayden cried out, "It wasn't me! It was Asher!"

What?! On instinct, he dropped the business cards, reached around his son's shoulders and slapped a hand over his mouth, pulling him back against his chest in an improvised headlock. He hissed in his son's ear. "Don't say another word!" *Asher!* Steven should have known that entitled little shit would get his son into trouble. Gretchen had been right to forbid Hayden from hanging out with the boy. *She's always right. I should've listened!*

Bustamente's brows rose. Luz stared at his son, her head tilted and eyes narrowed, assessing him. The dog pawed at her handler's leg, but Officer Luz didn't seem to notice.

Steven released his hand from Hayden's mouth. "May I have a word with my son in private?"

"At the station." Bustamente turned to Luz. "Call for a transport."

Luz squeezed her shoulder-mounted radio and requested a patrol car. Wondering why she didn't plan to transport Hayden herself, Steven looked past them to the cruiser at the curb, and saw that the back seat was outfitted as a dog kennel. Thank goodness Valerie, her husband, and their girls had already left for tonight's game against the Saginaw High School Roughriders. He'd seen them drive off a few minutes earlier when he'd gone outside to get the mail. Otherwise, Valerie would already be on the phone, spreading gossip that would surely get back to Gretchen.

Hayden began to shake and sniffle, swiping at tears escaping from his eyes. Steven's face heated in a knee-jerk reaction of embarrassment. *Who wants their son to be a crybaby?* But when he saw Officer Luz's expression soften, he realized his son's boo-hooing could have an upside.

A tiny blue Mitsubishi Mirage braked to a quick stop behind the cruiser, and a twentyish guy emerged with a large bag of food in his hand. The greasy spot on the side said their salsa might have leaked when the guy took a corner too fast. The delivery driver approached the porch, but stopped a few feet back, looking from Steven to his son, to the cops, to the dog. "Uh ... got food here for Steven Quinn?" He raised the bag.

"That's me." Steven went down the steps, took the food, and thanked the driver, who scurried back to his car.

A second patrol car pulled up to the curb, taking the spot as it was vacated by the DoorDash driver. At the wheel was a hulking cop with a cocky sneer and hair of flaming red, not the attractive rich ginger color that Gretchen and Hayden shared. The cop honked the horn twice, then unrolled his window. "Someone call for a taxi?"

Steven was not amused. Judging from their frowns, neither was the detective or Officer Luz.

Luz put a gentle hand on his son's shoulder. "Come with me, Hayden."

At the thought of being separated from his son, Steven panicked. The boy had never needed his father more than this very moment, and Steven didn't want to let him down. He'd let the boy down enough already. "Can I ride with him?"

"No," Bustamente said. "You'll need to take your own vehicle."

Dammit! "Keep quiet son," Steven admonished Hayden with a pointed look. "I'll call a lawyer."

He watched helplessly as Luz led Hayden to the redheaded officer's cruiser and helped him into the back seat. As the car pulled away from the curb, Hayden glanced back with such a pathetic, frightened look that Steven felt guilty for being relieved the cops were here about something his son was involved in rather than the fires he and Nash had set. But whatever involvement his son might have had in the shooting hoax, he'd likely get off easy. Kids were expected to do dumb-ass things, and judges were reluctant to punish them hard, especially for a first offense. Luckily, his son was still a juvenile, though barely. Seventeen-year-olds could be tried as adults in Texas. His son had less than a year until he reached that milestone.

Officer Luz opened the back door of her car, signaled with her hand, and the dog jumped up into its enclosure. As Luz and the detective climbed into her cruiser, Steven hurried back inside. He picked up the business cards from the floor in the entryway where he'd dropped them, and tossed them into the small bowl on the narrow table next to the door where Gretchen used to keep her keys. He rushed to his home office and booted up his computer. For the second time in weeks, he found himself in need of an attorney. Gretchen had broken his heart, and now his son was going to break his bank account.

50
BOYS WILL BE BOYS AND BOYS WILL BE IDIOTS

Megan

An hour and a half later, Detective Bustamente and I were sitting at a table in an interrogation room at the police station. Across from us sat Hayden Quinn, his father, and the lawyer his father had hired only minutes before. No doubt the attorney was charging an overtime rate for working on a Friday night.

The attorney had met privately with Hayden and his dad, and made Bustamente an offer. "Hayden had no prior knowledge that a crime was going to be committed, and played no knowing role in the commission of a crime. Even so, I've advised him to speak with you only if we are offered assurance that no charges will be pursued against him."

"I'll agree not to refer Hayden to juvenile court for prosecution," Bustamente said, "on the condition that Hayden provide his fingerprints and handprint. My agreement is revocable if evidence indicates Hayden played an active, knowing role in any crime."

Everyone agreed. I took Hayden's fingerprints and palm prints, no easy task when his hands were shaking, and Bustamente sent them to the lab for comparison to the prints found on the cell phone.

While the lab techs worked their magic, Bustamente began his interview by posing an open-ended question. "Tell me what you know about the active shooter report. Start at the beginning."

"Okay." Hayden's eyes were bright with emotion and his lip quivered. "I had a sleepover at my house for my birthday. Asher came. Two of my other friends, too. Micah and Cade. We were playing video games on our computers and my dad ordered pizza for us. After the pizza guy came, Dad went out for a little while. As soon as he left, Asher showed us a cheap flip phone he'd gotten. His parents had bought him the latest iPhone, so Micah asked Asher why he got another phone, especially a basic one like that. Asher said, 'So I could do this.' Next thing we knew, he had dialed nine-one-one and was telling the police that there were three men at the mall with guns. His computer was still logged into the game, and he kept pushing the key to make shooting noises."

I fought the urge to exchange a look with Detective Bustamente. We'd come here to get information about the call made from the stadium, but we were getting more than we'd hoped for—a break on the mall incident, too. Looked like the call from the stadium might not be a copycat, as we'd theorized. It had very likely been initiated by the same caller—Asher.

Hayden continued. "Asher talked in a high voice, like he was trying to sound like a lady. Then he hung up and laughed. The rest of us freaked out. We knew he could be in big trouble. Us, too. Asher told us we were making a big deal out of nothing and to 'chill the eff out.' Except he said the actual word, not just 'eff.'"

"Understood," Bustamente said. "Then what?"

"Then Asher took the phone out to the garage and smashed it with my baseball bat. He put the pieces in an empty pizza box and stuck the box in the big garbage can. Micah said we should call the police back and tell them it was a prank call, but Asher told him to 'stop being a pussy.'" Hayden glanced my way and blushed before looking down at his lap. "So, none of us did anything. Asher turned on the TV to see if there would be a breaking news report." He shrugged. "That's it."

Bustamante jotted some notes. "The Micah you referred to, that's Micah Peters, correct?"

Hayden's eyes flashed in surprise. He was probably wondering how the detective already knew his friend's last name. "Yes, sir."

The detective held his pen aloft. "And Cade is Cade Cox?"

"Yes, sir."

"And you were with these same three boys at Farrington Field last Friday night?"

Hayden nodded. "We hang out together a lot. At least Micah, Cade, and I do. Asher sometimes hangs with other people."

Bustamante turned his legal pad to a fresh page. "Tell me what happened that night at the football game."

The boy's brow furrowed. "Why?"

Hayden looked genuinely confused. Did he really not comprehend the connection—that false shooter calls were made on both nights? He must not have realized that we'd tracked the Camaro from the Walmart the night the call was made at the stadium. Bustamente hadn't yet mentioned it. The kid must think we'd been led to his house for some other reason. *Is he going to try to lie to us about that call?*

Bustamante filled in the blanks. "There was another shooter call that night, remember? Farrington Field was evacuated."

"But Asher didn't make that call," Hayden insisted, shaking his head. "He knew the rest of us were beyond pissed at him. He could've gotten us all in big trouble. He promised us he'd never do it again."

His earnestness said he was being sincere. I pitied the boy, naive enough to believe his troublemaking friend would keep his word.

Bustamante made a little circle in the air with his pen. "Tell me about that evening anyway. Start when you and your friends first met up."

"Hold up!" Hayden's attorney raised a hand in a stop motion. "I thought this was just about the shooter report at the mall."

Bustamante grunted and stared the man down. "You assured me your client wasn't directly involved in making *any* false police reports."

"I wasn't!" Hayden cried.

Both his attorney and his father shushed him.

"Can we have another moment?" The attorney's sharp exhale said that, no matter how much he was charging to be here, he didn't think it was enough.

"Of course." Bustamante rose from his seat.

Brigit and I followed the detective out to the door. We chatted with the officer at the booking desk until Hayden's attorney opened the door a few minutes later and beckoned us back into the conference room. "We're ready to proceed."

The attorney retook his seat. The detective and I did the same. Brigit flopped down under the table and rolled onto her side for a nap. She found interrogations far less interesting than we humans did.

"Go ahead," the attorney instructed Hayden.

Hayden gnawed on his lip. "Dad let me use his car that night, so I picked everyone up for the game. We drove to a Walmart first. The one on Jacksboro Highway. Asher had his older brother's driver's license and was going to try to buy us some beer." On admitting he planned to engage in underage drinking, the boy had the sense to look sheepish. "Asher put on a pair of mirrored sunglasses. He thought they'd make him look older."

Bustamante held his pen at the ready. "What else was he wearing?"

Hayden shrugged. "Jeans. An athletic shirt."

"What color was the shirt?"

Hayden's eyes narrowed as he thought. "Gray, I think? Black maybe? I don't remember for sure."

"Did he have another shirt with him?" Bustamante asked.

"Like an undershirt?" Hayden asked.

"Any kind of shirt," Bustamante said.

"Not that I saw," Hayden said. When Bustamante raised a palm, inviting him to continue, he said, "Asher went into the store by himself. He said the rest of us look younger than him even though I'm actually older than he is. He said if he was hanging out with us, the cashier might realize it wasn't really him in the driver's license photo and they might not sell him the beer."

"Was he able to get the beer?" Bustamante asked.

"No," Hayden said. "He told us he went to a male cashier because he thought the guy would be cool about it, but the cashier said he knew the I.D. was fake and that he could get fired if he sold Asher the beer. But the guy didn't call the manager or security or anything."

"Where did you and the others wait for Asher while he went inside?" Bustamante asked. "At the curb in front of the store? The parking lot?"

"No," Hayden said. "Asher said there was a chance he might have to make a run for it if the cashier called security, and that if someone saw the car they could get the license plate and call the police on us. So, we waited in a trailer park behind the store."

So far, his story was plausible and coincided with what we'd seen in the store's security camera footage and the doorbell camera footage.

"Did Asher buy anything else at the store?" Bustamante asked.

"No," Hayden said. "At least not that I know of. I guess he could have gotten some gum or something and put it in his pocket, but he wasn't carrying anything when he came back to the car."

Is he telling the truth here, or is he hedging his bets, pretending not to know that Asher had a new burner phone in his pocket? Had Hayden truly not realized that Asher had gone into Walmart to purchase the phone? That Asher hadn't even gone to the beer section at all? That he'd been wearing another shirt under the athletic shirt and evidently swapped them out? Thinking back on how my three younger brothers behaved during their teen years, how oblivious they could be to things going on around them, I realized it was entirely possible that Hayden had no idea what his friend had been up to.

"Then what?" the detective prompted him again.

"We drove from there to the game," Hayden said.

"Where'd you sit?"

"Fifth row on the thirty-yard line."

"Those are good seats," Bustamente said, "especially for a big game like that."

"Asher had some girls save them for us," Hayden explained. "Brooklyn and Makayla. We sat there and watched the game until a lady cop with a dog ran out onto the field at halftime and stopped the band." His gaze shifted to me and he cocked his head. "Wait. Was that *you*?"

"It was," I said. "Me and Brigit."

On hearing her name, Brigit raised her head from the floor below the table, but quickly put it back down when no order followed.

"And then?" Bustamente prodded the boy.

"And then the announcer told everyone to leave. We went back to the car and drove over to Waffle House and hung out there for maybe an hour. Then I dropped my friends off at their houses and went back home. Well, to my dad's house, I mean."

Steven Quinn sat bolt upright. He opened his mouth as if to say something, but then sat back, the rapid rise and fall of his chest telling me he was fuming. But why, exactly, I wasn't sure.

Bustamente asked Hayden whether he or his friends had left their seats during the game. "Maybe to get some food at the concession stand?"

"No," Hayden said. "We bought hot dogs and drinks on the way in. Micah got an order of nachos. Asher went down to use the restroom once, but other than that we stayed in our seats."

"When did Asher leave his seat to go to the restroom?"

"Near the end of the second quarter," Hayden said. "He said he wanted to beat the halftime rush."

Bustamente spoke slowly and deliberately. "So, Asher left you and your other friends in the stands around the same time a caller contacted dispatch, threatening to open fire during the halftime show." He stared Hayden down, as if willing the boy to realize his so-called friend was a lying, two-faced punk. When Hayden said nothing, the detective said, "That's awfully coincidental, isn't it?"

Hayden bit his lip and looked from Bustamente, to his father, to his attorney, and back again. "I-I ... I guess so." He shook his head, his voice rising with his desperation. "But I didn't know anything about it. I swear!"

"Did you ask Asher whether he'd made the call that night?"

Hayden lowered his eyes, looking sheepish again. "I didn't, but Micah did. Asher said he didn't do it. He said it must have been another copycat. He said he'd only made the call from my birthday party as a one-time prank and that he wouldn't have kept wasting money on junk phones just for kicks."

Steven huffed, seemingly irritated that his son could be so gullible, while the attorney rolled his eyes outright. He'd already negotiated immunity for his client. No need to pretend the boy wasn't a dupe.

Bustamente stared at Hayden. "We've recovered the phone used to call in the threat to the stadium. It was purchased last Friday at the Walmart on Jonesboro Highway. Just eight minutes later, your father's Camaro drove past a camera on a mobile home behind the store."

On learning that his so-called friend had made a fool of him, Hayden's mouth fell open, his braces glinting in the overhead light. His eyes darkened with hurt, humiliation, or some combination of the two.

After giving the boy a moment to process the information, Bustamente pressed Hayden for more details about what happened after he and his friends evacuated the stadium. "When you left Farrington Field, where else did you go prior to the Waffle House?"

Hayden appeared puzzled. "Nowhere. We went straight from the stadium to the restaurant."

"What about after Waffle House?" Bustamente asked. "Where did you go then?"

"I took my friends home, like I said. That was it."

"Did you go to Paschal High School any time that evening?"

"No, sir," Hayden told Bustamente. "I didn't go to the school."

"Do you know anything about the fire that was set there?"

"No, sir," the boy repeated, shaking his head vehemently.

Bustamente eyed Hayden in silence for so long that the kid began to tremble again. "You sure you don't know anything about the fire?"

Hayden nodded now, just as vehemently. "Yes, sir!"

Steven Quinn shifted in his seat, seeming uneasy about this new line of questioning. *Does he know something? Or is he just having a hard time watching his son being grilled?* Even though Bustamente was going relatively easy on Hayden, it couldn't be easy for a parent to see their kid under such stress.

"It seems like a very strange coincidence that someone called in a threat during a Paschal High School football game, and then a fire was intentionally set at the school on the same night. Wouldn't you agree?"

Hayden stammered again. "I-I guess so. But I didn't have anything to do with it. I promise!"

"Besides the phone call the night of your birthday party," Bustamente said, "are you aware of any other pranks Asher has pulled?"

"Just things that he did himself?"

That's a loaded response. Bustamente arched his brows in question. "Anything he was involved in. In any way."

Hayden gulped. "Asher got mad at a teacher once. His geography teacher. He found out where the teacher lived and asked me to spray paint his car. Asher wanted me to do it on a weekend when his mom was taking him to Houston to visit his grandparents. He said nobody would figure out I did it because I had never been in that teacher's class. Asher would have an alibi because he'd be out of town."

The punk was a budding criminal mastermind.

"Did he want you to write any particular message with the spray paint?" Bustamente asked.

"He wanted me to paint 'OK boomer.' The teacher is, like, kind of old." Hayden cringed, as if afraid he'd insulted the detective.

Bustamente chuckled. He wasn't far from retirement himself, but he took aging in stride. "Did you do it? Did you spray paint the teacher's car?"

"No," Hayden said. "I told Asher I couldn't do it because I was grounded that weekend and wouldn't be able to leave my house."

"Why were you grounded?"

"I wasn't, actually." A purple blush raced up Hayden's neck. "I made it up to have an excuse. He said I could sneak out after my parents went to sleep, but I told him our house had an alarm and that it would go off if any of the doors or windows were opened. I told him that my mom had changed the alarm code, and that she didn't give it to me so she could catch me if I tried to sneak out."

The kid had been afraid to stand up to Asher, to directly refuse to do his bidding. Why he'd want a friend who'd put him up to such shenanigans was beyond me. But I couldn't fault him too much. The teen years were difficult. Peer pressure could be intense, and nobody wanted to come off as a nerd.

Bustamente jotted a note, then looked back up. "Anything else he asked you to do?"

"No, sir."

Steven's face was pensive for a few beats, but then his eyes flashed bright as if he'd had an *a-ha!* moment. He sat forward and posed a question to his son. "Do you think some other kids might have set the fire at the school because Asher asked them to?"

Steven had posited an interesting theory. The caller who'd made the false shooter reports and initiated the SWAT responses had presumably done so because it gave them a sense of power. Forcing a response from the fire department would provide the same type of thrill. While Asher might not have set the fire at the school, he might have orchestrated it, recruited minions to do his dirty work, maybe students who hoped to get close to him to raise their own social status. He was obviously a popular boy.

"I don't know." Hayden's shoulders trembled as he raised his palms. "Maybe?"

Steven looked to Bustamente, a scowl on his face. "I wouldn't be surprised if Asher was behind the fire. He's one cocky kid. He had the nerve to ask me to buy alcohol for the sleepover. If he was willing to ask an adult to break the law, he'd have no problem asking kids to do it."

Bustamente shifted his focus from Steven back to his son. "Has Asher asked you to do anything else for him? Something illegal? Dangerous? Destructive?"

"No."

"What about your other friends? Micah and Cade?"

"If he did, they never told me."

Steven chimed in. "The boys haven't been friends all that long. They went to different middle schools and didn't meet until they all went out for the baseball team last school year." He exhaled a sharp breath. "Obviously, Hayden won't be spending any more time with Asher."

Ping! Bustamente pulled his cell phone from his breast pocket, opened the text, and reviewed the image before holding his phone out so I could read the lab report, too. Per the analysis, Hayden Quinn's palm print did not match the one on the cell phone found at the stadium. He wasn't the caller. *But had it been Asher?* Circumstantial evidence certainly seemed to point to him.

Bustamente slid his phone back into his pocket. "I've got good news for you, son. The lab cleared you. The prints on the phone aren't yours."

Hayden didn't look surprised, but his body relaxed anyway. He appeared glad to have his story confirmed.

Steven snorted in disgust. "I bet the phone was Asher's. He's spoiled and irresponsible. He left a water bottle at our house after the sleepover. A Yeti. That brand is expensive."

"He did?" Hayden asked. "I didn't see it."

"It was lying on your floor," Steven said, "with your dirty laundry. Still is, as far as I know."

I entered the conversation now. "You haven't returned the water bottle to Asher, then?"

"No," Steven said. "I figured he could get it the next time he came over."

I turned and exchanged a glance with Bustamente. "Should we compare the prints on the bottle to the ones on the phone before we head to the Burkes' house?" If the prints matched, we could bring charges against the boy at one time for both calls—the one falsely reporting the shooters at the mall and the one made from the stadium.

Bustamente agreed it was a good idea. "Might as well get all our ducks in a row." He asked me to round up the evidence and take it to the lab while he typed up his notes from Hayden's interview. Turning back to the trio across the table, he told them they were free to go. "Thanks for your cooperation."

Hayden released a long breath in relief. Steven reached over to give his son a supportive pat on the shoulder. The attorney checked the time on his watch and made a quick note in his phone, probably for billing purposes.

While Bustamente stayed behind to prepare his formal notes, the rest of us exited the building en masse. It was half past eight now, and the sun was low in the sky. Even so, the temperature was stifling, and I found myself wishing autumn would come early.

I loaded Brigit in her kennel and followed the Quinns back to their house, parking at the curb while Steven pulled the Camaro into the garage. He left the garage door open and waited for me inside. I rounded up latex gloves and evidence bags from my trunk, and brought them and my partner with me.

I glanced around as I entered the garage. A scooter leaned against a wall, the dust on the handles telling me it hadn't been ridden in quite some time. A topless plastic bin held a variety of outdoor children's toys, including a battery-operated bubble machine and several Super Soaker water guns, an essential summertime toy for young kids forced to suffer through the relentless Texas summers. A large bag of charcoal briquettes sat on the floor, with a pair of heat-resistant grilling gloves and a plastic bottle of lighter fluid beside it. In Texas, barbecue grills were considered a mandatory cooking appliance. Men here measured their masculinity by the horsepower of their pickup trucks and the size of their grills. Some opted for high-end high-tech propane grills, but the charcoal told me that Steven Quinn was old school. While the lighter fluid caught my eye, it didn't raise my suspicions. In fact, it would have been suspicious if there were no lighter fluid accompanying the charcoal, which could have meant that Hayden or Asher might have taken it to start the fire at the school.

In a corner was a tall stack of boxes with the neon green logo of Physical Force Supplements, the same brand as the sample Seth had brought home from the fire station. The boxes contained the Force variety according to the printing on the box, which read FORCE = MASS X ACCELERATION. I pointed to the boxes. "You must be a distributor." *Why else would he have so many cartons of product?*

Steven said, "I'm into fitness. A lot of my buddies are, too"

He was certainly in good shape. Some men had developed sizable beer bellies and B-cup man boobs by his age.

Steven opened the door that led to the kitchen, but I stopped him before he and his son stepped inside. "Hayden," I said, "show me the bat Asher smashed the phone with."

Hayden stepped over to a rack mounted on the wall. The rack held a half dozen bats. Some were made of wood, while others were made of metal. Hayden pulled a shiny aluminum bat from the rack and held it out to me. "He used the end to smash the phone."

I took a closer look. The end of the bat bore some minor scratches. "Where did he smash the phone?"

Hayden pointed to the floor under the rack. "Right there."

I handed the bat back to him, pulled my flashlight from my belt, and knelt down to look around. I turned the flashlight on and shined the light around the area. Sure enough, a tiny piece of black plastic about the size of a pencil eraser lay in the dust that had accumulated at the bottom of the wall. I donned a pair of gloves and picked up the piece. To my delight, I realized it was the zero key from the phone. The space bar icon appeared to the right of the zero on the tiny key. It looked like the key was winking at me, as if to say *We got him!* I slid the key into an evidence bag, and used a pen to mark on the bag, noting the place, date, and time I collected the evidence. I spotted no other pieces of the smashed phone on the floor. "May I inspect your garbage bin?"

"Of course." Steven opened the lid for me and even offered to hold my flashlight so I could better see inside.

Knowing the garbage had been picked up at least twice since the incident at the mall, I didn't bother looking through the bag inside. I lifted it up to see if any shards might remain in the bottom. None did. I set the bag back into the bin and closed the lid.

Steven motioned for me to follow him and Hayden inside. Brigit and I trailed them to the boy's room. The place smelled of adolescent body odor mixed with a musky deodorant spray. The aroma gave me flashbacks to when my younger brothers were in their Axe era. They'd coated themselves in the stuff.

I looked around but saw no water bottle on the dresser, desk, or night table.

Steven pointed down at the foot of the unmade bed. "I accidentally kicked the bottle under the bed when I was picking up laundry."

I crouched down and reached a gloved hand underneath to feel around. I pulled out a pair of rumpled underpants—ICK!—then a sneaker before my fingers encountered a hard metal cylinder. The water bottle. I pulled it out, too. The model had a black screw-top lid. I could hear and feel a few ounces of liquid sloshing around inside. Brigit stretched out her neck and sniffed it, probably disappointed it wasn't something to eat. I stood and held it up for Hayden to identify. "This is Asher's?"

"Yes, ma'am."

I bagged and notated the evidence. "Mind if I look around?"

"Feel free," Steven said. "I don't think Asher left anything else, though."

I was actually looking for anything that might incriminate Hayden, indicate that he'd lied to Detective Bustamente about his involvement in the shooter hoaxes or fire at the high school, maybe packaging or a receipt for a burner phone or feminine products. The boy's trash can held precious little. He'd left his empty soda cans and potato chip wrappers lying around his room. I took a quick peek in the secondary bathroom. Wet towels lay on the floor, and the tub and toilet both looked as if they hadn't been scrubbed in weeks. There was nothing unusual in the bathroom trash can, drawers, or cabinets. The guest room had been set up as a home office, and was neat and tidy. The master bedroom was also relatively clean. One side of the walk-in closet was empty, as were two of the three drawers in the bathroom. There were no women's products anywhere in the bathroom. Steven still wore his wedding ring, though. These facts told me that Steven and his wife must have separated fairly recently. It also told me that he might be hoping for a reconciliation. Otherwise, he'd have taken over her side of the closet and her drawers in the bathroom, and removed his wedding ring. *Is that why he seemed annoyed when his son referred to this place as his 'dad's house?'*

Having obtained what I came for, I thanked the two of them. "I'm done here."

Steven walked me to the door. "If we can be of any further assistance, just let me know."

"Will do. Thanks." With that, Brigit and I left.

I circled round to the station, where I picked up Detective Bustamente. Our first stop was at the home of Cade Cox. His mother answered the door in her bath robe. When we told her we were there to ask her son some questions, she invited us inside. The living room wall was decorated with an assortment of crosses, and a figurine of the Virgin Mary stood atop the fireplace mantle next to eight-by-ten-inch professional photos of a boy in a Paschal High School baseball uniform and baseball glove, and a younger girl in a soccer uniform, her arms crossed over her chest in a tough stance, her left cleat atop a black and white ball. Mrs. Cox offered us seats on the sofa, and hollered up the stairs to her son. "Cade? Come on down here!"

A few seconds later, we heard a door open upstairs and thundering footsteps as the boy took the stairs at warp speed. "I'm in the middle of a game. What do you wa—" He went silent mid word when he spotted Bustamente and me on the couch, and took the rest of the steps slowly and quietly. Cade had sandy blond hair and the bumpy face that often accompanied adolescence. His eyes were wide as he looked from me, to the detective, to his mother. "What's going on?"

She jerked her head toward an easy chair. "Sit. These folks have some questions for you."

Bustamente said, "We'd like to know what happened the evening you were at Hayden Quinn's birthday sleepover."

Cade squirmed in his seat. "Hayden's dad ordered pizza. After the delivery guy brought it, his dad left and we played video games all night."

"And?" Bustamente said. "Anything else happen you might want to share with us?"

The boy looked from Bustamente to his mother, appearing queasy. "I don't want to get in trouble!"

Bustamente's voice was gentle. "The best way to avoid trouble is to tell us the truth."

"Okay." He slouched back against the chair, seemingly resigned.

"I'm guessing you're here about the phone call that Asher made to nine-one-one?"

"Tell us about that," the detective said.

"None of us knew he was going to do it," Cade said, sitting up. "We were just playing games and then Asher pulled out this crappy phone and showed it to us. Micah asked him why he'd bought it. Next thing we know, he's talking to somebody and saying there's three people at the mall with guns. He changed his voice so he'd sound like a girl. After he hung up, he laughed his butt off while the rest of us flipped out. Micah said we should call nine-one-one again and tell them it was a mistake, but Asher said we were overreacting. He got one of Hayden's bats and used it to destroy the phone so it couldn't be traced. He turned on the television to see if they'd report what was happening at the mall. A few minutes later a breaking news report came on, and when he saw the SWAT truck in the video he laughed his butt off again. Then Hayden's dad came back home and we all pretended like we knew nothing about it."

While Cade had added a few more details to flesh out the story, none of what he'd said conflicted with what Hayden had told us. When Bustamente asked him about the following Friday at Farrington Field, Cade's story once again matched Hayden's.

Bustamente stood. "That's all we need for now. Thanks for speaking with us." He gave Cade a pointed look. "Don't tell Asher that we came to see you."

As Cade nodded, his mother said, "I'll make sure of that." She held out her hand. "Give me your phone."

Cade reached into the back pocket of his jeans, pulled out his cell phone, and placed it in his mother's hand before hanging his head.

"You're grounded for a month!" she snapped.

He looked up, mouth gaping. "But I didn't do anything!"

"It's what you *didn't* do that you're grounded for," she said. "I raised you better than this! You should've called the police from Hayden's house, or at least phoned me or your father and let us know what Asher had done so we could handle things."

I felt a little sorry for the kid, but I hoped he'd learn to stand up for what's right. Maybe four weeks at home would teach him that lesson.

Bustamente, Brigit, and I returned to my cruiser, and drove to the home of Micah Peters. We rang the doorbell. A few seconds later, a boy's voice came from the other side of the door. "My parents went out to dinner and a movie. They told me not to open the door for anyone."

Bustamente stared directly at the peephole. "I believe they'd make an exception for law enforcement, but if you'd like to call them first to ask, we'll wait."

Of course, Micah didn't want to call his parents. He opened the door a few inches and peeked through the crack. He had brown hair, fair skin, and a long face, thanks to an oversized chin. Still, he was a cute kid, with thick eyelashes and deep dimples. "Um … what … why …"

Bustamente got right to the point. "Tell us about the phone call made from Hayden Quinn's birthday party. If you're honest with us, you won't be in any trouble."

He stood straighter and opened the door a few more inches. "The phone call to the police? Asher made it. He didn't say anything before he did it or Cade, Hayden, and I would have tried to stop him. We thought maybe he'd prank call some girls, but we didn't think he'd call the police. We were shook. We tried to get him to call back and say it was a joke, but he wouldn't do it. He just kept laughing like it was hilarious, and he got all hyped up when he saw the news report on TV."

Bustamente asked him about the football game the following week. Micah gave the same story as Hayden and Cade. In return, Bustamente gave him the same admonishment not to notify Asher of our visit.

"I won't," Micah said. "I don't want to hang with him anymore, anyway."

"Smart decision." Bustamente gave the kid a dip of his head in goodbye and we returned to my cruiser. There, the detective got on the mic and requested an officer to meet us at Asher Burke's address for an anticipated transport.

Officer Spalding replied. "I'm two blocks away. I'll head over now."

I shifted the car into drive, and away we went to bag our prey.

51

SCENT OF A SUSPECT

Brigit had recognized the scent of the man who'd come to the door earlier, the one who'd later met them at the police station. She'd first smelled it at the high school, when Megan had directed her to track there. The water from the fire hoses had washed much of the scent away, or moved it to other areas, and Brigit hadn't been able to keep on the trail that night. But she'd done her best, leading them to the sewer. She'd smelled the man's scent again at the nursing home. That time, she'd tracked him all the way to where he'd climbed into his car. His scent hadn't been the only one Brigit had smelled. She'd detected the smell of another man, too, one who had also been at the high school. She'd caught a little whiff of the second man on some boxes in the garage. That man hadn't been at the house, though.

When she'd first recognized the man's scent at his house, she'd sat down on the porch and issued her passive alert. She'd looked up at Megan, hoping her partner would understand the message she was trying to give her, that this man had been one of the people she'd tracked before. But Megan hadn't looked down at her. Brigit figured Megan didn't know to look down at her because she hadn't issued her the order to track. She'd lifted her leg and gently pawed at Megan, but Megan had been busy listening to the others talk and paid her no attention. Brigit figured maybe Megan already knew that this man had been at the high school and nursing home, that maybe that was the reason why they'd come to his house. Still, she would have appreciated a treat for going the extra mile. *What's a dog gotta do to get paid?*

52
MALE BONDING

The Flamethrower

Steven's thoughts and feelings were all over the place, colliding inside him as he drove his son home from the police station. He was angry about the legal fees he'd have to pay the defense attorney, but he was relieved his son wouldn't be charged with a crime. He was upset that his son considered their family's residence to be his "dad's house" now rather than his home. He was annoyed and ashamed that his son didn't stand up to Asher after the prick had called in the false police report from their house. But mostly, he was gloating at his own genius for implicating Asher in the fire at the high school, even if only indirectly.

They'd driven in silence for a minute or two when Hayden sniffled and sobbed, "Please don't tell Mom!"

Steven had zero intention of telling his estranged wife that he and their son had ignored her direct order that Hayden not associate with Asher. Hell, Steven would be in more trouble than Hayden if Gretchen found out. She might even try to get full custody. Even so, Steven realized his son's request gave him a chance to play the hero. He wouldn't give in right away, though. The boy needed to learn a lesson. Fighting the urge to smile, Steven cut his son a sideways look. "A family shouldn't have secrets."

"But Mom will kill me!" Hayden cried. "I'll be grounded for life!"

Steven met his son's desperate gaze and pretended to think things over for a moment. "I don't want you to get in hot water with your mom. If you promise that you'll stay away from Asher, I won't tell her."

"I promise! Thanks, Dad!"

Hayden reached across him to give him a hug. Probably not the safest thing to do while Steven was driving, but it felt good to get some affection from his kid. It had been far too long since anyone had made him feel loved.

53
ARRESTED DEVELOPMENT

Megan

Detective Bustamente, Brigit, and I pulled up to the Burke residence in the Colonial Hills neighborhood and turned to take a look. The house was a sprawling classic two-story red brick model, with white columns, black shutters, and a broad balcony overlooking the meticulously landscaped front yard. It was nearly ten o'clock and the night was fully dark, but the bright beams of elegant up-lights illuminated the walls, emphasizing the height of the structure. An iron gate spanned the driveway, the metal adorned with a large letter B for Burke. Through the bars of the gate, we could see a shimmering swimming pool with a fancy stone waterfall, much swankier than the plastic above-ground pool back at my place. Even with the relatively affordable housing prices in Texas, the Burkes' property had to be valued at two million or more.

Leaning back against his cruiser at the curb was Officer Spalding, a beefy Black beat cop in his mid-thirties. Spalding was the strong, silent type, greeting us only with a lift of his chin as we emerged from my car.

Bustamente tucked the evidence bag containing Asher's water bottle into the inside pocket of his sport coat, and led the charge to the porch. Spalding and I flanked him, with Brigit on all fours by my side. The detective pressed the doorbell, which was a smart model with a camera and microphone.

A moment later a man's voice came through a speaker. "This is the homeowner."

Bustamente said, "We're from the Fort Worth Police Department."

"I can see that," Mr. Burke said. "I assume you've got a good reason for ringing my bell at this late hour?"

Sheesh. It was easy to see where Asher got his sense of entitlement. You'd think the guy would be concerned about police officers at his door. A visit from law enforcement typically meant there was some sort of emergency, a car accident or a family member who'd been a victim of violent crime. Then again, some people saw police as a nuisance—except when they were the ones to summon us for assistance. I'd learned fairly quickly in my police career that some folks considered the police to be their personal security service, existing only to protect them and their property, not to issue them citations for running their lawn sprinklers in violation of watering restrictions or speeding tickets when they tested the limits of their top-of-the-line Tesla.

Bustamente gave the camera lens a pointed look. "Come to your door, sir."

"It'll take a minute," he said. "We were in the hot tub. We'll need to dry off."

"We'll be waiting," Bustamente replied.

Shortly thereafter, the door opened and a White man and woman stood there, both tall, both attractive, and both in bathing suits and flip-flops. The man had short gray hair and a striped beach towel draped over his bare shoulders, while the woman had a towel in a palm tree print wrapped around her torso. Her dark hair, the same color as Asher's, was pulled up into a messy pile atop her head, probably to keep the bubbling water from getting it wet.

"What's this about?" Mr. Burke demanded.

Rather than immediately answer the question, the detective extended his hand. "I'm Detective Hector Bustamente. I assume you two are Mr. and Mrs. Burke? Asher's parents?"

"We are." Mr. Burke grudgingly took Bustamente's hand and gave it a quick shake before dropping it like a hot potato.

"We'd like to speak to Asher."

"He's not here." Mr. Burke didn't elaborate on Asher's whereabouts.

"When do you expect him?"

"I couldn't tell you. He doesn't have a curfew."

Mrs. Burke tilted her head. "What's this about?" Her breath held the unmistakable scent of chardonnay.

Bustamente said, "We're following up on our earlier discussion with him, about the cell phone we found at Farrington Field."

The Burkes exchanged puzzled glances. Asher must not have informed them that he'd been pulled out of class by law enforcement a few days prior.

Bustamente's brows rose. "Asher didn't tell you that we talked to him at the high school?"

Rather than answer the question, Mr. Burke narrowed his eyes. "Why all the fuss over a cell phone? And why do you think our son knows anything about it?"

"The phone was used to call in the threat of a mass shooting at the football game last Friday," Bustamente said. "Only one person's prints appeared on the phone. Asher's."

The two went rigid for a moment, their eyes on us, almost as if they were afraid that exchanging another glance would raise more suspicion. The volume and pitch of Mr. Burke's voice rose, along with his ire. "You took our son's fingerprints? Without our permission?"

"We didn't have to take his prints. We lifted them from his water bottle." Bustamente reached into his jacket and pulled the bottle from his pocket. Though it was still bagged, it was easily visible through the clear plastic.

Neither of them denied that the bottle was Asher's, though Mr. Burke asked where Bustamente had obtained it.

"From the Quinns' residence. Asher left it there."

Mrs. Burke flung her hand dismissively. "Asher carries that bottle everywhere. Anyone could have touched it. You must have compared the wrong prints."

"There was only one set of prints on the bottle. Logic says they're your son's."

"I disagree." Mr. Burke crossed his arms over his chest in defiance. "How do you know the bottle hadn't been washed?"

I chimed in then. "The bottle was on its side under a bed. There's still some liquid inside. If it had been washed, it would be empty and it wouldn't have been on the floor."

Rather than further argue the point, Bustamente addressed the other evidence against Asher. "We have three witnesses who say that Asher called in the report of the alleged shooters at Chisholm Trail Mall. All three also said that he left the stands at Farrington Field by himself just prior to the time that the threat to the stadium was phoned in to dispatch."

"Three witnesses?" Mrs. Burke pursed her lips. "You must be referring to those boys from the J.V. baseball team. They probably made up this ridiculous story because they're jealous. Asher's being moved up to varsity this year. They aren't."

Bustamente wasn't impressed with the explanation she'd offered. "It seems doubtful they would all be jealous enough to lie to the police. Besides, I interviewed each of them separately. Their stories matched."

Mr. Burke continued to dig in his proverbial heels. "That doesn't mean anything. They could have agreed on what to say." He raised his arm, putting a hand higher up on the door as if preparing to close it. "We're not going to accomplish anything here tonight. Why don't y'all come back tomorrow?"

"After noon," Mrs. Burke added. "Asher likes to sleep in."

Even Brigit seemed to understand how disrespectful and stubborn these people were being. She gave them a withering look with her big brown eyes.

Headlights came up the street behind us, a vehicle going much too fast. The driver hit the brakes as the car approached the Burkes' driveway. Because the house sat on a curve, the occupants must not have noticed the two cruisers at the curb. The car lurched to a stop at an angle on the drive. The passenger door flew open and Asher emerged, laughing at something someone in the car had said. He slammed the door, turned, and took three steps onto the grass before looking up and realizing six sets of eyes were on him. He stopped in his tracks. Though I couldn't hear his words, his lips clearly formed the words *Oh fuck!*

His friends noticed us now, too. The driver unrolled his window. "Dude! Why are cops here?"

Asher put a hand behind him and motioned for them to go. He turned his head to the side. "I'll text you later." He proceeded to take a shortcut across the lawn and stepped up onto the porch from the flowerbed on the other side of Officer Spalding. "Hey." His tone and manner were nonchalant as he looked from Spalding, to me, to Bustamante. "What's up?"

"We've got some more questions for you, Asher," Bustamante said. "We'd like to discuss them with you at the station."

Asher raised his palms. "Why can't I answer them here?"

I knew Bustamante wanted to perform the interview on his home turf so he could record the exchange before remanding Asher to the custody of the juvenile detention center. But he simply said, "A porch isn't the most comfortable spot for an extended conversation."

Asher cut a look up at his father, and his father turned his attention back to the detective, easing forward to the threshold. "Look. It's late. No sense staying up until all hours to discuss some harmless prank phone calls. Let's do this in the morning."

"No, sir," Bustamente said, his tone firm yet professional. "This conversation will take place tonight. The false reports were serious crimes. The SWAT team responded and mobile command centers were established. People were injured. Property was damaged. The cost to the public and the police department was considerable."

His arms hung by his side, and he surreptitiously twitched his finger, signaling Spalding to take Asher into custody. But before Spalding could take Asher's arm, Mr. Burke yanked Asher inside and shoved the door closed. Or at least he attempted to. *Swish!* I'd anticipated the move and been just a little quicker. I'd whipped out my telescoping nightstick, flicked my wrist to extend it, and swung it between the door and frame, preventing the door from closing. The door slammed against my baton and bounced back open, revealing three surprised faces.

Spalding seized the momentary advantage to grab Asher's upper arm, pull him out onto the porch, and wrangle the stumbling boy down the steps.

As the Burkes moved forward, Detective Bustamente held up his hands. "Stop!"

I swiveled my wrist, turning my baton crossways across the open doorway to form a barrier. While the Burkes seemed disinclined to respect Bustamente or me and both took another step forward, they halted when Brigit bared her teeth beside me, emitting a low growl that said they'd better do what we human officers told them to or else they'd have to deal with *her*.

"You're obstructing justice," Bustamente calmly told the Burkes. "Unless you would like to be charged with a crime, I'd suggest you move back and let us do our jobs."

This time, the couple complied with his request, but not without protest.

"This is absolute bullshit!" Mr. Burke hollered.

"A travesty!" Mrs. Burke cried.

While Spalding cuffed Asher and led him to his cruiser, Brigit danced on her paws beside me. She knew that when voices were raised, there was a good chance she was in for some fun. The Burkes looked down at Brigit again and, seeming to realize she was raring to tangle with them, took another step back.

Mrs. Burke's towel came loose and fell open, revealing her wet bikini. She was in remarkably good shape. Either she worked out, or she'd had cosmetic surgery. Maybe both. She wrestled the towel back into place. "You can't just take our son away!"

We could and we would. Still, there was no sense unnecessarily antagonizing these folks. Bustamente said, "You are welcome to join us at the station." He gave them the address.

Mr. Burke raised a finger and poked it in the detective's face, much closer than he should have. "You don't ask my son a single question until I get a lawyer. You hear me?"

Bustamente dipped his chin in agreement. "Yes, sir."

Mr. Burke slammed the door so hard in our faces that the porch lights rattled. We turned and headed back to my cruiser. Brigit looked disappointed that there'd been no action. I gave her a peanut butter-flavored doggie biscuit as a consolation prize.

It was half past midnight by the time the Burkes were able to retain an attorney and get him down to the station. By that time, we'd taken an official set of Asher's prints, and they'd been confirmed to be the same as those lifted from his water bottle and the cell phone.

The first thing Bustamente did was inform the Burkes, Asher, and his attorney that the prints taken from Asher at the station matched those on the phone recovered from the stadium. The detective looked Asher in the eye. "Did you place a call to nine-one-one reporting alleged shooters at Chisholm Trail Mall?"

"No," Asher said.

"What about a call from Farrington Field to report an alleged mass shooting to take place at halftime?"

"No. I didn't make that call either." Asher looked and sounded remarkably cool, but his relaxed demeanor was less likely a sign of innocence and more likely a sign he was a sociopath.

Though I knew Bustamente thought Asher was lying, he played along. "Do you know who made the calls?"

"Hayden Quinn made both of those calls. Or at least the first one. He said he wanted to 'stir up some shit' to make his birthday more fun." Asher used his index and middle fingers to form air quotes around the phrase. "That's why Hayden called in the fake report about the shooters at the mall. He brought another phone to the football game and dropped it in the bleachers. I picked it up for him. That's why my prints are on it."

It was an obvious lie or Asher's fingerprints would have appeared elsewhere on the phone, too, not just on the lower backside, but Bustamente continued to let the boy dig a hole for himself. The attorney did, too, having apparently bought the story Asher had fed him when they'd met privately. Or maybe the attorney didn't buy it, but figured if his client lied to him, it was at his own risk. He'd get paid either way.

Bustamente said, "Hayden told us you made the call from his birthday party."

"Hayden is a liar," Asher said in a matter-of-fact tone. "The other guys and I tried to get Hayden to call back and tell y'all that the call about shooters at the mall was a joke, but he wouldn't do it. We were afraid he'd get the rest of us in trouble. He swore to us that he'd never call in a false report again."

Asher was essentially telling the same story we'd heard from Hayden, Cade, and Micah, but switching his and Hayden's roles.

The attorney chimed in. "Asher mentioned that Hayden's parents are getting divorced and things have gotten nasty. Hayden and his mother have moved in with her new boyfriend. His mom and her boyfriend have been away in Europe for an extended vacation, and they dumped Hayden on his father. The boy must have made the calls to get some attention."

"Poor thing," Mrs. Burke piled on, shaking her head in a seemingly sympathetic gesture. "It can be hard on kids when their parents split. It's no wonder he acted out."

Bustamente cocked his head and stared intently at Asher. "What about the other two boys who corroborated Hayden's story?"

"Cade and Micah?" Asher shrugged. "They're way better friends with Hayden than with me. They all went to elementary school and junior high together. I didn't meet them until last year when we all went out for the Paschal High baseball team. They're mad that the coach is planning to move me up to varsity, but not them. I think that's why they threw me under the bus."

Bustamente retrieved his laptop from its bag under the table, booted it up, and said, "Tell me what's happening here."

He played the video footage of Asher buying the phone in Walmart. As the recording played, Asher stared intently at the screen. *Too* intently. His father sat stiffly, looking increasingly nauseated, while his mother chewed her lip and crossed her legs, swinging the top one so fast and furious she moved up and down in her seat like a dancer performing a can-can. After a few swings, Mr. Burke reached under the table and put a hand on his wife's thigh to halt her movements.

Bustamente paused the video as the boy walked directly under the camera at the exit. "Is that you, Asher?"

Though the detective had addressed his son, Mr. Burke interceded. "That can't be Asher. You can see the boy is wearing an Arlington Heights High School T-shirt. Asher doesn't attend that school."

Nice try. It was obvious Asher's parents recognized him in the video.

Ignoring Mr. Burke, Bustamente addressed Asher again. "Is that you, Asher?"

Mrs. Burke interrupted now, flapping a hand at the computer. "The recording is grainy. That could be anyone."

Disregarding her now, too, Bustamente repeated his question a third time. "Asher, is that you? Yes or no?"

Asher stared silently at the table as if trying to come up with a believable story, yet realizing the detective might have other evidence on him that had yet to be revealed. Asher hedged his bets. "I don't think so."

Bustamente took another tack. "Did you go into the Walmart on Jacksboro Highway last Friday prior to going to Farrington Field?"

Asher hiked a single shoulder. "I don't remember."

I fought the urge to roll my eyes.

Bustamente cocked his head. "Do you remember walking to the mobile home neighborhood behind the store?"

Asher's only reply was another lift of his shoulder.

"Maybe this will jog your memory." Bustamente played the feed from the doorbell camera.

On seeing the young man in the athletic shirt, Mrs. Burke emitted an almost imperceptible squeak and put her fingers to her lips. Mr. Burke cut her a warning look so sharp and cold she could have used it to carve an ice sculpture. Taking note, the attorney said, "I'd like another moment alone with my client."

Asher put up his hand. "It's okay." Turning to Bustamente, he said, "Look. I didn't want to get Hayden into any more trouble, but I don't really have a choice now. Hayden begged me to buy him the phone. He said he needed a second phone because his mother checks his texts and call history. She tells him who he's allowed to hang out with, too. She treats him like a baby. I thought I was doing him a favor. I didn't know he was going to use it to call in the fake report to the police."

Mrs. Burke nodded profusely. "See? Asher was trying to help a friend. That's all." She placed her hands palms down on the table, as if the matter were closed. It was anything but.

Asher's story had several holes, as Bustamente pointed out with his follow-up question. "Why couldn't Asher just buy the phone himself with cash? His mother would never have known."

Asher had another lie at the ready. "Because she keeps track of all of his spending, too. She makes him account for every cent he takes out of his bank account. At least, that's what he told me."

I had to give the kid credit. It was a clever response. Still, it didn't get Asher off the hook.

"You claimed that you, Cade, and Micah had been upset about the call Hayden had made to nine-one-one before, at his birthday party. Why would you buy him a phone when he might use it to make another false report to the police?"

"Because he promised us he wouldn't." Asher pulled a sad face. "I thought I could trust him."

Mrs. Burke sat up again, indignantly poking out her breasts. "Hayden's the one who should be in the hot seat here. Not Asher!"

Ignoring her, Bustamente continued to question Asher. "Did you also buy the phone used to call in the report of the shooter at the mall?"

Asher hesitated a few seconds too long, making it clear he was calculating the odds that the detective already knew the truth. "Nnnooo," he said, drawing the word out as if unsure.

Bustamente attempted to pin him down. "Did you arrange for someone else to purchase the phone?"

Asher turned his head, cracking his neck, again seeming to be trying to buy time to think. If he said yes, he'd have to explain why he felt it was necessary to have someone else make the purchase given that Hayden had yet to purportedly call in the shooters at the mall. There'd be no reason for him to suspect his friend was going to use the phone for an illegal purpose. If he said he hadn't arranged for someone else to purchase the phone, he could be caught in a lie. "No. I didn't arrange for someone else to buy the phone for Hayden."

Asher's response was so particular and precise that it was clearly intended to be deceptive and evasive.

Bustamente must have thought so, too, because he followed up with, "Did you have someone else buy the phone for *you*?"

Asher hesitated once more, then shook his head.

Bustamente stared him down. "What if I told you that I spoke to a man who claims he was paid to purchase the phone at a Dollar General store on Berry Street? And that the person who paid him fit your description, right down to the mirrored sunglasses?"

Asher raised his palms. "Don't know what to tell you, bro."

Bustamente asked another follow-up question. "If Hayden's mother kept track of his spending, how did he pay you back for the phones?"

"He got the money from his father. He plays his parents against each other so they'll give him more stuff."

I wasn't sure whether Asher was telling the truth about Hayden manipulating his parents but, if he had, he certainly wouldn't be the first child of divorced parents to turn a difficult situation to their advantage.

Bustamente went on. "Your teacher saw you walk away from the condiment stand where she found the phone was abandoned. She said you were alone. Her story corroborates what the other boys have said, that you left the bleachers a few minutes before halftime by yourself."

"That's not true," Asher said. "Hayden came down with me. I went to the restroom but he didn't. He told me to meet him by the concession stand when I was done. He must have made the call and hidden the phone while I was in the restroom. Mrs. Pollard talked to me before I met back up with Hayden." The boy had the nerve to look smug, thinking his story was airtight and would get him off the hook.

Bustamente pulled out the little notebook that he made notes in and flipped through the pages, refreshing his memory. "Mrs. Pollard said she saw you walk back up the ramp into the stadium alone."

"Hayden and I weren't talking," Asher said, with yet another shrug. "She must not have realized we were together."

"What about the girls you sat with?"

Asher's eyes went wide and he rose an inch or two from his seat, as if his fight or flight instinct had been activated. "What girls?"

"The ones who saved seats at the stadium for you and the other boys. I understand y'all had good seats. Fifth row, thirty-five-yard line." Bustamente consulted his notes again. "Brooklyn and Makayla." He looked up. "What do you think they'd tell me if I asked them who left the bleachers just before halftime? Do you think they'd tell me both you and Hayden left the stands, or would they tell me it was only you?"

"I don't know." Asher slouched back in his seat, his chest rising and falling more rapidly as he finally seemed to realize he wasn't as clever as he'd thought, that his story was unravelling. "They might lie, too."

Mr. Burke's jaw clenched and a thick vein throbbed in his neck. Mrs. Burke simply appeared bewildered.

"Why would they lie?" the detective asked. "They're friends of yours, correct?"

"They're friends with all of us, really. Makayla's been dropping all kinds of hints that she wants me to ask her out, but she's not my type. She could be angry about that. Hayden's been crushing hard on Brooklyn, and she seems to like him too, so she might lie to protect him. She's also Makayla's best friend, so, you know. She might lie to get back at me for not asking her friend out."

Teenagers could certainly be petty. Hell, so could adults. But I doubted that all three boys and both girls would lie to the police.

Bustamente continued his line of questions. "You were the one who asked the girls to save seats for you, Hayden, Cade, and Micah. Correct?"

Asher hesitated again. "I don't remember."

"You don't remember," Bustamente repeated.

Asher lost his cool and threw his hands in the air. "It's just seats! God! It wasn't a big deal."

Bustamente gave him a few seconds to calm down before continuing. "You're quite popular, aren't you?"

"I don't know." Asher jerked a shoulder again. "I guess."

"Do other kids often do favors for you?" Bustamente asked. "Like save seats at a football game?"

"Sometimes," Asher replied softly.

"Did you ask any of them to set the fire at the school?"

"What?!" Asher sat bolt upright, frantically looking from the detective to his parents and back again. "Fuck no!"

The attorney leaned forward so he could catch Asher's eye. "Let's watch our language."

Asher scoffed and threw his hands up for a second time. "Whatever! I don't like being accused of something I didn't do!"

Bustamente gave Asher another lingering stare. "I don't think you've been entirely truthful with me tonight, Asher. I'll be turning this case over to the prosecutor. We're going to take you into custody."

The Juvenile Justice Center on Kimbo Road had already closed for the weekend. Asher would be held in the adjacent lockup until the center reopened on Monday morning. *Maybe a weekend there will scare Asher straight.*

Mr. and Mrs. Burke bounced up from their chairs like a couple of jacks-in-the-box and turned to the attorney. Mr. Burke virtually snarled at the man. "What are we paying you for? Do something! Stop this!"

The lawyer made a downward motion with his hand, directing the couple to retake their seats. "There's nothing I can do right now. A judge will consider the matter on Monday. Asher will only be at the juvenile detention center a couple of nights."

Mrs. Burke covered her mouth with her hands, her shoulders shaking as she broke into sobs.

Mr. Burke looked from his wife, to the attorney, to the detective. "Can't we work something out here? We don't want our son tossed into a cell with criminals!"

The man hadn't yet accepted that their son was a criminal himself, having made a terroristic threat and recklessly endangering the lives of others, not to mention giving a false statement to police when we interviewed him at the school. The Burkes didn't seem to realize the enormity of the situation. But it wasn't my place to set them straight, so I kept my mouth shut.

Bustamente stood now, signaling that the discussion was over. "An officer will transport Asher to the juvenile detention center."

Asher stood, as if preparing to bolt. "But I didn't do anything wrong!"

Liar, liar, pants on fire. Then again, I wasn't sure about the fire, though I was certain he'd lied about the phone calls. I stood, too, ready to grab him if necessary.

"Simmer down, Asher," his attorney warned. "Things will get sorted out. The best thing you can do now is cooperate."

Asher didn't heed his attorney's advice. Instead, he raised his foot and kicked his chair over. It clanged to the floor, the top of it slamming down onto his mother's bare toes. She yelped in pain, probably wishing she'd worn something other than sandals. Brigit leapt to her feet under the table and barked. I yanked my handcuffs from my belt, circled around the table at warp speed, and pushed the boy up against the wall to disable him from further mayhem. Fortunately, his attorney helped me immobilize him, grabbing his upper arm tightly. "Stop, Asher! You're only making things worse for yourself!"

After I cuffed Asher, I ordered my partner to be quiet and sit. Brigit obeyed me, but not without giving me a look of disgust. She would have much preferred to take a chunk of meat from the leg of the boy who'd so rudely awakened her from her nap.

While Brigit and I kept an eye on Asher, Bustamente rounded up an officer from the station, who led the kid out to his cruiser for transport. The Burkes followed us out front. When Asher turned his big, wet brown eyes on his parent from the cruiser's window, Mrs. Burke erupted into a fresh wail and Mr. Burke fumed. He rounded on the detective, poking his finger in Bustamente's chest. "I'll have your badge for this!"

The attorney cut Bustamente an apologetic look before chastising his client. "Acting like this doesn't help your son!"

I pointed to the lens of my body cam, keeping an eye on Mr. Burke while speaking to Bustamente. "I've got that recorded, Detective. Would you like me to take Mr. Burke into custody?"

At the thought that not only would her son be taken into custody, but her husband might be, too, Mrs. Burke shrieked, "Noooo!"

Mr. Burke's face reddened, and he raised his hands to his shoulders as if in surrender. "I'm sorry. Truly. My emotions are just running high. Please accept my apology."

Bustamente simply said, "Go home and collect yourselves."

"Yes, sir," said Mr. Burke.

It's about time they showed the detective the respect he deserved.

As the Burkes and their attorney continued on to their cars in the parking lot, I stood by Bustamente's side and watched as the cruiser with Asher in the back seat drove out of the lot, turned the corner, and disappeared out of sight.

I held up a palm. "Congrats, Detective. You got another W."

The high five he gave me was halfhearted at best, but who could blame him? It had been a long, exhausting month. Good thing we had the Labor Day holiday to look forward to.

54
BOYS STINK

Brigit

Brigit was glad to finally be home, snuggling on the bed she shared with Megan, Seth, and Blast. It had been a long day, filled with so many scents that both her nose and brain were exhausted from processing them. *Teenage boys. Ugh.* So many stinky hormones! Not to mention the cologne they all seemed to coat themselves in. She'd forced herself to sneeze several times to try to clear the scents from her snout, but she could still smell them. She thrust her nose under the covers. The sheets smelled like her, Blast, Seth, and Megan—her pack. *Aaah.*

55
RELATIONSHIP STATUS UPDATE

Steven

The doorbell rang promptly at seven o'clock on Sunday evening. As usual, Hayden had waited until the last minute to start gathering up his and Mickey's things, so Steven would have to answer the door. Mickey followed him, his tail wagging like crazy.

When Steven opened the door, Mickey bounded out, yapping with joy at seeing Gretchen on the porch and leaping up on her. "I missed you, too, Mickey!" She bent down, laughing girlishly as the dog licked her all over her face and mouth. *Disgusting.*

As she scooped the dog up, a glint came from within his fur. Gretchen stood with the dog cradled in her arms, petting and sweet-talking the mutt, and Steven got a better look. On the ring finger of her left hand glittered a brilliant diamond, a much bigger one than he'd given her when he'd proposed.

Emotion sucker-punched him in the gut but, a moment later,

molten rage filled every vein in his body. "What's that on your hand?"

She sighed. "You know good and well what it is, Steven."

"You can't be engaged to someone else," he snapped. "You're still married. *To me.*"

Not for long! Though she hadn't said the words outright, he knew her well enough to read her mind.

She stared at him for a long moment, her face hard at first but then it seemed to soften. She set the dog down on the porch. "Despite everything that's happened, I hope you can find happiness in a new relationship, too. You're an attractive guy with a good job. You'd find someone in a heartbeat. Maybe you should start looking."

Start? He'd already been looking—online, anyway. All of the age-appropriate women had baggage. Kids. Exes. Aging parents. *Who wants to deal with that?* The few who didn't have baggage only made him wonder why. There was probably a reason no guy had ever wanted to walk down the aisle with them. But rather than share these thoughts with Gretchen, he changed the subject. "I was thinking I'd take Hayden back to Destin for Labor Day Weekend." The three of them had taken a vacation to the Florida beach town years ago, before Hayden had been old enough to start school, and they'd had a wonderful time. It was one of his happiest memories of the three of them as a family.

"But that's *my* weekend with Hayden," she said.

"Yeah, but I've kept him while you were in France. You owe me."

She frowned. "I don't owe you anything for spending time with your son. You should consider the extra time a bonus."

How dare she twist everything around, make him look like the bad guy! *Bitch.* "I can't believe you'd take a beach trip away from Hayden. The kid deserves to have some fun."

"He does," she agreed. "It's just not a good weekend. We've already made plans for Labor Day."

"He didn't mention them to me."

She let out a slow exhale, as if reluctant to share their plans. "If you must know, we're hosting a pool party."

"Where?"

"At our house. Doak had a pool put in."

Steven nearly blew a gasket. Hayden and Gretchen begged him for years to install a backyard pool, but he'd refused. They could have afforded it, but pools required regular cleaning and maintenance and a bunch of expensive chemicals. He already spent half a day every weekend mowing and trimming and edging the lawn. Winters were shorter now, and he hardly got a break from it. Something was always breaking around the house, too. A clogged shower drain. An off-kilter drawer. A burned-out light bulb. He hadn't wanted another damn thing to take care of. *Maybe I should have given in ...*

Before he could respond, Gretchen said, "Hayden's invited a girl. Brooklyn. He's been looking forward to it."

Steven scrubbed a hand over his face. He didn't want to get in the way of his son's social life. He only wished Hayden had mentioned the party—and the girl.

Gretchen threw him a bone. "Why don't you take him to Florida in October? He has a three-day weekend. They get a Monday off from school for Columbus Day."

"It's called Indigenous People's Day now."

She closed her eyes and took a calming breath before opening them again. "Do you want that weekend or not?"

Florida would still be plenty warm in October, and he could get off-season rates for lodging. But he wasn't about to let her off easy. "I don't really have a choice, do I?"

She ignored his barb and simply said, "Then it's settled." As Hayden came up behind Steven with his bags, she burst into a smile and her focus shifted from Steven to their son. "Hey, boy-o! Guess what?"

Before Hayden could venture a guess, Steven said, "Your mom's engaged."

Gretchen glared up at Steven.

Hayden appeared uncomfortable, as if he wanted to congratulate his mom, but knew it might upset his dad. His gaze darted between them. "Um ... wow. So that's happening, huh?"

Steven gave his son a pat on the back. "Take care, Hayden. See you for dinner on Wednesday."

The teen boy's metabolism took precedence over his mother's romantic life. "Can we get tacos?"

"Hell, yeah, we can get tacos!" Steven said with forced joviality.

Once Hayden had walked out the door, Steven closed it gently, turned, and punched his fist through the wall. Gretchen was marrying that bastard? *It's on now, motherfucker!*

Grimacing, he cradled his injured hand in the other and walked to the kitchen, where he filled a baggie with ice cubes from the freezer. After icing his knuckles for a moment, he shook his hand to get the feeling back and whipped his cell phone from his pocket. He pulled up Nash's name in his contacts and tapped the screen to place the call. He put the phone to his ear only to hear it ring and ring and ring. Nash didn't answer. Voicemail didn't either. *Dammit!*

56
GOODBYE SUMMER

Megan

Asher was released from the juvenile detention center late Monday afternoon after his lawyer negotiated his release. Rather than standing trial, his attorney had convinced him to accept a plea deal under which he'd serve one-hundred hours of community service and undergo counseling. He would be on probation until he turned eighteen. The kid was lucky. The names of juvenile offenders were not released to the media. All the media outlets could report was that an arrest had been made in the case. Hayden, Cade, and Micah were unlikely to tell others what happened, because they wouldn't want their reputations to be sullied, as well. What's more, juvenile records were confidential in Texas, meaning colleges and potential employers would not have access to them later. Asher would get a fresh start, a do-over. *I hope he'll keep his nose clean from now on.*

The rest of the week proceeded without incident. Now that there had been an arrest and the media fervor had settled down, any more would-be copycat callers had decided maybe it wasn't a good idea to make a bogus shooter report to the police. They wouldn't have a scapegoat to pin it on.

With our irregular work schedules, it was a rare treat for Seth and I both to have a day off together. But we got lucky on Labor Day. Neither of us was scheduled to work. We'd be able to enjoy an entire day together, just relaxing and having fun. Though the arson incidents had yet to be sorted out, the resolution of the swatting cases gave us an additional reason to celebrate.

That morning, Seth and I stood side by side in the kitchen as we prepared food for Captain MacDougal's pot luck pool party. Seth cut up the potatoes and boiled them while I rinsed grapes, oranges, blueberries, and strawberries, and layered them in a trifle bowl, turning a simple fruit salad into a colorful rainbow and work of art. Once the potatoes were tender, Seth drained them and dumped them into a large bowl so I could show him how to make my mother's Irish potato salad. We added red wine vinegar and egg-free mayonnaise. *Who needs the cholesterol?* While he chopped green onions, I chopped celery. We added those to the bowl and gave it a good stir to mix things up before putting it in the fridge to cool.

After a leisurely morning spent lingering over coffee and catching up on our favorite sitcoms, we gathered up our pool toys, beach towels, sunscreen, and lawn chairs, and stashed them in the trunk of Seth's Nova, along with a water bowl for the dogs. We changed into our bathing suits, and I grabbed the food while Seth rounded up Brigit and Blast. Captain MacDougal adored Blast, not only for his accelerant-detection capabilities, but also for his sweet nature. He'd invited the dogs to attend his party as well.

We drove over to the captain's house. The dogs snuffled along the walkway as we made our way to the porch. A handwritten sign taped to the door read COME ON IN, so we didn't bother knocking. Classic rock music played softly from speakers in the living room, which was furnished with a contemporary sofa, matching loveseat, and coordinating tables, most likely an economical buy-the-whole-room set. The house had an open concept floor plan, so we could see from the living room into the kitchen and dining area to the windows along the back wall of the house. As we stepped inside, a young dog with wiry gray hair bolted toward us, yapping up a storm. The tag on his collar identified him as Mickey. *That's odd.* He looked remarkably similar to the dog I'd seen at Steven Quinn's house. Mickey, Brigit, and Blast took turns sniffing each other's nether regions to get acquainted.

Several of the firefighters had already arrived, including Frankie. She waved us into the kitchen, where she was cutting up avocados to make guacamole. A pretty ginger-haired woman took the trifle bowl from me, giving us a smile in return. "Welcome! Thanks for bringing actual food. Most of the guys just brought beer."

"Because they are lazy butts!" Frankie called out, pointing an accusing knife at a couple of the men who stood nearby. The two looked up and around, whistling a lively tune and twiddling their thumbs, feigning innocence.

Captain MacDougal sidled up to the ginger-haired woman and wrapped an arm around her shoulders. "Seth and Megan, meet Gretchen. My fiancée."

"Fiancée?" Seth said. "I was only expecting a girlfriend."

The captain grinned. "I gave her a promotion while we were in Paris."

Beaming, Gretchen held up her hand to show off her engagement ring.

I took a close look. "It's gorgeous."

"Congrats, Captain." Seth tucked the bowl of potato salad under one arm and held out the opposite fist. The two bumped knuckles.

Gretchen looked from me to Seth. "I understand you two are headed down the aisle soon, too."

"That's right." Seth placed the bowl on the kitchen island. "Just three more weeks and Megan will be my official ball and chain."

On hearing the word *ball*, Blast looked up, wagged his tail, and issued an excited *arf!* He thought he was about to get some playtime. After we all shared a laugh, Seth pulled a tennis ball from the pocket of his shorts. "I'd better go toss the ball or he'll think I've punked him." Seth went out the back door of the kitchen, followed by Blast, then Brigit, then Mickey, whose paws had to work double time to keep up with the larger dogs.

I turned to Gretchen and asked if there was anything I could do to help. She grabbed a twelve-pack of Dr. Pepper and held it out to me. "Would you mind putting these in the cooler on the patio? My son's out back somewhere. He drinks this stuff by the gallon."

"No problem." I took the pack from her and strode out the rear door.

Wow. The captain's backyard was large and nothing short of spectacular. The patio was wide and deep. Three ceiling fans suspended from the cover provided a cooling breeze to those lounging on the padded wicker furniture. An enormous television was mounted on the back of the house. The TV was tuned to a Texas Rangers baseball game. In the yard, several large, leafy oaks provided respite from the sun. Colorful canvas sunshades had been strung between the trees to provide additional shade. A cornhole game was set up in one corner of the backyard, while a fire pit surrounded by Adirondack chairs took up another.

The captain's new pool was kidney shaped, with an elevated hot tub situated in the center curve and flagstone decking surrounding it. Ceramic pots filled with pink petunias and yellow lantana added splashes of color. A teenaged girl in a pink bikini lounged on an air mattress at the shallow end of the pool, while a boy in a striped bathing suit took a running leap off the diving board at the other end. He was launched upward, seemed to hang in the air for a second or two, and then pulled up his knees as he descended. He wrapped his arms around his calves, forming a perfect cannonball. He hit the surface with a smack, then *sploosh!* A plume of water erupted from the pool and rained down on the giggling girl. *What a couple of flirts.*

Seth stood at the back fence next to Zach, the two of them

chatting as the dogs ran after the ball Seth had just thrown. Zach raised a hand in greeting. With the heavy case of soft drinks in my arms, I couldn't wave back, but I called out a greeting. "Hey, Zach!"

I found the cooler next to the propane grill at the far end of the covered patio. I was bending down, arranging the cans in the cooler when the boy climbed out of the pool and walked up beside me, dripping water onto the concrete. All I could see were his bare feet and legs, and the hem of his striped bathing suit.

"Can I get two of those?" he asked.

"Sure." I grabbed a can of Dr. Pepper in each hand and turned to look up at him, holding them out. I recognized him immediately.

He was a little slower to place me, probably because my hair was down rather than pulled up into a bun, and I was wearing shorts and a tank top over a bathing suit rather than my police uniform. His eyes clouded in confusion for an instant, then went wide. "Oh, my God!"

I stood, putting us eye-to-eye. "Hello again, Hayden."

"Wh-what are you doing here?" he whispered as he took the cans from me.

I gestured to Seth. "My fiancé is a firefighter." I ran my gaze over the boy's features, realizing how much he resembled the captain's fiancée, right down to the ginger-colored hair. "Is Gretchen your mother?"

Hayden sucked his bottom lip into his mouth and nodded, his eyes alight with fear. "Are you going to tell her what happened?"

"You haven't?" I cocked my head in question.

"No." He gulped. "She forbade me from hanging with Asher. She'll be so mad that I went behind her back and did it anyway. I'm not friends with him anymore. None of us are. We used to think he had a lot of rizz, but he's a total Chad."

My conversations with my younger sister Gabby kept me up to date on the current Gen Z lingo, so I knew that rizz was short for charisma and that Chad was a derogatory term for a guy who was cocky and domineering, an alpha male defined by toxic masculinity. *Asher certainly fits the bill.*

I eyed Hayden for a moment, mulling things over. The boy seemed to have learned his lesson about associating with troublemakers. No sense starting some pointless drama or risk embarrassing Hayden, Gretchen, and the captain at their own party. "Don't worry. I won't say anything."

His shoulders relaxed in relief. "Thanks!"

Brigit trotted up and sniffed at Hayden's bare feet.

He looked down, laughed, and wiggled his toes. "That tickles!" He tucked one of the cans under his arm and reached down to give Brigit a pat, then turned and walked over to the girl, who'd folded her arms over the edge of the pool, her legs floating in the water behind her. Hayden handed a can down to her.

Seth and I set up our lawn chairs in the shade of a sprawling tree. We'd sat for only a few minutes before the heat became unbearable. I stripped off my shorts and tank top, and he removed his T-shirt. We sat on the edge of the pool and stuck our feet in to test the waters, then eased into the deep end. The cool water was refreshing. Blast and Brigit leapt in to join us, dog paddling around and loving every second of it. Seth rounded up the tennis ball from the lawn and tossed it across the pool. The dogs raced to retrieve it, each leaving a small wake behind them.

As the day wore on, the captain fired up his grill. The men grabbed beers and gathered around him to joke and talk sports as he grilled hamburgers and hot dogs.

Frankie came over with two cold bottles of hard lemonade in her hands and flopped down in the lawn chair Seth had vacated. After handing me one of the drinks, she angled her bottle toward me, and I clinked the neck of my bottle against hers. "Cheers!"

Gretchen emerged from the house with a pile of hot dog and hamburger buns on a tray, and placed them on a table near the grill before going back inside for the ketchup, mustard, and fixings.

Frankie finished her hard lemonade with a loud gulp, reclined in the lawn chair, and pulled her sunhat down over her face. Within seconds, she was dozing like the dead. *She must've worked the overnight shift.*

From behind my sunglasses, I watched Hayden interact with the girl. I'd heard him call her Brooklyn. I recalled Asher mentioning that Hayden had a crush on a girl named Brooklyn, who'd been one of the two girls who'd saved them seats at the football game. *She must be the same girl.* I watched the two for a while, amused.

A group had gathered in front of the television, and their excited chatter caught my attention. Leaving Frankie snoozing in her chair, I got up and wandered over to the patio, too, stepping into place beside Seth. He slid an arm around my waist without taking his eyes from the screen. The score was tied and the bases were loaded. The Dodgers were poised to take the lead. Everyone stared at the TV, rapt.

The pitcher threw a curveball and the Dodger at home plate swung, sending the ball arcing toward the far reaches of the field. The Rangers' outfielder ran after the fly ball and was about to catch it when a fan with a mitt reached over the wall and snatched the ball out of the air. The group on the patio erupted in shouts and curses, throwing up their hands in exasperation. The Ranger fans were furious. The camera zoomed in as they leapt from their seats, yelling and pointing at the offender. Two security guards rushed down the stands to eject the man from the game. When the camera panned to the umpire, who raised a fist over his head and grabbed the wrist of that hand with his other, my heart skipped a beat. *Isn't that the same signal one of the arsonists made at the high school?* The television announcer repeated the umpire's call. "Spectator interference."

A disturbing thought slithered into my mind. Hayden played baseball. So did his friends. They'd be familiar with the signals umpires used. The arsonist might have given the signal to indicate that a bus was approaching the school. *Could Hayden have been behind the fires at the high school and nursing home?* Maybe Hayden didn't like Captain MacDougal. Maybe he felt angry that the man had come between his mother and father. Maybe he blamed the captain for the breakup of his family and hoped his parents would reconcile.

The night of Hayden's birthday party, someone had set a fire with corn chips in a dumpster behind a fitness center not far from his father's house. In all the hubbub over the mall incident, I'd almost forgotten about it. *Had Hayden and his friends been the ones to start it?* Hayden's father hadn't been home much of the evening. It would have been easy for them to slip out, start the fire, and return without him knowing they'd left the house. But none of the boys at the birthday party were beefy. All were lean. Then again, maybe the person in the video was a boy who hadn't been at the party.

But if Hayden and his friends had started the fires, it seemed that Asher would have snitched on Hayden Friday night, when Bustamente was interrogating him and had asked about the fire at the high school. Asher had no qualms about implicating Hayden in the swatting incidents. Then again, if Asher had played a role in setting the fires, maybe he was glad that law enforcement was only after him for the false shooter reports and not arson charges, as well. He might have kept quiet about the fires and saved his friend's ass only because he thereby also saved his own. *Hmm.*

I was considering these possibilities when Hayden and Brooklyn stopped playing catch with a splash ball in the pool, climbed out, and walked over to the chairs where they'd left their things. He donned a tank top and she slid a knit sundress over her bathing suit before the two proceeded to the patio to help the captain and Gretchen with the food. When Hayden laughed at something Captain MacDougal said and the captain gave him an affectionate pat on the shoulder, I decided I was probably off base. The two seemed to have a good rapport.

Gretchen stepped to the edge of the patio and cupped her hands around her mouth. "The food is ready!"

The group gathered on the patio, filling our plates. Mickey, Brigit, and Blast milled about the crowd, begging for bits of burger or a potato chip to munch on.

Once they'd finished their dinner, Hayden begged off to walk Brooklyn home. "Can I hang at her house for a while?" he asked Gretchen.

"All right," she said. "But don't forget it's a school night. Be home by ten o'clock."

I watched the teenagers go, still wondering if Hayden was truly the relatively good kid he appeared to be, or whether he had us fooled.

57
IT'S A DOG-EAT-DOG WORLD

Brigit

What a fun day! Brigit and Blast had fun running around this new house and lawn, and sniffing new scents. They'd played in the pool with the yappy little dog she'd first met at the other house where the boy had been, too. The dog wasn't so bad once she got to know him. He was just a house pet, with no special skills and only average intelligence, but not every dog was made for tough jobs like her and Blast.

Megan and Seth had fed them bites of hamburger and pieces of hot dog. She hadn't had a hot dog since that night they'd gone to the football stadium. Megan had fed her lots of hot dogs that night. Maybe too many, if such a thing were possible. Her tummy had felt very heavy that night. Brigit had also managed to snatch up a few potato chips today when the party guests dropped them.

But now, she decided it was time for an after-dinner nap. She used her teeth to pull a cushion off a chair and plopped down on it.

Nice and comfy.

58
TOO HOT

Steven sat with a couple of buddies in Hail Mary's, drinking beer, eating nachos, and watching the Rangers game. There'd been lots of action. Some guy had even stuck his mitt over the wall earlier to catch a fly ball. He'd been promptly ejected from the stadium. *Asshole.* True fans didn't interfere in the game.

The door opened and Marco walked in, glancing around. Steven spotted him and waved him over. Marco slid into an empty chair. The server with the Live, Laugh, Love tattoo passed by with a tray perched on her shoulder. She stopped next to their table. "Can I get you something?"

Marco ordered a beer and hot wings.

As soon as the server left, Steven said, "Haven't seen your cousin around in a while."

"Nash?" Marco said, helping himself to a bean-covered nacho

from the platter. "He went back to Oregon. He said Texas was too hot."

Steven wasn't sure if Nash had meant the temperatures or the potential fallout from the nursing home fire but, either way, he wasn't wrong. Fortunately, according to the latest news reports, the fire department still had no leads on the fires set at the high school and retirement residence. *Heh.* Still, he was irked that Nash hadn't told him he was skipping town, and that he wasn't taking his phone calls. Steven had tried several times, but the phone just rang incessantly with no answer. Had Nash gotten a new phone? Blocked him? That was a shitty way to treat someone who'd bought thousands of dollars of his snake-oil supplements.

Steven finished his food and decided to call it a day, tossing a stack of bills onto the table to cover his tab.

Marco looked up from his messy plate of wings. "Leaving already, bro? The game's not over yet."

"I've got some things to do at home." It was true. The toilets needed a good scrubbing, the refrigerator was empty, and laundry had piled up. He missed having a woman around the house to take care of these things. *I should hire a housekeeper.*

After making a stop at the grocery store for a few essentials, he drove home. When his wife, son, and dog had lived with him, the house had been noisy and bustling—*too* noisy and bustling a lot of the time. The constant commotion had gotten on his nerves. Now, though, the house was too calm, too quiet, too empty. The sad place would soon be all his, too. Gretchen's attorney had responded to the property settlement offer and said she had no interest in the house, other than getting her share of the equity, of course. It wasn't a surprise since she was now marrying that asshat and the asshat owned a house—one with a new pool, no less. *Maybe I should sell this place and move.*

He put the groceries away and set to work on the house. As he cleaned the bathrooms, he tried not to think about the fun his estranged wife and son were having at the pool party, about the fire captain who had stolen his family from him. He was unsuccessful. He stewed, taking his anger out on the toilet rings and shower scum. He'd had nowhere to go today other than the sports bar, nobody to spend the holiday with other than a few of his buddies. He'd thought being free of responsibilities would be fun, and it had been, at first. But now, his life felt as empty as his house. At least the bathrooms sparkled after the rage-fueled cleaning he'd given them.

He grabbed a laundry basket from the top of the dryer and carried it into Hayden's room. *Sheesh.* The place smelled like sweaty feet and sausage. The cheap cologne spray did little to mask the teen boy funk. He grabbed the two shirts from the back of the desk chair and tossed them into the basket. He picked up at least a dozen dirty socks from the floor, along with a wet towel that had begun to mildew. *Dammit!* He'd have to rent a machine and clean the carpets. Maybe he'd make Hayden do it, teach the kid a lesson about picking up after himself.

After collecting the remaining clothing, he stripped the bed. The white sheets were yellowed with sweat stains. *Yuck.* He walked to the door and down the hall, where he started sorting the laundry into piles on the floor. Whites. Darks. Towels. Sheets. The mundane task required little concentration, and his mind wandered as he sorted through the items. He fumed, thinking about his wife and son having fun at the captain's house, enjoying the cool water of the pool and a lively party with friends. If Steven really wanted to make a fool out of the captain, he should start a fire at the fire station while the captain was throwing his party. *What better place to humiliate him than on his own turf?* He chuckled at the thought.

Then he stopped chuckling.

Even though it was a holiday, surely a few firefighters would be on duty. He'd never be able to drill holes in the back of the fire station without risking someone might hear the noise. He'd have to come up with a better plan. He pondered for a moment. *How can I set the place on fire without getting too close?* The last thing he needed was to get caught. A flamethrower would be the perfect tool but, of course, he didn't have a flamethrower.

Or do I?

He remembered the water guns in the garage, the ones he'd suggested the boys use for a birthday party battle. They'd be perfect for the job. They were made to hold liquid, after all. Hell, one of them held a full forty ounces! They could shoot up to thirty feet or more, too.

I'm a fucking genius.

He went to the garage and glanced around, spotting the guns in a plastic bin with a bubble machine that had entertained Hayden for hours on end when he was just a toddler. As Steven gathered up the guns, he recalled when he'd bought the first two they'd owned as a surprise for Hayden. His son had been around eight years old. Steven had snuck out to the backyard and surreptitiously filled them with water he'd chilled in the fridge. Then he'd opened the back door to summon Hayden outside. *"Come help me with some yard work!"* Hayden had begrudgingly come out the door wearing only a pair of superhero underpants. *"But it's so hot, Daddy!"* Steven had raised the gun and blasted Hayden square in his bare belly. *Splattttt.* Once he'd recovered from the surprise, Hayden had hooted and hollered, giggling with glee as Steven shot him with a second blast of cold, refreshing water. *"Arm yourself, son!"* Steven pointed to the second gun, which he'd left on the patio table. Hayden ran over and grabbed it. Steven demonstrated how to work the pump-action handle, and the boy was in business. Hayden had raised the full water gun as high as his skinny arms allowed. Realizing the stream would fall far short, Steven had dashed forward so the water hit him square in the nuts, giving the kid a win. Hayden had dropped the gun and fallen over onto the grass, holding his stomach as he laughed. *"Daddy! It looks like you peed your pants!"* Gretchen had peeked out the kitchen window to see what the commotion was about, and smiled when she spotted her son and husband having a playful moment.

Those days are long gone now. Hayden was probably bonding with

Doak now, challenging his soon-to-be stepfather to a cannonball competition in that damn swimming pool.

Steven choked up and blinked back the tears threatening to form in his eyes. *Grow a pair, you pussy.* The humiliation of his emotional reaction only strengthened his resolve for vengeance. He grabbed the two-gallon plastic gas can he normally used for the lawnmower, filled all three water guns with the flammable fuel and loaded them into his duffle bag. He donned the medical mask but not the windbreaker, deciding the jacket might attract attention on such a hot night. Instead, he put on a Texas Rangers ballcap to cover his hair and shade his face.

He decided to go to the station on foot rather than risk his car being picked up on security cameras near the fire station. He strode down the sidewalk in the dark, approaching the station a few minutes later. Keeping his head down, he veered into the parking lot of a medical imaging center next to the fire station, sticking close to the bushes marking the perimeter. It was after hours so no cars were around. The place had likely been closed earlier for the Labor Day holiday anyway. He crept around to the back of the center and hid behind a big metal trash dumpster, out of sight of any security cameras, but with a direct line to the rear wall of the fire station.

After setting the duffle bag on the ground, he crouched down and unzipped it, releasing an intense smell of gasoline that made his eyes water and his nose wriggle. He turned his head, fanned the air, and blinked his eyes several times, wishing he'd remembered the goggles. Once he could see again, he turned back, removed the guns, and lay them atop the bag. He took hold of the first gun and stood. As he raised it, a trickle of gas dripped from it onto the toe of his running shoe. The rubber seal on the gun's tank evidently had a small leak. Not a surprise given that the gun had been in their hot garage for years.

Spreading his legs so any further drips would fall on the asphalt rather than his shoes, he held the gun out in front of him. He gave the gun five quick pumps and aimed the barrel at the top of the back wall. He pulled the trigger, releasing a long stream of gasoline that hit the bricks with a *splat* and splashed gasoline across the back wall and down onto the dried grass. He moved the gun in a tight zig-zag pattern across the grass toward him, pumping it again when the pressure waned. The gun ran out of fuel just as the line he'd been drawing reached the edge of the asphalt his feet. *Perfect.*

He took a couple of steps back and whipped the lighter from his pocket. Chuckling, he crouched and flicked the lighter to ignite it. The flame lit up. So did his trigger finger. He'd forgotten the grilling gloves tonight. "Shit!"

On reflex, he dropped the lighter and fell back on his ass. The flames licked his skin, burning off the gas residue. He flung his hand out again and again, hoping the motion would put out the fire. It didn't. He lifted his opposite arm and jammed his hand into his armpit, clamping the arm down to smother the flame. He felt a momentary twinge of searing pain as the flames burned through the fabric and singed his underarm hair, but at least his finger was no longer on fire.

He'd been stupid to try to pull off this stunt on his own. He knew he should stop. Things were not going well here. But the pain from his burnt finger fueled his fury to the point that he could no longer control himself. He literally had skin in the game. *No way in hell I'm giving up now!*

He pushed himself up onto his left knee, his right leg crooked at the knee in front of him for balance. Using his left hand, he retrieved the lighter from the ground and held it to the gasoline-soaked dry grass. It took four awkward flicks for him to get a flame but, once he did, he held the lighter to the grass. The blades ignited with a soft whoosh, and he watched in evil delight as the flame zig-zagged over the station's back lawn, making its way to the building.

He shoved the lighter back into his pocket, grabbed a second gun and stood. He pumped the gun four times and forced his burned finger into the trigger, grimacing against the pain. He aimed higher this time, hoping to wet the roof of the station so the fire would spread upward. He knew the asphalt shingles were fire resistant but, at a minimum, they would scorch. To his disappointment, he was too far away for the stream to hit up high on the roof. Instead, the stream splattered down only two or three feet above the roofline, the gasoline running down into the gutters. *Damn!*

He reached down and grabbed the third and final gun. The back of the building was engulfed now, and he aimed the stream into the fire, moving the barrel to draw the flames to the holly bushes and cedar mulch on the side of the building. He fought the urge to cheer when the bushes and wood chips immediately burst into flame. He felt like a soldier in a one-man army, a force of justice wielding a flamethrower like some sort of destructive god. For a mere microsecond, he allowed himself to bask in the glow of the rapidly spreading fire. *Ha! That's what you get for putting your dick in my wife!*

With the last gun out of juice, he looked down for the duffle bag to repack it. It was behind him. As he'd sprayed the gun, he'd inadvertently moved forward. The grass at his feet was still on fire. Unfortunately, as he saw now, so was the toe of his right shoe. "Fuck!"

He stomped his right foot in a vain attempt to put out the fire. He quickly learned that stomping only works when the fire is *under* the shoe, not on top of it. All he succeeded in doing was fanning the flames. He stepped on the back of his right shoe with his left foot to hold it in place, yanked his foot out of the burning shoe, then kicked it over to extinguish the flames. By then, the fire had spread across the station and lit the area like a spotlight. He was exposed and vulnerable. *I've got to get out of here!*

He knew leaving the bag and guns behind could lead law enforcement to his door, but he didn't have time to pack them up. Instead, he hurled them into the flames, hoping they'd be consumed by the fire, or at least be damaged enough that no fingerprints could be lifted from them. He didn't dare leave his shoe though. The shoe could directly implicate him. He snatched it up. The last thing he saw before he turned to run was the dried leaves in the gutters igniting, the flame rocketing down the aluminum channel.

He sprinted away from the station, wincing each time he stepped on a pebble in his sock-clad foot. To get home faster, he cut through the woods in Forest Park. The route had the added benefit of helping him avoid security cameras that might be on the houses. He stopped near a tall oak, removed his undamaged shoe, and knotted the laces with the remaining four inches of lace on his burnt shoe. He stepped back and hurled the shoes up into the tree. The pair ended up tangled on a high limb where they'd never be found.

As he continued on, he wondered what was happening back at the fire station. Someone must have noticed the conflagration by now. He heard no sirens, though he hadn't expected any. After all, the trucks wouldn't have to leave the station to tend to this fire. Surely the captain would be summoned for such a strange event. Doak MacDougal would be the party pooper of his own pool party. The thought made Steven's upper lip quirk in a grin.

He exited the park and entered his neighborhood, sticking to the shadows along the tree-lined curbs. Once he arrived home, he transferred Hayden's sheets to the dryer, stripped off his clothing, and stuffed it into the washing machine. He poured in extra detergent to make sure the wash would remove the gasoline odor.

The immediate matters taken care of and the adrenaline wearing off, his burned finger and foot began to throb. His index finger and toes were red and raw, the edges of the wounds charred and blackened. Hot dogs and hamburgers weren't the only things that had been grilled today.

He went to the bathroom, where he took a shower, grimacing as the spray hit the burn wounds on his trigger finger and foot. After toweling off, he wrapped the towel around his waist and opened the medicine cabinet. Inside, he found a tube of ointment. He applied it to the raw flesh, cursing as it stung. He wrapped his finger and foot in gauze, put on a fresh pair of underwear, and went to the kitchen to treat himself to a celebratory beer.

59
GASSED UP

Megan

Just after nine o'clock, Seth and I were rounding up our towels, sunscreen, and dishes to leave the party when Captain MacDougal approached us in the backyard. He held his cell phone to his ear. Deep worry lines appeared between his brows. "Thanks for letting me know," he said into his phone. "I'll be there right away." He slid the phone into the breast pocket of his T-shirt and turned his attention to us. "Someone set a fire at the station. The back and the entire south wall were involved. Part of the roof, too."

My mouth dropped. *Arson at a fire station? Talk about irony!*

The captain said, "I'm going there now to take a look."

Seth was already looking around for his dog. "Blast can search the area for accelerants."

I volunteered the services of my partner, as well. "Brigit might be able to track whoever started the fire. I'll run home and get suited up as quick as I can." We hadn't had much luck at the last two fires, but maybe we'd get lucky tonight. If she tracked down the culprits, I'd need to be in uniform and have my handcuffs, radio, and other gear to make an arrest and arrange for transport.

Seth and I called to our dogs, who ran over to us, looking up at us expectantly. They seemed to sense the tension in the air. We went out to Seth's car and hurriedly loaded it. We drove to our house, where Seth unpacked the car while I changed into my uniform and pulled my hair up into a bun.

When we arrived at the fire station a short time later, we found the crew gathered in the parking lot. Fortunately, the floodlights on the front of the building were still functioning. We could see charred wood chips in the flower bed and scorched grass along the side of the building, as well as soot marks along the brick and roof. Seth and I donned protective booties so we wouldn't contaminate the crime scene. We also put rubber boots on the dogs to protect their paws from smoldering embers.

One of the firefighters on duty rounded up a large portable light and handed it to me. Rather than disturb the crime scene any more than necessary, the captain waited with the crew in the parking lot. Seth gave Blast the command to scent for accelerants. Brigit and I followed along as Blast sniffed his way down the side of the building and around to the back. I held up the light to help us better search for evidence and see where we were going.

Though we had yet to collect any clues, my mind was already working. *Why would someone do this?* The fact that this fire had been started at a fire station could indicate the arsonist had some sort of beef with the fire department. Then again, it could simply indicate that the arsonist had a warped sense of humor.

I shined the light along the back wall of the station. There were black marks along the building where flames had marred the bricks, but we found no tell-tale holes drilled into the bricks like we'd found at the high school and nursing home. Whoever had started this fire had used a different method—or *modus operandi* in police lingo.

Criminals tended to stick with methods that had worked for them in the past. Unlike the earlier fires, which had been started in a somewhat sophisticated manner, this fire appeared more rudimentary, the work of an amateur. Unfortunately, as with many fires, the flames had destroyed much of the evidence.

Seth pointed at a cluster of soot marks. "The burn pattern looks like splattered liquid."

"Molotov cocktails?" I suggested.

Our gazes went downward as we scanned the ground below the wall for broken glass. We saw none.

Seth gestured to the light in my hands. "Point that at the wall again."

I did as he asked, illuminating the back wall. While some of the soot marks resembled spattered fluid, others stretched in lines across or down the wall, a sort of scorched scribble.

He ran his gaze over the wall for a moment or two, then instructed me to shine it on the roof. The same sooty scribble appeared there.

Seth stroked his chin as he thought aloud. "The pattern of the burn marks reminds me of things I saw in the army. If I didn't know better, I'd say this was the work of a flamethrower." He pointed to the distinct lines. "See this? The marks are concentrated. Linear. Directional." He used his index finger to draw a line that followed the pattern on the wall. He looked around again. "Other than the grass, the fire didn't spread much. That's also typical of flamethrowers." He pointed out the lines of burnt grass that led from the back of the building toward the dumpster in the parking lot of the adjacent medical building. "Looks like they might have started the fire from there."

Seth ordered Blast to sniff for accelerants. The dog confirmed Seth's hypothesis by putting his nose to the ground and leading us in the direction of the dumpster. He sat down next to the charred remains of what appeared to have once been a duffle bag. All that was left was a blackened metal zipper, part of a vinyl handle, and a small remnant of fabric. Sitting atop the fabric was a messy pile of melted, smoldering plastic tubes, still giving off a noxious odor. Most of the melted plastic was white, or at least it had been before it was covered in soot.

"PVC pipe?" I mused aloud. It seemed like a plausible idea. PVC pipe was used to move water through houses and other structures. Surely, it could be used to concentrate and move a flammable liquid, too. But the liquid would need to be propelled through the pipe in some way. *Hmm.* After setting the light on the ground, I whipped out my nightstick and flicked my wrist to extend it. I crouched down and poked at the plastic, moving it around a little. Some blue and yellow plastic was visible now, too. *Was this some sort of toy?* "Could these be melted water guns? The big kind? Super Soakers?"

Large plastic water guns with big tanks were common in Texas. Kids could often be seen chasing each other with them around yards and parks. They were a cheap way to have fun and stay cool outside in the summer.

Seth's eyes narrowed as he considered the idea. "Water guns would explain the burn patterns. Whoever did this must have filled them with gasoline." He pulled out his cell phone and called Captain MacDougal, putting him on speaker phone so I could hear, too. "Whoever did this used the dumpster next door for cover."

"I'll be right over," said the captain.

A minute later, the captain appeared in the parking lot of the imaging lab with a spool of cordon tape. A firefighter had come along with him. While the crew member secured the area with the tape, I shined the light on what was left of the bag so the captain could see what we'd found. He crouched down, his head moving as he eyed the melted mess from several angles.

The captain stood, holding out a hand to take the light from me. "I called Lew Hamrick to see if he wanted to come to the station, but he can't make it tonight. He took his family to Galveston for the long weekend, and they're stuck in holiday traffic on Interstate Forty-Five. They've only made it to Corsicana. He'll be out here first thing in the morning to take a look. Seth, collect the evidence for him to examine. Megan, see if Brigit can track the culprit."

"Yes, sir," Seth and I said in unison, the casualness of the earlier pool party no longer appropriate now that we were all on duty.

I gave Brigit the command to trail the disturbance left by the arsonist or arsonists. She snuffled around on the asphalt near the dumpster for a few seconds before finding the trail. She set off at a trot, her snout only a few inches off the ground. I jogged after her, letting out the leash to give her the freedom of movement she'd need to stay on the trail.

She trotted down the road. I had to stop her at an intersection and wait for the signal to change before we could continue on into Forest Park. She led me into the dark woods, and I had to pull out my flashlight lest I turn an ankle stumbling into a hole or over a fallen branch. Dry leaves and branches crackled and crunched under our feet, accompanied by the sounds of critters skittering away. Brigit slowed, her sniffing intensifying. She stopped near a large tree and reared up onto her hind legs, sniffing at the air. When her front legs returned to the earth, she lowered her rear end and sat, issuing her passive alert.

A cold sweat broke out on my back. *Is the guilty person hiding nearby?* I shined my flashlight around, looking for anyone who might be crouched behind a tree trunk or standing still behind a wide tree. I saw nothing. That didn't stop me from calling, "I see you! Come out with your hands up!"

I waited a beat or two to see if anyone would respond, but the only sound I heard was the rapid chirp of crickets. The insects chirped faster at higher temperatures. The late-summer heat must pose a tough challenge for them.

Brigit raised her snout again, and looked up into the tree. My heart pounded as fast as the rhythm of the crickets. *Is someone hiding up there? They could be preparing to drop down on us.*

I shined my flashlight up into the tree but saw only tree limbs, no human limbs. I looked down at Brigit. If she'd led me here because a stupid squirrel had run up the tree, I'd be pretty darn pissed. But she knew better. I knew better, too. If there was one thing I'd learned during the time I'd been partnered with Brigit, it was to trust my dog.

Though I had no idea why she'd stopped here, I whipped a short length of cordon tape from my gun belt and tied it around the trunk so I'd be able to find this particular tree later. I fed Brigit a liver treat to thank her for whatever she was trying to tell me, then gave her the order to continue to track. Surely this couldn't be the end of the trail. Not unless a rascally raccoon had started the fire at the station.

Brigit set off again, and I jogged along behind her. Despite the fact that it was fully dark, the temperature was still sweltering. I'd say I was sweating like a whore in church, but it's time men took their share of the blame for illegal sexual transactions. So, let's say I was sweating like *a john* in church. Salty drops ran down my forehead and into my eyes, making them sting. I blinked to clear my vision, and wiped my eyes with the back of my hand.

Brigit led me out of the park and into the neighborhood surrounding Paschal High School. As she took a particular turn, it struck me where she was headed. *No! Please, no!* For the captain's sake, I didn't want it to be true. But when Brigit trotted up to the door of Steven Quinn's house, I was afraid I knew who had started the fire—the captain's soon-to-be stepson. *Hayden.*

60

CHICKEN-FRIED SUSPECT

Brigit

Brigit sat on the porch and issued her passive alert to let Megan know the trail stopped here. She could detect the lingering acrid odor of gasoline at the house, along with the flowery smell of lavender laundry detergent. Her nose was able to sort out many other scents, too, and take inventory. Bleach. Bath soap. Beer.

Though nobody had yet opened the door, Brigit could tell the man they'd visited here before was inside. She also recognized his scent from the high school and the nursing home Megan had taken her to days before. He smelled a little odd tonight, though, like some type of grilled meat Brigit hadn't tried before. She sure would like to get a taste of it.

61

TIPTOEING

Steven

After looking through the peephole, he sucked in a frantic breath and dropped to the floor, trying not to make a sound. It wasn't easy, especially when he twisted his burnt big toe while crouching down. *OUCH!* The doorbell rang for a second time, then a third, then a fourth. *Why won't that damn lady cop and her dog just go away!*

The dog must have tracked him from the fire station. Why else would the cop be here right now? His instinct was to continue to hide rather than answer the door but, when he took a deep breath to calm himself, his brain sparked with a clever scheme.

He scurried back down the hallway and called. "I'll be right there!" He hurriedly slid his feet into socks to hide the bandage and put on a bathrobe, tucking his fried finger into the pocket out of sight. He returned to the front door, taking another deep breath to slow his racing heart before unlocking it and opening it with his left hand. He forced a smile to his lips, hoping it didn't look as false as it felt. "Hello, Officer Luz. Sorry for the wait. I just got out of the shower and was au naturel."

"Good evening, Mr. Quinn." The cop looked past him into the house. "Could I speak to Hayden please?"

She thinks Hayden started the fire. Shit! He'd have to disavow her of that notion immediately. "He's at his mom's. Probably in bed already. She imposes a strict ten-thirty lights-out policy."

She hesitated a moment, then asked, "Did he come by here this evening?"

"No." Steven had to stifle a cheer. She'd given him a perfect opening. "The only person who's come by is Asher. At least I think it was Asher. Someone rang the bell about twenty minutes ago. I'd just gotten home from watching the Rangers game with my buddies at Hail Mary's and was getting into the shower. By the time I could wrap a towel around myself and make it to the door, he was down the block out of earshot. I got a glimpse of him as he passed under the streetlight. I'm not sure why he even came by, unless it was to apologize. Hayden has been steering clear of that kid. Asher is nothing but trouble."

The officer's eyes narrowed slightly as she appeared to be processing what he'd told her. He hoped he'd sounded credible. Asher already had a juvenile record for the prank shooter calls. Another black mark for arson wouldn't ruin the kid. Besides, he was still furious with the boy for lying to Detective Bustamente and trying to pin the bogus shooter calls on Hayden. The detective had informed him of Asher's lies when he'd called to let them know Asher had been detained and charged, and that Hayden was off the hook. *If that punk is punished for tonight's fire, he'll only be getting what he deserves.*

Officer Luz thanked him for his time. "Sorry to have disturbed you. Have a good evening." She turned to go and he'd nearly closed the door when she turned back around and held up a hand to stop him. "One more thing."

He opened the door a few inches and raised his brows as if happy to answer any additional question she might ask.

"I noticed when I was here before that you had several cartons of Physical Force supplements." She gestured toward the garage, where he'd stored the huge amount of product Nash had forced him to purchase. "Who'd you buy them from?"

The world went still as terror seized him. Nash hadn't been involved tonight. He wasn't even in the state! *Does she realize there's a connection between the supplements and the earlier fires, or is she asking for another reason?* He didn't want to get caught in a lie, so he decided to go with the truth—or at least as close to the truth as he dared to get. "I bought them from a friend's cousin. He convinced me to buy a big supply. I must have 'sucker' written on my forehead. Or maybe he could tell I was an easy mark since I mentioned I was concerned about staying in shape. It's much harder after forty than it used to be." He forced a chuckle, hoping to sound nonchalant.

"Any chance your friend's cousin's name is Nash Goshen?"

Fuuuuuuuck! His throat tightened and he fought not to squeak like a mouse when he spoke. "Yes. That's his name. Why do you ask?"

She shrugged. "He came by my fiancé's workplace a while back and gave everyone samples. I'd never heard of the supplement company before. I was just curious if it was the same salesman." She cocked her head. "Is there any chance the guy you saw walking away from your house earlier could have been him?"

Steven took a beat to process the question. If he said yes, the cops might go after Nash rather than Hayden, which would take the heat off his son. But Nash would surely turn on Steven and tell the police the fires at the high school and nursing home had been Steven's idea. *Better to say no, right?* After all, Hayden had been at the pool party all day, and had an easily verifiable alibi. Hell, Captain MacDougal himself could vouch for the boy! "No, the guy I saw didn't look like Nash. Nash is jacked. The guy I saw was too thin to be him. Besides, Nash didn't stay in Texas long. My friend said Nash couldn't stand the heat and moved back to the Pacific Northwest."

"Thanks for the information." She gave him a nod in goodbye. "Take care, Mr. Quinn."

"You, too."

He closed the door and released a shuddering breath. As he stood in the dark, his toes and finger throbbing in pain, he didn't know whether she'd bought his story. He knew only one thing—Officer Luz was too smart and dedicated for her own good. Even if she'd believed him, she'd seek corroborating evidence. She wouldn't find any ... *unless he manufactured it.*

He didn't remember her first name but, fortunately, he still had her business card from the first time she'd come by the house. He'd placed it in the bowl on the narrow table by the door where Gretchen used to leave her car keys. He snatched it up and took a look. *Megan.*

Armed with her full name, he went to his computer and typed it in along with the words *Fort Worth* and *address*. His search produced nothing useful. He logged into ChatGPT, and typed in a search: *How to find someone's home address online.* He hit enter and, an instant later, was given a list of suggestions. Addresses could be obtained through paid services such as Whitepages or Spokeo, or from government records such as property records or voting rolls in states where such records were made public.

He checked the property records first. There was no real estate listed in the name of Megan Luz in Tarrant County. It wasn't a big surprise that she didn't own a home. She appeared to be only in her late twenties, housing prices had risen rapidly in recent years, and she earned a measly cop's salary.

Are voting records public in Texas? He ran a quick search and discovered they were—or at least that you could access them if you knew a person's first and last name, the county they lived in, their zip code, and their birthdate.

He tried social media to see if Megan might have listed her birthday on her Facebook account. She hadn't. What's more, her account was private. But he found an account for a teenage girl named Gabby Luz who was Megan's younger sister. He searched her page for the word "birthday." The first two posts included pics of Gabby's brothers on their birthdays, but Gabby had also posted a photo of Megan behind a birthday cake, lips puckered to blow out the candles, along with text that read *Happy birthday to the best big sister ever!* He jotted down the date of the post. He didn't know the exact year of Officer Luz's birth or her zip code, but he could estimate her age within a few years' range. He found a zip code map online. He figured she probably lived close to her precinct, so he started with the zip code in his immediate area, then worked his way outward. It took him only a few minutes of trial and error to input the correct combination of birth year and zip code, and find out she lived on Travis Avenue in the South Hemphill Heights neighborhood.

Now that he had her address, all he needed was a new bag, another water gun or two, and more fuel. He donned a pair of dark blue lightweight nylon athletic pants, a dark blue long-sleeved T-shirt, and his second-favorite pair of running shoes. His favorite pair were now burnt to a crisp and hanging in the tree in Forest Park. He put on the medical mask and the Rangers ball cap, and slid his keys and wallet into his pants pocket before going out to the garage. He put his empty gas can in his trunk and drove to the nearest Walmart, which was open twenty-four hours. It was well past eleven o'clock when he arrived and the parking lot was virtually empty, but he parked at the far end anyway, in the shadows where the overhead lights didn't quite reach.

He went inside. The night crew was dismantling the seasonal back-to-school section at the front of the store, swapping out the school supplies for Halloween decorations and bags of candy. He grabbed one of the few remaining backpacks, a cheap basic black model, and held it by the attached cardboard price tag so as not to leave any fingerprints on the fabric. From there, he walked directly to the toy section, but found no large water guns. With Labor Day marking the unofficial end of summer, the store hadn't bothered to keep them in stock. *Dammit!*

He debated what to do. *Surely there has to be another way.*

He wandered the aisles, searching for inspiration. As he strode past the automotive section, he spotted a display of large car-washing sponges next to jugs of soap solution and microfiber drying towels. He might not have a water gun, but he did have a pitching arm and could throw like nobody's business. *These will do.* He rounded up ten large sponges in plastic packages. On his way back to the front of the store, he passed the hunting and camping section. He pulled his sleeve down to cover his fingers and grabbed a one-gallon rectangular metal can of camp fuel. The fluid was intended for use in camp stoves and lanterns, but it could serve his purposes just as well, and the container would fit easily into the backpack.

He rang himself up at the self-checkout, surreptitiously using a plastic store bag like a glove to ensure he didn't directly touch the backpack or camp fuel and inadvertently leave fingerprints. An older woman in a blue vest who was overseeing the area glanced over from her podium. "That's a lot of sponges. You planning to wash a bus?"

He forced a smile at her joke, glad he'd already bagged the camping fuel before she'd seen it. "They're for a car wash fundraiser. For my daughter's drill team."

The woman smiled back. "I hope y'all raise a lot of money."

Steven hoped he raised a lot of *hackles*.

He paid for the items in cash, collected his change, and was on his way.

62

WHO'S HOT AND WHO'S NOT

Megan

Once Steven Quinn had closed his door, I gave Brigit the order to continue tracking. She snuffled around a bit, then sat back down, telling me the trail ended there.

I pondered the situation as Brigit and I walked back to the fire station. I had no doubt that whoever had set fire at the station had gone from there to Steven Quinn's house. *But who was that person?*

Could it have been Hayden? Maybe even Hayden and Brooklyn? The fact that the fire had been started with water guns indicated a child or children could be the culprits. I remembered seeing large water guns in the garage when I'd looked around Steven Quinn's house before, though that didn't mean much. Nearly every boy in Texas owned at least one of the toys. Steven said he had returned home from Hail Mary's sports bar only a short time before. Though Hayden hadn't been at his father's house when Steven arrived home, he could have gone there earlier, while his father was at the bar. He might have gone to his dad's house after setting the fire to clean up and gather his wits. He might have known his dad was out for the evening, and figured he could get in and out quickly without anyone knowing. He might have left through the back door or garage, starting a new trail that, to Brigit, would be distinct from the one I'd asked her to follow.

Still, while it certainly seemed possible, even probable, that Hayden had started the fire, I had a hard time seeing the boy being so mischievous and brazen. He'd seemed like a nice kid who'd simply picked a bad friend when he'd decided to associate with Asher. He'd been so nervous when Detective Bustamente and I had shown up at the door to question him that he'd immediately blurted out the news about Asher being behind the swatting incidents. *A kid like that wouldn't intentionally start a dangerous fire, would he?* And even if Hayden was angry at Captain MacDougal for breaking up his family, would he take a chance on doing something like this on the heels of his former friend's arrest and detention? A smart kid would keep his nose clean—at least until things had died down. Then again, teenage boys weren't exactly known for their self control. They were immature and impulsive. They took stupid risks without thinking things through first.

Had Asher started the fire? He might have been trying something new, a different way to stir things up and cause a ruckus for first responders. He might have targeted the fire station because it wasn't far from his house. Or maybe he was trying to get back in Hayden's good graces, and thought he could win his friend back by acting out against the man who was behind Hayden's parents' divorce. Maybe he'd gone to Steven's house to tell Hayden what he'd done on Hayden's behalf. Or maybe Asher was trying to frame Hayden, to get back at his former friend for fingering him in the swatting investigation. Maybe Asher figured Hayden would be an obvious suspect in the station fire. There were multiple ways to interpret this potential scenario. Even though tonight's fire had been set in an entirely different manner, I wondered again whether Asher might have had something to do with the earlier fires at the high school and nursing home. He seemed to enjoy getting people in a dither.

Could Nash be behind tonight's conflagration? He might have been frustrated that he'd failed the written firefighter exam and set the fire to get revenge on the department. As a former professional firefighter, he could have easily come up with the scheme used in the high school and nursing home fires. Had he been on a weeks-long vendetta? Or maybe he'd been angry that the fire station crew hadn't bought a sufficient supply of supplements so that he could make ends meet. Or maybe he'd started the fire for some other reason. Maybe he'd come to the station with his supplement samples as a guise and had actually been there to scout the place. He could be a general, run-of-the-mill pyromaniac who saw starting a fire at a fire station as a challenge. Adult pyromaniacs tended to be unmarried and unemployed. Nash appeared to be both. When Steven said that Nash had moved back to the Pacific Northwest, there'd been no mention of a spouse moving with him.

Of course, it was also possible that the truth was much simpler. That Brigit had led me directly to the arsonist. That the person who had set the fire was none other than Steven Quinn. Maybe he wanted to give his wife's new man some hell, make Captain MacDougal look incompetent. *It's odd that Steven Quinn hadn't asked why I'd come to his house and asked to speak to Hayden, isn't it?* But would a seemingly upstanding man risk not only arrest, but also his relationship with his son and ex-wife just to settle a romantic score? It seemed like an extreme measure, one only someone with an inflated ego would attempt. Narcissists were known to be vindictive. But I didn't know Steven Quinn well enough to ascertain whether he might be a narcissist. Besides, he had an alibi. He'd been at Hail Mary's, watching the Rangers game. Of course, his alibi was as yet unverified. I'd noted the time I'd arrived at Steven's house. He'd told me he'd arrived home around twenty minutes earlier. When we met with Lew Hamrick in the morning, I'd offer to go by the sports bar and review the security camera footage to determine exactly what time Steven Quinn had left the bar. If it was significantly more than twenty minutes before I showed up, he'd have some explaining to do. The place was only a few minutes' drive from his house.

Brigit and I arrived back at the fire station. Captain MacDougal, Seth, and Blast were waiting in the parking lot. When the men saw Brigit and me approaching, they straightened and turned our way, their expressions disappointed.

"No luck?" asked the captain.

Due to the potentially sensitive nature of the prime suspects I'd come up with, I figured we should discuss the matter in private. "Can we talk in your office, Captain?"

His face clouded in apprehension. "Of course."

The captain led me, Brigit, Seth, and Blast inside and past the crew gathered in the main room. All of them watched us go by, but none posed a question. The expressions on our faces must have told them it was best not to make inquiries right now.

We walked down the hall to the captain's office. He closed the door behind us and held out a hand, inviting me to take a seat. Seth sat down in the chair next to me, while the captain dropped into his rolling desk chair.

I launched right in. "Brigit trailed the culprit from the medical office, through Forest Park, and into the neighborhood by Paschal High School." I took a breath before adding, "She stopped at Steven Quinn's house."

The captain's jaw went slack for a beat, then his hands fisted atop his desk. "*Steven* started the fire? That son-of-a-bitch!"

I raised a palm. "He's got an alibi. He told me he'd returned home shortly before Brigit and I arrived. He said he'd been at Hail Mary's watching the Rangers game. Of course, that alibi has yet to be verified."

The captain sat back, his fists loosening and dropping to his thighs. "Gretchen told me that Steven spent a lot of time watching sports with friends during their marriage. It was one of the reasons they grew apart. He wasn't home much. Besides his day job selling pharmaceuticals, he worked as an umpire during the spring baseball season. That kept him away from home on nights and weekends, too."

Steven was an umpire? The revelation sparked my suspicion. *Could he have been the guy we'd seen on the video from the high school seeming to make the spectator interference signal?* I wish I knew. I'd be sure to discuss the possibility with Lew Hamrick tomorrow. It was possible the gesture meant something else entirely, or even nothing at all. Throwing up their arms might have simply been the person's reflexive response to seeing the school bus coming. But something told me the raised arms and the gripped wrist meant more. Still, that fire had been entirely different from the one at the station tonight. *Are there multiple, unrelated arsonists, just like there'd been multiple, unrelated copycat callers?*

I went on. "Steven told me that he went straight for the shower when he got home, but that someone knocked on his door just after he'd stripped down. By the time he grabbed a towel and got to the door, they'd left. He saw them walking away down the street. He was fairly sure it was Asher Burke. If Asher started the fire here then went to Steven Quinn's house, that would explain why Brigit led me there."

Lines of confusion crinkled the captain's forehead. "Why would Asher go to Steven's house? He and Hayden haven't hung out for months. Gretchen won't allow it. Asher was a troublemaker."

I hated to burst the guy's bubble, but I had to tell him the truth, even if it meant breaking my promise to Hayden. I gave the captain the rundown on the swatting arrest, how Asher had been at Hayden's birthday sleepover, how Hayden had provided critical evidence that led to Asher being charged.

The captain's face went slack with shock. "So, Hayden wasn't directly involved, but he knew Asher made the call from his sleepover and didn't do anything about it?" He scrubbed a hand down his face, and his voice was somber when he spoke again. "If the kid didn't want to tell his folks, he could've come to me. I thought he knew that."

Though I hated to cause the man further upset, I had to go on. It was not only my duty as a law enforcement officer, but it was also the right thing to do. "When I saw Hayden at your party today, he begged me not to tell Gretchen that he'd been hanging out with Asher while he was at his dad's. He didn't want to get in trouble, of course, but I think he also didn't want to disappoint his mother."

"I can see why." The captain scoffed. "His father disappointed his mother on a regular basis." His expression was equal parts nauseated and bewildered as he thought aloud. "I just can't imagine Hayden would start a fire here." He looked down at his desk, slowly shaking his head. He took a shuddering breath, then looked back up at us. "Maybe there's another side of Hayden I don't know."

"The teen years are hard," I said. "Hayden probably has conflicting emotions about everything that's going on in his life right now. Besides, there's a chance that the person who started the fire was Asher." I told him the theories I'd come up with, that Asher might have done it either in an attempt to repair his friendship with Hayden or, on the contrary, to retaliate against Hayden by trying to implicate Hayden in a crime. "Asher might have gone to Steven's house to tell Hayden what he'd done, or to taunt him with it. If the boys haven't been in touch, Asher wouldn't have known that Hayden was at your house rather than his Dad's."

The captain's eyes narrowed and his head bobbed slowly as he considered the theory.

"I have another theory, too." I leaned toward him. "The night Detective Bustamente and I questioned Hayden, I took a cursory look around Steven Quinn's house. There were several cartons of Physical Force supplements in his garage, so many that I assumed he was a distributor. Steven told me tonight that he'd bought the supplements from Nash Goshen. Evidently, Nash is related to one of Steven's buddies. I know Nash failed the firefighter exam. I'm wondering if Nash might have been angry enough about failing the test to have a vendetta against the fire department."

The captain shrugged. "Don't know the guy well enough to say. I only met him the one time in person. He called the station after he flunked the test to see if I could give him some advice. I told him to study hard and try again." He raised his palms. "What else could I say?"

Seth looked from the captain to me. "Even if it was Nash who started the fire here, why would he go to Steven's house after?"

"Maybe because the house was close to the station and he hoped to clean up there, or at least to hang out until the coast cleared. He might have left his car somewhere nearby. Or maybe he was going to hit Steven up to buy more supplements. Maybe he was the person Steven saw walking away earlier. He could have left a trail then that Brigit picked up on." Nash's stocky physique was nothing like Asher's lean build, but it had been dark and the shadows cast by the streetlights could have distorted the image Steven said he'd seen of a guy walking away down the block. "The only potential problem with these theories is that Nash is purportedly no longer in Texas. Steven said Nash moved back to where he came from because it was too hot here."

The captain exhaled sharply. "I'm in a very awkward position here. I don't want to do anything that might jeopardize the investigation or appear biased. I'm not sure I should be the one to question Hayden tonight."

I offered a suggestion. "Let's get Detective Bustamente and Lew Hamrick on the phone."

Hamrick had made it to Waxahachie by the time we got the two investigators on the phone, but he still had an hour's drive to get his family home. Bustamente was already in his bed and not eager to get out of it. I, on the other hand, didn't mind working some additional unscheduled overtime if it meant further honing my interview skills and taking some of the pressure off Captain MacDougal.

Bustamante vouched for me. "Officer Luz can handle things tonight. I say we let her talk to the boy."

Hamrick concurred. "If it's good enough for you, Hector, it's good enough for me. See y'all in the morning."

Just like that, I was unofficially made a junior detective.

"I'll take Blast," Seth said. "He'll be able to tell if there's an accelerant on Hayden's skin or clothing."

We walked back out to the parking lot, again garnering looks from the rest of the crew as we passed them. Seth and Blast climbed into his Nova, while Brigit and I got into our cruiser and followed the captain back to his house. It was nearly midnight when we arrived. Gretchen had finished cleaning up when we arrived, and was sitting on the couch in her nightgown, barefaced and barefooted, sipping a glass of white wine.

She put down the wineglass and stood up as we walked in, grabbing a blanket from the sofa to drape around her shoulders for modesty. She seemed surprised to see me, Seth, and our dogs, unease flitting across her face. "Is everything okay at the station?"

"The crew is fine," the captain said. "I'll fill you in on the rest later."

I stepped forward. "Gretchen, can you tell me what time Hayden got home from Brooklyn's house tonight?"

Her brows drew together. "A few minutes before ten. Why?"

"Just trying to put things together." It was a vague response, I knew, but it was the best I could offer her at the moment. "May I speak with him?"

"But he's asleep, and it's a school night." She looked from me, to the captain, and back again, utterly confused. "Why do you need to talk to him? Is it important?"

The captain answered for me. "It's important, Gretchen. Get him."

She appeared taken aback, but said, "Okay."

She disappeared down the hall and returned a moment later with Hayden, who was dressed in a rumpled T-shirt and knit shorts, his eyes droopy and his hair wild. Mickey padded along behind him. Apparently, the dog had been sleeping in the boy's room. The dog looked just as tired as the boy, worn out from a day of energetic play.

"Let's all take a seat," I suggested. Once everyone was sitting, I turned to Hayden. "Where did you go after you left here this evening?"

He looked confused, as if he'd thought his mother or the captain could have already filled me in on his whereabouts. "I went to Brooklyn's house."

"Anywhere else?" I asked.

He shook his head. "No."

"Was anyone else at Brooklyn's?"

"Her parents and her sisters," he said. "We played Scattergories."

"Did you stop anywhere on the way there or on your way back home? Maybe your dad's house? To have some privacy, maybe?"

A dark blush raced up the boy's neck as he shook his head. "Brooklyn and I went straight to her house and I came straight home after. Why?"

"Someone set a fire at the fire station," I said.

"I know," he replied. "Mom told me when I got home."

I gave him a pointed look. "I'm trying to figure out who did it. Do you know anything about it?"

Gretchen's mouth gaped. "Why would *he* know anything about it?"

The captain raised a palm to calm his fiancée. "Let Officer Luz do her job, Gretchen."

I wondered if Gretchen would have sounded so surprised if she knew her son had disobeyed her and continued to hang out with Asher. Unless I had a good reason to betray Hayden's confidence, I wasn't going to tell her. I'd had no choice but to tell the captain earlier. Whether he chose to inform Gretchen was his business.

Hayden shook his head again, though his eyes were bright with panic. "I don't know anything about it."

Seth had a question for the boy now. "Did you take a shower when you got home tonight?"

"Yes," he said. "Mom makes me take one before I go to bed."

In other words, if he'd had any accelerants on his skin, they'd have been washed off.

Seth cocked his head. "May we take a look at the clothes you wore to Brooklyn's house?"

"Okay," Hayden said. "Do I bring them here or—?"

"Take us to them." Seth jerked his head to indicate the hallway that led to the bedrooms.

Gretchen followed as Hayden led Seth, Blast, Brigit, and me down the hall to his room. Captain MacDougal remained in the living room, probably praying we wouldn't find any evidence to incriminate his future stepson.

Unlike Hayden's room at his father's house, which scored the maximum of ten on the teen-boy-funk meter, this one ranked only a two. *Gretchen must have something to do with that.* The T-shirt, shorts, socks, and sneakers I'd seen Hayden wearing when he left the house earlier were scattered about the floor.

Seth put Blast to work, instructing him to scent for accelerants. Blast made his way around the room, scenting. After sniffing at a drawer on the boy's desk, he sat, issuing a passive alert. Seth went over, pulled the drawer open, and rummaged around in the assorted junk to find only a single, small forgotten firecracker, the kind that normally come stringed together in a bunch. It was broken and bent in two. "Good boy!" he told Blast, giving the dog a treat for his efforts.

Beside me, Brigit issued an irritated grunt. She seemed to think she deserved a treat, too. Though she'd done nothing here, I pulled one from my pocket and gave it to her.

Blast stopped at the pile of discarded clothing on the floor, his nostrils working. He spent a little more time on the shoes, but he didn't sit to give his passive alert. He apparently smelled no other accelerants in the room, and looked up at Seth from all fours as if to say *There's nothing here.* Seth gave him another "Good boy!"

We walked back to the living room, where we found the captain pacing, a hand on the back of his neck.

Seth gave him an update. "Blast found no evidence of accelerants."

The captain lowered his hand. "Thank God!"

Gretchen gaped again, her face hurt and angry as she glared at the captain. "Why would you think there was any chance Hayden was involved?"

The captain's eyes cut to me, then to Hayden, then back to Gretchen. Though Gretchen didn't clue in, Hayden did. He looked at me and bit his lip. Then he turned apologetic eyes on the captain.

The captain did a perfect job of covering for both himself and Hayden. "Cut me some slack, Gretchen. I'm new at this fathering thing. Hayden's a good kid. I knew he didn't start the fire. It just worried me that he was considered a potential suspect."

"Any blame is mine," I said, hoping to help get the captain off the hook. "I'm the one who suggested we speak with Hayden. I arrest teen boys all the time for doing dumb, dangerous things and, even though y'all all seem to get along great, I figured in theory Hayden might have some resentment toward Captain MacDougal for all the changes he's had to face recently."

Gretchen visibly relaxed, her shoulders coming down from her ears. "Are we done here? Hayden needs to get back to bed or he'll be a zombie at school tomorrow."

I looked to Seth. He nodded. "We're done," I said. "Thanks for your cooperation."

We stood and headed out the door. As I turned around on the porch to leash Brigit, I caught a glimpse of Hayden staring at her, that panicked look still in his eyes. *He knows why I asked whether he'd gone to his dad's house, doesn't he? He knows Brigit led me there.*

And he knows what that might mean.

63
SMOKE BREAK

Brigit

Finally, the four members of her pack were back home. It had been a fun, exciting day, but also a long, exhausting one. Brigit had already been worn out from swimming in the pool and playing all day when Megan had asked her to trail the person who'd fled from the fire station. She didn't want to smell any more smoke or track another person for days.

She used the last of her energy to hop up onto the bed. She settled lengthwise, lowered her snout to the soft sheets, and issued a contented doggy sigh.

64
FLAME AND FRAME

Steven

Before Gretchen had forbidden Hayden from hanging out with Asher, Steven had picked up Asher at his house on several occasions, then dropped the boys off at the batting cages, movie theater, or the Six Flags amusement park in the nearby city of Arlington. He remembered what the Burkes' house looked like—an enormous monstrosity with a pretentious letter B on their driveway gate. He knew the B stood for *Burke*, but it might as well mean *bougie*.

There it is. He drove past the house and down another block, taking a turn to park around a corner out of sight. He didn't want to take a chance that Asher might notice his Camaro.

Officer Luz lived four miles to the southeast, not a short distance by any stretch of the imagination. But Steven had no choice but to go on foot so the K-9 would track back to Asher's house. After removing the sponges from their plastic packaging, he squashed them into the backpack along with the grilling gloves and camp fuel, being careful again to pull his sleeve down over his fingers before touching the can so as not to leave prints on it. Ready now, he locked his car and set off at a quick walking pace, one that would get him to the cop's home in a reasonable amount of time without zapping the energy he'd need to sprint back to Asher's house, dump the tell-tale backpack and empty fuel can in the bushes, and get on his way before the dog could follow the trail here.

He set off, sticking to the shadowy curbs, the map on his dim cell phone screen guiding him. The night was hot as hell, and sweat ran down his face, neck, and back, streaming into his butt crack. By the time he reached Travis Avenue, the backpack felt glued to his shoulders. As he approached Officer Luz's address, he slowed to assess the area. Her cruiser was parked in the driveway behind an old blue muscle car with flames painted down the side and a tiny Smart Car. The bungalow-style house stood on the other side of the drive. *Perfect.* The cars would provide excellent cover.

He slipped between the cruiser and the muscle car, dropped the backpack to the ground, and knelt next to it. He opened the backpack, the *zzzzzip* sounding extremely loud, even against the racket the crickets and katydids were making. But his nerves were just making him paranoid. The windows were closed on all the houses, and the hum of the outdoor air conditioner condensers would drown out the noise, too. It was unlikely anyone had heard the sound but him.

After lining up the sponges on the driveway, he donned his grilling gloves, not about to make the same mistake he had earlier and risk burning his fingers again. He unscrewed the top of the can of camp fuel and poured the liquid over the sponges, dousing them. He returned the can to the backpack, zipped it, and picked up the first sponge. He held it away from his body so the caustic fuel wouldn't drip onto his clothes and hurled it at the house, aiming up high on the side wall. The sponge hit the wooden siding with a soft splash. The flammable fluid splattered and ran down the side of the wall, just as he'd hoped.

He continued to throw the sponges, one by one, until the side of the house was drenched. When just one sponge remained, he pulled out the lighter, eased out from between the cars, and stepped closer to the house. He flicked the spark wheel and held the small flame to the dripping sponge. With a *whoosh*, the sponge burst into fire in his hand, but he was ready for it this time. He pulled his arm back and pitched the flaming sponge at the house. In a split second, the wall exploded in a bright blaze.

With a smug grin, he reached down, grabbed the backpack, and took off like a rocket for Asher's house.

65
HOME FIRES BURNING

Megan

Woof-woof-woof!

The frantic sound of Brigit barking jerked me from a deep sleep. I lifted my head from the pillow to see her standing on her hind legs, her paws on the windowsill. The window glowed bright. *Can it be morning already?* Blast sat next to Brigit, as if he was issuing a passive alert on an accelerant. But Seth was still asleep and hadn't directed Blast to scent, so I figured the dog was simply sitting.

Still exhausted from the late night, I wasn't ready to get up yet. I patted the covers. "Come back to bed, you two."

The dogs stepped away from the window. Good thing, too. The fog of sleep hadn't entirely cleared my mind when the window glass exploded from the intense heat. I was fully awake in an instant, and realized the glow through the window wasn't sunlight but fire. I sat bolt upright and shrieked.

Flames filled the window, crackling and licking at the frame. The room began to fill with smoke as Seth woke and jumped out of the bed. "What the hell?"

To my horror, Brigit circled back into the room, then took off running for the broken window. Terror seized me as I realized what she was about to do. "Brigit! No!"

But it was too late. She leapt into the air and sailed through the jagged hole in the glass, disappearing into the inferno.

I've never moved so fast in my life. I threw back the sheets and raced in my bare feet to the front door, unlocking it and yanking it open. I dashed down the porch steps. The yard was hazy with smoke, but I could see that the entire north side of our house was on fire, the blaze lighting up the night sky. Past the driveway, I saw Brigit, a glowing rocket running across the yards. Her fur was on fire, the air rushing past feeding the flames. *She's going to burn to death! NOOOO!*

My eyes and nose filled with smoke, and my mind felt just as cloudy as I bolted after her, screaming her name. *I'll never be able to catch her!*

But then I had a flash of genius.

When someone's clothing catches fire, they're supposed to stop, drop, and roll, right? Brigit might not know *stop* and *drop*, but she knew how to roll. In her fiery frenzy, I had no idea whether she'd obey my command, but I had to try. I cupped my hands around my mouth and yelled as loud as my lungs would allow. "Brigit! Roll over!"

Not missing a beat, Brigit turned to an angle and performed three quick, graceful rolls in the direction she'd been headed, dousing the flames.

My knees went weak in relief. *Thank God she'd heard me! And thank God she'd obeyed!*

After the third revolution, she rose to her feet and took off again, leaving a smoky trail in the air behind her. I saw a figure a few yards ahead of her, running as if his own hair was on proverbial fire. But my partner was faster. She launched herself into the air, sailed across the space, and collided with his back. *Whump!* He dropped a bag he'd been carrying, lost his footing, and staggered a few feet before she took him to the ground, face first. Screaming, he wrapped his arms over his head to protect himself as she grabbed his collar in her teeth and growled point blank in his ear, warning him not to move or she'd rip him to shreds.

I rushed up to them. "Fort Worth Police!" I shouted. "Don't move!" I was in my pajamas with no gun, no pepper spray, and no handcuffs. But I had my best tool of all, Brigit, to keep this suspect under control.

I ordered her off the man, and she dutifully backed away a foot or two, sitting on the grass by his side, ready to react if he tried to get up. I didn't think much could smell worse than wet dog, but singed dog hair smells just as terrible. I ran my hands over Brigit to make sure any hot spots were fully extinguished before turning my attention to the man.

Still face down in the grass, he shook with either fear or rage. It became clear it was the latter when he slammed his fists into the grass three times in quick succession. "Fuck! Fuck! Fuck!"

I crept closer. "Mr. Quinn?"

He responded by slamming his fists into the ground again. "Fuck!"

I'd been right. Steven Quinn must have been behind the earlier fire at the fire station. *But why had he come here?* "Were you trying to kill me and my dog?"

"No!" he shouted into the grass. He rolled over onto his back and shook angry fists at the heavens. "I just want my life back!"

66

HEAT AND TREAT

Brigit

Brigit lay in her kennel in the cruiser, licking at her fur. It smelled funny, and it was short and prickly now, the ends poking her tongue. The intense heat she'd felt earlier must have something to do with that. She and Blast had acted on both instinct and training when they'd heard strange noises outside the house and smelled that strong, icky odor. *Someone had been threatening her pack, and she was going to make them sorry.*

Brigit figured whoever had started the fire must be on the other side of it, and she wasn't about to let him get away. She'd easily caught the guy, of course. Turned out it was the man from the house they'd gone to earlier, the same man whose smell she'd scented at the fire station earlier. She wasn't sure exactly what the man had been up to, but she knew it was no good. She knew *she* had done good, though, because Megan had fed her three liver treats and two peanut butter biscuits.

67
SPURNED, BURNED, COURT ADJOURNED

Steven

Why hadn't I just let Gretchen go? It would have been the smart, sane thing to do. But his ego hadn't let him. Now, he'd racked up thousands of dollars in legal fees, had lost not only his family but also his job, and was looking at over two-hundred grand in restitution for the damage to the high school, nursing home, fire station, and cop's house. He'd have to sell his house and liquidate his investment accounts.

On his attorney's advice, he'd remained silent. But the police had still somehow figured out that he'd been involved in the high school and nursing home fires, and that Nash had been involved, as well. Steven suspected Officer Luz was the one who'd put two and two together. *I should've gotten rid of those damn supplements!*

The district attorney had offered Nash a plea deal, and the guy had been all too happy to squeal on Steven in return for a mere one-year sentence. Steven was facing at least five years for first-degree arson. His attorney had suggested a bench trial. A jury might be tougher on Steven, especially if any of them had a vulnerable parent or relative living in a nursing facility.

Maybe the prison will have a baseball team ...

68

SOMETHING BORROWED,

SOMETHING BLUE,
SOMETHING BRIGIT

Megan

Despite everything Steven Quinn had done, a small part of me felt sorry for him. He'd put on a brave face, but losing his wife and son had obviously been much harder on him than he'd let on. Otherwise, why would the formerly law-abiding man have gone to such extremes to embarrass the man he blamed for breaking up his family?

The day after Labor Day, Brigit and I returned to the tree in Forest Park. Without the tape tied around it I'd never have found it. Frankie brought a ladder truck over from the fire station and used it to search the upper branches for us. When she'd descended the ladder, she'd had a charred pair of athletic shoes in her hands. They were a men's size eleven, Steven Quinn's size. I later found photos of him on social media wearing the shoes.

Bustamente and Hamrick had thanked me and Brigit for our help collecting clues. Brigit deserved most of the credit. She's the one who'd led me to Quinn's house from the fire station, and she's the one who'd taken him down in our neighbor's yard. He might have gotten away if not for her. The fact that his car was later located near Asher Burke's house told us he'd been attempting to create a false trail that would have led Brigit and me to Asher's house. Fortunately, Brigit had made sure he hadn't gotten that far.

I was proud to have realized the inventory of supplements in Quinn's garage was a clue. We tracked Nash Goshen down in Eugene, Oregon and, once a plea deal was arranged, he offered us a wealth of evidence against Steven Quinn. I'd followed up with the staff at the nursing home, and learned that Quinn made regular visits there to peddle his prescription drugs to the medical staff. The guy was looking at significant prison time in addition to a huge financial hit to cover repair costs. He'd lost his family, his job, his assets, and his freedom, but at least he'd be the MVP of his cell block's baseball team.

As Brigit and I left roll call a few weeks before my wedding, Captain Leone put a hand on my arm to stop me. Once the room had emptied, he closed the door. "Did you invite Derek to your wedding?"

"Yes. He's coming." I didn't want the jerk to be part of my big day, but I'd invited all the other officers and detectives from my station. The administrative staff, too. It would have been rude not to send him an invitation. I'd fully expected him to decline. To my dismay, his RSVP card indicated that he would be attending. He'd even jotted a note on the reply: **Stock the bar with Shiner Bock and seat me with the hot single chicks.**

A mischievous gleam shined in the captain's dark eyes. "I'm about to prepare the schedule. I could assign him to work the swing shift that night."

"Thank you, sir." A grin claimed my lips. "Consider it your wedding gift to me."

For days on end, our home was filled with the sound of contractors sawing boards and pounding nails, along with the noxious odor of fresh paint as they fixed the damage to our rental house. They completed the repairs just as our wedding day finally arrived.

Though I was nervous at the thought of standing in front of so many people and reciting my vows, I had no doubts about my decision to spend the rest of my life with Seth. He was a good man who had served both his country and his community with honor. I not only loved him, but I respected him, too. He returned these sentiments, supporting me and my dream of one day making detective, even if it meant I'd often be distracted and called away at odd hours. We enjoyed each other's company, no matter what we were doing. The fact that Seth was attractive and knew how to fix things were the icing on the cake.

Brigit served as flower girl, wearing an adorable veil in the same fabric as my own. She carried a basket of red rose petals in her mouth, and swung it side to side to drop petals along the aisle. Her fur had yet to fully grow back, but a professional groomer had evened out her coat. It was a miracle Brigit's skin hadn't been burned when she'd jumped through the window and into the blaze. Her thick fur had saved her. Blast followed Brigit down the aisle with our wedding rings attached to a D-ring on his white satin bow-tie collar. The dogs took their places on either side of the podium where the officiant and Seth stood, both turning to gaze down the aisle.

The pianist launched into the first few notes of the bridal march, and my father and I stepped forward. Our guests rose en masse and offered nods and smiles as we made our way down the aisle. I returned the nods and smiles, happy they could share our special day with us. In the front row on the groom's side were Seth's mother, his grandfather and Beverly, and his father, Pamela, and two half-brothers. Tommy's parents—Seth's grandparents—completed the row. As we reached them, I reached out and gave Lisa's hand a squeeze. Smiling through tears, she squeezed back, then dabbed at her eyes with a tissue.

Mom came out of her seat on the front row of the bride's side to give me a hug. Gabby blew me a kiss, while my brothers settled for a thumbs-up.

My father formally gave me away, then stepped aside. As he took his seat next to my mother, the officiant launched into the ceremony. With our dogs at our sides, Seth and I turned to each other, joined hands, and stared into each other's eyes. He gave me a grin and a quirk of his brows that melted away any remaining tension. We recited our vows, and I was thrilled to get through them without a single stutter. Seth retrieved our rings from Blast's collar, and we exchanged them, sliding them onto the other's finger with both certainty and joy.

I was Seth's wife now, and he was my husband. We shared a soft, warm kiss, then he took my hand in his again, stepping back with a big grin on his face. I felt my lips spread in an equally big grin. We turned to face our family and friends. The officiant said, "I present to you, for the first time, Mr. and Mrs. Rutledge."

Our guests rose to their feet, applauding and whooping, as Seth and I made our way back down the aisle together, our dogs trotting along behind us.

Our reception was so much fun! We were honored by heartfelt toasts from our parents, Detectives Bustamente and Jackson, and Captain MacDougal, who'd soon be going down the aisle himself. The food was delicious, the cake scrumptious, and the dance music a perfect blend that covered everything from disco classics to modern country tunes.

Our guests appeared to be having a wonderful time. Detective Jackson led the crowd in a line dance, with Summer and Officer Spalding serving as the detective's backup dancers. Tommy and Lisa grooved to an early nineties pop tune that had been a favorite when they'd dated all those years ago in high school. Seth, Pamela, Seth's half-brothers, and I joined them when an energetic Bruno Mars number queued up next. Lisa and Tommy had moved beyond what-might-have-been, and were able to enjoy the blended family they shared now. It was nice to see Lisa having fun, freed from the weight of the secret she'd carried so long. She'd also been freed from her financial burdens. Though she'd insisted it wasn't necessary, Tommy had paid her all the child support he would have owed her. The gesture could never replace the years Seth had spent without a father, but it relieved Tommy of some of the guilt he felt going off to college and unknowingly leaving a pregnant Lisa behind to deal with the enormous responsibility of having a baby on her own. On the next song, Gabby wormed her way in to dance with the older of Seth's half-brothers. My parents swayed to a slow song a few moments later, while Ollie and Beverly did the same.

When it was time for me to toss my bouquet, the single ladies gathered behind me. I knew Frankie and Zach had been considering marriage, too, and I hoped Frankie would soon be making a trip down the aisle. I fully admit that I cheated. I could see Frankie's reflection in the huge gilded mirror on the wall in front of me and, on the count of three when I tossed my bouquet, I aimed it in her direction. I whirled around to see Frankie step forward, her hands stretched up to catch it. But Brigit, who was used to me throwing balls and Frisbees for her, assumed the flowers I'd thrown were for her, too. She jumped into the air and snatched the bouquet with her teeth. The crowd burst into laughter as Frankie put her hands on her hips and cried, "I was robbed!"

When Brigit trotted over to me with the bouquet in her mouth, probably hoping I'd throw it again, I wiped the slobbery stems with a napkin and handed it over to its rightful recipient. "Here you go, Frankie."

"Thanks!" She took the bouquet from me and turned to Zach, batting her eyes. "Looks like I'm getting married next."

"Uh-oh." Zach made a show of tugging at the collar of his shirt, but he wasn't fooling anyone. He was as nuts about Frankie as she was about him.

I sat down on a chair, and Seth pushed the skirt of my dress up to my knee, reaching under the fabric to remove my garter. It was the single men's turn to gather now. Seth, too, used the mirror to his advantage, and tossed the garter over his head in Zach's direction. Like Brigit, Blast had other plans, and jumped up to grab it before Zach could get his hands on it. "Bad dog!" Zach said, wagging a finger at Blast. A jovial wrestling match ensued, with Blast finally releasing the saliva-soaked garter. Zach brandished it in victory.

Though the celebration went on for hours, it seemed to me that the festivities ended almost as soon as they had begun. The dogs, Seth, and I left the venue amid the glimmer of sparklers held up by our guests, an appropriate sendoff for a firefighter and his bride.

Our honeymoon couldn't have been better. The trip provided the perfect opportunity for Seth and me to enjoy romantic time together at a leisurely pace. The gorgeous scenery and rock formations in Arches National Park, Bryce Canon, and Zion were awe-inspiring. The dogs reveled in roaming the wilderness, getting in touch with their primitive natures, howling at the moon as it rose in the dark, desert sky. For grins, Seth and I howled along with them.

As we packed up the car on our last morning in Zion, preparing for the long drive back to Texas, I gazed down at the wedding ring on my hand, the symbol of my bond to Seth. I knew we'd have ups and downs over the years, suffer setbacks in our relationship like all married couples did, but what would cause them? What special memories would we make, those moments of deep, heartfelt connection? I had no idea. The only thing I could be sure of was that, whatever we'd face, we'd face it together, with our dogs by our sides.

THE END

ABOUT THE AUTHOR

Diane Kelly is a former assistant state attorney general and tax advisor who spent much of her early career fighting—or inadvertently working for—white-collar criminals. When she realized her experiences made great fodder for novels, her fingers hit the keyboard and thus began her Death and Taxes white-collar crime series. A proud graduate of her hometown's Citizens Police Academy, Diane is also the author of the Paw Enforcement K-9 series and the Busted female motorcycle cop series. Her other series include the House Flipper cozy mystery series, the Southern Homebrew moonshine mystery series, and the Mountain Lodge Mysteries. She also writes contemporary romance and romantic comedies, sometimes with a touch of fantasy.

Find Diane online at www.dianekelly.com, on her Author Diane Kelly page on Facebook, and on Twitter, Instagram, and TikTok at @DianeKellyBooks.

Visit the Newsletter page of Diane's website and sign up to receive book news, exclusive content, and more.

AUTHOR'S NOTE

Dear Reader,

I hope you enjoyed *Pawfully Wedded* as much as I enjoyed writing it for you!

What did you think of this book? Posting reviews online are a great way to share your thoughts with fellow readers and help each other find stories best suited to your individual tastes. Reviews are much appreciated by authors, too. ;)

I love to chat with book clubs! Contact me via my website if you'd like to arrange a virtual visit with your group.

Be the first to hear about upcoming releases, special discounts, and subscriber-only perks by signing up for my newsletter at my website, www.DianeKelly.com.

I'd love to connect with you on social media! Find me on my Author Diane Kelly page on Facebook or at @DianeKellyBooks on Twitter, Instagram, and TikTok.

See below for a list of my other books, and visit my website for fun excerpts.

Happy reading! See you in the next story.

Diane

OTHER BOOKS BY DIANE KELLY

THE HOUSE FLIPPER SERIES

Dead As a Door Knocker

Dead in the Doorway

Murder With a View

Batten Down the Belfry

Primer and Punishment

Four-Alarm Homicide

Dead Post Society

THE MOUNTAIN LODGE MYSTERIES SERIES

Getaway With Murder

A Trip with Trouble

Snow Place for Murder

THE SOUTHERN HOMEBREW SERIES

The Moonshine Shack Murder

The Proof is in the Poison

Fiddling With Fate

THE BUSTED SERIES

Busted

Another Big Bust

Busting Out

THE PAW ENFORCEMENT SERIES

Paw Enforcement

Paw and Order

Upholding the Paw (an e-original novella)

Laying Down the Paw

Against the Paw

Above the Paw

Enforcing the Paw

The Long Paw of the Law

Paw of the Jungle

Bending the Paw

Pawfully Wedded

THE TARA HOLLOWAY (DEATH & TAXES) SERIES

Death, Taxes, and a French Manicure

Death, Taxes, and a Skinny No-Whip Latte

Death, Taxes, and Extra-Hold Hairspray

Death, Taxes, and a Sequined Clutch (an e-original novella)

Death, Taxes, and Peach Sangria

Death, Taxes, and Hot-Pink Leg Warmers

Death, Taxes, and Green Tea Ice Cream

Death, Taxes, and Mistletoe Mayhem (an e-original novella)

Death, Taxes, and Silver Spurs

Death, Taxes, and Cheap Sunglasses

Death, Taxes, and a Chocolate Cannoli

Death, Taxes, and a Satin Garter

Death, Taxes, and Sweet Potato Fries

Death, Taxes, and Pecan Pie (an e-original novella)

Death, Taxes, and a Shotgun Wedding

OTHER BOOKS AND STORIES:

Almost an Angel

Don't Toy With Me

Five Gold-Smuggling Rings

Love, Luck, and Little Green Men

Love Unleashed

One Magical Night

A Sappy Love Story

The Trouble with Digging Too Deep

Wrong Address, Right Guy

Made in the USA
Monee, IL
18 February 2025